# UNTO A GOOD LAND

A Novel by

## Vilhelm Moberg

Translated from the Swedish by Gustaf Lannestock

SIMON AND SCHUSTER · NEW YORK

"And I am come down to deliver them . . . and to bring them up out of that land unto a good land and a large, unto a land flowing with milk and honey."

*Exodus* III:8

# CONTENTS

**PART ONE**

## In Search of Homes

| | | |
|---|---|---|
| I | A SHIP UNLOADS HER CARGO | 3 |
| II | BATTERY PARK | 16 |
| III | MILK AND WHITE BREAD | 19 |
| IV | A LETTER TO SWEDEN | 29 |
| V | THE MOST BEAUTIFUL STREET IN THE WORLD | 30 |
| VI | JOURNEY WITH THE STEAM WAGON | 46 |
| VII | VOYAGE ON THE LAKE STEAMER | 67 |
| VIII | PEASANTS ON A SEA OF GRASS | 84 |
| IX | DANGER SIGNS ARE NOT ALWAYS POSTED | 89 |
| X | THEIR LAST VESSEL | 105 |

**PART TWO**

## The Settling

| | | |
|---|---|---|
| XI | "WILL NO ONE HELP ME?" | 123 |
| XII | AT HOME IN A FOREIGN FOREST | 133 |
| XIII | DISTANT FIELDS LOOK GREENEST | 152 |
| XIV | A SMÅLAND SQUATTER | 168 |
| XV | . . . TO SURVIVE WITH THE HELP OF HIS HANDS | 176 |
| XVI | AT HOME ON LAKE KI-CHI-SAGA | 187 |
| XVII | GUESTS IN THE LOG HOUSE | 206 |
| XVIII | MOTHER AND CHILD | 223 |
| XIX | THE LETTER TO SWEDEN | 225 |

PART THREE

## To Keep Alive Through the Winter

| XX | THE INDIAN IN THE TREETOP | 229 |
| XXI | THE SWEDISH SETTLERS' ALMANAC | 240 |
| XXII | "MOTHER, I WANT BREAD!" | 253 |
| XXIII | THE LETTER FROM SWEDEN | 272 |
| XXIV | UNMARRIED ULRIKA OF VÄSTERGÖHL WEEPS | 289 |
| XXV | "AT HOME" HERE IN AMERICA—"BACK THERE" IN SWEDEN | 299 |
| XXVI | A LETTER TO SWEDEN | 308 |

# PART ONE

# In Search of Homes

# I

## A Ship Unloads Her Cargo

ON THE ELONGATED ISLAND of Manhattan, in the Hudson River, the largest city in North America had sprung up, already inhabited by half a million people. Like an immense hippopotamus resting immobile in his element, Manhattan sprawled in the water, at the mouth of the Hudson. The hippopotamus turned his head toward the Atlantic, and back of his enormous snout lay the piers of the East River, where ships with emigrants from the Old World tied up.

On June 23, 1850, there arrived in the port of New York the brig *Charlotta* of Karlshamn—Christian Lorentz, Captain—carrying seventy passengers, emigrants from Sweden, nearly all of whom were farmers with their families. The *Charlotta* was several weeks overdue, delayed by contrary weather; this arrival completed her seventh voyage as an emigrant vessel. The brig tied up at the East River pier between a tall, coffin-shaped English bark and a low Norwegian schooner heavily loaded with iron. Besides the human cargo in her hold, the *Charlotta* also had pig iron and sundry items of freight.

One of Captain Lorentz's first errands on American soil was to change his passengers' money. During the last days of the voyage he had collected the emigrants' cash and, carrying a leather sack, he now went to a bank on Wall Street to exchange Swedish daler and shillings for American dollars and cents. He did not accept paper money, only gold and silver coin; he knew nothing for sure about American bills, except that their value never was the same as the amount printed on them.

Sweating and puffing in the intense heat, he returned to his ship. Captain Lorentz had been in New York port during every season of the year; he was familiar with all North American weathers and disliked them all; this summer heat he abhorred. Down here by the docks there was at least some breeze from the Atlantic, but in the *Charlotta*'s hold the air was unbearably oppressive. To be tied up near Manhattan this time of year was one of his most distasteful duties as ship's commander.

In his tiny cabin the captain pulled out the passenger list. After each name he had noted the sum entrusted to him, and now he must figure out how much each passenger was to receive in American money. It was an annoying chore, a chore for shop clerks. He was not a counting man, he was a seaman; but a captain on an emigrant vessel apparently must also be a scrivener and a money-changer. Like a father with his children, he must look after his passengers and see to it that they weren't cheated or robbed.

And having sailed these Swedish peasants across the ocean from one

3

continent to another, Captain Lorentz now felt so great a responsibility for them he wouldn't even leave them to shift for themselves after they had landed. Hardly had his ship tied up at the pier when all those who made their living from the simplicity and inexperience of immigrants flocked around the gangplank like rapacious dogs at slaughter time. These *runners* and *grafters* and *brokers*, and whatever they were called in the language of this new country, watched for every newly arrived ship. There were agents from freight companies which the captain knew were fraudulent; there were men from taverns and quarters of ill repute; well-fed and well-dressed men in funny little round caps with large visors; lazy men who avoided honest work and whose presence was repugnant to Captain Lorentz. He would always place an armed guard at the gangplank to keep such rascals off his ship, for once on board they would steal all they could lay hands on, down to a single nail or a piece of rope. The rogues came from all lands, but they preferred to rob their own countrymen. By talking the language of new arrivals they gained their confidence and made easy victims of them. All European nationalities, it seemed, plundered and defrauded each other here on American shores: English robbed the English, Irish swindled the Irish, Germans preyed on Germans—while Americans plundered the immigrants from all countries, regardless of nationality. In this respect at least, thought the captain, the Americans honored equality among men.

The authorities in New York were too lenient. Lost and unsuspicious immigrants enjoyed no protection against the scoundrels lurking at the landings.*

The passenger list stuck to Captain Lorentz's rough, sweaty hands. His brain worked sluggishly in the infernal heat, and he lost himself in numbers as he figured daler into dollars. He was looking forward to evening, when he hoped to enjoy his supper and cellar-cool ale at Castle Garden. This tavern was conveniently close by, and it was the best eating place he knew of in New York—though not up to his standard in other ports. Its fare might do for the rich New York swine breeders who usually gathered there, but a man who sailed to Marseille, Bordeaux, and Barcelona had his own standards of good food. The Americans had lived such a short time in their country they hadn't yet learned how to prepare their food properly. There were too many other things to attend to. For example, they were said to be particularly good at building churches; he had heard New York alone had a hundred and fifteen of them. And he recalled what he once had read in a book by a famous Frenchman: The French had one hundred different sauces, but only one religion, whereas the Americans had a hundred different religions, but only one sauce. Captain Lorentz had, unfortunately, not yet had the pleasure of tasting this sauce.

* Not until 1855 was an official reception station for immigrants opened at Castle Garden.

4

He could never reconcile himself to the strange customs and ideas he met in North America. Here people of many races mixed, and the classes were so turned about that one couldn't tell which were the upper and which the lower. Lowly people considered themselves changed when they landed on American shores; they thought themselves equal to those of high birth and position. Every farm hand and servant wench assumed a conceited, disobedient, insolent attitude. Several times it had happened that able-bodied men of his crew had become so arrogant that they had boldly broken their contracts with him and had simply remained in America. Here, respect for authority and masters was disregarded, and consequently, the servant class was ruined. Here all felt at home, even those who smeared pork grease over their faces while eating, not yet having learned the use of a napkin.

The *Charlotta's* captain counted and wrote numbers, and the sweat from his face dripped onto his paper. For each passenger he must deduct the landing fee—two dollars and a half—which must be paid to the city treasurer immediately on arrival; Captain Lorentz must rob each one of these poor devils of six riksdaler and twelve shillings. The emigrants themselves certainly needed every penny, but the money went to the lean purse of New York—which no doubt also could use it. Here landed thousands of impoverished wretches, and when completely destitute, they were forced to remain in the harbor until provided for by that lean purse. Europe emptied her workhouses and literally shoveled the inmates over onto America; how long would the Americans meekly accept these discards from the Old World?

Including these passengers on his latest voyage, Captain Lorentz had sailed five hundred of Sweden's inhabitants to North America. A whole little town his brig had moved across the world ocean. Which one of the two countries ought to be more grateful to the *Charlotta* and her commander—the kingdom of Sweden or the North American Republic? Sweden got rid of her religious fanatics and other troublesome, law-breaking citizens, but at the same time she lost many useful and capable men. On every voyage, the *Charlotta's* human cargo was nine-tenths thrifty peasants. The lazy and useless ones, the rogues and the deserters, came mostly from other countries, on other ships. Also, of course, many enterprising Europeans found their way to New York; the captain had heard of some who immediately on arrival bought trunkfuls of guns and continued westward to seek a new way of living.

The gentlemen from the Commissioners of Emigration who pried about his ship as soon as it docked used to say that the North American Republic wanted healthy, work-willing, moral immigrants. But no one prevented the sick, lazy, immoral ones from landing, as long as they could walk ashore. The captain was responsible only for the incurably sick and was required to put up a bond. This time, he had to confess, the *Charlotta's* living cargo was badly damaged by seasickness, and scurvy too, after

5

ten stormy weeks at sea. Some of his passengers, during their first weeks in America, would no doubt be unable either to work or to lead immoral lives.

And this time, on arrival in port, Captain Lorentz had been met by a new proclamation: Captains carrying passengers must keep them on board for three days after docking.

The *Charlotta*'s gangplank was already lowered, and some of her passengers had gone ashore when the health officer arrived with the new order and sent them back aboard. His question indicated how things stood: Had there been cholera on board the *Charlotta*?

New York again was seized by the fear of cholera. Last summer the epidemic had frightened the inhabitants out of town, and this year, with the intense heat, it had flared up again. The authorities thought cholera was brought by emigrant ships from the Old World, and now every ship from a foreign port must be carefully inspected by health officers before the passengers were allowed to step onto American soil.

Crossed-out names on the *Charlotta*'s passenger list indicated to the inspector that eight passengers had been buried at sea, but Captain Lorentz could assure him with a clear conscience that none had died of cholera. He once had had that Eastern pestilence on board his ship, and he knew well the signs of the sickness: severe diarrhea, violent vomiting, and a thirst which burned like fire. But his passengers on this voyage had been free from these symptoms. And the inspector himself looked at those still sick and ascertained that the Swedish brig was not bringing cholera to New York. But he warned about an English merchantman, the bark *Isaac Webb* of Liverpool, arriving the same day as the *Charlotta*; on this ship the Oriental pest had raged so horribly that seventy-seven of the passengers had died.

Yes, Captain Lorentz had always known it, human beings were the most annoying and unhealthy cargo in the world.

There were now many additional troubles and complications in getting rid of this cargo. He must keep the passengers on board for another three days, for which he would receive no thanks from those crowded into the hold in this heat. Fortunately, now as always, the sick got well as soon as it was time to land; even the weakest wanted to look their best. Only one passenger caused him real worry and concern, a sixty-five-year-old farm wife from Öland. He had expected her to die before they reached port, he had been so sure of it he had made a mark after her name—like a small cross. He noticed it now as he read the passenger list: Fina-Kajsa Andersdotter. She had become a widow on the North Sea, where he had read the funeral service over her husband. The old woman was so weak from scurvy he had not believed she could survive. If she now were to be taken from ship to hospital, the commander of the *Charlotta* must post a bond of three hundred dollars with the mayor of New York.

Why in hell would a farm woman go out to sea at such an age? Why

6

should the shipping company be expected to pay three hundred dollars for an old, worn-out hag-body? One way to avoid the bond, perhaps, would be to keep her on board as long as the brig remained in port. While they unloaded the pig iron and other freight, the old woman would no doubt die, and then the health officer would come and fetch the corpse, and the captain wouldn't even have to think about the funeral.

It was always easier to get rid of dead cargo than living.

## —2—

THE PASSENGERS were now coming to the cabin to collect their money. A tall, husky man hit his forehead against the cabin ceiling as he came down the ladder. The captain said, "Look out for your skull! You might need it in America."

An unusually large nose protruded from the man's face; Captain Lorentz need not ask the name of this farmer, he remembered him well. One night during the voyage—while the worst tempest was raging—he had stanched a hemorrhage for this man's wife. The peasant had thanked him and said that his wife owed her life to the *Charlotta's* captain.

He consulted the passenger list: "Karl Oskar Nilsson. Paid 515 rdr. bko."

At the exchange rate of one dollar for each two and a half daler, the farmer had two hundred and six dollars coming to him. But from this sum the captain must deduct the exchange fee and the landing fees for man, wife, brother, and three children.

He told the farmer, "You have to pay thirty-seven and a half daler for six people."

"Is that the entrance fee to America?"

"We might call it that. There is also the exchange fee. Four dollars—that is, ten daler."

Lorentz counted and deducted: Balance to pay—a hundred and eighty-seven dollars. He counted out this sum in twenty-, ten-, and one-dollar coins, gold and silver, which he gave to the young farmer, who himself counted the money slowly and carefully. Then he put the coins, one at a time, into a homemade sheepskin belt which he carried around his waist under his shirt. The captain gave the hiding place a nod of approval.

The big-nosed farmer, having received his money, still remained standing in the cabin.

"Do you think you've been cheated in the exchange?" the captain asked.

"No. No, it isn't that. But I would like to ask you about something, Mr. Captain."

"Yes?"

Karl Oskar Nilsson continued: There were fifteen of them, eight full

7

grown and seven children, all from Ljuder Parish in Småland, who had undertaken the voyage together to this new country. Now they had been delayed at sea, the summer was already far advanced, and they were anxious to reach their destination as soon as possible, so as to be able to find land and get something planted before winter set in. All of those from Ljuder Parish intended to go to Minnesota, where land was said to be reasonably priced for people with little money. Now they wanted to continue their journey without delay; would the captain be kind enough to advise them how to get started inland?

"Have you any definite place in mind?"

"Yes. Here is the name."

From his purse Karl Oskar took out a soiled, worn piece of paper, once part of an envelope:

Mister Anders Månsson
Taylors Falls Påst Offis
Minnesota Territory
North-America.

"Who gave you this address?" asked the captain.

"An old woman on board the ship. Månsson is her son. She's going to him and we'll all be in the same company; they say there's good land where her son lives."

"You rely on the woman? What's her name?"

"Fina-Kajsa. She is from Öland; her husband died in the first storm."

Captain Lorentz suddenly straightened. "You mean the old woman who is so sick?"

"She is better now, she says; she feels so well in her body she'll be able to go with the rest of us."

"Then you'll take the old woman in your company and be responsible for her?"

"Yes. She has money for her journey. And we'll look after her as best we can. When we get there, perhaps her son will help us find land."

The captain's face had suddenly lightened; it was not the first time Providence had helped him out of a difficult dilemma. This time, apparently, Providence had chosen the farmer to get him out of his difficulty with Fina-Kajsa Andersdotter, and thus save his company three hundred dollars.

He handed the important piece of paper back to Karl Oskar.

"It's a long way to the territory of Minnesota. About fifteen hundred English miles, I believe."

"Is it so . . . so . . . far away?" Karl Oskar's face fell, and he scratched his head with its unkempt hair, yellow as barley straw, grown very long during the voyage from Sweden.

"Of course, it's only two hundred and fifty Swedish miles," the captain hastened to assure him. He did not wish to frighten the farmer by dwelling on the journey's length, but rather to encourage him to undertake it. He continued: Every time he had transported farmers in search of land he had advised them to go as deep as possible into America; the farther west they went, the richer the soil was, and the broader were the regions to choose from. Most of the distance they could travel on river steamboats.

"Two hundred and fifty miles! It isn't exactly next door."

The infinitely long road which had worried Karl Oskar at first had shrunk to one-sixth, but it was still two hundred and fifty times the distance from Korpamoen to Ljuder church. He thought to himself, he must be careful how he spoke of the distance to others in his company; it might dishearten them.

"I will arrange the contract for the journey," Captain Lorentz assured him. "Including the Widow Andersdotter, there will be sixteen in your company?"

Karl Oskar had never seen this taciturn, unobliging man so talkative and willing to help as he was today. The captain spoke almost as to an equal: Yes, he often arranged contracts with honest companies for transportation inland. His conscience bade him help immigrants leave New York as soon as possible; they couldn't stay here in the harbor, they couldn't settle in Battery Park. And he knew an honest Swedish man in New York whom he often asked to guide the immigrants and act as their interpreter. The man's name was Landberg, he had once been carpenter on this very ship, the best carpenter Lorentz had ever had. But several years ago, when the captain was transporting a group of religious fanatics from Helsingland, followers of the widely known prophet Erik Janson, Landberg had been so taken by their religion that he had left the ship in New York and joined the group. After half a year, Landberg had lost faith in the prophet, who had plundered him. The poor man had been forced to flee from Janson's tyranny penniless and practically naked. Landberg now earned his living by acting as interpreter and guide for Swedish immigrants. He spoke English fluently, and it was Captain Lorentz's custom to send for him as soon as the ship docked in New York. This time also he had notified the one-time carpenter, and Landberg had been given a pass by the health officer to come aboard the brig.

"How much would the interpreter cost?" Karl Oskar asked.

"It depends on the distance he must accompany you. I believe he charges three dollars for each grown person as far as Chicago."

"Hmm . . . Well, we can't manage by ourselves. None of us can speak this tongue."

The captain thought, to leave these poor, helpless peasants to shift for themselves would be almost like driving a flock of sheep into a forest full of wolves. He said, "If you would like speedy transport inland, you must take the steam wagon from Albany. Landberg will get contracts with all the companies concerned."

9

"Thank you, Captain, for your great help."

It had been reported to the captain during the voyage that this big-nosed peasant had been dissatisfied with his quarters, had complained of the small ration of water, and had been insubordinate to the ship's officers. But Lorentz no longer disliked the man: Karl Oskar undoubtedly had a good head; and then, he was the tool of Providence.

". . . And you think the old woman is strong enough to be moved?"

"She says she is. She was on her feet again today."

It was indeed strange; a few days ago the Widow Andersdotter had been shaking in every limb with the ague, fallen off to the very bones from diarrhea. But such miraculous recoveries had happened before, and even though Lorentz had little use for the customs of the North American Republic, he had to admit that the mere sight of the country worked like magic on people; one day they were lying in their bunks sighing and crying and ready to die, unable to lift head from pillow, and the next day they were on their feet again. When semi-corpses saw the shores of America, they returned to life.

—3—

As KARL OSKAR felt the new money in his belt, it seemed to him that a hundred and eighty-seven dollars was a poor exchange for five hundred and fifteen daler. His property had somehow shrunk on his arrival in America. And what he now carried in his belt was all he and his family owned in worldly possessions; it was all they could rely on for their future security.

He went to tell his fellow passengers that the captain would arrange for their continued journey; all were anxious to get away from the crowded ship's quarters and were disturbed over the delay on board.

On the deck he met Jonas Petter of Hästebäck, the oldest one in their company; he should really have been the one to plan the journey, to act as leader for the group, rather than Karl Oskar.

"Ulrika is stirring up the women," Jonas Petter told him.

On the foredeck, next to the watchman whose duty it was to prevent anyone from going ashore, stood unmarried Ulrika of Västergöhl, the Glad One, talking to a group of women, gesticulating wildly, loud, upset.

"She insists our captain is a slave trader," Jonas Petter said.

What had the Glad One started now? Karl Oskar had long been afraid she might bring shame on their company.

He went to Ulrika; her cheeks were blossoming red and her voice was husky with anger.

"So it's you, Karl Oskar! Now I've found out the truth! Now I know why they won't let us land!"

"It's because of the cholera," said Karl Oskar.

10

"No, it's not! It's the captain! He keeps us confined here because he is going to hold an auction and sell us! He is going to sell us as slaves to the Americans!"

The women around Ulrika listened fearfully. They might have been listening to the auctioneer she predicted calling for bids on them; one woman had folded her hands as if praying God for help.

Karl Oskar seized Ulrika by the arm. "Come and let's talk alone." He pulled her away from the others and they walked over to the mainmast. "Don't spread such lies," he warned her. "You might have to pay for it."

"It's the truth," insisted Ulrika. "We've been swindled! We are to be sold on arrival—that's why the captain keeps us penned in on the ship!"

"What fool has put such ideas into your head?"

"You don't have to believe me if you don't want to. But I'm going to run away; I'm not going to stay here and be sold as a slave!"

Ulrika's eyes were flashing. As a little girl in Sweden she had been sold, she knew what it meant; she had been a four-year-old orphan when she was sold at auction, to the lowest bidder. The one who had offered to take her and bring her up for eight daler a year had been a peasant in Alarum, and he had raped her when she was fourteen. The only difference between Sweden and America was that in this new country you were sold to the highest bidder, instead of the lowest; perhaps it might be considered more flattering to be sold to a high bidder, but nevertheless she would have nothing to do with it; she had left that hellhole Sweden to get freedom in America. Now she was going to take her daughter with her and escape from the ship.

"But this is a lie!" exclaimed Karl Oskar. "The captain is not a slave trader."

"Ask your brother if you don't believe me! He is the one who told my daughter."

"Robert? What do you mean?"

"I'll fetch him. Then you can hear for yourself." And Ulrika of Västergöhl hastened to find her daughter Elin and Robert, Karl Oskar's younger brother, dragging them with her as she returned.

"Now tell Karl Oskar what you heard!" she demanded.

Elin looked trustingly from her mother to Karl Oskar. "Robert said the captain is keeping us on board until he gets permission to sell us to the Americans."

The youth looked reproachfully at Elin. "I only said one of the crew told me so."

Karl Oskar turned sternly toward his brother: "Now, tell the whole truth!"

Robert's jaw fell in embarrassment and he looked down at the worn and splintered deck: he had asked one of the seamen why they weren't allowed to land, and the man had said they must stay until the Americans

11

came and got them; they were to be sold at auction. Last voyage, he said, the captain had sold all the passengers to the Turkish Infidel for ten thousand dollars; this time, he didn't wish to rush things, and that was why he kept them aboard. Last time he had sold everyone except two old, worn-out hags who couldn't be used for work or aught else. And no complaints had been raised, for no one had had any relatives in America on whom he could call for help.

The seaman had said he was telling all this to Robert because the captain had refused to share his ten thousand dollars with the crew. The seaman was angry that he couldn't share in the profits from the slave trade in New York, and that was why he had warned Robert and other passengers to get away from the ship before the auction was advertised.

Robert admitted he had not believed the seaman; if the captain wanted to sell people to the Infidel, he would undoubtedly have sailed to Turkey, where the Infidel lived, and not to North America. There was no sense in shipping people back and forth across the Atlantic. Moreover, Robert knew from a book he owned—*Description of the United States of North America*—that it was forbidden to sell white-skinned people as slaves; a person had to have curly hair, and black skin to boot, before he was allowed to be sold.

Robert had told the seaman's story to Elin only because it struck him as funny.

"But you didn't say it was a lie," Elin protested.

"I thought you would know I wasn't serious," Robert explained in embarrassment.

Thus Karl Oskar killed the rumor. And he urged Ulrika to quiet the anxiety she had aroused in the other gullible women. Neither she nor anyone else on board need fear slave chains or sale at auction in North America. The captain was an honest man who was doing all he could to help them, he had even promised to help them get started on their way inland.

Ulrika now turned her anger on Robert: "You brat! You're responsible for this! Karl Oskar, better keep your brother in line from now on."

And Robert was severely reprimanded by Karl Oskar for sowing lies in the mind of a credulous girl. Suppose these stories reached the captain; then there would be trouble. Now they must go and find the man who had started the rumor.

"He isn't on the ship any longer," Robert said hastily.

"You just come and show me the liar!"

"I can't find him. They say he has run away."

Karl Oskar gave his brother a stern look; it had happened before that Robert had been caught in a lie, and it did seem strange that the man had vanished. But this time Karl Oskar let Robert off with a strong warning: If he didn't stick to the truth he might get himself and others into great danger. He was now seventeen years old and he must begin to have some sense of responsibility; he must remember that here in a foreign land unknown dangers awaited them.

Robert felt he had been betrayed by Elin. He had told her this story about the slave trade in strict confidence. The way it had happened was this: Not far from the ship stretched a park, a real manor-house park, with tall, green, thick trees, below which lay cool shadows. But Robert was not allowed to go there, he must remain here, on this rotten ship, in the burning sun. So he had just had to talk to someone to make the time pass more quickly. This he could not explain to his older brother, but he thought Elin might have understood. He certainly would tell her no more stories if she must run to her mother and repeat them.

—4—

The *Charlotta*'s ex-carpenter entered Captain Lorentz's cabin, stooping so as not to hit his head against the low ceiling. Long Landberg, as he was usually called, was the tallest man ever to sign on this vessel—almost seven feet. His lengthy arms hung loosely against his narrow body. A well-trimmed full beard half hid his healthy smile.

The captain greeted him with a warm handshake. "Any news since last time? This infernal heat is the same." He could easily see that the man he had sent for was eager to unburden himself, and even before Landberg sat down he began: "Yes, I have news this time. You haven't heard, then, Mr. Captain? Wheat-flour Jesus is dead!"

Lorentz stared at him.

"Yes, it's true. Wheat-flour Jesus was murdered. Last month."

"Whom are you talking about, Landberg?"

"Erik Janson, of course. A prophet even in the old country, where he traveled about and sold wheat flour. That's why they called him Wheat-flour Jesus."

"The prophet Janson? Murdered?"

"Yea. He was shot like a dog at Cambridge, in the court where he had brought suit. The defendant shot him."

The captain was not surprised by the news. He thought he had some knowledge of the handling of legal matters in this country. Perhaps, tacked to the wall of the courtroom, was the same notice he had seen in a saloon in New York: "Shoot first! Live longer!"

But he realized that the *Charlotta*'s old carpenter was much excited by the happening.

Long Landberg, the apostate, continued: Erik Janson was the worst scoundrel ever to tramp the ground of North America. Landberg had seen him daily during many months and he knew the prophet's creed. Janson called himself the new Christ and had chosen as his apostles twelve be-fuddled louts whom he kept in attendance, like a tyrant king. Indeed, he

13

had been a cruel tyrant to his followers, plaguing them enough to make angels weep, if there were tears in heaven. No doctor was called for the sick; when one of the disciples lay at death's door, unable to move toe or finger, Janson ordered him to rise up and be healthy, and if the sick one could not, Janson condemned him for sin and lack of faith. Janson, of course, was free from sin and righteous in all ways.

Once, Landberg had defended some poor sick sectarians against this tyranny, with the result that Janson had seized everything he owned, including most of his clothes. Without means, he had been unable to bring suit against the prophet. Janson had said that he was equal with God. . . . Well, the fact was, humanity could thank the man who had shot Wheat-flour Jesus; through this splendid deed he had freed North America from a beast. Janson, a raw, presumptuous peasant boor! Yes, said Landberg, he even looked like the Evil One, his teeth were like tusks, no doubt he was possessed by an evil spirit and had been sent into the world by the devil.

Captain Lorentz, when he had transported some of Janson's followers, had heard them speak of their leader as a Heavenly Light, lit for them in the dark heathen land of Sweden. They had been honest in their faith; to them he had been the returned Christ. And now, after his murder, they would undoubtedly say that, like Christ, he had sealed his religion and faith with his blood.

Was Erik Janson sent by God or by the devil? Perhaps by neither; who could tell? One had to be satisfied that God Himself knew.

Now Lorentz asked his former carpenter how things were with these sectarians; how were they getting along in that vast prairie land of Illinois where he had heard they were settled?

"Janson said he founded a new Jerusalem," Landberg retorted with derision. "But the fact is, he founded a new hell."

It was true that the community which Janson had built and named Bishop Hill, after his home parish Biskopskulla, had been called Bishop Hell by the Americans, and letters so addressed had reached their destination. But the Janson followers, Landberg admitted, were fine, industrious farmers; they had greatly improved their situation; no longer did they live like beasts in earth huts, but had built themselves houses of bricks, which they made. Nor were bricks the only things they made: though in Sweden they had been temperance people, in Bishop Hill they had built a still, operated by steam and capable of making three hundred gallons of brännvin a day. When they got drunk, they blamed this on the Holy Ghost "filling them," as they called it.

Last spring the sectarians had sent a group of their men to California to dig for gold in the name of God. Even two of their apostles had been sent. Could anyone imagine Saint Peter or Saint Paul digging for gold? But Janson did not seek first the kingdom of God and His righteousness; he was said to have grown so rich that he had the tusks pulled out of

14

his evil mouth and replaced by pure gold. Could a mortal here on earth descend to lower depths of vanity and conceit?

Landberg continued: The people in Bishop Hill believed Erik Janson would rise from the dead in the same manner as his predecessor, Christ. They went about their chores now, making their brick, distilling their brännvin, while waiting for their master's return. Jesus arose on the third day, but six weeks had already elapsed since Janson was shot, and nothing had been heard from him so far as anyone knew.

And this much Landberg said he wished to add: Should Wheat-flour Jesus return to the American continent alive, there were many who would be glad to shoot him a second time.

Captain Lorentz thought to himself, Janson had undoubtedly been in many ways a fine man. But he realized how important it was for Landberg to give vent to his feelings, so he had not interrupted him. Now he returned to their business at hand: "Now you must again help me unload my human cargo."

"Gladly, Captain. I am free at present."

Landberg was pleased to get a new commission; his income had been poor lately, since no emigrant ship had arrived from Sweden for some time. For a while he had helped English captains. But most immigrants this year were German or Irish. If only he had known German, then his income would have been better. It was hard this year to earn an honest living, he told the captain. The swindlers and the runners were as fast as ever, but an honest agent was recognized by all captains: a thin man!

"And tall as a mast," added Captain Lorentz.

"Precisely, Captain! And how large is the cargo this time?"

"Seventy. Most of them are going inland."

"Fine. The immigrant transfer, *Isaac Newton*, runs now every second day up the Hudson to Albany."

The two men began to go over the list of passengers and their destinations. While so occupied, Landberg remembered that he had a message to the captain from a well-known countryman: The Methodist pastor, Olof Hedström, on the Bethel Ship here in the harbor, sent his greeting and intended to pay a call the following morning.

"Hmm. So Pastor Hedström is still preaching on his old ship. Tell him he is welcome. A fine fellow; he might help the people a great deal."

Through fortunate circumstances, the Swedish Methodists in New York had been permitted to unrig an old ship and turn it into a church. Lorentz had been on board the Bethel Ship after she had been converted into a God's House and he had liked it there. Now that the *Charlotta* was beginning to rot, perhaps some other sect might buy his ship and make a church of her, here in New York Harbor. He mused that it might mark great progress for Christianity if all old, worn-out ships, those nests of sin, could be stripped of their rigging and turned into churches.

Pastor Hedström undoubtedly was coming to invite the immigrants to a

15

sermon and Holy Communion aboard his Bethel Ship. And Lorentz thought he must ask the minister to make it clear to the passengers that he belonged to the Methodist religion before he gave them the Sacrament. After the *Charlotta*'s previous voyage, some of the Lutheran immigrants had received the Lord's Supper on the Bethel Ship, and only later had it been made fully clear to them that they had been given the Sacrament by a sectarian minister, a teacher of heresy. They had been thrown into great anguish and fear of eternal judgment; they had prayed to God that He might let them throw up the false tokens of grace, but their prayers had not been heard. Yes, even the souls of the emigrants were the responsibility of the captain of an emigrant ship.

"Yes, my old carpenter—three days from now you'll get another load of Swedish farmers for the North American Republic."

And on June 26, early in the morning, when the three-day quarantine was over, the brig *Charlotta* of Karlshamn could at last discharge her living cargo on the pier near Castle Garden in New York Harbor.

## II

## Battery Park

AFTER SEVENTY DAYS AT SEA, the seekers of new homes were again on solid ground—though the restlessness of the Atlantic Ocean remained a while within them. As they set foot once more on the trustworthy, immovable earth, they were well satisfied to part with those great masses of water which the Creator on the Third Day had called Sea, and they blessed in their hearts that dry part which He had called Earth. They gave thanks to the Lord God Who in His mercy had helped the brittle planks to carry them over the terrifying depths to the longed-for harbor.

On an outjutting tongue of land in the East River stood Castle Garden, the old fort, now transformed into an amusement place, and near by, separated from the river piers by a broad walk, Battery Park spread its greenery. This piece of wooded land so near the harbor resounded daily with heavy peasant tramping and foreign tongues. The Old World people, having passed through the portals of the New World, found here their first resting place on American soil. Battery Park was to the immigrants a cool and shaded grove on their day of landing.

Here they sat down and refreshed themselves in the comforting shade of spreading elms and linden trees, here rested side by side men, women, children, and aged ones, surrounded by their possessions—chests, baskets, bags, and bundles, filled with essential belongings. As many knapsacks and bundles as they had been able to carry they had clutched in their hands when walking down the gangplank, holding them so tight that their knuckles whitened, and their cheeks reddened with fear lest hustling foreigners snatch their belongings from them. Never during the whole journey would they leave these important possessions out of sight, these inseparable bed companions during the transport across the ocean.

Rough, broad-shouldered peasants, their faces marked by all the seasons of the year, stood here with hands behind their backs, their eyes appraising the new land. On their bodies hung heavy wadmal clothes, wrinkled and baggy. (These woolen garments—such splendid protection against the bitter cold of the North Sea—were now drenched with sweat and a burden to their wearers on America's sunny shores.) There was a constrained lust for action in these men's hard muscles and sinews; their bodies were power restrained. Crowded in narrow ship's space for many weeks, their hands had had no chores to perform. They had arrived on a new continent anxious to resume accustomed duties, their hands eager to hold the familiar ox thongs and plow handles. Their hands possessed much knowledge, acquired from childhood, inherited through centuries. When now again they stood on solid ground, they felt the lust for work spring up after the painful time of inactivity. But yet a while must their forced rest last, yet a while must they carry their hands behind their backs.

Mothers sat leaning against tree trunks in the park, feeding their babies from the breast; the women emptied their scrawny breasts without filling the stomachs of their babies. The milk gave out long before the babies' hunger, and the little ones cried and fretted, irritated by the heat and discomfort of the heavy woolen garments in which they were bundled. And the mothers rocked their children on their knees—mother-love's cradle, the softest and most comfortable cradle on earth—and tried to lull them to sleep. But the babies whimpered, they wanted to stay awake; now that their eyes saw for the first time the land their parents had chosen for them, it seemed as if they wanted to take in everything; this was the land where they were to grow up, the land that was to be their home.

A five-year-old boy, wrapped in a coat that hung to his ankles, sat on his haunches in the grass, chewing a crust of rye bread, a coarse, dark loaf; spots of mildew testified to the fact that this bread had not been baked yesterday, nor on this continent; it came from an old oven in a hidden, stony part of Europe. The boy chewed ravenously and swallowed with determination; the bread in his hand disappeared until only a few crumbs were left; these he tossed into his mouth. The loaf was finished but his hunger remained, and the child looked questioningly at his empty hand: Why did food end before hunger? Mother said: "It is the last loaf I have, the last one from home; now you will never get any more bread from home." And the boy pondered this . . . Why no more bread from home?

In Battery Park the immigrants took stock of their food baskets; they counted their loaves of bread and scraped away the mildew; many were

17

those who ate their last slice in confidence that the soil of the new country would feed them from now on.

An even stream of people moved along the river road which separated Battery Park from Castle Garden: these were the inhabitants of New York, the people who lived in the greatest city of North America. Here walked leisurely men in tall, black hats, dressed in tail coats and tight-fitting trousers which enclosed their legs almost like cloth skin. Here walked women in bonnets and tightly laced waists from which hung skirts of generous proportions, reaching the ground. Others had skirts spread out like birds' beautiful tail feathers, and of all colors: red, white, green, and gold; checkered skirts, polka-dotted and striped. Over their heads the women held parasols in bright colors, like small-paned canopies of heaven. The men carried Spanish canes.

The walkers paid no attention to the people camping in Battery Park. The appearance of immigrants under the trees in the park was neither new nor unusual—they saw immigrants almost every day when walking along the river. Shiploads of immigrants arrived daily and would continue to arrive; the people landed, waited in Battery Park for inland transportation, moved on and were gone. A new group arrived in their place—new people gathered here constantly, waiting under the trees. This was the endless train of aliens, outsiders; the immigrants were one of the permanent sights for promenading New Yorkers; they would always be there, they were part of the park, they belonged to it, like the leaves on the trees and the grass on the ground. The immigrants, it seemed, would always wait there, under the trees in Battery Park.

The immigrants came from places where they knew everyone and were known; they had seldom seen a stranger. Now they had arrived in a land where everyone was a stranger; the inhabitants of New York were a new and strange sight to the immigrants. The people in the park looked at the stream of people on the road: the newly arrived looked at those who were established here; these were the Americans, settled, comfortable, having found their place in the new land, able to move unhindered, walking in security, free of worries, and able to speak to any one they met. The immigrants were strayed wanderers, seeking a place to live and work; the others had found what they were seeking; the homeless observed those who had homes.

The home seekers stopped a moment in Battery Park, alien, confused, bewildered, insecure. They were overtaken by surprise at their first meeting with the unknown country. But they were to participate in the breaking of the land and the changing of the character of the country they had just entered, these waiting here in the cool grove on the East River.

# III
## Milk and White Bread

THE DAY THEY LEFT SWEDEN the emigrants from Ljuder Parish had counted sixteen in their group. For one of them a watery grave had opened during the voyage, but as Fina-Kajsa from Öland had joined their company, they were still sixteen when they gathered together on the American shore in Battery Park.

Danjel Andreasson of Kärragärde sat by himself, a little to the side of the others, next to his America chest. He was reading in his psalmbook, his head was bent down, and his bushy, brown beard swept the book, open at Hymn 344—"At the Death of a Mate." A dried flower, a reseda, lay as bookmark between the leaves; it had grown in the flower bed at home, cared for and tended by his wife. The page with the psalm was badly worn from much use.

> O Death, why hast thou snatched away
> My bosom Love from me?
> In sorrow and despair I pray,
> But comfort flees from me. . . .

Danjel Andreasson had arrived in the new land to which the Lord had guided him with four motherless little children. He had lost Inga-Lena, his dear wife and earthly helpmate; the Lord had stricken him and trampled on him; he was now only a wretched human worm, wriggling under the heel of the Lord.

He had searched his inner self and arrived at a new understanding: he had sinned the sin of self-righteousness. In his presumption he had considered himself better than others and had believed that his sins once and for all had been washed away and tied up in Christ's napkin cloth that bound His head at burial. He had held himself righteous, unable to sin any more. But on the ship, as he had lain in all his wretchedness covered with his vomit, listening to the tempest and feeling the depths below him, he had learned that he had been found wanting in the eyes of the Lord.

In his vanity he had believed that when he reached the harbor he would be able to praise God in the foreign language; in his conceit he had considered himself an equal of Christ's apostles who were visited by the Holy Ghost on the first Whitsuntide, and he had thought that the outpouring of the Holy Spirit would take place in him so that he would be able to use the American tongue. His Creator had already given him a speaking tongue, and this in itself was so great a miracle that it was presumptuous to expect God to give him the ability to use this tongue for all languages.

Sitting here now, he heard the buzz of this foreign language which he had expected his ears to understand and his tongue to imitate. But his ears recognized no sounds and his tongue remained dumb. The words of the language he heard did not reach him, he could not use them in his mouth. No outpouring of the Spirit filled him, no cloven tongues appeared, no visions were seen. He could not prophesy in the new language; his ears were closed and his tongue lame.

Danjel Andreasson entered North America a mute and lost stranger among all other strangers in this multitude of people, races, and tribes here gathered. Once, in Babel, the Lord had confused human language so that men could not understand one another; because each was a sinner, his tongue was capable of his native language only. And because Danjel had thought himself righteous, the Holy Ghost had failed him in the new land; he was not worthy of spiritual outpouring.

Danjel was stricken to the earth, God had chastised him, left him naked in all his frailty and faults. He beheld one vision only, a terrifying one: Man was smaller than the worm, because he was the food for worms—he, Danjel Andreasson of Kärragärde, was food for crawling creatures of the earth.

Once he had conceived this picture of himself, he ceased to explain God's word to his fellow travelers on the ship; how could he explain Holy Writ when he hadn't rightly understood it? How could he advise and admonish others when he himself had committed the grossest of sins? How could he be a spiritual guide for others if he were unable to guide his own soul?

"At the Death of a Mate"—Danjel knew this hymn by heart and he closed the book and laid it on the ground. Then he knelt down and folded his hands over the lid of his America chest: "In Thy presence, Father in Heaven, I crawl in the dust."

On the ship Danjel had given a promise to the Lord—he would build an altar of thanks in the new land. The old clothes chest from the loft of Kärragärde became a Lord's altar on American soil, and next to it now knelt a crushed man, praising and thanking God; with a full heart he thanked Him for the trial which had been sent for his betterment; he thanked the Almighty Who had snatched away Inga-Lena, taken from him his earthly helpmate; he thanked the Lord Who had taken the mother from four little children; he blessed and praised the Lord God for the ills, sufferings, and persecutions he and his beloved ones had had to endure; he thanked his Creator with the warmth of his heart for all the evils which had been bestowed upon him.

God had sought out Danjel Andreasson who now bent like a worm under His foot. At his entrance into the new, young, and healthy world, he prayed for a rebirth, he prayed to be washed clean from that vanity and self-righteousness which clung to him from the Old World. And he felt that God had come close to him now, closer than He had ever come to him in the country he had left.

—2—

KRISTINA LAY WITH HER HEAD on the bulging knapsack; it was a hard and knotty pillow but to her it seemed the softest down; the knapsack had come with them from home—it was something intimate and friendly. She lay still; she was weak from her severe illness, every limb was weak and weary. If only she could rest, rest a long time; if only she could lie like this, quite still, stretched out on her back in the grass, without having to move even a little finger or a little toe. Such were the delights she desired. If she could remain still, perfectly still, then the tiredness would leave her body. But as yet she could only find momentary rest, soon they must move on again.

A few feet away from her another woman was sleeping, no doubt more tired than she—old Fina-Kajsa lay there with open and gaping mouth. She had pulled up her skirt in a roll around her waist, exposing a worn-out, mended, dirty petticoat which once must have been red. In her arms, tight against her chest, she held a wooden casket decorated with green and yellow dots. It contained her most treasured possessions. The casket had no lock but was tied with heavy string, and the sleeping old woman held it close to her breast the way a mother holds her little child. Through her pointed, toothless mouth, which opened like a black hole, Fina-Kajsa snored. At her feet stood her iron pot, now wing-broken and crippled, one leg lost during the voyage. No wonder people had ill endured the crossing when even iron vessels were broken.

Uncle Danjel's large white linen sack, once Inga-Lena's pride, was now frayed and dirty, having fared badly on the ship. Ulrika of Västergöhl, who was looking after Danjel's belongings now he was a widower, had just opened the sack and was searching for something in it. She was dressed today in Aunt Inga-Lena's best dress; she and her daughter had divided the dead one's clothes. Kristina never spoke to Ulrika more than was absolutely necessary; for her uncle's sake Kristina had endured Ulrika's company, but Karl Oskar had promised that they would separate themselves from the former parish whore as soon as possible. Kristina did not begrudge the Glad One her aunt's clothing; both she and her daughter must have something to cover themselves with, and they had earned the garments now that they were taking care of the poor children who had lost their mother.

The dress Elin was wearing had also belonged to Inga-Lena, and it was too big for the sixteen-year-old girl. It flowed in large billows and bags about her lithe body. She sat with a small chip basket on her knees

21

and it reminded Kristina of berry-picking time. What kind of berries might there be to pick in this country? Wild strawberries, so sweet to taste, and with such delicate white flowers in the spring? Blueberries which colored the fingers black in summer. Fiery red cranberries on the tussocks in autumn? Elin held the handle of her basket firmly, as if just about to go out into the berry lands—she held on to it as one holds to a single worldly possession.

And Kristina sat up, the better to keep an eye on her family belongings. There stood their chest—five feet long and three high—reinforced with broad iron bands which had held it together unharmed across the Atlantic; only one corner of the lid was scraped a little. On the front of the chest glowed the letters, still red, painted there before departure: *Home-owner Karl Oskar Nilsson, North America.*

And there stood their sacks and their food basket. The small bundle next to Kristina moved at times, it was alive—in it slept little Harald, the baby. Karl Oskar had gone back to the ship to pick up something forgotten and he had the two other children with him.

From where she sat among the trees Kristina could see the harbor and the long row of ships at the piers. Right in front of her was a tall, yellow-green house with a round tower which it carried like a crown. The house was built on an islet, and people went to it across a bridge. High up on the wall over the entrance there was something written in tall black letters, visible from where she sat: CASTLE GARDEN. It was, of course, the name of the house, whatever it might mean. In front of the round house on the same isle there was a smaller and lower house, one wall of which was almost covered by an inscription: LABOR EXCHANGE; the name of that house was painted in the largest letters she had ever seen.

They put names on the houses in America. And the incomprehensible writing she saw reminded her that she was now in a land where she understood not the smallest word of what people said; they might speak into her very ears, yet she wouldn't hear them; she might talk, and they would not hear her. From the first moment here in America she suffered from two defects—deafness and dumbness; she must go about among strangers a deaf-mute.

It was gentry she saw walking about there near the big house with the tower; the women had umbrellas like the ladies at home in Sweden. But it wasn't raining, it was entirely clear, the sun shone in a cloudless sky. Why did the women carry umbrellas today? Perhaps they had brought them along for show.

Yes, the sun was shining, there was an unmerciful heat in America. The air was oppressive and she breathed with difficulty; she had the sensation of inhaling pungent steam while bending over a pot of boiling water. But her happiness in being on the earth again was so great that it almost obliterated the discomfort of the American heat. On the

22

ship she had believed that she never more would get out into God's clear daylight; she had felt she would end her life enclosed in the dark hold; she had thought she would never again see a patch of grass or a green leaf. But now she lay here on the green earth in the sun. She could just as easily, like poor Inga-Lena, have been lying on the bottom of the ocean, her body lowered for monsters of the deep to devour. But she had been saved from them, she and her loved ones—what else mattered?

To go out on the ocean in a fragile ship with three small children—she felt it had been to tempt the Lord God. In a long and fervent prayer she thanked her Father in Heaven Who in His mercy had let them reach solid ground in health.

She almost felt as if she had been dead and awakened to life again, as if a miracle had happened to her. How wonderfully still everything about her seemed! The joy of lying here on the peaceful, quiet earth could only be fully appreciated by one who had long lived in a constantly moving and heaving bed, one who had been tossed about on high, restless billows. At last she was liberated from the ship's swing which had thrown her up and down, she was free from the dizzy journeys to the top of the waves and into their valleys. She had always loved to play with a swing but never again would she be tempted by the swing of the sea; with this she was sated for life. Never again would she desire to see this terrifying ocean, never again would her feet leave solid ground.

She felt thirsty, her tongue was parched, and her appetite was returning now that she was on land; she must eat well now that she had one more life to feed.

She put her hand against her abdomen: again she could feel the stirring within her. Many days had passed since the last time she felt the child move, and she had begun to wonder if it still could be alive. It would not have seemed strange to her had it died, so ill and weak she had been from seasickness and scurvy. A joy filled her as she now felt it stir: once having conceived a child, she wished to bear it alive; a stillborn child was a shame and God's chastisement—the woman was not worthy to carry into the world the life He had created within her.

When was it due? She counted the months on her fingers: she had conceived it sometime in the middle of February—March, April, May, June—she was already in her fifth month. July, August, September, October, November—her childbed would be sometime in the middle of November.

About half the time left until she was in childbed. Would they have a bed by then, a bed in which she could bear her child?

The child was alive. A life that had traveled free across the ocean had come into the land. It stirred and moved in its hidden nest, stronger than the mother had felt it before. Not only had she herself come to life

23

again, the child within her seemed to have gained new life, now that she had carried it into the New World.

—3—

"ARE YOU ASLEEP, Kristina?"

She had dozed off. Karl Oskar stood by her side, wiping his sweaty face with his jacket sleeve.

"What a heat! They can fry bacon on the roofs here!" He took off his wadmal coat and threw it on the ground. Johan and Lill-Märta came rushing to their mother.

"Guess, Mother! Father has bought something!"

"Guess what Father bought!"

In one hand Karl Oskar carried a paper bag, in the other their own large pitcher. He held up the bag to Kristina's nose. "You want to smell something?"

"Look in the bag, Mother!" shouted Johan. "Father has bought sweet milk and wheat bread!"

"Sweet milk and wheat bread!" Lill-Märta repeated after him.

Kristina inhaled a pleasing odor which she had not smelled for a long time. She stuck her hand into the bag and got hold of something soft: fresh, white rolls, wheat rolls!

"Karl Oskar—it isn't true."

"Look in the pitcher!"

"Mother! It's sweet milk!" shouted Johan.

Karl Oskar held up the pitcher, so full of milk that it splashed over. "Be careful. Don't lose any," she warned.

"Now you must eat and drink, Kristina."

"Karl Oskar, I don't believe my eyes. How could you buy it?"

"The Finn helped me. Eat and drink now. We have already had some."

Sweet milk! Fresh milk! When had she last tasted it? Not one drop had they been able to obtain on the ship. It was in their quarters in Karlshamn that she had tasted milk last time; long, long ago, in another world, in the Old World.

Kristina took hold of the pitcher with both hands, carefully; she mustn't let it splash over. Tears came to her eyes; she had to see what milk looked like, she had forgotten. This milk was yellow-white, thick and rich; no spoon had skimmed off the cream; and it smelled as fresh as if it had just been milked into this pitcher.

Karl Oskar opened the knapsack and took out a tin mug which he filled with milk from the pitcher. "Drink—as much as you are able to. You need it to get well."

Kristina held the mug. "But the children? Have they had enough?"

No mother could begin to eat and drink before her children had been

24

given food and drink. But Karl Oskar told her that Johan and Lill-Märta had eaten themselves full and drunk until their thirst was quenched back there at the store where he had bought the food.

Kristina drank. She emptied the mug in a few swallows, and Karl Oskar filled it again; she drank until she felt satisfied; never before had she realized that milk could be so good. She herself had sat on the milking stool and pressed out hundreds of gallons of milk from cow udders, she had strained milk for her children morning, noon, and night, she had fattened calves on milk, she had brought up piglets on milk—during her whole life she had never longed for milk until she started on this voyage. Now she accepted the pitcher of milk as a gift from God; she felt she would cry.

She said the milk was cream-rich and good. Then she took a roll from the bag and looked it over; this roll was almost as big as a small loaf at home.

They still had a little left in their food basket. The ship's fare had been rancid, bitter with salt, smelling of old chests and musty barrels; Kristina still had a taste in her mouth from the dried, hard rye loaves. Toward the end of the voyage there had been worms in the bread, and they had been forced to soak it in water and fry it in pork fat before they could eat it; much of the fare they had been given on the ship had been little better than pig food.

After those hard loaves, how delicious it was to bite into a soft, fresh wheat roll! The rolls looked a little puffy, but she soon saw that they were well filled under the crust. At the very first bite she felt that she was eating festival food.

"They bake mighty fine bread in America," said Kristina.

"Here they eat wheat bread on weekdays as well as on Sundays," said Karl Oskar.

"I've heard so. Can it be true?"

Kristina was a little skeptical. To her, wheat bread had always been a food for holidays and festival occasions. She used to buy a few pounds of wheat flour for a baking at Christmas, Easter, and Midsummer. Then she counted the loaves and locked them in the bread chest so the children couldn't eat them unless allowed; such food had to be carefully portioned out, each one getting his share.

"It's swarming with people here in New York," she said. "Is there enough wheat bread for all of them?"

Karl Oskar said, that, according to what he saw with his own eyes, there must be plenty of food in this country; in several stores he had seen quantities of wheat loaves, piled high like stacks of firewood at home, and he had seen whole tubs full of sweet milk. He was sure that both she and the children could eat and drink all they needed to regain their strength.

The bundle at Kristina's side began to move and a sound came from it; Harald had awakened and cried out. The mother picked him up and his cry died as soon as he felt the sweet milk in his mouth. The little one swallowed the unfamiliar drink in silence, he simply kept silent and swallowed: surprise overwhelmed him.

It hurt Kristina's heart to see how fallen off her children were, how pale their faces, how sunken their cheeks, how blue their lips, how tired and watery their eyes. When she took them in her arms their bodies were light, their arms and legs thin, the flesh on their limbs loose; it was as if muscles and bones had parted from each other. They had dwindled this way from having been kept so long in the dark unhealthy hold below decks. How often had she worried about them when she lay sick, unable to care for them, while all three of them crawled over her in her bed. How often had she reproached herself because of her inability to give them a single bite of fresh food, or a mouthful of sweet milk. How she had longed for the moment when she could walk on shore with Johan, Lill-Märta, and Harald. These poor, pale, skinny children certainly were in need of America's good sweet milk and fresh wheat rolls.

Johan had been told to guard his father's coat lying there in the grass, and he said impatiently: "Father, you forget the apple! The apple for Mother!"

From the pocket of his father's coat he took a shining red apple, almost as big as his own head. The boy handed it proudly to his mother.

"Have you ever seen such a big apple?" said Karl Oskar. "I got it for nothing!"

Near the pier, he told her, they had met a woman carrying a large basket filled with beautiful apples. Johan and Lill-Märta had stopped and looked longingly at the fruit. The woman had spoken to them, but they had not understood a word. Then she gave the children each an apple, which they immediately gulped down. He, too, had received an apple—which he had saved for her.

"Karl Oskar—you're good. . . ."

She weighed the large apple in her hand; it must weigh almost a pound, she thought; it was the largest one she had ever seen. The children's eyes were glued to the fruit in their mother's hand, and Kristina asked Karl Oskar to cut it in four equal pieces, so that all would get even portions. He pulled out his pocketknife and divided the apple carefully; each quarter was as big as a whole apple at home.

And the immigrant family ate and enjoyed their first American fruit, which was full of juice and cooled their mouths.

"Is it a new apple?" exclaimed Kristina when she tasted it.

"Yes, doesn't it taste like one?"

"I thought it was fruit from last summer."

"Here in America the apples ripen before Midsummer," said Karl Oskar.

26

Yes, the sour-fresh taste in her mouth convinced Kristina. It must be true what Karl Oskar said—she was eating a fruit of the new crop; yet it was only Midsummer.

Midsummer—the holidays had passed, a Midsummer no one had celebrated. Enclosed on the ship, they could not celebrate, they could only talk of the Midsummer holidays in the land they had left.

Just a little more than a stone's throw from where she sat Kristina could see the pier where the *Charlotta* was still tied up, discharging the rest of her cargo. She recognized the Swedish brig by its familiar flag. After unloading, it would sail back again. The ship would once more have to find her way across the restless, endless water. It had been a bleak and misty spring day when she left the Swedish harbor; perhaps it would be a bleak and misty autumn day before she returned to the same harbor. Then their ship would be at home. *At home*—the thought cut Kristina to the quick, and she chewed more slowly on her piece of apple.

Midsummer at home—Father putting young birches on either side of the door, Mother serving coffee at their finest table, which had been moved out into the yard and placed under the old family maple; Maria and Emma, her sisters, picking lilacs and decorating themselves for the village dance. The house would smell of newly scrubbed floors, smell clean, inside and out, smell of lilac blossoms and flowering birches. And when they gathered around the table under the family maple—the guardian tree of their home—they would all be dressed in their Sunday best, and there would be much fun and much laughter. At home it was always so for Midsummer.

Did they speak this year of one who had been among them before? Did they mention her name—Kristina, who had moved away with Karl Oskar to North America? Did they ask how it was with her this moment, this afternoon, this Midsummer Eve?

*She* knew how it was at home, but those at home did not know how it was here.

She had traveled a long road, almost endlessly long; she knew the sea that separated her from her homeland, that incomprehensibly wide water which separated *home* and *here*. She would never again travel that road, never again traverse the sea. So she would never again be with them at home.

Now for the first time she began to think deeply into this: *Never again be with them at home*.

The thought suddenly disturbed her profoundly, not less because she could still see the ship, over there in the harbor, the ship that was to turn about, to sail home again. This ship on which she had suffered so horribly, what did it mean to her now? Did she want to go back with it again? Did she want to stay another ten weeks in a pen in the dark

27

hold? No! No! Why was it then that her tears were breaking through? Why? She did not understand it.

Karl Oskar sat down and wiped the perspiration from his forehead with his sleeve; even in the shade the heat was melting.

"We are to board a ship and ride on the river this evening," he told her.

She was thinking of the road behind them—he was thinking of the way ahead.

"We are late getting started," he said.

He was afraid they might have arrived too late in the season. No one could have imagined they would sail the sea until Midsummer. He had expected them to reach their place of settling by now and have time to hoe some land, sow some barley, plant some potatoes. What would happen to them next winter if they didn't get something into the earth before it was too late this year to grow and ripen?

Karl Oskar agreed with what Kristina had said, and it worried him: this town of New York swarmed with people; perhaps the whole country was already filled up. No one in their group had ever seen so many human beings in one place. Great numbers must have come before them, this they could see with their own eyes, and every day new ships arrived, with great new flocks of people. Perhaps they had been deceived, perhaps it was too late, the best land already taken; perhaps America was entirely filled up with new settlers.

But he must not disturb Kristina with these thoughts on their very first day in the new land. He must, rather, try to cheer her up, she was so weak and depressed after her illness. He had just given her a foretaste of the delicacies offered them on entering an American store, and he must assure her that all he had seen and heard so far was promising.

"I think America is a good land. We need have no regrets; that I must write home."

Kristina swallowed hard and turned her head. Karl Oskar must not see her tears today, their day of landing. And why did she cry, after all? She was on solid ground, she had all her loved ones around her. They were drinking sweet milk and eating fresh white bread—what more did she want?

Karl Oskar continued: For the past three evenings he had been writing a letter to Sweden, and now while they were waiting here in the park he must finish it. He could write on the lid of the America chest, it made a good table, then he could send the letter back with the ship. It would be September before it reached home, it would take from spring until fall before the nearest ones at home would hear anything about their voyage.

Kristina had not spoken for a long while; she had not said a single word since he had told her that American apples ripened before Midsummer. Could that have surprised her so much? He turned and looked

28

at her. Something must have made her sad. But he would not ask her—whatever it was, a question now would only increase her sadness.

He handed her the bag with the bread: "Eat some more, Kristina."

"It tasted awfully good. If you think there'll be enough for . . ."

She ate one more white roll. And her first day on American soil was ever after to be a memory of sweet milk and fresh bread—milk and wheat rolls.

# IV

## A Letter to Sweden

North America, 26 Day of June, 1850

Dearly Beloved Parents and Sister,

That you may Always be well are my Deep Wishes to you.

I will now let you know about the journey from our Fatherland. We completed it in 10 Weeks and arrived in the town of New York. The Swedish Ship reached the American strand safely on Midsummer Eve.

There was great Joy among us as we beheld the New Land, the Americans are noble folk, letting all foreigners through their Gates, none asked us One word about our Situation, no one is denied Entrance. We were not asked if we were Poor or Rich.

All in our family are with Life and Health. The Sea heaved considerably but we endured the Journey well. I must tell you that Danjel of Kärragärde was stricken by the great Inconvenience that out at Sea He lost his wife Inga-Lena. Her time was up. But it would be too cumbersome to describe our Journey.

New York is a large town and the Houses are large and high. It swarms with People of all kinds of the known World, Black, Brown, and Colored in Skin. But they are People. We are met with kindliness by all.

The Americans are Thin and Pale, they say it comes from the Heat. The air is warmer here than at home.

All strange Phenomena can be seen here—they can not be described in a Letter. They say the Time in North America differs six Hours with the Time in Sweden in such a Way that all Clocks and Watches have been turned back Six Hours. Swedish Paper Money is not allowed to be changed here, except with the Captain on the Ship, but Gold and Silver have their value here the same as at home. Our Swedish money is less in value than American money.

Carry no Sorrow for me, kind Parents. Here we are well taken care of. I left satisfied my Fatherland. If Health and Strength remain with me I shall fairly well take care of Myself and Mine here in North America. When I get something to work on with my Own Hands I shall look well after it, I think it will not be hard to get along here.

On our Arrival we met a Nobel Woman who gave us Apples from her basket. Apples in America are uncommonly large. Many Fruits are offered

29

here but not Planted in Sweden. The Americans eat wheat Bread at nearly every meal and use Good food.

Our dear Children are healthy and well, they talk much of you. Go with Our Greeting to Kristina's Beloved Parents and Family in Duvemåla, say to them their Daughter has arrived in America with health and Satisfaction.

Our Ships Captain has bespoken a Boat which will freight us deeper into the land. On the enclosed piece of Paper I have written down a Place where we intend to Stop and settle. Will you, Sister Lydia write to your Brother, we wish next time to hear of the changes at Home.

Be kind and let us know the date when this letter arrives in Sweden so that I may figure out how long Time it takes from North America. Do not Pay the Freight for the Letter, then it is more sure to Reach us.

I send my Greetings to all friends and relatives in Our Parish, we are alive and well bodily and Our Souls, Nothing in this world is Wanting Us.

Written down in great haste by your Devoted Son

Karl Oskar Nilsson

# V

## The Most Beautiful Street in the World

IT HAD BEEN generally understood on the brig *Charlotta* that about half the inhabitants in the town of New York were loose people—thieves, rogues, robbers, and criminals. Consequently, none of the immigrants dared go alone on the streets of this town. But the second mate had promised Robert and Arvid, who was Danjel Andreasson's servant, that he would go with the boys and show them New York as soon as they arrived. And on the afternoon of the day of landing he had to do some errands for the captain and invited the boys to accompany him through the city.

The second mate had been kind and helpful to them during the voyage. They had never heard his real name mentioned—when anyone spoke to him, he was called Mr. Mate; when anyone spoke of him, he was referred to as the Finn. He was a talkative man and the only one of the ship's officers they had come to know.

The Finn now went with the two youths, walking by the long row of ships tied up at the piers; on the East River there were piers along the whole shore, it seemed. And the Finn pointed and explained: In this port flew all the flags of the world, side by side; over there lay a frigate with the American flag, strewn with stars and stripes. They must learn to recognize this flag, now that they were to settle here. This vessel was an East Indiaman, as seafolk called it. It had a beautiful sail. American ships had nice hulls. The ship over there, the one like a barge, was a Dutchman; nothing fine about that one; it was called a smack. And that long ship loaded with planks was Norwegian, or half Swedish, for after all the two countries had the same king. But they had better not mention that to any Norwegians they met, they might get their heads knocked off.

On the broad river arm the ships were crowding each other, steamboats, sailing ships, sloops, rowboats, ferries, and barges in one great galaxy. In the middle of the river, boats moved with the aid of sails; nearer the shore, wheels under the water drove them. The tall narrow smokestacks of the steamers rose like a forest of black, burned tree trunks over the harbor. The Hudson and the East River, with their bays, estuaries, and canals, flowed around the city of New York, encircled it in their arms, and the city of New York pushed its piers and embankments into the rivers and broke them up. Smoke from house chimneys and steamer funnels flowed together into great clouds, floated by a weak westerly breeze toward the Atlantic.

A small vessel without sail, wheels, or oars moved with great speed across the water and aroused Robert's interest. He asked what made it move so speedily. The Finn said it was a steam ferry. Didn't they see the smoking funnel from a small house in the center of the ship?

The *Charlotta*'s second mate pointed out and explained things to the boys; he spoke of barks and smacks, schooners and galleasses, but of this they understood little. From the deck of a large sailing vessel came song and loud, gay voices. A group of men in broad-brimmed hats, apparently passengers, were making merry on the ship. The boys wanted to stop and listen to them; they were quite curious.

The Finn said that this was a clipper ship from California, ready to sail for San Francisco. The ship was a new, fast sailer, sheathed in copper; the men on board were California bound, to dig for gold.

The ship's name was *Angelica*, and from her prow hung a red, flapping pennant with jolly words: *Ho! Ho! Ho! For California!* This pennant did not resemble the flags on other ships, nor did the passengers resemble other ships' passengers; these men were laughing, noisy, singing lusty songs. It seemed to the boys as though the ship had no command.

The Finn further informed the boys that a shipload of women, both white and colored, was to sail from New York for the gold fields. There was a scarcity of women throughout America, in San Francisco there were only fifty, and the gold diggers were said to be languishing from lust. Cases of attacks on mules and mares had been reported—woman hunger could drive men insane.

But there was plenty of gold out there, it grew in the earth as potatoes grow in Sweden. In the rivers they could fish for gold lumps, big as eggs. The Finn himself had seen samples of twenty-three carat California gold right here in New York. Beggars in California, of course, went about in rags, as did beggars the world over, but California beggars were dressed in glittering golden rags. A hundred ships had arrived in the port of San

31

Francisco, and every crew member had run away to the gold fields. The gold would soon be spread all over the world, and in a few years the whole world would be rich.

But very few men returned alive from the gold fields. The Finn had heard that the passengers on the *Angelica* had ordered their tombstones in New York and were taking them along—this to save money, since it was cheaper to have them engraved here.

Robert came to new life, seeing and hearing about this clipper ship; he looked wonderingly and longingly at the *Angelica*. She wasn't like the *Charlotta*, either in name or otherwise. She was a happy ship with happy passengers; as soon as the men finished one song they immediately started another:

> Blow, boys, blow for California!
> There's plenty of gold,
> So I've been told
> On the banks of the Sacramento. . . .

The men waved, hats in hand, to the crowd on the pier. The passengers on the Swedish *Charlotta* also had sung, but mostly hymns, funeral hymns, and seldom had any of her passengers laughed. And while Robert didn't understand the words of the songs from the *Angelica*, he didn't think her passengers were singing hymns. Yet these singing gold diggers were traveling with their own engraved tombstones. How could people be so boisterous and happy, sailing with their tombstones? Perhaps, thought Robert, they were happy and sang because they were doing the wisest thing people can do in this world: their course might be perilous, but anyone wanting to get rich in America must, danger or no, head for the place where gold could be picked from the earth itself.

"They have fun on that boat," said Arvid with a touch of envy.

"The men on the gold-rush ship are drunk," explained the Finn. "I wouldn't be surprised if they drink up their tombstones before they leave."

The *Angelica*—Robert looked at the clipper ship's stern where the name was painted. *Angelica* and *Charlotta* were two women's names. *Charlotta* was heavy, hard, dour, stern, harsh, and commanding; *Angelica* easy, soft, light, and gay. *Charlotta* sounded like the name of a fat farm mistress, authoritative, masterful; *Angelica* like a tender, delicate girl, like a bird's twitter in a flowering meadow early in spring; there was joy and freedom in that name.

The next ship he would travel on must have such a name.

Now the passengers on the clipper ship began jumping about in wild leaps.

"Those men must be dancing the polka," said the Finn.

"What kind of dance is that?" asked Robert.

"It's a new Hungarian war dance; in fact, an unchristian whore dance. Let's get on, we've lots to see today."

Reluctantly, Robert left the *Angelica* with her fluttering red banner; there were many hundreds of ships in the New York Harbor, but only one he wished to board.

They left the piers and turned off to the left, cut across the Battery, and went into town. If they wished to get a good view of Manhattan, the Finn said, they must go over to Weehawken; unfortunately, he didn't have time to go with them, but once up there they could see thousands of houses and hundreds of churches; up there they could feel they were really seeing the world.

In his description book Robert had read about New York, and he knew it was the New World's largest, most active town, that houses were six stories tall, and streets sometimes seventy-five feet wide. Now he wondered whether it were true that half of the inhabitants were murderers, robbers, and swindlers.

"It's a little exaggerated," said the Finn. "Only one-tenth are criminals." And he added: It might be better to put it this way: every fourth house they passed was a saloon, every fifth woman they met was a whore, and every fifth man a criminal. Perhaps it would be better not to say exactly, but rather thereabouts, as far as a visiting seafarer could judge.

Robert began to inspect the people they met on the street more closely, particularly the younger women.

"Every fifth woman a whore, Mr. Mate?"

"Yes, maybe thereabouts, yes, just about."

The Finn continued: There were in this town twenty thousand known and public sluts, besides all the private ones whom only God could count. There were two thousand whorehouses, open day and night, seven days of the week, except for the hours of service on Sundays. There were ten thousand saloons, and every saloon keeper had in his pay an undertaker, who came with his cart and dragged away the corpses of those who drank themselves to death. The American brännvin was the strongest in the world, and some saloon keepers even put a pinch of poison into the drink to make it smoother and more tasty; from childhood Americans had hardened themselves to spiced and poisoned drinks, but a foreigner might fall dead on the floor as he stood at the bar. In the most notorious nests, like the Old Brewery at Five Points, the saloon was on the first floor, the whorehouse on the second, and the morgue in the cellar. The guests got drunk in the saloon, then went upstairs to the girls, where they were robbed, murdered, undressed, and pushed through a chute to the morgue in the cellar. Yes, it was true, there were places here in New York where one was served speedily and efficiently. The police never dared go near such places. One den at Five Points had been demolished a few years ago when more than a thousand corpses were found.

Robert and Arvid felt their scalps tingle at the Finn's stories. But,

33

fortunately, remembered Robert, he carried nothing of value with him, and if you didn't carry anything on a walk, you couldn't be robbed. His inheritance had been used for the voyage, and only a few Swedish coppers remained in his purse.

But Arvid clutched the watch chain which hung across his vest and whispered into Robert's ear: He had brought along his watch, perhaps it was risky, what should he do about it? Robert didn't even have a watch; no one could rob him even though each tenth person was a thief.

The boys from Ljuder knew very little about towns. Before coming to New York, they had passed through only one town, Karlshamn. (Arvid had not even read about towns, as he couldn't read; before Robert had shown him a geography schoolbook, he had thought the whole world consisted only of Sweden.) But the boys did not wish to appear ignorant, as though unused to people. Robert therefore asked the Finn, with an intonation reflecting familiarity with the subject: Were the women in the New York whorehouses born in this country or were they immigrants?

The Finn answered that nearly all such women were born in the Old World; some had fallen into sin while crossing on the ships; others, perhaps, ran out of traveling money when they reached New York, and when they couldn't get beyond the pier, they sold that which could be sold most easily and quickly. But a whore's life in North America lasted only four years at the most. Then came death. That is to say, if she were healthy and sound at the beginning. Most of them became venereal cases, their bodies covered with stinking sores, their limbs rotting away, falling off one after the other. The poison buried itself inside their bones, he had heard; there it reproduced itself, from generation to generation. In this way God's law was fulfilled, as it was written in the commandment of the catechism: the sins of the fathers were visited on the children, unto a third and fourth generation "of them that hate Me."

When they rounded a corner, their guide stopped and pointed to a stone pedestal near the street: "On that foundation stood the last king who reigned in America."

The mass of stone was at least twenty feet high. Robert asked: "What was the king's name?"

"I don't remember. He was an English king. He was made of lead!"

"Oh, I understand; it was a statue?"

"That's right, boys! It was a lead statue of a king!"

The Finn explained: The English king reigned so poorly and so tyrannically that the Americans went to war to get rid of him. But they had a scarcity of bullets for their guns, so they melted down this leaden image of their king. When the English came to chastise the obstinate Americans, they were greeted by pieces of lead from their own king. The fine bullets hit them right between the eyes! So the Americans won the war and became a free people. That's what happened to the last king in America.

And who could tell—perhaps the European people one day would put their king statues in pots, and boil and melt them and make bullets of them. Then they too might be free.

Robert nodded; he understood: because kings were forbidden in America, one might speak as one would about them.

Now they turned right and entered a wide street. In great pride the Finn held both his hands out over the street as though to show something particularly his own, something his hands had made: this was Broadway, the most beautiful street in the world!

They had been sucked into a solid mass of people moving slowly about their errands, as it was impossible to hurry, giving way always to the right to avoid bumping against one another. So the boys did likewise. The walkers did not look each other in the face when meeting, no one stared in curiosity at anyone else. Robert and Arvid kept as close to the Finn as they could; they were jostled and pushed a little when they failed to give way fast enough, and they felt dizzy and bewildered in this multitude, faced with the endless horde passing on this street, said to be the world's broadest.

Robert tried to estimate the breadth of Broadway and he thought it must be more than seventy-five feet wide. The Broad Way, he knew the meaning of the name from his language book. Once he had seen a picture with the same name, and this picture had illustrated the road Man walked through life, crowded with people indulging in sin. That road had led to the Gates of Hell. On this street, also, wherever it led, was a jostling crowd. Most people he saw had white-skinned faces and were shaped like his own people. But the great difference in dress surprised Robert. Here walked men in elegant, well-brushed, expensive clothes, with clean, white-shining linen around their necks and polished boots on their feet. He saw other men, too, in worn-out, ragged garments, dirty shirts, and with their feet wrapped in old rags; some even went barefoot; they must burn their feet on these hot stones. He thought those poorly dressed men must be new arrivals in this country; they had not yet had time to get rich.

He saw many Negroes, all going about free and unchained. He had thought that black people held as slaves were in chains and led by guards, like dogs on leashes. He noticed Negroes laughing so broadly that their teeth gleamed white against their dark lips; but others looked so sad, shy, and downtrodden that the sight of them hurt him deep inside. He guessed that those who laughed had kinder masters than the others.

The Finn said the houses on this street were the highest ever built in the world. Some were, indeed, as tall as six stories, and taller houses could not be built.

"Danjel says we have arrived at the Tower of Babel," volunteered Arvid.

"Babel's Tower fell long ago," Robert informed his friend.

They looked at the houses along Broadway; some were built of wood

35

and stone, and painted in many colors—white, clear red, black, and yellow. Some houses even had walls with white stripes of plaster; this was a curious sight, striped houses.

In the middle of the street rode men in black coats and high hats, their horses well fed, newly curried, with flanks shining. Wagons rolled by, gilded spring wagons bearing women in fine clothes; there were plain carts loaded with ale barrels, carriages with white teams, cabs, gigs, clumsy wagons drawn by oxen, light vehicles drawn by horses small as colts, four-wheelers, two-wheelers, big and small wagons, light and heavy ones. Everything that could be put on wheels and pulled by animals rolled by on this street.

Arvid pointed in amazement at a small, gray, long-eared, long-haired animal which stood quite still between the shafts of a cart: "That thing is neither horse nor ox!"

"It's an ass," said the Finn.

Robert hurried to show what he knew: "One can ride on them too," he said. "It's told in the Bible that Jesus rode on an ass into Jerusalem."

"On an animal like that?" asked Arvid. "How could he sit straddle-legged on such a puny creature?"

They slowly continued their walk up Broadway. A great fat sow with a litter of pigs was poking about in the gutter on their side of the street. The mother sow was as long legged as a calf, but her teats hung so low they almost reached the ground; the little piglets were light brown, almost like whelps, and ran between the legs of the walkers so that Robert almost tripped. Arvid counted fourteen in the litter and observed that American swine were longer legged than Swedish.

Robert said the Americans didn't seem afraid to lose their pigs, letting them run around at will, but the Finn informed him that every owner marked his swine with an ear cut; moreover, there were so many swine in America, no one cared much if an occasional litter were lost. All garbage and sweepings were thrown into the streets, and the swine kept the town clean, he added. Here slops were lying in piles, and some of the houses they passed smelled as though more slops were being prepared inside.

But the street smell of pigsties was familiar to the two youths from Swedish peasant communities. In Sweden or North America, in Ljuder Parish or New York City, they could find no noticeable difference in the smell of swine dung.

From time to time the Finn stopped and peered into windows as though he were looking for some particular place. Arvid and Robert stopped also, but as far as they could judge, every house was a shop, and every entrance had something written over the door in large, gilded letters.

At last the Finn stopped in front of a small house, not much bigger than a shed; it could be a shop, but there were no shop articles in the window. The Finn pointed to a placard nailed to the door:

### NOTICE!

*This shop is closed in honor of the King of Kings,*
*Who will appear about the twentieth of October.*
*Get ready, friends, to crown Him Lord of All.*

"Now we're near the place I'm looking for," said the Finn. "This same notice was on the door last fall when I was here."

Robert, who had begun to learn English from his book during the voyage, tried to read the notice on the door. He recognized some of the words but could not understand their meaning; he wanted to ask the Finn, but Arvid took the question from him: "What do the words say?"

The Finn explained: It had been predicted that the Day of Doom would take place in New York during October last year, and the owner of the shop had closed in advance to honor Christ on His return. The King of Kings had not appeared, but the shop still remained closed; perhaps the owner had starved to death by now.

There was another notice a little lower on the door, and the Finn bent down to read it: *Muslin for Ascension Robes. Muslin to meet the King of Kings. 20 cents a yard.*

The boys wanted to know what this notice said.

"Oh, just that the storekeeper sold wedding gowns for Christ's brides," said the Finn.

And now the Finn must attend to the captain's errands. He told the boys to find their way back to the ship alone; it was not difficult, only turn right about and then to the left. And if they wanted to go to the end of the street, they could do so. Broadway was about three miles long and ran right through Manhattan. They would not lose their way if they stayed on Broadway.

The Finn nodded good-by and they saw him enter a saloon with the name *Joe's Tavern* on the window; it was next door to the little shop which had been closed for the arrival of the King of Kings.

—2—

ARVID AND ROBERT continued alone up Broadway. It was only today that they had been released from their long imprisonment. A feeling of unaccustomed freedom filled them now that they were free to move unhindered on solid ground. Boldly they decided to walk to the street's very end, however far it stretched. Then they would turn straight about and walk back to the harbor and their fellow passengers.

And so they continued along the most beautiful street in the world;

37

they stopped and looked at the tall houses, they examined inscriptions over doors: *Store, Steak House, Coffeehouse, Lodging House, Brown's Store, Drugstore*. They tried to interpret the inscriptions and guessed at their meaning. Could this be a tavern? Was that a hawker's shop? Or an apothecary? The word *store* in particular impressed them, it appeared on one building after another. At last Arvid espied a small house, which he thought must be an outhouse, and he pointed for Robert to look, and laughed: "Look at that one! They call that a store too!"

"They must be bragging," said Robert. But he did not mind this exaggeration; it was always true that the smaller you were the more you needed to seem bigger.

He tried to understand words and sentences he overheard, but everything was unintelligible, senseless jabber; not even one word, not a single syllable, was he able to recognize from his language book. He felt discouraged and disappointed. When he had stepped ashore he had thought he knew enough English to understand what he heard, even if he couldn't answer properly; he began to think they had cheated him in Karlshamn by selling him an unreliable book.

The boys arrived at an open square where many booths had been erected, and they thought this must be a market day. Here they stood long and gazed; Robert had said they shouldn't stand and stare because they might be laughed at, but this market fascinated them.

Wooden barrels stood in long rows, running over with potatoes, turnips, cabbages, carrots, peas, beets, parsnips, and many other roots which they saw for the first time; barrels in great numbers were filled with fruit—yellow, red, green, striped—apples, cherries, plums, and other fruits and berries which they never before had seen and the names of which they did not know. Between the barrels were long rows of baskets full of eggs and tubs full of butter, so fat that it seemed to perspire; on poles hung yellow, round, fat cheeses, big as grindstones; carcasses of animals, legs of pork, steaks, shortribs, and sides of bacon were stacked like firewood in high piles. Sizable, well-stuffed sausages hung in lines over tables on which stood vessels of ground meat and salted hams. There were booths with fowl: chickens, ducks, game birds; other fowl were stacked in hills of feathers, of all earthly bird colors, with a sprinkle of blood here and there on heads, necks, and wings. Four-footed beasts of the wild hung here in great numbers, hairy bodies of stags and does, hares and rabbits, known and unknown animals. In other stands were large tables with fish, long and short, broad and narrow, fat and spindly, black and white, red and blue; fish with striped bodies, misshapen fish, all head and protruding eyes, fish with ravenous jaws and sharp teeth like dogs', fish with fins as sharp as spears, and fish with long tail fins by which they hung on hooks, swinging like pendulums as the shoppers brushed against them. On the ground stood wooden boxes in which crawled and crept shellfish, horrible-looking sea monsters, lizardlike creatures, frogs, crayfish, mussels, snails, animals in shells that opened up like caskets, and shellfish that crawled about and resembled who knew what; nothing they had ever heard of, seen, or known, now or ever in all their living days.

The barrels, baskets, tubs, tables, boxes, and buckets in this market place were filled to overflowing; the whole place seemed flooded with fruit and meat, pork and lamb, fins and feathers, shell and hides, flooded with food of endless variety. People shopping here tramped in food, hit their heads on food, were enveloped in food, tumbled about in food. Who would skin all these animals, pluck all these birds, scale all these fish? For strangers and new arrivals, there was a booth in the market offering samples of all the food products which the new land offered its inhabitants. Here they saw the Creator's many gifts, fruits and berries, roots, herbs, and plants; they saw crawling, flying, swimming creatures, and meat from the cattle and beasts which God had created on the Sixth Day, before He created Man.

The two youths beheld the earth's abundance in a market next to the most beautiful street in the world. This much they understood: there was food in sufficiency in North America; it would be enough for them too, and for the seventy immigrants who had arrived with them today; they knew, from what their own eyes told them, that they had entered a new world.

—3—

THE DAY WAS nearing its warmest hour, the heat lay like a heavy weight over the city, making breathing difficult for the crowds on the street. People sought the shade and sat with their backs against house walls, drowsy, resting with their eyes closed; little babies slept at their mothers' breasts, women sat leaning their heads against men's knees. A half-naked Negro boy with a shoebrush in one hand and a jar of shoe blacking in the other strolled about, calling: "Black your boots! Black your boots!"

Robert and Arvid dragged their steps, burdened by their heavy wadmal clothes. Their hair, grown long during the voyage, felt sticky and uncomfortable. They pushed their way among brown pigs poking in the gutter, they squeezed themselves in between the carts of fruit sellers; now and again they were hailed by peddlers offering them wares; once a man stopped and spoke directly to them. Robert had learned what to say when accosted by an American: he had the sentence ready on his tongue, he was glad to use it now for the first time: "I am a stranger here."

But the man only stared at him. Robert repeated the words, carefully, clearly, he pronounced each syllable as directed in the language book. But the man only shook his head.

How could this be possible? He had practiced this sentence so many

39

times. Yet the American failed to understand him. The book must be wrong.

A man in fiery red pants and a tall black hat kept following them. On a leash he led two sharp-nosed, starved-looking dogs. "You want to buy a dog?" Robert did not understand these words. He looked at the dogs whose long, red tongues were hanging out of their mouths; they seemed fierce and dangerous. Robert was afraid of the obtrusive man; now he had taken his arm. He did not know what the man wanted, but he wanted to get away. At last he managed to free himself from the man's grip, and he and Arvid hurried their steps until the stranger was lost in the crowd.

Now Robert began to contemplate their situation, and he became fearful: here they walked about, entirely alone, in a town where everyone was a stranger, every tenth man a criminal; they were unable to say anything to anybody, they understood nothing that was said to them. If danger should overtake them they could not even call for help. Perhaps the Finn had exaggerated, probably only one man in twenty was a robber, but even so it was unpleasant. They did not know what robbers in America looked like, but they had seen many faces behind which an evil and treacherous soul might be hidden. He suggested that they return to their company. He did not wish to scare Arvid, he only said the others might be apprehensive if they stayed away too long. He was not afraid for his own sake, nor did he think Arvid had anything to fear; still—

"I have my nickel watch," Arvid reminded him, and began nervously fingering the broad, yellow brass chain which hung on his vest.

When Arvid left home his father had given him this watch, his dearest and most expensive possession. The father had said that the watch must be considered his paternal inheritance, given to him at this time because of his emigration. It was of fine nickel and had cost twelve riksdaler with the chain. During the forty years Arvid's father had worked as cotter under the name of Kråkesjö, it was all he had been able to save as inheritance for his son. The cotter would not have given Arvid his inheritance in cash, even if he had had any; he would have been afraid Arvid might spend it on snuff and brännvin. But a watch he would always keep with him: he had admonished his son never to sell or lose his Swedish inheritance.

Now Arvid was walking about in the dangerous town of New York, surrounded by robbers and swindlers, and he was carrying the watch with him.

"Put it in your pants pocket," advised Robert. For it occurred to him that the shining brass chain on Arvid's stomach might attract robbers. Arvid unhooked the chain and put the watch in his trousers pocket.

So they continued their walk up the street. Arvid wanted to go farther, he was happy today; Robert had never seen him so excited and gay. Arvid said that as long as he was back on land again, he wanted really to use his legs, he wanted to walk all the way to the end of the street. Now

40

that they were in America and could go anywhere dry shod, he was willing to walk the whole way to where they would settle, however far it was. He was sure he could walk there, because he was one of those who could use their legs.

A blond girl in a red dress held out a basket of fruit to the boys—black-red, juicy cherries. Robert shook his head; in vain he tried to remember a suitable English word from his language book; he would have liked to tell the girl (even if it was not true) that he had just bought a bagful of cherries.

But the girl remained standing in front of them, smiling at them in a kind, friendly way, and they each took a handful from her basket, as though wishing to taste her cherries before deciding whether to buy. The girl said something that sounded rather kind and went on her way. The boys were a little ashamed of their daring, and Robert regretted that he hadn't at least said "Thank you." That much he knew in English.

The juicy cherries were a treat to their dry mouths, and they ate them eagerly and spit the stones about them. A fat woman offered big loaves of wheat bread for sale. The loaves had been made in the form of rings, and she carried them hanging around her arms; the boys thought this quite ingenious: to use one's arms for bread poles. The smell of the fresh bread aroused their appetites—they felt hungry.

A black-haired, ragged little man, carrying a hand organ on his back and holding a monkey on a leash, stopped them with a stream of words. But they understood not a single syllable issuing from his mouth. Neither one of them had ever seen a monkey before. The creature went on two legs like themselves, and it had a hairless behind, red and swollen like an open wound. Arvid, in great disbelief, stared the monkey in the face and said with great emotion: The creature looked impudent—it was inexcusable of an animal to resemble a human being so closely.

A cart loaded with fruit turned over in the gutter with much noise and commotion. Large, yellow, and bigger than apples, the fruit rolled into the horse and swine spillings of the street and was allowed to remain there. The driver turned his vehicle back on its wheels and drove on, his cart empty. None of the walkers paid any attention to the accident, none made the slightest move to pick up the fruit. Only Arvid and Robert remained standing there a few minutes, but they were afraid to gather any of the beautiful unknown fruit.

The sight of so many edibles increased their hunger. But they had no money, they must wait to eat from their own food baskets—Robert would have to eat with Karl Oskar's family, Arvid with Danjel Andreasson's.

The boys would not admit to each other that their stomachs were calling loudly for food, nor would they disclose their astonishment during this walk. They had never imagined that all these things existed in the world, these tall houses, these shops with inscriptions over their entrances in glittering letters, all these valuable things that were hung or spread

41

in the store windows: glittering jewelry, gold, silver, precious stones, watches, rings, chains of gold and silver; expensive materials, cloth of gold and of silver, linen, wool, silk, velvet in quantities that could have covered this whole, long street; the expensive, gilded carriages, the light-footed, agile horses in glittering harnesses; all the things with names and uses they did not know, which they could only look at, admire, and guess about.

Before they recovered from one surprise, another even more amazing met their eyes. Two tall men in striped green and white coats and trousers, each carrying an upright pole with a placard on its upper end: *See the Anaconda! See the Serpent Charmer! See the Great Boa Constrictor! Five Cents!* The men stopped at the corner, calling loudly, and Robert tried to interpret their message. From his book he recognized the word *boa constrictor*. And in an open place near by he espied a reddish tent with the same inscription; then he understood what it meant and explained to Arvid: Over there in the tent one could see the boa constrictor, the most dangerous snake in the world, it might be as long as forty feet; it cost only five cents to go in and see. . . .

The boa constrictor? ruminated Arvid. Hadn't Robert once read to him from his *History of Nature* about this peculiar crawling reptile? He seemed to remember: ". . . the boa constrictor can be dangerous because of its great size and strength; it has happened that it has crushed and swallowed people; it grows to be almost forty feet long. . . ."

"If only we each had five cents!"

It hurt Robert that they must miss this opportunity to look at the world's greatest snake; a snake forty feet long that swallowed people, to be seen for only five cents. . . .

"Is the beast bound?" asked Arvid.

He looked toward the tent where a crowd of people thronged; he was not as anxious as his comrade to see the man-eating snake. From the very beginning, he had been worried about American reptiles; in his night-mares, America had been filled with hungry, hissing snakes, a veritable snake nest. He now wondered if it could be healthy to look at a snake that big. For himself, a snake five, six feet long would satisfy him, he wasn't so interested in snakes. Perhaps they could see part of the snake, maybe its tail; that might be cheaper.

Robert said it didn't matter, since they had not even one cent. He suddenly felt depressed and disappointed. All day long he had seen beautiful things for sale, and it had bothered him that he was unable to buy anything; now he actually suffered from having to leave the tent with the large snake.

Truly, on this, the most beautiful street in the world, there was everything one might strive for in this world, all one's heart might desire was here. And Robert felt that the street would have been still more beautiful had he a purse full of American money.

But the very thing he lacked, he had come here to earn; he had come to America to be free—but in order to be free, he must first become rich.

—4—

THE HUMMING IN ROBERT's left ear suddenly began again, so intensely that it drowned all the street sounds. It was an echo from that box on the ear received at home in Sweden many years ago; it was a reminder of the servant law—"suitable chastisement." This his master had given him for laziness in service. The windy weather at sea had worsened his ear injury, and again a yellow, malodorous fluid ran from it. The humming sound, which sometimes increased to a roar, was constantly and depressingly with him. It had followed him from Sweden to North America, he could not lose it. Something was hurt inside the ear.

The hum carried with it a memory from his farm-hand service, a memory which troubled him day and night, year after year. Because of this memory he did not wish to serve as farm hand ever again; he did not wish ever to have a master; he wanted to be free.

He had tried to reconcile himself to the throbbing, had tried to make friends with the sound; it was a voice in there, wishing him well, comforting him when something went wrong, warning him when danger lurked. He had noticed that the hum began when something was happening to him, or about to happen; perhaps his friend in the left ear now wanted to comfort him because he had been unable to see the forty-foot, man-eating snake. . . .

Suddenly the sound was drowned by a loud outcry from Arvid: "Look, Robert! Look over there!"

"What is it?"

"A corpse! Look!"

"What?"

"Can't you see—there's a man lying there dead!"

They crossed the street and saw a man lying stretched in the gutter on his back; he was half naked, dressed only in a pair of worn-out pants which hardly covered his legs. His upper body was black with dirt or paint, but the skin of his face was white; he was not a Negro. His eyes were closed and his mouth open, disclosing toothless gums.

Arvid bent down over the body, bustling and excited: "He's dead! The man is dead! Stone dead!"

Robert, too, looked closer. The man's chest did not heave, his mouth did not move, he did not seem to breathe. With his foot he lightly touched the foot of the man; he did not move. "I believe he *is* dead."

Here a corpse was lying in the street, and people went by without noticing. Living people passed by the dead man, stepped over his outstretched legs, but no one paid any attention, no one noticed he was dead.

43

It was extraordinary. Robert thought this must be because of the great size of the population: there were so many living people jostling each other here in America that no one could pay attention to the dead ones, who were so silent and so still. He and Arvid noticed the body because they were new in the country and not accustomed to seeing corpses lying about.

They looked at each other in consternation: What should they do? Perhaps they should report their discovery, but how? They probably ought to call the police, but they did not know where the police were, and they could not talk, could not ask. Robert remembered there was a sentence in his language book to be used when calling the police. But that was in case of attack on the street. . . . And he couldn't remember the sentence, anyway, either in Swedish or English. And the police might wonder about them, perhaps even suspect them of having murdered the man lying there in the gutter. It seemed he had only lately died, the corpse was still warm, and it didn't smell as might be expected in this heat. Perhaps the man had been murdered. Yes, Robert was sure they would be suspected. And they couldn't say a word, couldn't deny it, couldn't defend themselves. No doubt they would be put in prison for murder. It would be best to forget about calling the police. They might stop a passer-by and point to the corpse, and then let him fetch the police. But in that case they might be held as witnesses. It would be best just to walk on and let the dead one lie there.

"We'll pretend we haven't seen anything," advised Robert. "Come, let's go!"

But Arvid remained leaning over the man. He had made a new discovery: "He smells of brännvin!"

He poked the man carefully between his naked ribs: "Yes, I believe he is—"

Next moment Arvid jumped backward with an outcry: the man had suddenly risen from the ground like a Jack-in-the-box. In front of them stood a heavy-set giant, a living man, swiftly resurrected and roaring furiously.

At this threatening apparition Robert crouched in fright, and Arvid, in his backward jump, almost landed on top of him. They grasped each other's hands.

Arvid never had time to finish his sentence that he thought the man was alive. Nor did he need to: they could see it—they heard it; they saw and heard a furious, insulted giant standing on his feet, though a little shaky. He took a few steps toward them, and from his enormous, red throat flowed a stream of words which the boys did not think were of a friendly kind. A few words Robert thought he understood: *Damned—thieves—bastards.* Never in their lives had they heard such terrifying sounds come from a human throat.

The passers-by stopped in the street, people began to gather around

44

them, attracted by the resurrected one's roaring. The boys held each other's hands as they backed away. The man so suddenly sprung from the ground spurted spit and fury, he bent forward as though ready to spring at them; something gleamed in his right hand, it flashed in the sun.

Arvid cried out at the top of his voice: "A knife! He'll stab us—Run, run!"

The boys took to their heels and ran. They ran into the middle of the street, still gripping each other's hands, down the street the same way they had come; they ran until they lost their breath and felt a burning in their lungs; they ran past riders and wagons, carts and carriages, horses and asses, they slid between animals and vehicles, they ran for their lives—to get away from the man who sprang at them with a flashing knife in his hand, from the dead man who had come back to life. They had no trouble finding their way, they knew it—all the way down the broad street, the whole length of Broadway, until it ended, then a turn to the left where they would see the harbor and the ships.

During their race they jostled people, and angry voices were heard from the crowd. At last Robert held Arvid back: they must slow their pace and be more careful or people would become suspicious of them.

As they reached the market place they stopped for a moment and looked back, puffing and breathless. No one was following them, they were saved. And they resumed their leisurely walk, protected and hidden by the crowd.

"He was a dangerous man," said Arvid, still shaking. "He might have killed us!"

In a flash Robert could see himself and Arvid lying there stretched out in the street, knife slashes through their throats, like pigs at slaughter time, their blood gushing like ale through a bunghole; their legs kicking a last, weak kick, a helpless kick against death; a feeble twitch of their limbs—then death overpowering them. And there they would be lying, dead in the street, people walking by, no one noticing or taking care of their corpses, nor shrouding them, nor burying them, nor grieving over them here in a foreign country. And when they began to rot and smell, they would at last become food for the swine in the street. So it might have happened.

Robert had seen something glitter in the man's hand but now, as he recovered his breath, he thought it might not have been a knife; it looked more like glass, perhaps a small bottle. But Arvid insisted he had seen the gruesome man pull out a slaughter knife, a real sticking knife with a point as sharp as an awl.

Robert was still trembling a little, and now he felt ashamed of it and wondered if they hadn't run simply because of their own fear. He told Arvid they must agree never to let fear overtake them here in America.

"Silly to run away! If the man had touched us, we could have reported him to the police."

45

He had just remembered from his English instruction book how to call the police in case of robbers and murderers on the street: *Please listen to me, Mr. Policeman! I appeal for your protection against this unfriendly person who is annoying me.* This was a long sentence, requiring much time to say. . . . He thought one would have to be very quick if one were to finish the whole sentence before being murdered. He realized he must learn English as soon as possible; he must know the language in order to save his life in case of sudden attack, if for no other reason. He had forgotten, earlier, that he had something of value he might lose; now he remembered: his own life!

But what had happened was really Arvid's fault: "I told you to let the man alone!"

"I thought he was dead from drinking. He stank of brännvin."

"But why did you poke him in the ribs?"

"I like the smell of brännvin, and I thought a corpse couldn't be dangerous."

Robert lectured him. He had been foolish and curious, and as a result almost got them killed. Finally Arvid agreed that he had been careless; but he had felt happy and reckless today, walking along this broad, beautiful street. Now he became dejected and sad; he promised on oath, using God's holy name, that it would never happen again. If he found droves of corpses here in America, if people lay dead in piles on every street and road, he would never bother to stop. No, he wouldn't even cast a glance at a single one of the corpses, no one could ever persuade him to look at dead men, or poke at them—even if they smelled of brännvin ever so much. He and Robert shook hands on this.

They were a little disappointed not to have reached the farther end of the street, not to have seen where Broadway ran—either to the portals of Heaven or Hell. But now they trailed dejectedly and cautiously back to its beginning, where they had started out, near the green grove, the manor park. They went back to join their families, both of them anxious to tell the others about their walk on the most beautiful street in the world, where they had almost been robbed of the only thing they owned—their lives.

Arvid soon consoled himself, and his happiness returned as he stuck his hand into his trousers pocket and felt his watch still there.

# VI

## Journey with the Steam Wagon

*Contract for Transportation of Immigrants*

*The undersigned agrees to carry the immigrants, who have arrived on the*

46

*Swedish brig* Charlotta *of* Karlshamn, *from New York to Chicago, on the following conditions:*

*1. From New York to Albany by steamer, from Albany to Buffalo by steam wagon, and from Buffalo to Chicago by steamer.*

*2. For every adult person the fare is 8 dollars, children under 3 years free, children between 3 years and 12 years half fare.*

*3. The same fare entitles the traveler to 100 lbs. baggage free, and 150 lbs. on the steam wagon.*

*4. The baggage of the passengers is transferred free of charge from the vessel in New York to the steamer, and likewise in Albany and Buffalo, the whole way through to Chicago.*

*New York, June 26, 1850*

THE IMMIGRANTS traveled up the Hudson from New York to Albany on one of the largest steamboats plying the river, the *Isaac Newton.*

The steamer left New York at eight in the evening, loaded to capacity with passengers and baggage. The immigrants were crowded together on the lower deck, while their belongings were piled almost as high as the smokestacks of the steamer on the upper deck toward the bow.

This was a night without rest for the travelers; there were no sleeping accommodations, and the immigrants sat or stood on deck, so closely packed together that no one could lie down. Parents held their children in their arms, older children and grownups stood upright. When they were tired, they tried to find rest by leaning on each other. Fortunately, they were to travel on this boat for only one night.

And this night they might have been able to sleep without concern for their lives if only there had been room to stretch out; this was not a dangerous voyage over a heaving ocean, violently pitching and rolling; this was a steady, easy passage on a calm, protected river. The Hudson stretched serenely before them, dotted with islands and inlets, following its furrow in quiet power. Through the night, mist towered over the high, steep shores. They were like secret dark fortress walls or silent sentinels, which guarded their water passage on either side. The journey on this water, where they could see land on the right and on the left, was to these ocean travelers almost the same as a trip on solid ground.

The *Isaac Newton* was driven forward by its great stern wheel, which dug deep into the river, stirring up whirls of foam; the wheel twirled the water like a giant egg whisk. The Hudson's even current slowed the progress of the heavily laden, deep-lying vessel. The stern wheel cut a deep furrow through the white foam, a wheel track in the water, evened out, obliterated, and gone as soon as its wake had passed. Behind the vessel

47

the river flowed as before, calm, slow, even, majestic, on its way to the Atlantic.

One hour after daybreak the *Isaac Newton* tied up at the pier in Albany. Tired, limp, worn-out by lack of sleep, the immigrants left the boat and were divided into groups by their guides and interpreters, who marched with them on a road along the river to the railway station. They were shown into a large hall in the station house, and here the different groups—the English, the Irish, the Germans, the Swedes—were told by their respective guides in their own languages to remain absolutely still; no one was allowed to move from his indicated place. They were not told why they must stand so still, but gradually they learned: two American inspectors went about among them, pointing their fingers at each one, counting them. The men came back, pointed and mumbled once more, and again the immigrants were told by their guides to remain absolutely still; a few had moved and confused the inspectors in their counting.

The immigrants were counted like sheep in a pen, their numbers must check with the numbers in the passenger contracts. Then they were let out of the station to board the steam wagon.

—2—

AT HOME, the immigrants from Ljuder had heard stories about these newly invented wagons, which were driven by steam and rolled along on iron bars strung over the ground. But until now none of their group had seen or used the railroad. To them this newfangled method of transportation seemed dangerous, possibly disastrous. But Karl Oskar had said that the steam wagon was the fastest means of transportation inland, and as their interpreter had told them the same, they had agreed to try the new way of traveling.

They considered themselves lucky in obtaining so tall a Swede to be their interpreter and guide; the ex-carpenter Landberg was a whole head taller than anyone in this great multitude of travelers, and wherever he happened to be, they could easily see him, they would not be likely to lose him. And Landberg was careful not to lose any of them. He stayed close to the group from the *Charlotta*, explained things, and was helpful in all ways. Now he led them up to the steam wagon and told them to be careful when climbing on board, so as not to fall and hurt themselves.

Some twenty wagons, high and covered with roofs, were tied together in a long row, and the immigrants gaped at them wide eyed, half from fear and half from curiosity. Each wagon was built on eight iron wheels and had windows. They thought it might be strong and steady. The wagon at the forward end was unlike the others; as it was first, it must be the one that was to pull, the real steam wagon. It had only four wheels, but these were three times as large as the wheels on the other wagons. Then there

48

were two small wheels, in the very front end. The steam wagon had a tall chimney, broad at the opening and narrowing downward; it sat there like a huge funnel stuck in the throat of a bottle. At the fore end this wagon had iron bars twisted together to form a large scoop or shovel.

Thick, black smoke belched from the chimney and sent red-glowing sparks whirling into the air. The steam wagon had fire inside, it burned there, and this worried the immigrants.

They had always been taught to be careful with fire, to carry burning candles cautiously, to handle lanterns and firesticks with utmost wariness; they harbored a fear, implanted in them from childhood, of fire on the loose. And now they must ride in a row of wagons drawn by one with fire burning inside it; it smoked, crackled, sputtered, and sparks flew from the wagon's bowels. How easily one spark could fall on the roof of a following wagon and ignite it! They realized that they were to be exposed to continuous fire hazard, at least while the fire burned inside the steam wagon. They had also heard that a steam wagon might easily explode and fly to pieces in the air.

Robert had read about steam engines in his *History of Nature* and tried to explain to the others: Inside the steam wagon they were boiling water in a great big kettle, and it was that kettle which pulled the whole row of wagons. But he did not know what purpose was served by the large iron scoop in front of the steam wagon, and he asked Long Landberg about this. Their guide said that this contraption shoveled away wild animals if they stood between the rails and threatened to overturn the train.

Ulrika of Västergöhl said she wanted to ride as far away from the burning wagon as possible. She expressed the desire of all in their group.

When they were ready to take their seats, the guide showed them into the fifth wagon from the engine; they were disappointed not to be farther away from the fire. They climbed a small ladder, slowly and cautiously. Their wagon was about fifteen feet long and half as wide. A bench had been built on either side with a narrow passage in the middle. The seats were made of carelessly nailed-together rough boards. Two more groups, somewhat smaller than their own, were to share this wagon with them. Their knapsacks, food baskets, boxes, and bundles took much room, and they had to crowd together in order to find space for all. Those unable to find room on the benches stood or lay down on the floor. The immigrants felt as though they had been packed into a good-sized calf coop.

On the end of one bench a place was made for old Fina-Kajsa, so that she might ride half-sitting; she was weaker than she would admit and could stand on her legs only a few minutes at a time. For the third or fourth time she inquired of the guide about her iron pot, and for the third or fourth time she was given the information that the pot rode with the chests and other heavier pieces in a special wagon.

"But where is the grindstone?" asked Fina-Kajsa. "Where is it?"

The grindstone, brought along by her husband who died on the voyage, had, through carelessness at the New York unloading, fallen into the harbor, and all said this was good luck for Fina-Kajsa, who need not now pay the expensive inland freight for it. But she thought they were telling her a lie. Her son Anders in Minnesota had written home that grindstones were scarce in America, and now she thought the Americans had stolen her stone as soon as they laid eyes on it.

And Fina-Kajsa kept on complaining: "Oh me, oh my! What an endless road! We'll never arrive!"

In great harmony the immigrants shared the wagon space with each other; no one tried to spread out, all made room; they had learned on this journey to live closely packed in narrow quarters, and they endured it good-naturedly. In the wagon, too, they had more space in which to move than they had had on the river steamer. But the air in the wagon seemed thick and stuffy after a score and a half people had pushed their way into it. At daybreak a heavy shower had fallen and cooled the earth, but now the sun already felt burning, in spite of the early hour, and they understood that the day was to bring intense heat, hard to endure.

As yet the wagon stood still, and the passengers were quiet in silent anticipation and wordless worry: What would happen when they began to ride? Unknown dangers lurked on this journey; what mightn't take place when the wagon with fire inside it began to move? They had heard that some persons could not stand being freighted along on the railroad; it was said to be so hard on them that they fainted and lay unconscious for hours.

Kristina had heard the same as the others; she sat in a corner of the wagon with Lill-Märta and Harald on her knees. Johan had climbed up on the knapsack standing between the bench and her feet. The oldest boy had also wished to sit on her knees, and she would gladly have let him if she had had three knees. But Johan wouldn't understand that she had only two. The boy had grown impatient and troublesome since they landed.

He pulled his mother's arms: "Aren't we going to live in a house now, Mother?"

"Yes, soon—I've told you so."

"When is soon? When shall we live in a house?"

"When we arrive."

"But Father says we have arrived in America now."

"Yes, we have. Please keep quiet."

"It isn't true, Mother! You said we would live in a house when we got to America. Now we are in America—aren't we going to live in a house?"

"Yes, yes—please keep still, can't you, boy?"

Johan tired her beyond endurance, and she didn't know what to do with him, except to let him be until he tired himself. After the night on the river steamer without a moment's sleep, she was too exhausted to answer her children. All she wanted was to stretch herself out somewhere and

50

rest; she wanted to lie still, still, and sleep, sleep. But there never seemed any rest on this journey, no real rest, no satisfying sleep; now that they were to travel on this dangerous steam wagon there would be no sleep tonight either.

Karl Oskar stood pressed against the wall near her and talked to Jonas Petter and Danjel about the new form of transportation. Danjel said that now the prophesy had been fulfilled which said that toward the end of the world wagons would move without horses.

Danjel had asked himself if it could be God's will that His children use the steam power as beast of burden; if this power were something good and useful, why had the Lord kept it secret from man ever since the creation of the earth—nearly six thousand years? It might be that the steam power emanated from evil powers. But thus far the Lord had helped them on their journey. On the steam wagon they were still in His hands.

Kristina remembered Dean Brusander's words at a catechism examination, to the effect that the steam wagon was a wicked human device, tending to estrange the soul from its Creator, and, like all mechanical contraptions, leading to disaster for poor and rich alike. Steam power weakened and undermined soul and body, encouraging idleness, fornication, and immorality. The dean had therefore prayed God to spare them this curse and prevent steam wagons from ever being used in Sweden.

Kristina wondered if they sinned against any of God's commandments by riding the steam wagon; she thought, if she had understood the dean rightly, it must be the sixth commandment.

She knew nothing in advance of what might happen on this steam journey, but as she and her loved ones were in the clutches of the wagon it was too late to regret it. She felt as though she had stepped into a conveyance which had been harnessed to a wild, untamed horse in the shafts for the first time; a romping, ferocious beast capable of anything, which might run off the road, bolt, or roll over on the ground in play. She could not forget the belching sparks from the steam wagon's bowels; she felt that this was the most perilous part of their journey thus far. As yet nothing dangerous had happened to them in America, but they hadn't got far from the shore: anything might still happen.

Danjel had opened his psalmbook to the "Prayer before Starting a Journey," and when Kristina saw her uncle fold his hands, she did the same. She, her husband, and children already had risked their lives at sea, now they must do it on land as well; in silent prayer she invoked her Creator's protection.

—3—

In each end of the wagon was a narrow door, and over both doors were identical inscriptions in tall black letters:

51

DANGER!

WATCH YOUR STEP!

Karl Oskar had seen the same inscription near the pier in New York and as he now recognized it he asked their interpreter to tell him the meaning. Landberg said that these four words warned of dangerous places; when they saw the sign they must watch their steps and look carefully where they set their feet. Inexperienced travelers could easily take a false step when entering or leaving the wagon, and fall off.

Karl Oskar in his turn explained the words to Kristina, who said it was thoughtful to nail up placards in dangerous places in America; she too was going to keep in mind the four words signaling danger, they were so black and threatening she could never forget them.

Outside their window was a tall, white-painted signpost with several lines of foot-high letters:

SAFETY SIGNALS FOR TRAINS

A WHITE FLAG BY DAY

A WHITE LAMP BY NIGHT

SHOWS

ALL CLEAR

Karl Oskar wondered what this placard might mean; no doubt it concerned the travelers, therefore they ought to know. And it annoyed him that he understood not a single syllable of the new language, that he couldn't decipher a word. It was like the first day at school, when Schoolmaster Rinaldo had held the ABC book to his eyes for the first time. But now he was a full-grown man, twenty-seven years of age, with three children of his own; yet in this country he felt like a schoolboy once more; he must learn to spell all over again, he must learn to recognize words. His inability to read the language did not seem so bad, but it vexed him not to understand the spoken words; it hurt him to hear people speak in his presence without understanding them; he felt inclined to believe they were talking about him, and he was ashamed and annoyed to be talked about before his face, disregarded. Here in America one could stand face to face with people who insulted one, yet one couldn't do a thing about it; only stand there and stare, awkward, helpless, dumb. Since stepping ashore in America not many hours ago, he had felt foolish more often than during his whole life in Sweden.

But he refused to believe his intelligence had suffered from the emigration.

Their guide Landberg was standing at the entrance, his tall head concealing the inscription; he was speaking English to a man in a blue coat with yellow buttons; the man had a yellow sign on his cap, he must be one of the American guards, or steam-wagon officials. Karl Oskar surmised they were talking about the travelers inside the wagon. He listened with his ears open, trying to understand something that at least *reminded* him of words he understood. But the language of the interpreter and the American did not sound like human speech, rather like the buzz of a bumblebee in his ear; the sounds were distorted, mixed up, crazy through and through. The men twisted their mouths and made knots of their tongues in order to emit strange sounds; it seemed they imitated each other, made faces at each other as children might in play. To Karl Oskar's ears the American language seemed an unaccountable mixture of senseless sounds, and he grew more depressed each time he listened to it; he would never be able to teach his mouth to use this tongue.

The official left the wagon after he had seen to it that both doors were closed, and now Landberg spoke in Swedish: "Hold on to your seats, good people! Our train is starting to move!"

The warning was followed by a long-drawn-out, piercing, evil yell from the first wagon. The immigrants had never heard the like of this horrible howl, produced by neither beasts' nor human beings' throats, but by a lifeless thing and consequently much more terrifying. When it stopped, there was silence in the wagon, a silence of fear and apprehension. Faces turned pale, hands grasped hands, the travelers clutched each other or sought support against benches and walls, against anything within reach.

The moment had arrived; the steam wagon was moving. They could hear the wheels thunder under them as they rolled along on the iron bars, they could see through the windows that they had started ahead.

Their wagon jolted and shook, it cracked and creaked. A minute passed, and two, it pulled still harder, and the wagon rolled and leaned over a little to one side. Some of the travelers crouched in terror to weigh down the other side with the weight of their bodies; Fina-Kajsa shrieked to heaven. It was like the shriek of a dying person; she said she was being choked. Ulrika of Västergöhl hurried to her and loosened her vest, and soon she grew quiet and breathed more easily.

"It's turning over!" Johan screamed and gripped his mother's legs. "It's tipping over, Mother!"

"Keep quiet, boy!"

"I'm afraid!"

"Don't be afraid! It isn't dangerous!" Karl Oskar reassured the boy. "Lill-Märta and Harald aren't crying. You're the biggest, you mustn't cry."

Johan wanted to crawl up onto his mother's knees, already occupied by the smaller children, but the closest he could get was to cling to her legs; he held on with all his strength while the wagon rolled on, and great tears rolled down his pale cheeks.

Kristina was as much afraid as the child holding on to her, but she forced herself not to cry out. As she looked through the window and saw houses, trees, and the very ground itself move backward, she felt nauseated, her eyes blurred, her throat closed, her head swam. She wanted to see nothing, feel nothing—she closed her eyes and clenched her teeth. She must drive away this dizziness. She held her children closer to her, she clenched her teeth still tighter, she mustn't faint. . . . Perhaps she might escape it by sitting quite still, eyes closed. . . .

And while the train increased its speed, faster and faster, Kristina sat with her eyes closed. The engine blew out smoke and sparks from its interior, it belched and sputtered, it drew its breath heavily, in and out. The wheels rolled, creaked, and thundered, the wagons rocked and jerked, pulled and shook. And the people closed up inside sat in tense turmoil, each moment anticipating calamity.

But their wagon did not leave the rails, nor did it turn over, nor catch fire; nothing happened.

After a long while Kristina opened her eyes. She saw through the window how trees, bushes, hills, fields rushed by her with dizzying, indescribable speed, and her feeling of faintness returned. They were traveling with frightful speed, she could not endure to see how fast they moved, her head could not stand it; she was forced to close her eyes again.

And the immigrant train continued inland. Pale, silent, serious, the travelers felt they were moving with the speed of the wind.

Karl Oskar said, perhaps they were the first from Sweden to ride on a steam wagon.

—4—

THE PASSENGERS gradually grew calm, they began to talk to each other and move about. But they suffered sorely from the heat that pricked their skins with a thousand invisible pin points. As no air was admitted, it grew more and more oppressive inside the wagon, breathing became almost impossible; the children grew restless and irritable.

Karl Oskar turned to their guide: "Couldn't we open the windows ever so little?"

"The windows are nailed and cannot be opened."

"Couldn't we open the doors, then?"

"The doors are locked. They won't be opened until we stop."

And Landberg admonished the travelers to be calm and to rely on him; they were in his hands and he would look after them the way a shepherd watches his flock.

Landberg continued: It had happened that traveling immigrants had fallen off the wagons during the journey and been killed; it was in concern for their lives that the doors had been locked. But he would see to it that they got the air they needed during the journey. He knew that locked doors, too, could be dangerous. Last year a gruesome disaster had happened

54

to an immigrant train. When it had arrived in Buffalo, and the doors of one windowless freight car had been opened, five travelers were dead of suffocation. Three of those stifled had come from Sweden. All the other passengers were far gone. They had cried and begged to have the doors opened, but no one had understood them as there was no interpreter in their company. So, Landberg pointed out, the travelers could readily see how useful a guide was to newcomers. Since that tragedy, the railroad companies had been instructed to open the doors every time the train stopped. Landberg would see to it that sufficient air was admitted to keep his flock alive; no one would suffocate on this journey.

And the ex-carpenter, their tall countryman, smiled encouragingly at them. He had a mouthful of teeth which glittered white and handsome, and his cheeks were covered with a black, well-kept beard. He was a man whom women looked at. When unmarried Ulrika of Västergöhl asked him a question, she stuck her finger in a buttonhole of his coat so as not to let him get away. Long Landberg was kept busy answering questions, as they had no one else to ask, no one else to hear complaints; but he was never impatient or short.

Hardly had the passengers got their promise of fresh air than they were disturbed again: the sound from the wheels had suddenly grown more intense and hollow. They looked out and saw water streaming on either side of the wagon. They were riding over a bridge that crossed a broad river. The Americans had laid the iron bars for the railroad right across the water! The guide said the Americans were very daring people; above all, they liked to risk their lives; they did it frequently, as a matter of course.

Robert and Arvid sat together on the wagon floor and spoke to each other in low voices. Arvid did not feel well, he had a toothache; he wished he had continued the journey on foot. The first day on land he had had the motion of the waves in his legs and had felt as though he were walking over a quagmire; now when all his limbs were in good order again he must sit locked up in this calf coop. He was sure the wagon had been used for cattle transport—under one bench he had found dry cow dung. Robert showed this to Landberg, who said yes, maybe the wagon had been used for freighting cattle before it had been turned into an immigrant wagon.

Arvid asked if they could trust the wheels to follow the iron bars all the way. Robert told him there were rims on the wheels which forced them to follow the bars. It might, of course, happen that a wagon would lose a wheel, particularly as they drove with this terrible speed; they must be going eighteen miles an hour, or three times as fast as an ordinary spring wagon. That was how fast and strong the steam was.

Arvid looked at him in disbelief: "They say steam is nothing but mist?"

"Ye-es. The kind of mist one sees when water is boiling."

And Robert explained the power of steam to his friend: Once he and some other boys had picked up an old, discarded gun pipe; they had

55

plugged one end, filled the pipe with water, and then plugged the other end too; they had made a fire in the forest and laid the gun pipe over it; soon it became red hot and blew up; it made a terrific explosion, and the pipe burst into a thousand pieces. One of the boys had had three fingers torn off—so strong was steam power when loosed.

If they were unlucky, it might well happen that the steam in this train would break loose and tear all of them to pieces like a mash of meat so intermingled that flesh scraps and bone chips could hardly be separated.

Arvid chewed one of his knuckles, as was his custom when uneasy. "You think the steam will break loose?"

"No. I said, only if we are unlucky."

Robert meant to recount all he had read in his *History of Nature* about iron roads and steam power, so that his friend might feel comfortable and safe on this journey. But Arvid's face showed that his mind was in a turmoil. He whispered: "Do you remember what we promised each other? Always to stick together. Whatever happens, we must stick together."

"That we must, Arvid." Robert suddenly became very serious. "I do not forget a promise. Whatever happens to us in America, we must be friends."

Once, in their farm hands' stable quarters, back in Sweden, they had clasped hands and promised always to stand by each other. After their lives had been endangered on New York's broadest street, they had renewed this pledge.

Robert nodded toward his elder brother, he told Arvid he did not care for Karl Oskar's masterful ways, he did not like masters, he would rather be in Arvid's company. To be such friends as he and Arvid were counted more than blood relationships.

The train was slowing down, and soon their wagon stood quite still. Landberg kept his promise: the doors were opened at both ends of the wagon, and fresh air came in to ease their breathing. Through the windows they could see a few tall houses along a street and many small houses clustered near by, some no larger than woodsheds.

At last Kristina dared open her eyes and she gazed out as long as their wagon stood still. Karl Oskar asked how she felt after this first stretch.

"Not too bad. A little dizzy."

"It's because the wagon runs so fast, of course."

Across from Kristina sat Ulrika of Västergöhl, who had been looking out the window ever since they left Albany and did not seem to have suffered from dizziness. She was still as rosy cheeked and healthy as when she left Sweden, she had suffered no inconvenience during the long voyage, she had not missed a single meal at sea, she had never been seasick for one minute, nor had she thrown up one bite of all the food she had eaten. Scurvy did not attack her, lice did not come near her. No other passenger had remained as well as she. It had been given to her to step

56

ashore in America in full health, with all her strength intact. And now she sat here, unruffled by the terrifying speed; it agreed with her to ride behind the steam wagon.

Kristina wondered how this woman was created, what she could be made of. Most remarkable of all was the fact that twenty years of whoring had left no visible marks on the Glad One. Since embracing Danjel's teaching she no longer followed her profession, and lately Kristina had begun to believe that Ulrika's nature had improved; she was kind to Danjel's motherless children and took good care of them; this everyone had remarked on. Perhaps she wanted to expiate her life of whoring. Surely, in God's redemption book much was written concerning Ulrika of Västergöhl; each time her body had been used for fornication was noted. (Ulrika, however, thought that Christ's blood had washed her clean and that her sins, like a bundle of soiled linen, were tied up in the Saviour's napkin cloth.)

It had always bothered Kristina that she was forced to use the same privy as Ulrika; she could never forget the great number of men the Glad One had consorted with. In one end of the wagon was a small booth serving as a call-of-nature room for the passengers. Someone was always waiting near the booth, as the immigrants suffered from a severe diarrhea, which had attacked them after landing. But diarrhea was to be expected when they first arrived in America, said their interpreter; it was a special kind of immigrant diarrhea, caused by the change of country and different weather conditions; hardly one newcomer escaped it. Now all of them had been running to the privy this last day, at least once an hour—all except Ulrika of Västergöhl. She seemed to have normal, undisturbed bowels. She had escaped all ills and evils, even the diarrhea. God had verily shown her great patience, even though she was so deeply sunk in sin; yet He had severely tested Uncle Danjel, who always strove to live righteously. The ways of the Lord were inscrutable. But Kristina was grateful that Ulrika did not often use their privy here in the wagon.

For the third time since boarding the train Jonas Petter emerged from the little stall at the end of the wagon, fumbling with his trousers. He had lost weight during the crossing, and his face was pale and sunken. He complained to Karl Oskar: "This plagues one's bowels!"

"Diarrhea is not dangerous to life; it will pass as soon as the bowels are accustomed to the climate." And Karl Oskar pulled out his knapsack: "I heal myself with pepper-brännvin. Have a swallow, Jonas Petter."

He poured the brännvin from its earthen jug into a tin mug, and from a small bag added pepper until the brännvin looked as black as dung water.

"Pour it down fast!"

Jonas Petter emptied the mug of dark pepper-brännvin and made a wry face. "It's like swallowing burning coals."

"But it closes the hole. Take another drink in the morning—then you won't be forever running."

57

Jonas Petter said it was a strange invention to sit on a wagon and ride while attending to one's needs. What would the people at home say if they knew how comfortable they were, traveling with such a contraption! He admitted Americans were smart. This invention saved much time; should the train have to stop each time someone needed to cleanse his bowels, they would have traveled scarcely more than a stone's throw a day. But he wondered if anyone collected all this human dung so that the earth and the crops might benefit. Or perhaps American soil was so rich that no manure was needed.

Karl Oskar offered some of the pepper-brännvin to Kristina, but she refused it, thinking it too strong for her; she had tried it on the ship but threw it up again. Perhaps this was because of her pregnancy, which also caused her to suffer more than the others from the heat. She had often wondered why God inflicted so many miseries on pregnant women when He Himself created the human lives inside them.

As half her time had passed now, it would soon begin to show that she was with child. No one in their company except Karl Oskar knew as yet how things stood with her. But it couldn't be kept secret much longer. It was the women who first made such discoveries in each other; they always noticed the signs. Indeed, probably Ulrika already knew—she had seen the shameless creature, from time to time, look searchingly at her body, and even before they left Sweden the Glad One had said to Kristina, in a meaningful tone, that seasickness was much like being in the family way. Kristina had no hiding garment to don; she had not found time to sew herself a forty-week apron before they started out on their journey, and she did not think she would have opportunity to sew one here in America; she had a needle and thread, but not the smallest piece of cloth.

At home it was the custom for a woman to hide her pregnancy as long as possible. But why should she need a forty-week apron far away in a foreign country where she didn't know a single person and no one knew her? And perhaps no one in this country was offended by women showing their pregnancy. Perhaps they had different customs in North America. She had heard that no one cared how other people lived here or what they did.

But there sat Ulrika staring at her again, as if wondering in which month she might now be. This look on Ulrika's face angered her; she had a full right to be with child. She lived with her husband in a Christian marriage, she had a known father for her child. But how had it been with Ulrika's own brats? Who was father to Elin, the girl next to her, now looking after Danjel's children, sitting this moment with little Eva on her knee? There had been rumors about tramps; the churchwarden in Åkerby had also been mentioned. And who had been the fathers of those children she had lost? Their fathers were known only to God. Ulrika ought to remember this before she stared at honest women.

Kristina would have liked to sew a forty-week apron—if for no other reason than to irritate Ulrika.

—5—

THE IMMIGRANTS from Ljuder rode on the steam wagon through a green and fertile country. From their train they saw vast fields covered with a thick fell of beautiful crops; in other fields the crops already had gone to seed. They saw meadows with tall fodder grass where cattle grazed in great numbers; in places the grass was so tall that they saw only the animals' backs. They thought the cattle here must tramp down more grass than they ate; they counted as many as fifty cows together and wondered if such large herds might belong to one single owner. They passed through forests of tall, lush leaf-trees and recognized oaks, maples, elms, and birches. They saw groves of unknown, low trees and wondered what the name of such beautiful little trees might be. Danjel Andreasson thought they might be fig trees, of which Jesus often had spoken in parables and which grew also in the land of Canaan.

They passed through a smiling landscape—it was a fertile world they saw here. A verdant ground promised food for both man and beast, ample crops, and security. Where the earth grew green, there life throve; it marked a good place for people to live.

They were looking for such green places with rich growth in which to build their own homes—here they would have liked to stop and settle, if others hadn't arrived before them.

Karl Oskar was pleased with what he saw: the earth here seemed rich, and his eyes did not discover a single hindering stone in the fields. As he looked out over the cultivated land he remembered the picture of a wheat field in North America which he had seen in a newspaper at home; the picture had spoken the truth—the American fields lay before his own eyes now, as vast and stone free, as even and fertile, as they had been in the picture. And it was said that still vaster fields existed farther inland.

At times they passed through poorer regions, they saw hills and mountains, morasses, plateaus, and forests of pine trees. But Karl Oskar had not expected the whole American continent to look like the picture of the wheat field.

The journey on the steam wagon was long, hour after hour passed, and new landscapes came into view, new fields, new pastures, new forests, new crops, and new meadows with more large herds of grazing cattle. Karl Oskar noticed that the cows were larger than those in Sweden, they were white or light yellow in color, like milk and butter; at home they were red or sometimes black. The American horses too were taller than those in Sweden; he wondered if they might be wild horses that had been tamed. The sheep were black and white, fat and round, with bodies like barrels.

59

He saw black and red-brown pigs in the pastures; but the hogs were lean and long legged, not at all resembling those at home. Thus he observed that cattle in the New World were not shaped like the kine at home: cows and horses were larger, sheep fatter, with shorter legs, hogs leaner with longer legs.

Seldom did he see workers out in the fields or forests. There seemed to be a scarcity of people but an abundance of cattle. Seeing the multitude of people in New York, Karl Oskar had begun to worry that America already was overcrowded, that they had arrived too late. He now discovered that his worry was groundless. This country was so vast that it still had room for many more; it wouldn't be filled up tomorrow, or next year. And he recalled how crowded it had been at home, people had even said there wasn't enough room for his big nose, and perhaps they had been right. But here there was room for all in his group, here he was sure he would find a place to settle, large enough to turn about in and do as he pleased, and where others would not be disturbed by him or his big nose.

Danjel Andreasson had long been silently watching the green fields on either side of the railroad. At last he said, "This land is fertile and fruitful. It is a good and broad land, a blessed land. We must humbly thank the Lord God for His grace in letting us enter it."

—6—

LANDBERG SAID that when all went well, about twenty-four hours were required for the journey on the steam wagon to Buffalo. But delays were likely to occur. Once, for instance, the steam wagon had been delayed six hours because the iron rails were covered with a thick layer of grasshoppers.

Ulrika was disappointed that their journey on the steam wagon would come to an end so soon. In her whole life she had never before experienced pleasure like this. The poor back home in Sweden were never treated to such entertainment. Most of them were not allowed to ride on any kind of wagon until they were picked up by the corpse cart. And the gentry in Sweden would have preferred to see them walk to the grave as well.

Their guide nodded to her with a broad smile: "You, my dear *Fru*, will ride on the steam wagon many times in America."

He had several times called her Mrs., and it sounded strange to those in her company. She had always been called Unmarried Ulrika of Västergöhl. Under that name she was registered in the church book, and everyone called her so. It was as if it ought particularly to be emphasized that she was unmarried, and it sounded as if she were more unmarried than any other woman. Now they could all see that Ulrika sat there, greatly enjoying it that the first man she met in America raised her to a married state, nay, even to the level of gentry, by calling her Mrs.

60

She guessed what the others were thinking and she said, half mockingly: "Perhaps I ought to change my name as well."

It happened often that Swedes changed their names when they came to America, Long Landberg replied. Many took entirely new names. Those named Andersson and Larsson at home had here assumed high-sounding names like Pantzarskiold, Silverkrona, or Lejonstjerna. But it was, of course, mostly rogues who felt in need of changing their names; it was of no use to an honest person, nor did it help a useless one, for here no one got along better because of a noble name, as people did in Sweden.

That was exceedingly just, Ulrika of Västergöhl remarked, although she wouldn't mind being called Mrs. Ulrika von Lejonstjerna. For a lonely, poor woman, a noble name would be a comfort. But she was sure menfolk would find nothing different in the body of a noble lady than in a simple woman: each was made in the same way.

Landberg laughed heartily, but the members of Ulrika's group who knew her past did not smile. They were familiar with her talk. And now she was making up to their guide, who couldn't know what she actually was.

From his bag the guide now took out a number of medicine jars which he was accustomed to sell to immigrants during his trips. *Painkiller* was the name on the jars, and he explained what it meant. These were pills which healed all ailments attacking newcomers during their first weeks in America. *Painkiller* healed fatal diseases as well as small wounds and scratches: cholera, red soot, diarrhea, fever, ague, yellow fever. A jar cost one dollar, leaving Landberg with a profit of only five cents. But he was not one to take advantage of his countrymen.

Danjel and Jonas Petter had bought a jar of the *Painkiller*, mostly to be agreeable to the seller. Karl Oskar declined; his family was in good health at the moment and not in need of medicines. Landberg kept urging him—it would be well to have a jar handy in case of sickness; there were many fatal diseases in America, neither young nor old could be sure of tomorrow. But Karl Oskar could not forget how the money in his skin pouch had shrunk; he had paid twenty-four dollars for their passage to Chicago; if they were to have any money at all left when they arrived in Minnesota, he must confine himself to buying the food his family needed on the journey.

Arvid complained of his toothache to Danjel, who bought another jar of *Painkiller* for his servant. Landberg told Arvid that in case the pills didn't help the toothache he could have all his teeth pulled painlessly with the aid of gas at only twenty-five cents a tooth. Then he could buy new teeth. A professor here in America had recently discovered how to make teeth of gutta-percha; they were comfortable and indestructible; they cost only ten dollars a row, or a dollar apiece. He advised Arvid to get a whole row, since this was cheaper.

61

Danjel again opened his purse with the broad brass lock and took from it a new silver dollar. He looked carefully at the strange American coin before he handed it to Landberg: on one side was an eagle with extended wings and searching eyes; the bird held some silver branches in one talon and some sharp arrows in the other; turning the coin, he saw a bare-armed woman dressed in flowing robes; she held bunches of flowers in her hands and sat there like a queen on her throne, surrounded by a wreath of beautiful silver stars.

"They have nice money in America," said Danjel. "It's decorated with the stars of heaven."

"The stars represent the first thirteen states," explained Landberg.

"What does the searching eagle represent?"

"I don't know. The Americans have no king to put on their money. Perhaps they find a bird of prey more suitable."

Karl Oskar also had taken out a silver dollar to inspect; it might be well to familiarize himself with the coin of the country.

"There is writing under the throne where the woman sits," he said. "Mr. Landberg, can you interpret it?"

"Yes, that I can. It says 'In God We Trust.' "

"What are you saying, man!" exclaimed Danjel. "Is our Creed printed on the money?"

"Yes, that's so. These words are printed on all money in this country."

A ray of happiness lit Danjel's eyes, and he began to examine his silver dollar with renewed interest and wonder: "Can that really be true? They have faith in God, those who make the money in this country. That's good to hear; no heathenism exists in this country."

And Danjel of Kärragärde was pleased and satisfied as he sat there inspecting the shining coin in his hand; at home the coins carried only the picture of King Oskar I and his name; in Sweden they thought it sufficient to serve and worship an earthly ruler. But those in charge of money matters in America knew that no coin could be reliable and sound without God's name stamped on it; here they put their foremost trust in the heavenly king.

"In God we trust," he repeated to himself.

To Danjel Andreasson this silver dollar had gained a new and greater value through its four-word inscription; he had come into a land where the rulers had imprinted on the country's coins the uttermost tenet of their faith. Now he knew that North America had a God-fearing government, that it was a Christian land. He understood now that the Americans in a faithful, humble spirit remembered the Lord God each time they held a dollar in their hand. They were thus ever reminded that gold and silver were only dust, to be eaten by worms and corroded by rust, and that they themselves in the presence of their Creator were the like of worms. "In God we trust!" In a land where such coin passed,

62

honesty and confidence between fellow men must rule, and no one could be tempted for sordid gain to cheat his fellow brethren.

Danjel held the coin up to the window so that it glittered in the bright sun: "Behold! God's silver dollar!"

Then he gave the interpreter the coin as payment for Arvid's medicine, and Landberg collected his jars of *Painkiller* and walked on to offer them to other passengers.

Arvid had become very curious about the American coin and he asked Karl Oskar if he might see it. He showed it to Robert and asked who the beautiful woman in the flowing robes might be: "Could it be the queen of America?"

"When they don't have a king, they couldn't have a queen," Robert instructed him.

"Hmm. That's so. They have a president instead."

"And the woman has no crown either."

Arvid looked once more at the picture; then he exclaimed in great excitement, "Now I know who she is—the president's wife, of course!"

Robert supposed his friend had made the right guess. The bare-armed woman in the flowing robes, sitting on her throne among the stars, with flowers in her hands—she couldn't be anyone except the wife to the president of the North American Republic.

–7–

THE CHILDREN whined for food, and for the third time since leaving Albany Kristina brought out the food basket. By now there was not much left of their provisions from Sweden—a couple of rye loaves, a dried sausage, the end of a cheese, and a piece of dried leg of lamb. But these were precious scraps and must be carefully rationed. They could buy no food in the railroad wagon; those without food baskets must starve.

From Karl Oskar's purchase in New York Kristina had saved two wheat rolls for the children, from one of the rye loaves she cut slices for her husband, brother-in-law, and herself, and among them she divided the sausage the best she could. The rye bread was dry and hard, and she had been unable to scrape away all the mildew. But they all ate as if partaking of fresh Christmas bread.

Jonas Petter also took out his food basket and began to eat. Danjel's two boys, Olov, fourteen, and Sven, eleven, sat next to him and looked longingly as he chewed and swallowed. And now Kristina remembered that she had not seen her uncle or anyone of his family eat a bite today.

"Aren't you going to eat, Uncle Danjel?"

Danjel looked shamefacedly at the wagon floor and said they had not the slightest crumb left in their food basket.

63

This was poor management, thought Kristina, as she remembered what an enormous food basket Inga-Lena had brought along—a score of big breads, many fat cheeses, half a side of pork. Yet, her family couldn't sit here and eat their meal and let Danjel's motherless, hungry children look on. She could see the boys following every bite with their eyes and she knew how starved they must be.

She cut the rest of the loaf in slices and divided them among Danjel and his four children. A piece of the cheese crust she gave to Arvid, to whom Robert already had given some of his portion. But because of his toothache Arvid wasn't very hungry and stuck mostly to his jar of pain-killing pills.

Kristina's hand, still holding the bread knife, fell on her knee: there were two hungry people in her company who had nothing to eat, Ulrika of Västergöhl and her daughter Elin. They belonged to Danjel's household and had shared his food throughout the journey. But now their food basket was empty, now Ulrika and her daughter must sit and look on while others ate their meal.

Kristina's hand, a moment before so busy cutting and dividing the bread, lay now quite still upon her knee. Not for one moment would she entertain the preposterous thought that she should divide her food with the Glad One—no, certainly not.

Ulrika was looking out the window, gazing at the landscape they were passing as if she weren't aware that the others were eating. Elin had picked up her little berry basket in which she found a dried bread crust; this she chewed with an expression of contentment, as if she were sitting at an overloaded table. Neither mother nor daughter seemed aware that they were being left out of the meal.

Kristina reflected that Ulrika had taken charge of the family food basket at Inga-Lena's death. But she was not one to save or be stingy with the possessions of others; she had been so generous with the food that already it was gone; she had only herself to blame.

But it was true that the Glad One's healthy body required much food, and she never willingly missed a meal. As she had put nothing in her stomach the whole day, she must be thoroughly hungry, must ache with hunger, even more now that she saw the food the others were eating. Kristina could not help feeling sorry for her! as she now shared her food with all the others, could she pass by Ulrika and her brat? It said in the Bible to break one's bread with the hungry.

Kristina had only one bread loaf left, one single loaf. Must she cut this for the Glad One's sake? She had a hungry husband, brother-in-law with a heavy appetite, and three small children, lean and pale, who needed regular meals. She did not know when they might be able to buy more food. Could God mean that she ought to take the bread from her own poor children and give it to a person like Ulrika, a harlot, an evil creature? How she had insulted other women, this Ulrika of Västergöhl! How

64

detested and looked down on she had been in the home parish! And how Kristina had suffered from being forced to travel in her company! If she now offered the infamous whore food from her own basket, then it would be as if she invited her as a guest to her own table. It would be accepting her as an honorable woman, and equal. Giving her food would be like taking her hand; it would be a humiliation to Kristina, a debasement, if at last she gave in to the Glad One, as though wanting her for a friend.

One could hand a piece of bread to a beggar. But Ulrika had never begged; she was proud, she was more than proud, she was haughty. When she was in prison for breach of the sacramental law, she had refused to eat; she had spit in the porridge, it was said. She would accept nothing unless it was offered to her as to an equal. And Kristina did not wish to consider her an equal.

Her hand with the bread knife was quiet on her knee. Mixed with the rumbling of the rolling wheels she could hear the sound of eagerly chewing jaws; but she who had divided the food had not yet begun to eat.

Kristina's heart beat faster, so greatly was she perturbed. Should she cut the last loaf—or should she save it? She had a vague feeling that what she did now would be of great importance to all of them. She had a foreboding that fundamental changes awaited them in this new land, everything seemed different from home, they were forced to act in new and unaccustomed ways. And as they now were driven through strange country, with everything around them foreign and unknown, they were more closely united—it seemed more and more as if they were one single family. Then they must try to endure each other, at least not irritate each other. Otherwise, how would things work out for them?

Ulrika suffered hunger, and any one able to give her food but withholding it increased her suffering. Could Kristina be so cruel as to let another human being suffer when she could help her? She had many times asked herself why people plagued each other so mercilessly in this world; now she put the question to herself: Ulrika is hungry—why do you let her suffer? You say she is proud—what are you? Is it not from haughtiness that you pass her by?

Kristina's hand took a firmer hold of the knife handle—but this was the children's bread. They were weak and needed every bite. She thought, you cannot take it away from them! To cut that bread is like cutting your own flesh. The Glad One is big and strong, vulgar and forward, she will always manage, she'll never starve to death. It's different with your helpless little ones. If there were plenty of food, more than they needed, then . . . Now—never!

But it couldn't go on like this. They couldn't continue to hurt each other. They were all of them poor wretched creatures, lost in the New World; no one knew what awaited them in this new country, no one knew what they might have to suffer. One loaf would save no one's life in the long run. And if one could help another . . . Help thy neigh-

65

bor! The Glad One too was her neighbor; she too had been given an immortal soul by her creator. He had from the beginning considered her as worthy as others; she too was made by God, Who must care for her as for others. Kristina felt He would see to the little children also, so they needn't starve. . . .

She took out the last loaf, cut generous slices, and handed them to Ulrika of Västergöhl and her daughter: Wouldn't they please share her bread? It was old and dry, but she had scraped off the mildew as best she could. . . .

Mother and daughter accepted gratefully. "Thank you very much," Ulrika said, and this sounded strange when all she got was hard, old bread. Nor did Ulrika seem surprised at the offer; she only looked grateful, truly grateful. And Kristina also handed them the knife and the smoked leg of lamb that they might cut themselves meat for the bread. They both chewed slowly, with restraint, but it was apparent they did so with effort, trying not to reveal their ravenous hunger.

Kristina herself began to eat and she wondered: What would the people at home think of this? What would they say, if they could see her cut her last loaf from home in order to share with Ulrika of Västergöhl, the parish whore?

—8—

IN THE EVENING the twilight was short, and soon it was dark as a potato cellar outside the windows of their railroad wagon. Everything went faster in this country, even the twilight passed more quickly than at home. And the thick darkness which now fell over them on a night so near Midsummer surprised the travelers. At this hour it would still be full daylight at home. But it seemed as if everything American was opposite to Swedish: here they had dark summer nights instead of light, white cows instead of black.

Their train stopped and remained standing a long time. At least an hour passed, and still they did not move. They could no longer see the landscape outside the windows; perhaps this was one of the towns where the interpreter had said the train stopped for a long rest: Schenectady, Utica, or Syracuse. Those were difficult and unusual names for towns, almost like Biblical names, towns in Canaan. Then some of the company with good eyes reported that they were in the middle of a wild forest—there were huge, thick tree trunks on either side. Their guide had gone to another wagon, and they had no one to ask about this.

Perhaps the train couldn't go on during the night when it was so dark; perhaps they had to stay here until daybreak.

No light was lit inside the wagon, and the passengers couldn't see each other's faces, but they sat close to one another and each knew

66

where his own family and his belongings were. They were not in need of light and they were thankful to have air; those in charge of the train had opened the doors at both ends of their wagon as soon as it stopped; the cool night air refreshed them. But none of the travelers dared step outside.

One more hour passed, and the immigrant train still stood there. They began to grow restless, they wondered and worried. Outside the windows they could see sparks from the steam wagon, whirling about in the dark like a swarm of fireflies, and this increased their anxiety. They began to fear that some accident had befallen their vehicle, or was about to happen. Why hadn't their guide returned? Someone suggested that perhaps Landberg had deserted them.

They could hear the wheezing and hissing from the steam wagon in front, and they saw the flying sparks; they were in the depths of a dark forest, and here they sat clustered together, blind, like chickens perched in darkness, and could not even ask anyone if they were in danger. They knew nothing, therefore they feared everything.

At last they began to confer with each other: shouldn't they elect someone to step out onto the ground and try to discover what was the matter with their unmoving train? Even if he couldn't talk, he might learn something with his ears and eyes.

They were talking this over when the doors suddenly slammed shut, and the train started up with such a jerk that the passengers tumbled against each other. And suddenly the man they had missed stood among them; Long Landberg had returned, friendly and calm, and he explained: There was a steep, difficult hill ahead of them on the railroad, and one more steam wagon was required to pull them uphill. Their train had been waiting for the extra steam wagon, and now it was added to the back of their train, and would help push the wagons up the steep hill.

So their journey continued; the immigrant train pushed on through the night, seeking its way into North America. As yet nothing dangerous had developed, but anything could happen, they did not even know what to fear.

# VII

## Voyage on the Lake Steamer

IN THE FORENOON of the next day the immigrants arrived at Buffalo. That evening they started across Lake Erie on the steamer *Sultana*. The whole remaining part of their journey was to be on water—across lakes, up rivers, and through canals. Just ahead of them lay three great lakes over which they must pass. They had embarked on a vast, restless, inland water, but on this voyage they at least could see land on one side of the ship. At intervals, the *Sultana* touched shore to discharge or take aboard passengers, cargo, and firewood for her engines.

The *Sultana* was a fairly large steamer with one water wheel on either side; she was overloaded with people and cargo. The immigrants were given quarters below, on the middle deck, and when they were sent to their quarters, they learned another English word, *steerage*. Cabins were built in three rows in the hold, each one four feet wide, and each one accommodating two full-grown persons of the same sex, or a married couple. Two children under eight years of age were counted as one grown person; children under three years of age were transported free of charge, but no one asked the little ones' ages, and all children carried aboard by the parents were allowed free passage, however old they were.

Kristina took charge of Harald while Karl Oskar carried Johan on one arm and Lill-Märta on the other. Johan was four, but tall as a six-year-old. Other parents carried children even larger, never before had such big two-year-old babies been seen. But it seemed as if all Americans loved children: they brightened and smiled as soon as a child came near them, and no one spoke harshly when the youngsters were noisy or caused trouble; children were the most welcome of all immigrants, it seemed.

Kristina was uneasy each time she boarded a new means of transportation—she was afraid her family might be separated during the journey; she wanted them to hold on to each other all the time.

The American steamer was new and the middle deck roomier, lighter, and drier than the immigrants' living quarters on the old Swedish ship; nor did this vessel smell musty. But when all had gone aboard and packed themselves in down there, it was just as crowded and uncomfortable as it had been on the *Charlotta*. The passengers' belongings were stacked together helter-skelter on the lower deck, and the owners had to look after them and watch that nothing fell overboard. On the *Charlotta* they had been allowed the unrestricted use of the upper deck in fine weather, but here they were confined to the lower deck. Yet they could see there was plenty of space on the upper deck, where only a few passengers walked about. The immigrants enviously watched these fellow travelers who had their individual cabins and more room than they needed: why was that deck up there in the fresh air and daylight reserved for only a few, while such a great number of people must stay below, packed together?

Long Landberg explained that the upper deck was first class, which cost much more than a berth in steerage, and the ladies and gentlemen up there were wealthy travelers on a pleasure excursion.

Kristina noticed that the passengers on the upper deck were dressed like the people she had seen walking about near the harbor in New York: the women in silk skirts and velvet shoes, the men in tall hats and long coats of costly cloth. And here, too, the women went about with open umbrellas even though it wasn't raining. Those passengers up there

68

were not, like themselves, traveling to find homes; they already had homes. Why did they travel when not forced to? How could anyone, of his own free will, roam about on lakes and seas? If Kristina ever found another home in this life, she would certainly stay there.

And these passengers who traveled just for fun were allowed to keep the whole upper deck to themselves, while the immigrants, forced to find new homes, were crowded and jostled down here. Kristina thought that the passengers in first class were like the gentry at home in Sweden, and she asked her brother-in-law Robert, who had learned so much from all kinds of books, to explain this: Hadn't he said that the inhabitants of North America were all alike and not divided into gentry and ordinary people?

Robert tried to make himself clear: He had only said that different classes did not exist in the New World, no one was born into a class. But there was, of course, a difference between people, in that some were rich and others poor; some could afford to spend more, others less; some could afford first class, others could not. There were only two kinds of people in North America: those who had lived here long enough to grow rich, and those lately arrived and still poor.

There was no other difference between people, Robert insisted. Kristina could observe for herself—did she see anyone who took off his hat or cap to another? Did she see any man bow or any woman curtsy? Here one didn't stand on ceremony, the poor didn't kowtow to the rich as they did at home in Sweden.

The ship's fare was ample, even abundant, but to the Swedish peasants it seemed oddly prepared and peculiarly flavored. American food consisted mainly of things mixed together, and one's tongue was unable to distinguish one kind of food from another; the immigrants did not always know what they were eating. But still more foreign than the food were their fellow passengers in the hold. They were lodged with other immigrants, people who, like themselves, came from countries of the Old World, each speaking his own language. Their fellow passengers were dressed in outlandish clothes, they laughed and sang and behaved in the strangest ways, and they were loaded down with an amazing variety of things: axes, hoes, spades, harnesses, saws, tubs, barrels, cradles, clocks, pots, yarn winders, ale kegs. The Swedish immigrants began to feel that they had arrived empty handed in North America when they saw what these others carried along. Many of those who crowded the ship with their belongings were Germans, the guide told them; a German was wedded to his possessions and would not part with them when emigrating. But when they saw a spade with a six-foot handle, said Landberg, they might be sure the owner was Irish: the Irish were too lazy to bend their backs while digging; at work they stood upright.

He pointed out some tall men in skin jackets who carried guns and hunting sacks and had knives in their belts. They were fur hunters on their way to the forests of the West for autumn game.

But strangest of all the steerage passengers were two Indians. The immigrants studied them with timid wonder. The two men were draped in pieces of red-striped woolen cloth which covered them from head to knees and which they usually held closely around themselves; they wore trousers reaching the middle of their thighs and held in place by strings to a belt around their waists; on their feet they wore skin shoes but no socks. From the Indians' ears hung beautiful glittering silk bands; the color of their faces was sooty brown, and their sloe-black eyes lay deep in their skulls, lurkingly under their brows.

Most of the time the Indians sat immobile, staring moodily before them, each holding his blanket tight around his body as if this garment were his only possession. No one addressed the brown-hued men, and they themselves seemed inclined to silence. When they spoke to each other they used a language which sounded like a series of short grunts. These Indians could not be wild, as they were allowed to travel unhindered among white, Christian people. But they sat apart from the other passengers, who walked by them in silence and with some uneasiness; perhaps they were heathens after all; one couldn't know for sure; there was something dark, threatening, and cruel in their looks, something inspiring fear. The immigrants did not know what to think of or expect from these curiously draped figures.

The steamer had a large crew—bosuns, engineers, stokers, and deckhands. Negroes served in many capacities; those black men with hair like wood shavings prepared the food and served it, loaded the ship, cleaned it, and busied themselves everywhere. The black crewmen were free, but among the passengers in steerage were two Negro slaves shackled in foot chains, because they were said to have wild tempers.

Kristina felt pity for the two black-skinned men sitting there chained together, unable to move. Why were people put in chains and foot irons when they had done no wrong? The slaves' owner was among the pleasure travelers on the upper deck: Kristina would have liked to ask him to unshackle the poor Negroes, had she been able to speak his language.

Little Johan watched the Negroes for a long time in silence. Then he asked his mother: How long had their faces been so terribly black?

"They have always been that way."

"Are they black both morning and evening?"

"Yes. Negroes are always black."

"But, Mother—how can they know when they need to wash themselves?"

"I don't know. . . . Quiet, now."

But the boy insisted: "Tell me, Mother, how do the Negroes know when they are dirty?"

Kristina was unable to give Johan this information. She herself was deeply disturbed by the dirty white passengers in steerage. No Negro could help it that the Lord God had made him black, but when God had

70

given people white skin, then they owed it to their Creator to keep it white. Children and menfolk seemed to crave a little dirt for comfort's sake, but Kristina demanded more from women. Here she saw womenfolk who were sorely in need of a thorough scrubbing in boiled lye-soap, and their children appeared never to have touched water since they were baptized. Fina-Kajsa, to be sure, wasn't very clean, and washed herself unwillingly, but compared to these foreign women she stood out as clean as an angel. They were probably too lazy to keep dirt from them; slothfulness bred uncleanliness and uncleanliness bred vermin; among these people they must be careful or they might again become lice infested.

In the hold there were no spittoons, which seemed strange; one would expect to find them in nice places, among cleanly people. The deck soon was awash from the tobacco-chewing menfolk's spittle, and Kristina had to hold up her skirts as she walked over it; she was horrified to see little children crawling and creeping about on their hands and knees on this bemired floor; only with great effort was she able to keep little Harald away from it.

Washing buckets were set up for the steerage passengers, but the water was never changed. After a score of people had dipped their hands and rinsed their faces in the tubs, the water became as thick and black as though blood sausage had been boiled in it. And the same towel passed from one hand to another—there was only one for this multitude. Perhaps the ship's command felt: If fifty people have dried themselves on the towel before you, then it's good enough for you too! But Kristina washed neither herself nor her children in water used by dirty fellow passengers. The very first morning on board she asked their guide for help, and as soon as the steamer touched shore he managed to get her a tub of clean water. Then she used her own towels, which she had brought along and laundered during the voyage.

But in spite of her annoyance at this lack of external cleanliness, Kristina was unable to dislike her fellow passengers. These foreign people —poor, dirty, and badly dressed—appeared so friendly; only kind eyes and smiling faces were turned on her and her children. When strangers spoke to her, Kristina realized they spoke no evil, but rather something kind and cheering, wishing her only well. She felt ashamed that she could not answer them with the same kindness, that she could not make herself understood by them. All she could do was to smile back as broad a friendliness as she could and shake her head for the rest. She longed to enter into conversation with them; she suffered from being unable to do so and felt as though she were doing the strangers a rudeness. Besides, here she could have found honest friends, and these friends she turned away, again and again, through her silence.

Kristina suffered and worried over the lot awaiting her in the new land: to walk like a deaf-mute among other people.

71

IT HAD BEEN AGREED that the interpreter Landberg was to accompany the immigrants to Chicago and from there return to New York.

While he still was with his countrymen he tried to advise and inform them about the things they needed to know. Landberg said he had traveled all the great seas, he had seen much of the world, on land and water, but he had found himself most at home in North America. Nowhere had he been less disturbed by the authorities, nowhere had he been so free to make his own decisions, nowhere were people so helpful to each other as here. His deepest needs—freedom to move as he pleased, and sufficient food—he had found in North America. Yes, more freedom and cheaper food than anywhere else on the globe. Just as an example—pork could be bought for three Swedish shillings per pound, pork so tasty and fat that the grease spurted between the jaws while one was eating it. Long Landberg called the North American Republic the Land of Liberty and Fat Pork.

But, he reminded them, they must remember that here, as elsewhere in the world, people were good and evil, industrious and lazy, generous and greedy, honest and crooked. They must be particularly on their guard against two types: the runners, who wanted to rob them, and sectarians, who wished to snare them into their fold. Among the latter he warned them against the Jansonites, who had come earlier from Sweden. Their prophet, Erik Janson, had been a plague to humanity, a torturer of his followers. First he had forbidden marriage in his sect, as childbearing interfered with the women's work, but when his adherents grumbled at this, he was forced to allow it, and prepared a wedding for fifty couples at one time. But the sectarians were allowed no will of their own; when a married man wished to sleep with his wife, he must announce his wish to the prophet far in advance and obtain his permission. And when the tyrant gave his assent to the bedding, he insisted also that husband and wife must perform it in full view of all the other sectarians. Many hesitated at this. Landberg himself had for a while been a member of this sect, but he had soon left it, with many others, who, like himself were unable to put up with Janson's demands.

They must also be on the lookout for the Shakers, who served God by making their bodies shake and shiver, nay, even danced and hopped about, singing and howling until, exhausted, they would fall to the ground and faint. The dancing and the shaking themselves into insensibility were supposed to illustrate the ascent into Heaven by the saved ones. These sectarians maintained that the praising and blessing of the Lord should not be confined to the tongue only—the whole body, head, and limbs had the same right to share this joy. (To this point Landberg was inclined to feel there was some reason.)

Another dangerous sect was the Whippers, who exorcised evil spirits by beating each other with scourges until their bodies were a bloody mass. Sometimes the evil spirits might resist the mistreatment and remain in the body until the soul had left it. Yes, these sectarians actually whipped each other to death.

Landberg himself had by now returned to the church of his forebears, the Evangelical-Lutheran religion, and he earnestly begged the Swedish immigrants to remain in the faith of their fathers, to stick to the only right God here in America; they must not allow themselves to be led astray by irreligious and false prophets. He was pleased to see that they had brought along their Bibles and psalmbooks, so that they could hold their own services.

Kristina asked how it would be possible for Swedish Lutherans to partake of the Sacrament out here. Their last Sunday in Sweden, before they started out on their fateful journey, she and her husband had received the Lord's Supper. At that time she had felt as if she were undertaking a death journey. Now again she was in great need of the Sacrament. At home they went to the Lord's Supper table every month; three months had already elapsed since they had enjoyed the Sacrament, and man sinned in many matters daily. How much time they'd had to sin in the last ninety days! Idleness breeds sin, according to the old saying, and they had long been idle. Kristina had lately felt the burden weighing on her, disturbing her mind and soul. Original sin clung to her like an invisible, loathsome mange; it was a degradation. She longed to be cleansed in Christ's pure blood, and no doubt there were many in their company who were in need of forgiveness for their sins, and absolution; how long would it be before they might again enjoy the Sacrament? The Swedish pastor who had come aboard their ship in New York had promised them communion, but when they heard he was a Methodist, not one among them had dared follow him to his altar.

Long Landberg answered: In Chicago there was a Swedish Lutheran minister by the name of Unonius; he was an upright man and a true Christian. Landberg said that a few ministers of the right religion were to be found also in Andover and in Moline, both places in the state of Illinois. When they arrived in Chicago, he would himself look up Pastor Unonius, who surely would be happy to give the Sacrament to all wishing to partake.

Landberg said that he intended to leave Chicago as soon as he had performed his duties there. This town was the only place in North America he detested. But it was the gateway to the West, which all travelers must pass through, although most thanked the Lord they could journey farther. Chicago was a swamp hole and a blowhole, built on the low shores of a lake and a river. On one side was the lake and on the other the prairie, with no protection against the winds, which blew so intensely that eyebrows and hair were pulled off people's heads. The town had only three decent streets: Chicago Avenue, Kinzie, and Clark Streets. Yard-

73

high stumps still stood in the other streets, and almost all the surrounding country was desolate wasteland where cows grazed. The houses were newly built, yet gray, dirty, and unpainted, for the hurricanes blew the paint off the walls. And the whole town stank from the mud and ooze of the swampy shores. Pools of water abounded, filled with crawling snakes and lizards and other horrible creatures. Thirty thousand people lived in Chicago, and of these, several thousand earned their living as runners, robbing immigrants passing through. Grazing was fine in Chicago, and cattle lived well in that town. But honest people, non-runners, could ill endure an extended visit in the place. Landberg thought Chicago would within twenty years become entirely depopulated and obliterated from the face of the earth.

Pastor Unonius worked zealously advising all his countrymen to settle in Chicago, but the guide thought that on this point the minister had wrongly interpreted God's will.

Landberg was indeed like a father to the immigrants, and all agreed he had well earned the three dollars each person was to pay him.

"He is an upright man and an honest guide," was the way Karl Oskar summed up their feeling. And he worried a little about their future when they would no longer have an interpreter to help in their dealings with the Americans.

Landberg had given Robert a new English textbook: *A Short Guide to the English Language*. This book had a chapter entitled "Instruction in Pronunciation for the Swedes." Here were enumerated those English words in common use, as well as advice in general for immigrants. Landberg's gift was quite a small book, hardly bigger than the almanac; Robert could carry it in his pocket and take it out when he needed it. Landberg had explained Robert's difficulty with his first language book. The Swedish youth had been unable to comprehend why the sentences in English were spelled in two entirely different ways, one sentence always within parentheses. Now he was informed that the words were to be pronounced according to the spelling within the parentheses. Robert had learned English altogether wrong from the very beginning.

The first thing he had tried to say to the Americans was: "I am a stranger here," and he had pronounced the words carefully, according to their spelling and Swedish pronunciation. But people had only stared at him, he had been unable to make a single soul understand that he was a stranger. From this new book, he learned how the words were supposed to sound: *Aj äm ä strehn' djër hihr.*

And Robert began at once to practice the pronunciation of the twenty-six letters of the English alphabet. He hurried his study of the language, in order to help himself and to lend his mouth to others of his group when their interpreter left them. He must show the others what he could do, and they would then value him the more and show him the respect due to learning. From now on he read in his language books every free moment, and always without Elin's company. He told her, somewhat sarcastically, she was supposed to know English already; hadn't the Holy Ghost filled all the reborn ones?

After her disclosure in New York of his secret concerning the captain's "slave trade," there was no longer the same intimacy between them. Moreover, Elin had difficulties with the foreign language, she moved her lips too much and pushed out her tongue too far while speaking English. How many times he'd told her to keep her mouth still and pull her tongue back; but she did not obey him. Not all people were so fortunately born as to be able to learn a new language; not even the rebirth seemed of any help to Elin.

Robert had been in danger of his life and he knew the importance of learning English. Moreover, Landberg now told him of a terrible thing that had befallen a newly arrived farm hand from Sweden: the boy had been one month in America when he met a cruel, heartless, cunning woman who inveigled him into going with her to a priest, who married them. The farm hand understood what was happening but he didn't know one word of English, he couldn't even say "No" at the wedding, and this the wicked woman knew. And now her victim had been ordered by the court to support her for the rest of her life. So Robert understood that there were many reasons why it was necessary to learn the language—in order to escape the many dangers that lurked in this land.

—3—

KARL OSKAR AND KRISTINA were standing at the starboard rail where they could keep an eye on their belongings—their bulky linen sacks and the great America chest—stacked with other movables against the ship's wheelhouse. The lake heaved moderately, the breeze was cooling, the heat did not seem a plague when the steamer was in motion. Karl Oskar complained of the slow speed: he was constantly worrying lest they arrive at their place of settling too late for sowing and planting. If they were unable to gather any crop this summer, they would be in ill circumstances. Now he was a restless man, he would not be at peace till the day when he could start to work.

Kristina watched the purring drive wheel, whipping the water like a dasher in a churn full of cream. When she used to make butter, the cream would splash up in her face, and now, as the wheel threw water against the side of the ship, the spray splashed on her face and into her eyes; it felt refreshing.

Ulrika of Västergöhl came up to them hurriedly. She addressed Karl Oskar in agitation: "Now I know the truth! Just try to explain this away!"

He turned slowly toward her: "What is it this time?"

75

"You have deceived us! You've swindled and cheated us and made us travel this long way!"

"What in hell are you accusing me of?"

"You said it was only two hundred and fifty miles!"

"That's what the captain of the *Charlotta* said."

"But our guide says it's fifteen hundred miles! Six times as far as you said! Landberg doesn't lie, but you've lied to lure us along! Now comes your day of reckoning, Karl Oskar!"

Ulrika's lips quivered, her eyes flamed, her whole body shook with anger: "Because of your notions the rest of us have to travel many hundreds of miles unnecessarily! Because you lied to us, Karl Oskar! Why have you deceived us? Answer me, you—you—lying—" She called him an obscene name.

His cheeks paled at this insult, and Kristina grew frightened lest he lose his head.

Ulrika did not give him time to reply. She continued to rant: How could he be so low, such a scoundrel, as to cheat his own countrymen in a foreign land, so shabby as to lure them all this way, so deep into America? Not one of them would have followed him had they known what an eternal distance it was. He was certainly the most selfish and cruel and false of all the menfolk she had met. They must sail sea after sea, only because of him! They were all tired to death of this endless traveling! They wanted to settle down somewhere, they wanted to arrive! But now he couldn't deceive them any longer, now it was over! Now his true colors were discovered! Now he was at an end with his smirking, his lying, his cheating! Now was the time of reckoning, now he must answer!

His anger seethed within him so he could hardly speak. He burst out: "You accuse me? You insult me? You—you—you dirty old sl——"

He stopped short. But Ulrika egged him on: "Yes, say it right out! Say what you started—'You old slut'! That's what you meant—say the whole word! Say it quickly!"

By now both of them were shouting at the top of their lungs. Long Landberg hurried to them. Danjel Andreasson and Jonas Petter suddenly appeared.

"Ulrika accuses me of deceiving you about the distance!" Karl Oskar shouted.

Landberg explained soothingly: When Karl Oskar had said it was two hundred and fifty miles from New York to Minnesota, he had spoken the truth, because such was the distance measured in Swedish miles. And when he, Landberg, had told Ulrika that the distance was fifteen hundred miles, then he too had spoken the truth, for he had meant American miles. An American mile was only one sixth of a Swedish mile.

Both Karl Oskar and Ulrika were in the right; they might as well end their quarrel.

76

But the words uttered on both sides had been too insulting. Karl Oskar was deeply offended: "If anyone thinks I have lied and cheated our group —step up!"

Kristina held on to his elbow: "Be calm, Karl Oskar! It was only a misunderstanding."

"No! Now I want to tell the truth!"

And Karl Oskar continued angrily: It concerned no one but his family that he had decided to settle in Minnesota. He had never asked anyone to accompany him; the others had followed of their own will. Why? Why did they ape him? They could go and settle wherever in hell they wanted—it didn't concern him. He had never asked to be the leader of their group. But when they had come to him, he had done their errands gladly. And now he got his reward. Ulrika and the others need only say the word if they wanted to leave him and travel alone. He would not cry over their departure; he wouldn't shed one single tear for those outside his family. It would be less trouble for him to travel alone with his wife and children. He wanted to hear one word only, if the distance was too great!

"Ulrika was excited, pay no attention to her," advised Jonas Petter. "We rely on you, we're grateful to you, all of us."

Then Danjel Andreasson attempted a reconciliation: "There is no quarrel between the two of you. Shake hands, now!"

"Shake his hand!" sputtered Ulrika. "Did you hear what he called me?"

"You called me a lying—" Karl Oskar could not make himself repeat the obscenity in his wife's presence.

"Take back your words, both of you," urged Jonas Petter.

"Be Christian and forgiving," admonished Danjel. "Forgive each other as our Lord Jesus forgives all of us."

"If a group of immigrants want to succeed, they must live in harmony," Landberg said.

Karl Oskar and Ulrika, surrounded by curious fellow travelers, stared fixedly into each other's eyes, silent, immobile, neither one yielding an inch.

Robert and Arvid had heard the commotion too and approached the group as Long Landberg left, shaking his head and muttering that Swedish peasants found a peculiar enjoyment in personal quarrels, at home and abroad.

"Be at peace, good people," Danjel entreated once more, deeply concerned. "Won't you shake hands?"

Karl Oskar and Ulrika remained silent. Both had calmed down and each would have taken a proffered hand. Ulrika knew that Karl Oskar had acted in good faith, and that she had unjustly accused him of skulduggery. Karl Oskar regretted the words he had uttered; there was reason enough to call Ulrika of Västergöhl an old slut, but it was unnecessary and foolish to dig up dirt from home to throw at her in a foreign land.

77

Both admitted inwardly that it would be right to retract; both were ready to shake hands in forgiveness. But neither one offered his hand, each feared the humiliation of refusal from the other.

And so no hand was offered. Danjel bowed his head in sorrow, his shaggy, unkempt beard sweeping his chest.

Elin called her mother from their cabin, and Ulrika departed with long strides, proudly.

Jonas Petter looked after her and said in a low voice to Robert and Arvid: Ulrika of Västergöhl was getting ill-tempered because of lack of close male company; what she needed most of all for a few nights ahead was a man.

Karl Oskar and Kristina walked over to the wheelhouse.

"I can't stand the Glad One any longer!" he said. "We must part from her."

"But she is part of Danjel's family," protested Kristina. "She is like a foster mother to the children. You don't want to take her away from the poor motherless children?"

Karl Oskar kept silence gloomily, wondering what to do.

"And how can you get rid of Ulrika?" continued Kristina. "You can't throw her into the lake."

"You've always disliked Ulrika before. Now you defend the old whore!"

"I didn't defend the way she acted just now. But I can stand her better in this country."

Kristina pointed out that Ulrika had softened a little since sharing their food on the train the other day. She was more friendly and talkative, and the two women had these last days talked with each other as if no unfriendly feelings had ever existed between them. Ulrika had spoken many words both true and wise, and Kristina had enjoyed her company. Earlier, she had avoided the Glad One as one avoided vermin, she had thought her full of hatred and ill will, always trying to hurt others. But Ulrika wasn't entirely wicked and evil; there must be something good in a woman who was so kind to Danjel's offspring, poor little ones. And perhaps injustice had been done her at home in Sweden, ever since her childhood when they sold her at auction. That was why she always thought the worst of people. If they mistreated her and scorned her, then she acted the same way in return; and she could give ten for two; she could act like a viper if tramped on, biting, spurting out venom. If now they were to be considerate of her, if they made her feel one of them, perhaps . . .

"There will be no peace in our group until we get rid of her," Karl Oskar insisted. But what Kristina had said seemed to him worthy of thought, although he wouldn't admit it now.

Kristina also harbored an opinion of her own, well hidden from Karl Oskar: she felt the same way as Ulrika about this long journey inland.

They had barely started; the guide said several weeks would elapse before they reached their destination. Why must they travel such an unfathomable distance? Why hadn't they settled on a nearer place? It was Karl Oskar who wanted it that way, the responsibility was his, his will was being carried out. He had decided that they were to travel with the old woman, Fina-Kajsa, to her son in Minnesota. The others were willing to follow along: they thought what he did was best. He gave advice, and the others listened. But who could tell if he were right? Need they traverse so many lakes and rivers to find a home? Couldn't they have found one nearer?

This was Karl Oskar's great shortcoming: he never let well enough alone. All other men were satisfied at last, satisfied some time—never he. Many would have thought a move to another country quite sufficient—he wasn't satisfied until they moved to another continent. To others it would have been enough to travel two, three hundred miles inland—he must travel fifteen hundred miles, five times as far; he must get as far inland as he possibly could, before he would be satisfied. He said he wanted to find the best soil. But was it so sure (he acted as though God had said so) that the best land lay farthest away? Such was Karl Oskar's nature: things far away were better than those near by; what he couldn't reach was better than what he had, and the best of all lay farthest away in the world.

And now they were on a ship again, even though it didn't move by sail, but by steam and wheels. And she who had made up her mind never again to travel on water! The others too had come along. Ulrika alone had murmured, she was not afraid to speak her mind. Her unfair accusations against Karl Oskar were inexcusable, but what she had said about this eternal traveling could just as well have come from Kristina's own mouth. It was well for him to hear it! He should know that there were those among them who were tired to death of this journey. Kristina was. Three long months had elapsed since that morning when she stepped onto the wagon in Korpamoen for a ride to the sea; she was still riding! And deep within her she marveled that her little children had survived this dangerous, unending journey; it would not have surprised her had it killed them all.

How intensely she longed for a place where she could stay. Where she could be by herself and make her own decisions, where she wouldn't have strangers with her always, where she could rest in her own bed, under her own roof, where she could make a home for her husband and her offspring! How fervently her heart longed for a home again, how desperately she prayed that she might see the place where she was to live.

—4—

THE STEAMER *Sultana* entered a sound which soon turned out to be a river mouth; shortly they tied up at the pier in Detroit.

The immigrants were now approaching the northernmost boundaries

79

of the United States. In this harbor the *Sultana* was to remain long enough so that anyone who wished to go ashore was allowed to do so.

Detroit was an old town, well built and of pleasing aspect. It was not a settlement village with streets crowded with cattle and tall tree stumps; it had well-ordered streets, almost like a town in Sweden, as Landberg said. From the boat it seemed that Detroit stood on a high bank along the river; they could see rows of well-built and well-looked-after houses, topped by church towers and steeples; next to the pier there was an extensive market place. Coming up the river they had seen vast orchards on either shore, filled with apple and cherry trees, their branches overloaded with delicious-looking fruit. The country around the town was fertile and good as far as their eyes could see.

Nearly all the *Sultana's* passengers went ashore. Of the group from Ljuder, the two smallest children were left behind, Karl Oskar's son Harald and Danjel's little daughter Eva, and Fina-Kajsa also remained on the ship to take care of the babies.

The older children were much excited by the prospect of walking on solid ground again; they asked if they might go back to where they had seen the cherry trees, but the parents told them there would not be time. Kristina took Johan by the hand and Karl Oskar held on to Lill-Märta, so as not to lose them in the crowd. They walked about the town for a few hours, looking at many strange things, but it was surprising how soon both children and grownups tired from walking: they had been freighted about for so long that they had no strength to walk any distance. The heat was more infernal on land, too, and they were almost glad to return to the ship.

By the time the passengers were back on the pier, the *Sultana* had finished unloading her freight. A wide barge loaded with cattle was tied to the steamer's side. Half a dozen sturdy men, their upper bodies bare and their heads covered with broad straw hats, were bringing the cattle from the barge onto the pier. Then an accident befell one of the animals: a large bull refused obstinately to walk onto the landing plank: he skidded and fell into the water. The river was quite deep near the pier, and only the head and back of the bull could be seen above the water. A curious crowd gathered immediately to see the beast rescued. The bull struggled in the water like a sea monster, snorting, bellowing, and squirting quantities of water through his nostrils, until the men finally succeeded in getting a rope around his horns and pulling him on shore.

While the others of their group went aboard, Karl Oskar and Jonas Petter had remained behind to watch the rescue of the bull. As Karl Oskar turned to climb the gangplank he was met by Kristina.

"Are you alone?" she asked.

"Yes. Is anyone missing?"

She stared at him, fear in her eyes: "Isn't Lill-Märta with you?"

"No. I thought she was aboard."

80

"She was with you. Only Johan came with me."

"The girl is not on the ship?" Karl Oskar asked breathlessly.

"No."

"Are you sure?"

"Yes—I told you, the girl was with you. Where is she?"

"She was on the pier when you went. . ."

"You let her out of your sight?"

"I thought she went with you."

"Lord Jesus! Where is Lill-Märta?" Kristina shrieked. "Lord in Heaven! The child is left behind somewhere!"

She rushed down the gangplank, followed by Karl Oskar. They ran back and forth on the pier, looking for their missing child. The men, a moment before busy with the drowning bull, turned their attention from the now safe beast to the man and woman who ran about on the pier, calling out their child's name. No one answered. They looked everywhere for the little one, on the pier and near it, among the unloaded freight, behind barrels and boxes and sacks and coils of rope; they searched behind cords of wood and stacks of boards, they examined every place imaginable that might be a hiding place, every nook and corner where a three-year-old might have crawled. On the pier were only grownups, there was no child in the crowd. They looked up toward the market place and along the shores, as far as their eyes could reach. But there was no sign of Lill-Märta. Their child had simply disappeared.

She had been on the pier a short time ago, when Karl Oskar stopped to watch the bull in the water; he had thought she followed her mother aboard. But the child had been in his charge, he felt the blame was his.

The *Sultana's* bell rang piercingly, it was time for the boat to leave. The bull responded with a long-drawn-out, angry bellow, as if wishing to chase the boat off, and Karl Oskar glared at him fiercely: if that damned beast hadn't fallen into the river—if he hadn't stopped to watch it . . .

Kristina turned to the man who had done the unloading: "Have you seen a little girl, about three years old?" She grabbed hold of the arm of a bearded giant, wailing in despair: "A very little girl . . . in a blue dress . . . red ribbons in her braids?"

The man stared at her helplessly, mumbling some words in his own language. Kristina ran to the next man, she ran from one to another, and asked, and asked; she had forgotten that none of them understood a word: "A girl . . . haven't you seen her . . . our little girl?"

Karl Oskar searched in silent anguish; he remembered that he was among strangers, that here he was no better than a mute.

Their child had disappeared, and they couldn't tell a single soul that she was lost. No one could tell them if Lill-Märta had been seen, no one could tell them where she had gone, no one could help them, because they couldn't ask anyone for help—no one could help them search for a little girl in a blue dress and red ribbons.

"Maybe she has fallen off the pier . . . into the water," he said to Kristina.

"It was you! You let her get away from you!" Kristina broke out accusingly.

"Yes . . . it's my fault . . . I forgot . . . for only a moment. . . ." Remorse swept over him.

"Lill-Märta! Lill-Märta! Lill-Märta!" Hysterically, the mother called her child's name, and no one answered. She broke into tears. "We've lost our child! She was with you!"

"Yes, Kristina. She was with me."

"Our first girl. Anna. You remember?"

As Kristina mentioned Anna, their dead child, memories of the past flashed through Karl Oskar's mind: He carried a small coffin in his arms, he was on his way to a grave, he walked with heavy steps carrying the coffin he himself had made, had hammered together of fine boards, the finest, knot-free boards he had been able to find. That was Anna, that was the other time, the other child whom they had lost.

The *Sultana's* side wheels were beginning to churn, foam whirled about, the bell rang again, and a man on deck shouted, "All aboard!"

Some of the crewmen made ready to pull in the gangplank—no one was aware that two passengers had gone back on shore.

Karl Oskar stood on the pier as if paralyzed. But suddenly, at the sound of the bell, he came back to life: "The ship is leaving us!"

"We cannot leave Lill-Märta!"

"The boys are on the ship! All we own is on the ship!"

"I stay here on land. I must find our child." Kristina sank down on a packing box among the freight, unable to move.

Karl Oskar looked wildly in all directions, searching for the lost child; he looked at the ship, ready to depart; he looked at his wife, sitting on the box, forlorn and shaking with sobs. In that moment he was a thoroughly bewildered, helpless human being, not knowing what to do next. Yet within the minute he must know, his decision must be made.

Two of their children were on board, one was here on land. If they went on board without the girl, they would never see her again. If they remained on shore, their sons would be left to themselves on the ship. What must they do?

He would never give up in despair, never consider all lost; he must do the best he knew how, he had always done so in critical moments, he must do so now.

He would rush on board and find Landberg; their interpreter might persuade the captain to delay the ship until they found . . .

But now the gangplank was hauled in.

Karl Oskar made two jumps to the edge of the pier, waved both arms and shouted as loudly as he could: "Wait! Wait a little! Have mercy, people!"

A crewman came to the rail and shouted something back, something he didn't understand. But suddenly he heard another voice, a voice he understood, a voice shouting in his own language, louder than all the noises of the ship, louder than any human sound around him: from somewhere on shore came a woman's voice, a coarse voice, a penetrating, fierce, furious voice, rising above all the din and bustle on the pier: "Wait, you sons of bitches! I'm still on shore!"

A woman came running along a footpath that followed the shore, and she called, short of breath and angrily, while running, yet louder even than the bellowing bull: "Put down the gangplank, you bastards! I'm coming as fast as I can!"

Karl Oskar recognized the voice; it belonged to Ulrika of Västergöhl, who, it seemed, was also in danger of being left behind. But Ulrika was not alone as she came running to the pier, she carried a burden, she carried in her arms a kicking, obstreperous child, and because of this burden, and the fear of being left behind, Ulrika was short of breath and angry. In her arms the Glad One carried a little girl in a blue dress with red ribbons on her hair. Panting, she put the child down next to Karl Oskar and yelled once more toward the ship: "Those sons of bitches! Trying to get away!"

While Karl Oskar and Kristina fell upon their child, the gangplank was once more lowered.

"The girl was back there under the trees," said Ulrika. "She was eating cherries."

Near the shore, Ulrika told them as they hurried to the gangplank, she had seen a grove of cherry trees, and thinking their boat would remain a while longer, she had gone there to pick some fruit—her throat was dry in this awful heat. The child was already there, reaching for the cherries. But Lill-Märta had been unable to reach the branches, she was too short, so Ulrika had picked her a handful. The child had wanted to remain and eat cherries, and that was why she had kicked and fought so hard when Ulrika carried her back.

Lill-Märta was still restive; when Kristina pressed her hard to her breast, the girl began to cry: the mother had squashed one of the cherries which she still held in her hand.

The crewmen greeted Ulrika with happy smiles and gestures as the four belated passengers walked up the gangplank. Who knows, perhaps they would have been equally friendly had they understood the words she shouted at them a few minutes earlier.

Slowly the steamer *Sultana* glided out of the Detroit harbor, with none of her passengers missing.

As soon as they were inside the rail Karl Oskar held out his hand to Ulrika; he shook hers violently, he pressed it in his own, he would not let go of it for a long while: this was the hand that had brought back their child, had saved the little girl and—the parents. But he was unable to speak, not a syllable would cross his lips, not a sound. He felt something in his throat, something he couldn't swallow. Only a few times before had he had this feeling, it came over him instead of tears.

Karl Oskar wept, wept inwardly like a man, with invisible tears.

—5—

AFTER SIX DAYS' sailing across the Great Lakes and the rivers and sounds which separated them, the steamer *Sultana* reached Chicago. Waiting for a river steamer, the immigrants remained three days in this town, lodged in quarters Landberg had found them. Meanwhile, their guide was busy making arrangements for their continued journey. Pastor Unonius, the Swedish Lutheran minister, unfortunately had gone to visit a new settlement outside the town; consequently, the immigrants were unable to participate in Holy Communion while in Chicago.

On July 6, early in the morning, Landberg escorted the group on board a steamer in the Chicago River which plied a canal to the Illinois River and which was to carry them to the upper Mississippi. With this last service the guide finished his obligations. Landberg bade his countrymen farewell, wishing them health and success in their new homeland. They were now entirely dependent on themselves, but he commended them all to the hands of Almighty God.

The immigrants had passed through the portals of the West. They were on a new ship, and on the new ship they met a new sea, a sea unlike any they had ever seen or traversed: the prairies' own Sea of Grass.

# VIII

## Peasants on a Sea of Grass

THROUGH THE VAST FLAT LAND the Creator's finger had carved a crooked furrow and in this furrow flowed the river, carrying the vessel of the immigrants. The shores of the waterway lay close to them, just beyond the boat's rail. The solid earth on either side gave the travelers a feeling of security. Fear for their lives, their constant companion on the ocean voyage, was no longer with them; they traveled on water, yet they were near land.

But their sense of being lost, astray in the world, remained with them on this river journey as it had during the ocean voyage.

They were passing through a vast level country, an endless emptiness of open, grassy, flat land. No more here than on the ocean could their eyes find a point of focus: no trees, no groves, no hills, no glades, no mountains. They saw one sight only—stretches of wild grass, herbs, and

84

flowers, fields of tussocks, hollows of grass, billows of grass, springing from the ground on all sides, rolling forth in infinity; the same green billows extended all the way to that narrow edge where the flat land flowed into the globe of heaven, all the way to where the eye could see no farther. Like the Atlantic Ocean, this treeless expanse seemed to them one region only; nothing under the sun separated one landscape from another. The grassy tussocks swayed and sank and came up again from the hollows; the tussocks were like billows, always the same, everywhere; when they had seen one, they had seen them all. This unchanging, monotonous expanse was called the prairie.

For seventy days they had traversed the Atlantic Ocean—a sea of water. Now they traveled across the North American prairie—a sea of grass.

Here blossomed a hay meadow, vast as a kingdom, yet here no cattle grazed. Here was hay to harvest in such abundance that all the barns in the world would not suffice to hold it; here a haymaker could go forth with his scythe and cut one straight swath, day after day, mile after mile; he could continue his straight swath the whole summer long, the meadow was so vast he need never turn. Here were blossoming fields and grazing lands, here abounded flowers and fodder. Here, spreading before them, the travelers saw a verdant ocean which they might have walked through dry-shod, which they might have traversed without a ship.

This was not the sterile sea with darkness in its depths, existing below the firmament before dry land was seen: this was a growing and yielding sea where crops had as yet never been harvested.

Over this sea, too, the winds wailed, sweeping through the grass, stirring waves that rolled on endlessly. The fierce wind fell upon the grass, flattened it with all its power, rolled over it, pressed it down, so that it lay there as slick as if it had been combed with a comb. But when the wind lost its force and the pressure slackened, the soft grass rose again, straightening its blades. The sea of grass lay there again—living, irrepressible, billowing back and forth in its eternal way, unchanged since the creation of the earth.

The immigrants had lived in woodland regions in Sweden, they were at home in forests, they were familiar with trees, bushes, and thicket paths, they were intimate with valleys, glades, ridges, and hills. In the woodlands at home they had easily recognized familiar landmarks to guide them. But in this sea of grass they could find nothing to notice and remember: no roads, no wheel tracks, no paths, no cairns. In whichever direction they looked, from the deck of the river steamer they could see only a wild, untrampled expanse, where nothing indicated that man had passed. Without a guide, a wanderer over these flat lands would be lost, swallowed up; how could he find his way when one mile was forever like another?

The peasants from the forest regions passed over the prairie and shrank from the land opening before their eyes in all its incomprehensible vastness. They desired nothing more than to till smooth, level ground, but this prairie was not what they wanted. There was something missing in this flat land: God had not finished His creation. He had made the ground and planted the grass and all the other growing herbage, but the trees were missing, the bushes, the hills, the valleys, the swales. Moreover, this grass sea was too immense; it frightened them. Anything stretching farther than their eyes could see aroused fear, loneliness, a feeling of desolation. They feared the sea of grass because they were unable to see its end, they feared it in the same way that they feared eternity.

The prairie stung their hearts with its might and emptiness. The grassland lay on this side of the horizon and it lay beyond, continuing into the invisible, encircling them on all sides; they wanted to shrink and hide within themselves in their helplessness; the farther the earth stretched, the smaller man seemed.

Here was fertile soil, offering itself to the plow, a ground of potent growth. Where the earth is green, there people can live and feed themselves. And the rivers and brooks had cut into the land and watered it with their flow. What more could a tiller wish? Yet, here they would not like to settle, not under the best conditions; this land was not what they were seeking.

Born in the forest, they would never feel at home on the prairie. They wanted *all* of God's creation around their homes; they wanted trees which gave shade and coolness in summer, warmth and protection against winds in winter. Here was not a single tree to fell for house timber, hardly a shrub to cut for firewood. They wanted to live within timbered walls, to gather high piles of wood for fires in their stoves. Settlers on the prairie must dig holes in the earth and live the life of gophers, and when above ground they must bend their backs because of the unmerciful winds. The woodland peasants would languish from the monotony of the unvarying, desolate, empty endlessness which would surround their homes if they lived here. They would wither away from loneliness and the sense of loss. Delivered into the infinity of this sea of grass, they would perish, soul and body.

No, the prairie was not a suitable place for permanent settlement. From the deck of their moving steamer they looked out over this flat land, satisfied to pass through it; they thought of the prairie as a thoroughfare, another sea they must cross.

Their journey continued in the river furrow, and more great stretches of prairie opened up. The new country was showing its size to them, and the more they saw of its vastness and immensity, the smaller they felt themselves; more than ever before during this long journey they felt lost and strayed in the world.

86

AT NIGHT, darkness was upon the face of the deep, and on this sea of grass. The wind held its breath and died down. From the ground rose a surge like dying billows on a calm water. Grass and wild flowers were veiled by the cloak of darkness, the verdant ocean was hidden by night. In the firmament—stretched over the earth by the Creator on the Second Day, and called by Him Heaven—the stars shone with clear brilliance. The world down here was great, but the heavenly firmament and the lights up there were greater still—so it seemed when night descended with darkness over the land, comforting those who felt too small for the great earth.

One evening at dusk, they saw a bright light in the sky ahead of the steamer. Somewhere far away a fire was burning, reflecting its gold-red flames in the heavens. On the earth a fire was throwing its flames so high that it wove red stripes into the gray clouds all the way to the top of heaven: the sea of grass was afire.

Far into the night the immigrants stood and gazed at this fire, so brilliantly reflected in the firmament ahead of the steamer. A wall of fire and flames rose into the sky, and they could discern thick clouds of smoke spreading above their heads like the wings of a black bird of prey. The stars faded away behind this red-glowing heavenly wall. A fire was sweeping the prairie, devouring the grass, feeding on a sea of fuel.

To the immigrants, watching from a distance, it seemed as if God's heaven were burning this night, and a burning heaven is an awesome sight to see. Even the children noticed the fire in the heavens above them, and asked about the angels and wondered if they could fly away before their wings got burned.

The immigrants were reminded of the altar picture in their village church. It showed the Last Judgment and Christ's return to earth. In the picture, too, fiery clouds and smoke belched forth, heavy and dark and so real one could almost smell the smoke. And from on high Jesus came riding down on a burning cloud, in snow-white mantle, surrounded by a host of white angels. The people who were to be judged stood in fear on trembling legs, while the earth was lighted by pale rays from a darkened sun. It was daylight, yet it was dark as night, because it was the Last Day, the Day of Doom.

And now they were seeing the heavens burn in a fire which spread a fearsome light over the earth: their village altar picture was now hanging before them in the firmament, immensely enlarged and brought into living reality.

As yet that part of the picture which gave meaning to it remained undivulged: as yet Christ remained invisible in the fire-wreathed clouds. Christ and His angels had not yet made their appearance.

But many among them would not have been surprised if during this night He had descended from on high, in the glare of the heavenly flames, to judge living and dead.

They recognized the signs, they saw them in the very skies: like this it must be on the last day of the world. The seas and the winds would make much noise, and the heavens would tremble. Any moment now the world's Judge might descend from His heavenly throne, the burning skies lighting His way to the earth.

But even if this were only an earthly fire—the prairie turned into a burning sea—they were nevertheless drawing closer to this fire each moment. The steamer followed the river, and the river flowed right into the red wall of flames and smoke. They would have liked to ask the captain why their ship didn't moor, why he continued to steer right into the fire. Did he with intention bring his boat into the flames, to destroy it with passengers and crew? But unable to speak the language, they could not ask. All they knew was that the fire appeared closer and closer, and the boat approached the fire: the boat and the fire must meet.

Would it be possible to pass through a burning wall and yet remain alive? The alarmed and anxious immigrants sought comfort in their Bibles, where the prophet Isaiah had written the Lord's words: "When thou passest through the waters, I will be with thee; and through the rivers, they shall not overflow thee: when thou walkest through fire, thou shalt not be burned; neither shall the flame kindle upon thee."

All stayed awake through this night; those who went to bed rose at short intervals to look at the burning skies; many prayed in anguish and despair; if it were so that their last day was upon them, hadn't it come too suddenly? Would the heavenly King recognize them as His own, or would He say to them: "Depart from Me, ye cursed!"

Toward morning they could see the fire and the smoke far to the right of the steamer; during the night they had passed a turn of the river, to the left, and were drawing away from the fire.

In clear daylight, it paled and diminished, losing its terrifying effect on those who had taken it as a sign of approaching Doomsday. During the day, the flames gradually disappeared, and at dusk could no longer be seen from the deck of the steamer.

Far, far away they had seen a fire on the prairie. But all around them, all the way to the horizon, the flat land remained green and untouched by flames.

Earlier the immigrants had crossed the *stormy* sea and had safely reached shore. Now again they thanked their God Who had helped them: He had saved them from the *burning* sea.

—3—

THE RIVER STEAMER brought them farther West, following the deep furrow which the Creator had cut through the land of grass, where the bil-

88

lows rose and fell under the wind's persistent comb. Down in the river the drive wheel churned its circular way, hurling the glittering drops into the sunlight.

Since leaving their homes, the immigrants had traveled by flat-wagon and sailing ship, by river boat and steam wagon, by canal boat and steamer. They had been pulled by horses and transported by winds, they had moved by the power of steam. They were still traveling through night and day, traveling across this country which seemed to have no limit. And every moment drew them farther from the land that had borne them. Their native village was now so far behind them that their thoughts could scarcely traverse the distance from the point on the earth where their journey began, to the place where they now were. They shuddered when they tried to comprehend the whole distance they had traveled across land and water. Trying to remember, they were unable to reach back—not even their imagination could undertake a return journey. The distance was too overwhelming; the earth which God had created was too large and too wide to fathom.

A realization which their minds had long resisted became fixed in their hearts and souls: this road they could never travel again; they could never return. They would never see their homeland again.

# IX

## Danger Signs Are Not Always Posted

A BELL RANG on the upper deck, the steering wheel turned, and the prow of the river steamer headed shoreward. The boat moored to a lonely bank deep in the forest; there were no signs of people or human habitation. The gangplank was thrown out, and two of the crewmen went on shore, carrying an oblong bundle between them. Two other men with shovels followed them. All four disappeared behind the thick wall of trees and bushes which grew to the water's edge.

After a short while the men returned to the ship. But now they carried nothing except the shovels dangling in their hands. The bell rang again, the gangplank was pulled in, and the steamer backed into the river, resuming its course after this short, unscheduled delay.

These stops at wild and lonely shores took place every day, some days many times. Except for the ringing of the bell, the stops made not a sound, indeed, they happened so quietly and unexpectedly and were of such short duration that at first the passengers hardly noticed them. Otherwise they might have asked why the steamer made shore; no passenger disembarked, they saw no freight unloaded, no firewood or timber was taken aboard. And at the mooring places not the smallest shed could be seen, there were no piles of wood, no stacks of lumber; untouched

89

wilderness was all that could be seen. Why was time wasted for these stops?

Only the most observant travelers had noticed that a bundle was carried ashore, they had seen the men with shovels, and on closer inspection had seen earth clinging to the shovels when the men returned to the boat. And so they had figured out that the men remained ashore long enough to dig a shallow grave.

Soon all had guessed the riddle of the frequent stops in the wilderness, so quickly and silently undertaken. Something—wrapped in a piece of gray cloth—was carried ashore. Some one of the passengers was taken on land, not alive, but dead. A corpse was removed from the boat, a funeral was performed during the brief interval while the steamer was moored to the bank.

Some passenger died every day; and there were days when several died. Soon all on board were aware of this and counted the number of times the bell rang and the men with shovels went ashore.

No one on board had died by act of violence or by accident, no one had starved to death, no one had frozen to death in this summer heat. A disease was killing the passengers, a disease which in a few short days transformed the healthiest person into a corpse. And the sickness which had stolen aboard the river steamer was so greatly feared that it could not be called by its name, it was the *disease*, nothing else. To call it by name would have been to challenge the dreaded scourge, make it appear sooner. People became sick from fear. In terror they watched for the signs: when the bodily juices dried up, when the skin turned blue-red and coarse, when the nose grew sharp, when thirst burned the tongue and the membranes of the throat, when the body could retain nothing, neither fluids nor solid matter, when the limbs felt cold and cramped, when the eyes sank into their sockets, when nasal slime and saliva stopped, when all tears dried up—then it had entered the body! And if the miracle didn't happen—perspiration breaking out over the whole body within two hours of the seizure—then death had prepared his work well and would finish it within twenty-four hours.

It was a painful sickness. Yet it could be called merciful because it killed within a fairly short time: in a day—perhaps two—it forced the warmth of life from a body, leaving the chill of death in its place. The strongest and healthiest suffered the worst agonies, because the stronger and more capable of resistance life was, the more painful the death struggle.

The murderous disease was the Asiatic epidemic, the cholera.

For the past two years this disease from the East had been sweeping over North America. The Old World had given the New World its most deadly epidemic. It was a gift out of Bengal, from the Holy Ganges, the river of swampy death lands and poisonous waters. The emigrants from Europe had brought this pestilence with them, they carried it with them inland as their journey continued, it was spread from place to place, from boat to boat, from river to river: the pestilence of the East had come to the West.

No one had announced to the passengers that cholera was with them on the steamer: it was not registered in the passenger list, it was not entered on the list of cargo. Inconspicuously, hurriedly, the bodies of the victims were removed. There was need for haste—in this heat.

When the mysterious visits on shore had continued for some days, the name of the horrible disease began to be whispered among the passengers. Then not only the unrelenting pestilence but also the fear of it paralyzed all on board: here, in the midst of them, it had stolen in, invisible, yet it was everywhere; death was close upon them.

—2—

KARL OSKAR remembered the sign he had seen on the steam wagon, which their guide had translated for him, that sign which cautioned about places to be avoided, places where one must be careful: DANGER! WATCH YOUR STEP! He kept his eyes open wherever he went, he was always on the lookout for these English words of warning. But this sign was not posted in all dangerous places in America: he had not seen it on their boat. The passengers had boarded the steamer in confidence, unaware that it was tainted.

At home they had heard of the cholera as a scourge. But the pestilence had little power in Sweden, where the climate was cold. In the heat of this country, Karl Oskar realized that the pestilence might flourish and spread; the very air seemed to burn, it was the worst heat he had experienced since landing in America. He did not know how to combat it. Against cold weather he knew what to do; when the cold grew intense, one could put on heavy clothing. In hot weather one must remove one's clothes, and here he went about as much undressed as he could without feeling ashamed. But it did not help. Even stark naked he would have suffered; it wouldn't have helped to remove his skin!

Against cold one could light fires, one could crawl all the way into the fireplace, if necessary. But where could one flee to get away from the heat? There was no place to crawl into, nowhere to hide from it.

And in this melting heat the steamer fare seemed foul and dangerous. Sometimes the food smelled bad: the nose performed its duty and warned the mouth to refuse it. No fresh food would keep; the blowflies buzzed everywhere and laid their eggs, which hatched almost immediately. Worms crawled in newly slaughtered meat, and soon no one dared touch even the fat pork, swimming in its thick grease, and until now eaten greedily by all.

The cholera must be something living, something that entered one's

91

body through food or drink, some little worm or creeping thing. It might be a tiny creature floating about in the drinking water, perhaps a worm so small that the eye couldn't see it. The cholera might hide in every bite they swallowed, in every drop of water they drank. The murderous pestilence might lurk in their eating vessels or drinking mugs—how could they avoid it when they couldn't even see it? Never before had Karl Oskar felt death so close upon him; it was here everywhere, yet invisible to all.

Not all passengers ate the steamer fare; those who had money bought their own food. Karl Oskar noticed the travelers on the upper deck: each time the steamer stopped at an inhabited place, the first-class passengers went on shore and bought fresh food; they returned with heavy loads of bread, butter, milk, eggs, pancakes; even hens and chickens, which their Negro cooks prepared for them. The passengers up there could eat special, healthy food. And Karl Oskar recalled he had not yet seen a corpse carried ashore from the upper deck. But in steerage, a room for the sick had been prepared with beds all over the floor.

One day when the steamer sought shore three times to accomplish its hurried errand, Karl Oskar said to Kristina: "Those who leave the food alone keep healthy. From now on, we starve."

Kristina agreed, and they let the meals go by; they could starve many days without endangering life. Their appetites had greatly diminished due to the heat, and in a few days they would leave the contaminated steamer. But thirst plagued them sorely, and they had to use the drinking water on the ship. They mixed some vinegar into it; vinegar killed all poisons in water, according to Berta, the Idemo woman who had healing knowledge.

But the best remedy against cholera was said to be a handful of coarse salt, taken a few times daily and washed down with brännvin. Karl Oskar had brought along some wormwood-seed brännvin, which had so far kept his body in good order. Now it was all gone. Fortunately, they had some camphor-brännvin left, and they drank this; Kristina gave the children spoonfuls of "The Prince's Drops" and "The Four Kinds of Drops." Fresh milk was also said to be good against the pestilence, but there was no milk on the boat, neither fresh nor sour. "All gone," they were told, and Robert explained that this meant the milk had been drunk to the last drop.

Jonas Petter borrowed Karl Oskar's bleeding iron and let his blood several times. He said he must get rid of his bad blood to be on the safe side. He also used the iron on Fina-Kajsa, who had long been asking for it. She, being the oldest in their group, was more afraid of the sickness than any of the others, and having lately been near death from another illness, she thought it would be unfair were she again to be laid down on a deathbed. She also tied one of her woolen hose around her throat and after this she felt comparatively safe. Arvid ate conscientiously from his box of *Painkiller*, and he shared the pills with Robert until not a single one was left. Ulrika of Västergöhl prepared plasters of mustard, which she placed across her stomach and Elin's; these plasters would draw the pestilence poison from the entrails where its home was.

The only one of their group who used no remedy against the cholera was Danjel Andreasson; he did not fear the pestilence. He refused to believe that the epidemic was contagious. Who had contaminated the first person to die of cholera? Could anyone tell him? To Danjel, no contagion existed; the cholera was sent directly to each one by the Lord God. God was now visiting His people, already He had decided which ones among the passengers were to die. How could anyone believe this decision might be changed? Danjel saw his fellow immigrants, each one using his medicines and plasters, and he asked: Why not leave the healing to their Creator? Were they so weak in their faith as to doubt God's omnipotence? And he asked his relatives Kristina and Karl Oskar: Did they actually believe they could escape if God had chosen one or both of them to die? Did they think they could hide from the face of the Almighty?

Kristina answered: Man should not sit with crossed arms and shovel everything onto the Lord. She believed God might be more inclined to look after her if she tried to help herself a little.

Danjel was more sad than ever when he learned that Ulrika, his obedient disciple, tried to protect herself against the pestilence with a mustard plaster. He reproached her for this and said she committed the heavy sin of doubt when she relied more on a plaster made by herself than on her God. Did she think, while preparing this plaster with her own sinful hands, that she could do more than the Almighty? She provoked the Lord with the mustard plaster on her stomach, and he entreated her earnestly to remove it.

After Inga-Lena's death, Danjel had admitted to Ulrika that he himself had been mistaken in his belief that one reborn was rid of sin forever: no human being on earth could be free from sin as long as he remained in a mortal body; neither he, Danjel, nor anyone else. All were wretched sinners, burdened by fallen man's body as long as they lived. There was no hope except through God's grace and mercy.

When Ulrika heard this, she was deeply upset and perplexed; how could Danjel fail her thus? Weren't all her sins washed away, once and for all? Did Jesus no longer live in her body? She had believed what Danjel had told her, and now he retracted what he had said. But she didn't want her sin-body back, under no conditions did she wish her old corpse back. Nor had she sinned with any man since coming into Danjel's house and eating his bread. She had been cleansed—why then did not Jesus wish to remain in her? Ulrika felt cheated and insulted: she had confidently relied on Danjel's word, and she demanded that he, as the Lord's prophet, stand by his word. She had long obeyed him and been subordinate to him in all things, but now doubt stole over her: Was Danjel too weak a man to be the Lord's messenger? Yet he looked so much like a prophet, with his long, wild-grown beard.

Now Danjel tried to frighten her with God's wrath because of the mustard plaster she had prepared. She felt irresolute, wondering what to do. But she was not convinced within herself that she had angered God because of such a little thing. She left the mustard plaster in its place.

—3—

EVERY UNFORTUNATE VICTIM chosen by the cholera sickened so suddenly that one moment he stood erect and strong, and the next, he almost fell to the floor. In the sickbed he immediately grew so weak that he was unable to lift his head, he shook in convulsions and moaned pitifully; some screamed in agony before they sank into the merciful depths of unconsciousness. After this the shrouding cloth was soon brought forth.

On the *Charlotta*, Kristina had not been conscious when anyone died; at the time of the deaths around her she herself had been desperately ill. But now she remembered the night on the ship when she nearly bled to death: a few times she had heard a woman's weak voice: "The poor little ones! I don't want to die!" It had been a low, moaning cry, and she had wondered whence it came. She had learned afterward that Inga-Lena had died that same night; it was Inga-Lena who had cried.

And as she now sat with her children about her, Kristina thought: "I do not wish to die and leave them!"

She had seen other creatures die: she had seen the animals at the slaughter bench. She had always had a feeling of compassion for them and had tried to avoid being present at the slaughter. But sometimes, when the men had no other help, she had been forced to hold the bucket for the blood. She had seen the dying animals suffer, she had heard their moaning and bellowing as they lay there, chained down, feet tied, and had seen their helpless kicking and struggling as long as they could move. She had often cried over people's cruelty to innocent creatures who had never done them harm, and she was often aware of her own share in this as she stood at the slaughter trough and received the butchered animal's blood in her bucket.

As she now heard the victims of cholera she was reminded of the times when she had helped with the slaughter. Now it was human creatures who suffered, and when their agony was over, they were hastily buried in unconsecrated ground in the same way as carcasses of diseased cattle were flung into shallow graves in the wastelands.

God must help her; He was the only one she could turn to. She herself would do all she was able to, and then God must help her.

The youngest one of their group, Danjel's daughter Eva, who had not

94

yet learned to walk, was suddenly seized by the pestilence one morning.

The child's face turned blue, her small limbs were contorted with convulsions, her body twisted itself into a round bundle. It seemed as if the arms and legs of the little one had been pulled out of their joints. She cried pitifully, and at times lay still and moaned; she could not describe her pains, but if anyone touched her she screamed. Ulrika gave her all the medicines and pills at hand, but she refused to swallow anything, either dry or fluid. She lay in the vise of cramp, and no one could help her.

After a few hours the child's moaning died down. She was still, now, as if in deep slumber. Her breathing could still be heard, her heart still beat in her little body, but her breast fluttered up and down so quickly the eye could not follow its movements. Her last sounds were like a little bird's peep in a bush. In the late afternoon she grew entirely silent.

Eva Maria Emilia, not yet a year old, died in Ulrika's arms. And Ulrika would not give up the little one after her breathing had stopped. She sat with the dead child in her arms, her weeping shook her whole body. Danjel sat next to her, immobile, his hands folded. He did not weep, he prayed. God had again touched him and he uttered his prayers of thanks for this: he had been too deeply devoted to this his youngest child, and because of this God had taken her away from him. He could not belong to the Lord soul and body while he loved a living creature here on earth. He had idolized little Eva, now the idol was removed, and he thanked his God that He had taken her.

Danjel was beyond human compassion, nor did he seek mortal comfort. It was Ulrika of Västergöhl who was in need of comfort at this moment, she who had been a good foster mother to Danjel's tender daughter, this daughter who had left the earth before she had learned to walk on it. And Ulrika remained sitting with the dead child in her arms until one of the crewmen came and took the little body away from her, and wrapped it in a piece of gray cloth.

At sunset the bell rang on deck, the prow turned shoreward, the steamer moored at an outjutting cliff. Two men with shovels in their hands went on land, one man carrying a small bundle. A flock of half-grown wild ducklings were disturbed and lifted from among the reeds; they flew noisily in circles over the cliff; they were mallard ducks, with beautiful feathers in changing colors. While dusk fell the men dug a hole behind the cliff. Soon they returned on board with their shovels; only a small grave had been needed this time.

Little Eva's funeral was over. And while the steamer put out again and darkness quickly fell over land and water, the flock of ducklings, still disturbed, kept crying plaintively as they flew about over the promontory behind which was the newly dug baby grave.

## 4

THEIR GROUP had now lost one of its members. When, after this, they spoke to each other about the terrible pestilence, there was always in the mind of each: Who will be next?

Ulrika, up till now free from all pains and ailments, began to complain of diarrhea and aches in her legs; she hoped it was only the usual immigrant diarrhea that bothered her; and so it seemed. Karl Oskar suggested that she use the bleeding iron and get rid of some of her blood. Kristina had lost so much blood during her sickness on the *Charlotta* that she did not consider it necessary to be bled, nor did she think they should bleed their children; the little ones were so pale, they probably had no more blood in their bodies than they needed.

Kristina interpreted the smallest discomfort in herself or her children as a sign of the pestilence. All except Danjel kept away from the unhealthy ship's fare and starved themselves. The grownups went about starving in silence, but the children begged for food. Children could not starve day after day; yet they mustn't eat the food either. Kristina said they must get fresh food, at least milk, for their offspring; they still had the means with which to buy it.

The silver in Karl Oskar's skin pouch had melted away during their journey inland, and he had less than a hundred dollars left. Their transportation from Chicago to Minnesota had cost more than he had figured, and they had spent more for food than they had expected. How much would be left on arrival?

One night little Johan was seized with intense vomiting. It continued until green bile came up. Except for pain in his stomach he did not suffer, but Kristina watched in anxiety for the usual sign: the thin limbs twisting in convulsion.

Next morning the steamer made shore at a settlement where firewood for the engine was to be loaded. This stretch of the river flowed through a forest region, and groves of evergreens and leaf-trees grew on either side. A group of bearded, long-haired men met the boat at the pier; they were woodcutters, waiting to load the steamer. These men of the forest had revolvers and knives in their belts and did not look very kind.

A narrow strip of land had been cleared along the river, and behind tall stacks of firewood and piles of lumber a row of houses could be seen. People lived here, so it should be possible to buy food. Kristina entreated Karl Oskar: "Go on shore! Try to get some milk for the little ones."

Karl Oskar picked up their large tin pitcher and went on shore. Robert had seen a map and he said that this was a town, but to Karl Oskar it seemed no more than an out-of-the-way farm village. Not much building had taken place; there were a few houses on the cleared strip, recently built of green lumber, and a little farther away, near the edge of the forest, he could see some primitive huts, not larger than woodsheds; probably the woodcutters lived there. All the houses seemed to have been hammered together in a hurry. A road had been staked out through the village, and work on it begun, but it looked more like a timber road; it was uneven and full of ruts, winding its course between piles of logs and stumps many feet high. Karl Oskar had noticed these tall stumps in many places: apparently the timbermen in America did not bend their backs but felled the trees while standing upright. This left ugly stumps and wasted lumber.

He looked at the row of houses, trying to find a store where food could be bought. He had made up his mind not to return to his children with an empty pitcher.

The biggest house had a sign painted in yard-high letters on the wall toward the river: BANK. Karl Oskar spelled the word twice to be sure, b, a, n, k. A word from his own language was painted on a house far away in the American wilderness! How could this be? Was it done to help arriving Swedes, unable to understand English? Or was the owner a Swede? Robert was not there to inform him that bank was spelled the same in both languages. Karl Oskar decided to go in and ask the bank master where he could buy some milk and wheat bread.

The door below the sign was locked. Karl Oskar knocked, but no one answered. Not a single person was in sight, neither inside the house nor near it. He walked farther, and through a window noticed some men standing at a counter of packing boxes. Behind the counter were shelves, and he thought perhaps this was a store.

Upon entering he immediately realized his mistake: on the counter stood a keg with a tap in it; a man in a white apron behind the counter was pouring a dark-brown drink from the keg. Karl Oskar recognized it as the American brännvin. The men at the counter were drinking, the shelves were filled with bottles, but there was no sign of food. He had entered a saloon.

He did not want to buy brännvin, he wanted milk. He turned in the door, mumbling something about being in the wrong place. It vexed him that he couldn't ask where to buy fresh food and milk for his children. It was pitiful the way he had to act—like a suckling, not yet able to speak, unable to ask for food when he was hungry.

But the few words Karl Oskar mumbled as he left the saloon had an unexpected result. One of the men at the counter followed him through the door and called after him: "Hallo! Are you Swedish?"

Karl Oskar turned quickly. At first he only stared, the Swedish words surprised him so much.

Many Swedes had moved to North America before him, but it was the first time in this country a stranger had spoken to him in his own language.

"You are Swedish, aren't you?" the man repeated.

The stranger was about his own age and size, somewhat thin, with large hands and feet. He was dressed in a red-striped woolen shirt and

97

well-worn skin trousers, held up by a broad, richly ornamented belt. A wide-brimmed straw hat hung on the back of his head; his cheeks were puffed out as if swollen with a toothache or mumps, but his tobacco-spotted chin and lips divulged the secret of the swollen cheeks: they were filled with tobacco quids. Karl Oskar had seen many Americans dressed similarly and equally tall, gangly, and swollen cheeked; the stranger did not look like a Swede.

"I'm a countryman of yours!" the man said.

"Did you come from Sweden?" Karl Oskar was still dubious.

"Yes! Can't you hear me speaking Swedish?"

The stranger wasn't speaking exactly the way Karl Oskar did, but perhaps he had forgotten some of his Swedish. And Karl Oskar was well pleased to have met someone he could converse with.

He pointed to the sign on the building near by: "Are you the Swede who owns the bank?"

The man laughed: "No, I'm sorry. Mr. Stone owns the bank. My name is Larsson. I came from Sweden five years ago."

Karl Oskar listened carefully—yes, the man must be Swedish.

The stranger smiled, he had dancing brown eyes, lying deep under his forehead, and his grin exposed a row of long, grayish-yellow, pointed teeth, spaced far apart.

"What can I help you with, countryman?" he asked. "I guess you came with the steamboat?"

Karl Oskar told him there was a group of Swedish immigrants on board. He was careful not to mention the cholera, he only stated his errand on shore: "I want to buy some food for our children. They can't stand the ship's fare."

"Oh, yes, I understand. I'll show you a store."

"Have they milk and bread?"

"As much as you and your children can eat. Come along, I'll show you. If you have no money, I'll pay for it."

"I can pay for myself," said Karl Oskar. He wanted to make it clear to the stranger that he could pay for anything he got. He was no beggar, he told Larsson; he had been a farmer at home, all his life he had been able to meet his obligations and he intended to do the same in America.

"But it's hard here for a new settler," Larsson said kindly. "We immigrants must stick together, we must help each other."

Karl Oskar was in need of aid; he needed someone to show him the way to a store; and for once luck seemed to be with him.

"I have a wagon over here. Come along!" said Larsson.

They turned a corner and found Larsson's horse, harnessed to a kind of gig, a two-wheeler with a double seat and the driver's seat behind. The vehicle reminded Karl Oskar of similar contraptions in Småland, called "coffee roasters." Larsson untied the horse and asked Karl Oskar to climb in while he himself mounted the driver's seat.

98

"Is it a long way?"

"Only five minutes."

"I don't want to miss the boat."

"The steamer loads here for several hours," Larsson told him. "You'll have plenty of time."

His new acquaintance kept addressing Karl Oskar with the intimate Swedish *thou*, something a stranger in Sweden never would have done, and Karl Oskar found it difficult to be equally familiar.

The gig turned onto the rutty road. The horse was a black, powerful, ragged animal, with dried-up dung clinging to his flanks and legs and a long, uncombed tail. Karl Oskar asked if he were young, and the driver confirmed it: "He's just been broken in; hard to handle."

The two-wheeler hopped about and shook on the rough road, though they drove quite slowly. They left the row of houses and, as the road turned away from the river, passed the small huts so much resembling woodsheds. Heavy logs were piled high on either side of the road, the ruts became deeper, the stumps more numerous, and as they passed the last shed, the thick forest lay only a few hundred yards ahead of them.

"Is the store in the wood?" asked Karl Oskar, puzzled.

"Just inside; only three minutes more."

Then Karl Oskar began to be suspicious. Why would they build a shop in a wild forest, far away from the other houses? How much did he know about the stranger who had offered to take him to the store? Landberg, their honest guide, had warned the immigrants particularly to beware of their own countrymen, who could cheat and rob them the more easily because they spoke the same language. "Never confide in the first stranger you meet just because he speaks your language!" Landberg had said that more than once. Yet Karl Oskar had confided in this man he had just met and had climbed into his carriage. He had been careless enough to say that he had money; in the sheepskin belt next to his body he carried all he had left in cash.

A robber wouldn't commit his crime near houses. He would wait until they were in the forest where no one could see them; in the forest Karl Oskar would be alone with the stranger.

He glanced back at the unknown man sitting behind him on the driver's seat. In America he had seen many men with guns, pistols, or knives, but Larsson had no weapon in sight. Karl Oskar would have felt more comfortable had a weapon been carried openly. As it was, he didn't know what kind of arms the man might have hidden on him. He himself had only an old pocketknife in his hip pocket.

He looked about—perhaps it would be best to jump off the gig while he still could see the houses back there by the river.

The vehicle rolled along, the driver tightened the reins and squirted tobacco juice quite calmly into the wheel tracks: "Where do you intend to settle, countryman of mine?"

99

"In Minnesota, we had thought."

"Don't know that country. Why don't you stay here—you can make two dollars a day in the forest."

Larsson went on: He had helped many Swedes find good jobs. But not all of them had been reliable, he had been cheated and robbed by Swedish crooks when he himself had first arrived in America. As a good friend he wanted to warn Karl Oskar: he must never rely on or confide in anyone; he must be careful.

Karl Oskar felt slightly embarrassed: his new acquaintance seemed to guess his thoughts.

But Larsson seemed as friendly as before, he laughed and talked with the same geniality that he had shown earlier. Judging by his looks and speech, he must be an honest man. And why should Karl Oskar think he was a bandit? Nothing indicated he had evil intentions. One shouldn't think ill of a stranger only because he seemed anxious to help. He felt a little ashamed of his suspicions; he was here for his children's sake, to get them food which might save their lives. Yet he was full of fear and suspicion when he met a helpful countryman. It wasn't like him to be so timid. His father used to say, if you weren't afraid within yourself there was nothing to be afraid of in the whole world. Of course he dared drive a short distance into the forest with this man!

They had reached a stream and were about to cross it over a newly laid bridge of wooden planks, when the driver reined in his horse; on the bridge stood a man holding up one hand and saying something in English. The driver greeted him with a broad grin and a stream of English words. It seemed that the man wanted to ride along with them, and he climbed in and sat next to Karl Oskar.

"Max is an American friend of mine; he is coming to pay me a visit. I have not seen him for a long time," Larsson said and again showed his thin, sharp teeth in a broad grin.

The two-wheeler drove on across the bridge, and now three men were riding in it, two in the low seat and one on the driver's box.

The newcomer was a thickset man with a round face and curly, black hair. He spoke English rapidly and smiled broadly at his neighbor on the seat, as though in Karl Oskar he had met a close relative after long separation.

And the fact was that Karl Oskar did recognize the man who had just jumped up beside him. He had noticed him in the saloon, in the company of Larsson.

Larsson had said that he had not seen Max for a long time, and the two now acted like long-lost friends. Karl Oskar did not need to know English to understand that this play was put on for his benefit. After all, it was not more than minutes since he had seen them stand side by side in the saloon.

Apparently they considered him more simple than he was; now he knew

100

for sure that two robbers were driving him into the forest. Larsson had followed him outside in order to get him into the gig, and meanwhile Max had sneaked away to meet them at the bridge. Now Karl Oskar had two men to handle, one beside him and one behind. The gig kept rolling closer to the edge of the forest; ahead of them the road swung in among the heavy close-standing trees; within two or three minutes he would be alone with two robbers in a thick forest.

He carried his money next to his body when asleep or awake; without it, he and his family would be destitute in this country. No one was going to take it away from him, without first killing him.

He had fallen into a trap. He had been led to believe there would be a store in the wilderness where he could buy milk and bread; he had ridden along like a meek beast to slaughter. But he was not going to ride another step with these robbers.

They had left habitations behind, and not a soul was in sight. He must use cunning, he must pretend he had to get off on an urgent matter, "to call on the sheriff," as the authority-hating farmers at home used to say, when they had to go behind a bush.

But it wouldn't be wise to mention the sheriff now, it might arouse suspicion. With forced calm, he turned to the man on the driver's seat: "Would you mind stopping for a minute, Larsson? I've got to relieve myself."

"All right. Whoa! Whoa!"

The Swede calling himself Larsson spit on the road and reined in his horse. The gig came to a stop. On the right were some bushes, on the left a tall pile of logs. Karl Oskar had been sitting on the left side of the gig, and he jumped off in that direction.

The driver had believed Karl Oskar's excuse valid and had not objected when he wanted to get off; now he became suspicious. Karl Oskar had been in too much of a hurry to get off the gig, he had lost his feigned calmness; and he could see the two men exchange quick glances. They saw through his ruse.

Larsson rose from the driver's seat, and his genial look disappeared; his pointed yellow-gray teeth showed in a sarcastic, malicious grin: "You almost dirtied your pants, I believe. Perhaps I'd better help you unbutton them."

For a fraction of a second Karl Oskar stood paralyzed, his tin pitcher in his hand. Now he could not sneak away from behind the bushes as he had intended to do; now they would not let him go, and there would not be a single person to witness what they might do to him in the forest.

He glanced at the pile of logs beside the road; one log was sticking out toward the hindquarters of the horse. This gave him an inspiration: the logs and the horse must save him. The horse was young, barely broken in; the horse must run away with the robbers, since Karl Oskar couldn't run away from them.

101

Larsson said something in English to his fellow bandit and handed him the reins. A sarcastic grin was still on his face as he said to Karl Oskar: "You can stay right there and use your pitcher! Don't move, countryman, I'll be right down to help you."

But in the split second before the man jumped from the wagon, Karl Oskar gave the outjutting log a kick with his iron-shod heel; he kicked with all the strength in his body, and the added strength of a man fighting for his life.

The pile of logs started rolling onto the road. The young horse tossed his head, his whole body trembled, he snorted excitedly, jumped sidewise, and then bolted off in a wild gallop, pulling the light vehicle with the two men behind him, barely missing being crushed by the rolling logs.

Karl Oskar saw the gig disappearing with the two men clinging to the seats for their very lives; they were still hanging on as the vehicle disappeared among the trees. Karl Oskar felt pleased—the kick had been sufficiently hard, they made good boots in Småland.

But in his excitement he forgot all about the rolling logs behind him. Suddenly one of them hit his left leg with such force that he fell face forward over a small stump. He had the sensation of a sharp knife blade being stuck into his chest, and he heard himself cry out. He was in such intense pain that a wreath of red-hot sparks flashed before his eyes.

He ground his teeth together and managed to rise. He had fallen over the stump of a small tree which had been felled by an ax, leaving large sharp splinters sticking up, and these had cut him like knife points. He pulled out one splinter sticking through his shirt: blood oozed out. He was aware of pain in his left leg, it felt stiff and useless. A shudder of terror ran down his spine—suppose his leg were broken?

But he was able to stand on it. Slowly he moved the leg; he was able to walk. He noticed the milk pitcher which he had dropped in the fall, and he stooped to pick it up; then he limped along the rutty road, back toward the village; every step was painful.

He did not look back for the bolting horse, the gig, and the two strangers. He had no further interest in his countryman who had promised to show him the way to a store where he could buy as much milk and bread as his children could eat; he was in a hurry to get back, back to the houses and the steamer, and to his own family. Slowly he hobbled along; the return took him a long time. He could still see sparks before his eyes, but his head was clear, and his injured leg was good enough to help carry him back.

The steamer was still at the pier loading firewood. One passenger—gone ashore to buy milk and bread—returned, limping on his left leg.

## 5

KARL OSKAR made his way toward the steerage. He walked slowly to hide his limp. Lill-Märta came running toward him, crying out jubilantly: "Here comes Father with milk!" For he still carried the tin pitcher in his hand. Kristina and Johan also ran to him expectantly. "Father has brought us milk! Come!"

Silent and embarrassed, Karl Oskar stood with the empty pitcher in his hand.

"You took your time," said Kristina.

He dropped his hand with the pitcher so they could see for themselves; it was empty.

"We've been waiting for you," Kristina was saying; then she broke off as she looked into the pitcher. "You haven't any milk?"

"Not a drop."

"Not a single drop?"

"No. No bread, either."

Kristina's lower lip quivered in disappointment. "No luck?"

"No, this time I had—no luck."

Johan pointed to his father's chest: "There's blood on Father!"

"What are you saying, boy?" Kristina exclaimed.

Karl Oskar's shirt was of a reddish color, and the blood didn't show much. But she touched his chest, and her fingers became sticky with blood. "God in Heaven! You're bleeding! What happened?"

"I fell over a tree stump, got a small splinter in my chest. Nothing to bother about."

"Mother, I was right!" Johan cried triumphantly. "There's blood on Father!"

"Only a very little blood," corrected Karl Oskar. "Just a scratch from a splinter."

"I must bandage it! Go to your bed and lie down," Kristina ordered Karl Oskar.

Karl Oskar went over to their bunk and removed his shirt. Lill-Märta ran after him: "I want milk. Mother promised!"

"Be quiet, child," admonished Kristina. "I must bandage Father."

"But you promised us milk, Mother!" the child insisted.

"Father fell down. Go away, children."

"Did you lose the milk when you fell?" Johan asked.

"Did you lose every drop?" Lill-Märta echoed.

Kristina took the children by the hand, led them to Robert, and asked him to look after them while she took care of Karl Oskar. She was relieved about Johan, who had improved during the day, having vomited up all the poison of the pestilence—if the sickness had been that. But now that her son was better her husband was hurt.

Karl Oskar had a deep wound just below his right nipple, blood had coagulated around the hole. The left side of his chest hurt when he breathed; he thought perhaps a rib was cracked.

"How did it happen?" Kristina asked.

"I told you, I fell on a stump. Accidents will happen."

Karl Oskar had not told a lie; that was how he had hurt himself. But how much more he should tell her, he didn't as yet know.

After her long sickness at sea Kristina had gradually regained her strength, but at the sight of coagulated blood like a wreath of fat leeches on her husband's chest, she felt wobbly in the knees. Nevertheless, she had learned as a girl to look after wounds, when she had stayed with Berta, the Idemo woman, to have a gangrenous knee treated, and now she soaked a piece of linen cloth in camphor-brännvin and washed the wound clean. Then she applied a healing plaster which Jonas Petter had brought along. She tore up one of her old linen shifts into bandages which she tied around her husband's chest. Berta had said that bandages must be tied as hard as though horses had helped pull them, in order to stanch the blood. Kristina tied the bandage as hard as her fingers were able to, but she thought regretfully she had not the strength of even half a horse.

"I'll change the rags if it bleeds through," she said.

Resting on his bunk, Karl Oskar reflected that he now had two bandages around his body, one of sheepskin and one of linen, one for his money and one for his wound. He had got the second because he must defend the first; the security belt for himself and his loved ones was still intact around his waist. But how near he had been to losing it—he had gone in a cart with a stranger, and this alone had been sufficient to endanger the lives of himself and his family. Yet who would have refused to go with the friendly Swede who offered to find as much healthy food as he and his family could eat?

Sitting close by him, Kristina was still wondering: "How could you fall so awfully hard, Karl Oskar? You're usually steady on your legs."

"When ill luck wills it, one might fall on an even floor."

"You must look where you step in America. They have signs in dangerous places."

"There was no sign in this place."

Those danger signs they had seen so often should be painted not only on posts and walls in this country, they should be written in flaming letters across the sky of all North America; from above they would shine as a warning to immigrants in every part of the country.

"Your luck has left you," mourned Kristina. "In spite of your big nose."

For this "Nilsa-nose" which Karl Oskar had inherited was said to be lucky.

Yes, he, the father, was bleeding, and his children were without milk and bread. Another day and another night they must remain in this pest house with its unhealthy fare. But a little blood and a hurt leg could not be counted among the irreparable disasters of life. A whole family need

104

not be destroyed by these misfortunes. He had merely fallen and hurt his leg, and a splinter had pierced his chest. Later, when all traveling dangers were behind them, he would tell the whole truth to Kristina. Then he would let her know how close she had come to continuing the journey without him, staking out and building the new home alone, a defenseless and penniless widow with three children.

It was not long before the bandages around his chest were saturated with blood.

"You won't bleed to death?" Kristina's voice quavered.

"Nonsense!" He smiled at her. "Only a little blood keeps dripping."

"It goes right through the rags!"

"It drips a little from my nipple, like milk from a woman. It will soon stop."

He reassured Kristina: His superficial scratch would soon heal, his flesh was of the healing kind; he was in good health and could well afford to lose a quart of blood; it was good against the cholera; he had thought of bleeding himself anyway, now he needn't use the bleeding iron. It had been different when a woman called Kristina had bled streams from her nostrils one night at sea; she must have lost many quarts that night. Then, indeed, it was a question of her life. It had been the most horrible night he had ever lived through.

A warmth came into Kristina's eyes: "You were good to me that night, Karl Oskar. If you hadn't gone for the captain, I would not be alive today."

Then he had taken care of her, now she bandaged and cared for him. Then he had tried to stanch her blood, now she tried to stanch his. Blood was the very life inside one; when the blood ran away, life also ran away. Karl Oskar and Kristina were concerned for each other's lives. It was between them as it ought to be between husband and wife: they were joined together to ease each other's burdens, heal each other's wounds. They were two people who in God's presence had given the promise to love each other through shifting fortunes as long as they both should live.

# X
## Their Last Vessel

> The boatman is a lucky man.
> No one can do as the boatman can.
> The boatmen dance and the boatmen sing,
> The boatmen are up to everything. . . .
> (Old Mississippi River Boat Song)

*The Boat*

The *Red Wing* of St. Louis, B. Berger, Captain, Stuart Green, clerk, was an almost new side-wheeler, having started its runs on the Mississippi only two years earlier. It measured 147 feet in length, 24 in width, had one engine for each wheel, and a capacity of 190 tons. Toward the prow two tall funnels rose close together, like a pair of proud twin pillars. The Red Wing lay in the water like a floating house, long and narrow, well cared for and newly painted white. On either side of its prow a great wing had been painted, spreading its blood-red feathers. The steamer was named after a famous Indian chief, and its wheels plowed the same waters on which warriors of his tribe still paddled their primitive canoes.

New steamers, new sounds: on the Red Wing's deck no bell rang, instead the booming of a steam whistle reverberated through the river valley, drowning the sounds of Indian powwows. The steam whistle was new and alien in this region where until lately only the sounds of the elements and of living creatures had been heard on land and water.

The rivers were the immigrants' roads inland, and the Mississippi was the largest and most important of them all. No less than eight hundred steamers churned its waters, a fleet of eight hundred steamboats moved the hordes of travelers northward to a virgin wilderness. The Red Wing of St. Louis was one of the vessels in this river fleet, proudly displaying on its prow the Indian chief's red feathers, as it plowed its way upstream, loaded with passengers.

*The River*

Broad and mighty, the Father of Waters filled his soft bed, like a mobile running lake with two shores, a lake now rising, now falling, yet never draining. From the lakelets of Minnesota in the north to the levees of Louisiana in the south the river flooded its shores and let them dry again; low, swampy shores, tall, rocky cliffs, grassy meadows, sand banks, and sandy bluffs, shores of tropical lianas, cotton fields, giant trees shadowing the water with their umbrageous crowns. Vast and varying was the river's domain: now choppy as a sea whose mighty waves have been arrested after storm, now flowing smoothly, and overgrown with twisted brushwood, tangled masses of thorns, willows, sycamores, alders, vines, brambles, and cedars; here flowering blossoms stood high as altar candles in the swamplands, the nesting place of wading birds, here mountains and cliffs rose on either side, like tall, dark, triumphal arches through which the river roared like the procession of a proud ruler passing with much fanfare.

Trees and bushes grew not only along the shores but also in the water. The river bed itself was a mass of root wreaths; when the trees fell, they fell into the water, and there they lay, their branches stripped of bark, naked, like fingers feeling the stream, like drowning human hands grasping for something to hold. The waves from the steamers' wake washed the wooden skeletons along the shores, hastening their disintegration. Trees lost their foothold on shore and floated into the current; whirling, spinning in circles, the trees floated about, twisted together, caught in each other's branches, as though seeking protection on their uncertain, thousand-mile voyage to the sea. Veritable islets of trunks, roots, branches, bushes, brush, bark, and leaves swam about on the surface. And down deep, in the river bottom, was the grave of dead forests.

The Father of Waters embraced in his bosom other rivers, streams, brooks, becks, creeks; went on shore and stole plants, pulled trees out of the earth to make islands, seized all that was not anchored to the very rocks; the Mississippi, since the beginning of time the earth's mightiest concourse of running waters—going onward for all eternity, onward to the sea.

### The Captain of the Steamer

The travelers from Ljuder had seen many ships and boats since they left Sweden, but the steamer *Red Wing* of St. Louis was the most beautiful of them all.

When they stepped on board and showed their tickets, the captain himself came up to them and spoke in a mixture of Swedish and Norwegian which they could understand: "Ah, *Svensker!* Welcome aboard! I'm a Norseman—we have the same king."

Captain Berger of the *Red Wing* was well past middle age, with gray hair, and a beard that grew thick, covering his face to the eye sockets, except for his red nose tip. The immigrants had observed many bearded men, both at home and during their journey, but Captain Berger was the most richly bearded man they had ever seen. He was also the first Norwegian they had met.

"We *Norsker* arrived before you," continued the captain. "We were wondering how soon you Swedes would come along."

They couldn't understand all the Norwegian he spoke through his beard, but by and by he and his passengers were able to carry on a conversation. At last on this journey they seemed to have come upon good luck; after the cholera-infested steamer, they were now on a clean boat where the pestilence had not made its appearance, and where the captain himself welcomed them warmly as if he had long known them. The *Red Wing* was their sixth vessel, and here they felt more secure than on any of the other five, even though Captain Berger warned them that the river was so crooked a steamer sometimes met itself on the curves.

### The Passengers

The travelers were now on the last stretch of their journey; the Mississippi was their last river, the *Red Wing* their last vessel.

The Father of Waters was emigrating to the sea, the steerage passengers on the side-wheeler were immigrating against the current to the northwest country. Yet both the river and the travelers were on the same errand—seeking new homes. Captain Berger said that all types of people

107

were aboard his ship: settlers, traders, fur hunters, lazy rich men, restless farmers, high government officials, cardsharps, honest working people, happy-go-lucky adventurers. But the greatest number of his passengers were immigrants on the last lap of their journey.

There were German peasants who said *Bayern* at every second word—was it the name of their home parish? They were blond and wore blue linen shirts over their clothes, shirts with outside pockets like coats. Their women had thick legs covered with blue woolen hose; both men and women wore small, funny-looking caps. Among all the immigrants, the Germans alone still had something left in their food baskets. A sausage was always discovered in some bundle; the Germans were always eating sausage.

The Irish immigrants spoke loudly among themselves, seeming to be in a constant quarrel. About half of them were dark haired, the rest red haired. They drank whisky from large wooden stoups, as calves would gulp down sweet milk. Captain Berger said an Irishman would not work unless someone stood with a club over his head: he would no longer use them as crewmen, he preferred Negroes. But a German must be threatened with a club before he would quit work. The two races differed in another way: an Irishman could never get enough to drink, a German never enough to eat.

Then there was the large Jewish family which the bearded captain pointed out to the Swedes: a father bringing his ten sons, four daughters, five daughters-in-law, four sons-in-law, twenty-two grandchildren, and three great-grandchildren; all together forty-nine people. The old father, the head of the family, was a little man; he had a longish face with a black beard and a long crooked nose; he didn't seem over fifty or fifty-five years of age. He always wore a small round cap without a visor, and when the family gathered together, he was always in the center. The little family father sat there, calm, silent, sure, smoking his long pipe, surrounded by his many descendants. Captain Berger guessed that this Jewish family was the largest one that had ever emigrated to North America, which to the children of Israel was the New Canaan; Jacob and all his sons were well represented here.

Karl Oskar asked himself how he could be so filled with concern for his own family of six, when he saw this little Jew with eight times as many.

The crewmen on the *Red Wing* were both colored and white; there were also men with yellow-brown skin, offspring of white fathers and black mothers. All seemed dirty, as if rolled in mud. All were half-naked. Deep down in the steamer's bowels they stoked the engines; in the evenings they gathered on their own separate deck, sitting in clusters, singing their songs—or song, for it seemed they sang the same tune over and over again. In the evenings, when heavy darkness fell over the river, their song rang out over the black, wandering Mississippi:

We will be free, we will be free,
As the wind of the earth and the waves of the sea. . . .

—2—

ON A SMALL DECK near the prow, set aside for steerage passengers, the immigrants from Ljuder were gathered in a group. The deck was roofed but open at the sides, and in the melting heat the passengers sought their way up here to find coolness; some even slept here at night. They had lived so long on the water that a deck now felt like home to them.

A heavy thunderstorm had passed over the valley in the early morning, and fiery swords of lightning had crossed each other over the blue mountains; but the relief it brought had been of short duration. They could feel in the air that the thunderstorm was still near. The travelers from cooler regions sat listless and lazy in the stifling heat and gazed apathetically at the green countryside with its immense fertility, plants and herbs in great numbers spreading far on either side of the river. They pointed out to each other an occasional tree, a bush, or some clinging vine with unusual leaves; or their eyes might follow the flight of some unknown bird, whose name they would ask.

From time to time the river narrowed or broadened; at its greatest width they thought the distance must be about two American miles. At times the strong current slowed down their speed. But the steamer kept to the center of the stream and met the oncoming current with such force that water splashed over the forecastle. Behind them the smoke from the funnels hung in the air like serpentine tufts of hair behind a fast runner.

Time dragged for the immigrants; at sea the wind had delayed them, here on the river the stream hindered them. It was already the last week in July.

Fina-Kajsa lay outstretched full length on the dirty old blanket which she had shared with her mate before he was buried in the North Sea.

"Oh me, oh my! We'll never get there, never! Oh me, oh my!"

From the lips of the old woman two questions constantly issued forth: Had anyone seen her iron pot? Would they never arrive?

With each day since landing in New York her health had improved, and by now she was as well as anyone in their company. She liked the heat; her old backache, a constant plague in the wet climate of Öland, had entirely disappeared. If they could put Fina-Kajsa into a well-fired oven and keep her there for a while, Jonas Petter had remarked, she might come out with new life and hop about like a young girl.

"Oh me, oh my! We'll never get there! Oh me, oh my!"

If they ever arrived, they would meet Anders, her only son, who had emigrated five years before. And now as they were nearing their destination her fellow travelers began questioning Fina-Kajsa about him. She told them: As long as he had stayed at home he had been an obstinate and unmanageable scoundrel; she and her husband had beaten him harder than an unbroken steer to make him tractable. He was lazy, evil-tempered, drunken, and ready to fight anyone; he had spent his time in the company of loose women, obeying neither father nor mother. When he was only ten years old, they had realized his nature: at one time they had refused to let him go with them to a Christmas party, they had locked him up. When they returned, the boy had broken out and given vent to his unchristen nature by smashing nearly all the furniture, from their fine chiffonier to the porcelain chamber pot. But after he had gone out into the world he had regretted his behavior; a few years ago he had written from America, asking his parents' forgiveness. Out here he had become a different person, he worked hard, and he was capable. And he had written and told them about his fine home and the extensive fields he owned in Minnesota. She was sure she would find security and comfort with her son Anders as soon as they reached his beautiful farm. And he would help them all get settled, for whatever else she might have said of her son, he was capable, he knew what to do. According to his letters, there would be farms for all of them where he lived; as soon as they reached Anders all their worries would be over.

"But America has no end. We'll never get there! Oh me, oh my!"

Karl Oskar still kept the piece of paper with Anders Månsson's address. "Have patience a little longer, Mother Fina-Kajsa. We'll get there," he comforted the old woman.

Robert and Arvid were looking down into the water, trying to figure out how fast they were traveling. Robert had read in his book about the Mississippi that it drained a greater area than any other river in the world, and that it flowed with a speed of four miles an hour. And their bearded Norwegian captain had said that the boat could move with a speed of two miles an hour. This didn't seem to make sense; if the river flowed faster than the steamer moved, they wouldn't get forward at all, rather backward.

Robert deducted the speed of the steamer from the speed of the current —two minus four—then he said: "Now I've figured it out. We go two miles backward an hour! We'll soon get back to the ocean again."

"Christ in heaven!" Arvid exclaimed in terror. "Not back on the ocean again! I told you we should have walked once we were on dry land!"

But Robert's figures did not give the truth of the matter. By watching the shores they could see for themselves that their boat was moving upstream. Luckily, Robert had been mistaken.

He asked his brother how the boat could move faster than the river even though the river moved faster than the boat? Karl Oskar said, perhaps Captain Berger had counted in Norwegian miles. But he did not wish to be drawn into arguments about miles and distances, he had already had enough trouble with the difference between Swedish and American miles.

Ever since Ulrika had found Lill-Märta in Detroit, harmony had reigned among the group; there was no longer talk of anyone's leaving it. They realized that in their situation they could be of help to each other. After reaching these distant regions where their language separated them from other travelers, their group had become more unified than before: they owned one thing in common—their language. Since Landberg's departure in Chicago, they had been left to rely on themselves, and a greater intimacy had sprung up among them. Kristina said if they all stuck together, they would get along; she told them the secret of success was that none must be proud. No one must feel above anyone else. They mustn't act the way they used to at home in Sweden.

And they all agreed not to dig up old quarrels and scandals from their homeland; the past must be dead and buried forever. Ulrika had been the parish whore and spent time in prison; Danjel had many times been punished with heavy fines for breach of religious laws and had been threatened with exile by the authorities; both were now banned by the church in Sweden; but who cared about that out here? The deeds for which they had been punished in Sweden were not considered crimes in America. Moreover, no one here cared what they had done in Sweden. Why then bring it up among themselves? More and more they began to realize that Sweden was an antiquated country, behind the times, her unjust laws written by the masters that they might dominate the simple people. Here in America they could tell both the bishop and the sheriff to go to hell. As Jonas Petter put it, they could tell all of them—the bishop, the dean, the warden, and the sheriff—to kiss their bottoms.

The health of the travelers was improving. At little Eva's death, on their previous boat, nearly all had felt pains and aches, but they had escaped the cholera. Ulrika had become perfectly well the moment she stepped aboard the *Red Wing* though at first sight of the steamer she had refused to go near it: one wheelhouse had an inscription in tall letters —PACKET. In Swedish *packet* meant rabble, mob, loose people. If they were to be lodged in the part of the ship called packet, she refused to go near it. Here in America all were supposed to be equal, and no one group ought to be called packet. She calmed down only after the Norwegian captain's explanation that packet meant his steamer carried mail.

The captain had risen in unmarried Ulrika's estimation since he addressed her as *Min Fru*. Apparently all men in America raised her to married status. Now, too, she was well again and without pain. She believed the mustard plaster had saved her from the cholera. In spite of Danjel's friendly remonstrance, she had used it, but for a few days she had worried lest God punish this disobedience to His apostle. Never before had she disobeyed Danjel. However, the Lord God had not taken revenge because of her plaster, and now she wondered if she should always follow Danjel's advice and warnings. She had noticed he was not as stern as before; it seemed as if he sometimes doubted that he had been chosen to guide their souls.

Kristina looked after Karl Oskar's wound, which was healing well, but his chest was sore and blue all over and it hurt when he breathed. In his left leg some stiffness remained, and he still limped a little. His Swedish good luck had deserted him in America, Kristina insisted.

Since they had now been a whole month on their journey from New York, Karl Oskar was thinking of writing another letter to Sweden; but he decided to wait until they arrived at their place of settling. There was nothing new to tell his parents; nothing had happened that was worth mentioning in a letter.

As they sat together on deck they spoke for the first time in a long while about their old homeland, and now it appeared Karl Oskar was the only one who had written home to Sweden. Danjel had no one to write to there; after the church had pronounced its ban, none of his relatives would have anything to do with him, no one expected a letter from one who was exiled, no one cared what happened to him after his departure. His servant Arvid could not write. Jonas Petter could write, and he had his wife Brita-Stafva to write to, but after twenty years of daily quarrels they had at last reached complete disagreement, so he had left her; he was in no hurry to write to the cause of his emigration; nor would he have anything to say to his wife, except that he was glad to be rid of her, and that she already knew.

When she heard them speak of letters home, Ulrika of Västergöhl exclaimed: "Write to Sweden? But that country doesn't exist any more! That hellhole is obliterated from the face of the earth!"

Jonas Petter asked what she meant by this, and Ulrika explained: When leaving Karlshamn, Danjel had said that their old homeland would immediately perish. The Lord's vengeance would smite the land which had put His faithful in prison on bread and water. The Lord God had long intended to destroy Sweden, but He had to wait until Danjel and his followers had left. Soon four months would have passed since their ship had sailed away, and undoubtedly divine judgment had by now been meted out; the Almighty had surely stricken Sweden and erased her from the earth. If they wanted to send letters home, Ulrika suggested they address them to Hell Below, if mail were delivered there.

Danjel admitted in a low voice that at the departure he had made a prophecy concerning the homeland's imminent destruction. But he did not know whether the Lord had as yet carried it out. Perhaps the Lord in patience held back His avenging hand.

Kristina looked at her uncle and shook her head: Surely the Last Judgment could not have taken place in Sweden without having been noticed here in America? Or what did he think?

Danjel turned his kind eyes toward his sister's daughter: He would never again prophesy the Day of Doom; he had now learned that this happening was not postponed until the end of the world but that every day, for every mortal, old or young, was a day of doom. For the Last Judgment was the judgment of conscience within one's soul, it was meted out in the heart of every pious Christian each time he committed a sin.

Robert had this to add: They must all realize that when the world was destroyed, then the whole globe would be destroyed in one moment. That little part of the earth's surface called Sweden could not fall out by itself and disintegrate.

Ulrika said: "I wouldn't send a letter to that hellhole, whether it has sunk below or not!"

She continued in bitterness as her memories rose within her: To whom would she write? To the dean in Ljuder who had chased her away from the Lord's altar and forbidden her the Sacrament, and who many times had called her a child of Satan? She had always answered him: "Yes, dear Father, I hear you calling me!"—Or should she write the sheriff and thank him for putting her in prison? Or the judge of the county court who sentenced her to bread and water? Or should she send a letter to the prison guard who gave her this fine fare, who brought her the dirty water and the mildewed bread? Should he receive an epistle of love from her, was he worth it? And all those in the home parish who had spit at her and thrown filth after her—should she remember them with a letter? Was any single creature among that damned *packet* worth a letter? All they did was to serve the devil every moment of their lives.

Only one person in Sweden would Ulrika like to honor with a letter—the King himself. She would like to thank His Majesty for the feast she had enjoyed in the royal prison, and she would like to tell him that she daily thanked her Creator for having liberated her from being a subject of His Majesty. She would also like to ask the royal person on his high throne how his conscience could let him rule a kingdom where little children were sold at auction, their whole childhood through to be mistreated by greedy, cruel peasants. She would like to tell the King how happy she now was to have escaped from his kingdom, to have arrived in a country where neither he nor any of the lordships at home had any power, a country where she was considered one of God's own creatures.

Yes, indeed, next time she got hold of paper and writing tools she would send the King of Sweden a farewell letter from one of his former subjects. And before she put this letter into an envelope addressed to the "King by God's Grace" at Stockholm Castle, they could guess what she would do with it!

They all laughed at the Glad One's letter to the King—they all knew she couldn't write.

Karl Oskar said: "Forget the old! It's over."

What purpose could be served by harboring grudges against Sweden? Now that they had arrived in a new, young country, it was better to forget

113

all that old stuff, throw it away as they threw away old rags. They must not keep their homeland so much in their minds that it depressed and irritated them; this would only hinder their success in America.

Ulrika agreed on this point, as did Danjel and Jonas Petter. But Kristina sat silent the whole time and let no one know how she felt about the danger of thinking too much of her homeland.

—3—

Every day Robert read in his language book, every day he practiced the new forms and positions indicated for his lips and tongue. The most useful sentences he learned by heart: how to ask one's way to inns and lodging places, to food stores and eating places; how to ask the price of food and quarters; how to find work, and above all—the salary paid for work: *How much wages do you pay?* He must be sure to ask the right question in each instance. He also learned the numbers in English, as he considered these of the greatest importance to avoid being cheated when receiving change or pay.

Not only was it important to ask rightly; it was equally important to answer correctly when the Americans asked questions. He studied the exercises on getting a job: *What can you do?* In Sweden he had been a farm hand. But he didn't like the English word farm hand. *Farm hand!* It sounded too lowly an occupation, as if he were one hand of the farmer, a piece of his master's body, another farm tool used by the master. In Sweden he had actually felt that he was nothing more than a tool, a most insignificant and helpless tool, used by the masters as they saw fit. But here the servant was as good as the master, and he had emigrated to America because he didn't wish to be a tool used by masters; he didn't want to have any masters, he wanted to be free.

No, he wanted to tell the Americans what he could do: *I can plow and tend cattle!* It sounded more like a *man* talking, inspiring more confidence than to say, *I am a farm hand*; it sounded more capable and grown-up, as if he worked with his own hands and not with the master's.

The Americans were polite and considerate and always asked a stranger how he was. Robert wanted to be equally polite and he had learned by heart the reply: *Thank you! I am feeling very well!* True enough, he wasn't quite well, his ear still bothered him, but he wasn't going to admit that, not even if he were worse than he was. He didn't want to cause the friendly Americans anxiety in any way. He didn't want them to go about worrying over his health; they had so many other things to worry about, and so much to do.

If he were offered some food that was spoiled or tasted bad (for in America, too, he had discovered such dishes), then he would be courteous, like a man of the world; he would say that he didn't have time to eat and

114

drink just now, he had *a few things to attend to*. The Americans, themselves so industrious and thrifty, would hardly blame him for attending to his business.

The language book gave advice about conversations with people of different trades and positions: *Conversation with an Innkeeper, Conversation with a Watchmaker, Conversation with a Hatmaker, Conversation with a Shoemaker, Conversation with a Laundress, Conversation When Purchasing a Country Place, Conversation When Building a Log House*. Each conversation listed a dozen questions and answers, and as soon as one knew the person concerned, it was merely a matter of opening the book and starting off. Under different headings were lists of words most frequently used: *Time, Nature and the World, Man, Mental Qualities, Bodily Attributes, Plants and Flowers, Metals and Stones, Animals—Wild and Tame*. If Robert wanted to report to the police that he had found a corpse in the street, he would only have to look under *Man*. And if he wanted to compliment someone on his great intelligence, he would look under *Mental Qualities*; if he wished to tell a girl how beautiful she was, he must turn to the heading *Bodily Attributes*. And when he had become rich and wanted to buy a riding horse, a thoroughbred stallion, he must choose the words for this transaction under *Animals—Wild and Tame*. Having bought the stallion, he might also wish to buy a golden watch, and instruction for this purchase might be obtained under *Stones and Metals*, or perhaps under *Conversation with a Watchmaker*.

Robert had written down on a list the names of all the dishes he liked: veal, mutton, pork sausage, rice porridge, pancakes. He had learned to name forty-three different dishes and twelve kinds of drinks. He wanted to have everything in order for the day when his riches were accumulated so that he could order anything he liked and finish up the order with this sentence from his book: *Put all the dishes on the table!*

He had heard stories of immigrants who in a short time had accumulated immense fortunes but had been unable to handle their riches. Greed had eaten them up or dried them up, or gluttony had made their stomachs swell to abnormal proportions. Some rotted away in unmentionable vices. Money was their destruction. Robert felt a warning in this for himself. Ever since entering the portals of the New World in New York, he had pondered his ambition in America and how best to effectuate it. He would neither become puffed-up and haughty in prosperity, nor would he worry in adversity, like a weakling. He would not wish for everything he saw, he would be satisfied with sufficient possessions, a small fortune, easy to handle; moderate riches would not be dangerous, would not tempt him to destroy himself.

But all the steerage passengers on the *Red Wing*, whatever their language, were as poor as he, and all wanted to get rich.

Robert's purpose in coming to America was perhaps best expressed in a song which he had heard from the crew's quarters many evenings. Their voices could be heard from their place of gathering on their own deck, where he could see their half-naked bodies in the semidarkness. At first he had only been able to understand one word of their song—*free*. But after listening for a few days he could interpret the whole meaning:

> We will be free, we will be free,
> As the wind of the earth and the waves of the sea. . . .

This was the crew's song in the evening, it was the song of the wandering river, it was the song of Robert's aim in America.

## —4—

FROM THE DECK of the *Red Wing* Robert and Arvid saw a constant change of scenery: the shores, the river itself, the many passing steamers with strange names, logs floating along on the current, pieces of lumber, bushes, trees, boxes, barrels, dead birds. Once they saw a corpse sail by, only part of the head sticking out of the water, a gray-white face and black hair entangled in a mass of green grass and branches; they thought it was the corpse of a woman, floating along with this unusual bridal wreath on her head.

They watched for new trees and plants along the shores, for Arvid had heard that shirts and pants grew on trees in America, and he wanted to see these trees. Robert said he must have in mind the cotton bush which grew only in the Southern states; they would not see it here.

Robert was looking for crocodiles; he had read in his book that these monsters inhabited the Mississippi. And one day Arvid pointed out an animal, swimming near the shore, so ugly that the like of it he had never seen before; it must be a crocodile. But the captain assured them that crocodiles didn't swim this far north, and the ones in the swamplands near the river mouth weren't really crocodiles, they were alligators.

One night an immigrant from Scotland, sleeping on the deck, fell into the river. No one missed him until morning. He left a wife and six small children on the boat. A collection was taken up among the passengers for the destitute family, and each one contributed something. In all, more than thirty dollars was collected as comfort and aid to the fatherless family; but the widow and her six children continued to weep just the same.

Arvid was horrified at the thought of the Scotsman; not only did the poor man lose his life, if his body floated toward the sea, he might be eaten by the gruesome crocodiles. How could he, on the Day of Doom, rise up from the stomach of a crocodile?

One morning Arvid called to Robert in consternation: "Look over there! The wild critters have come!"

On a cliff overlooking the river stood a group of strangely immobile figures, all facing the steamer, which passed them at a distance not above a gunshot. Feathers on their heads indicated they were Indians; some had bows in their hands. All watched the steamer intently, its funnels spewing smoke, its wheels rolling along through the water, splashing like large fins. The Indians stood like trees grown out of the rock, petrified by the sight of the steamer.

Undoubtedly these were wild Indians, Robert said.

Several times during their journey inland they had seen Indians, but they had been civilized. Now, for the first time, they saw wild Indians, Indians in the bush. And Robert understood that the immigrants were now approaching the vast, unknown, dangerous wilderness, a much larger and much more dangerous wilderness than they had traveled through before.

"They might shoot arrows at us!" Arvid said, looking for a place to hide.

But the Indians remained like statues, straight and silent, intently watching the puffing, pushing steamer on the river.

Suddenly the stillness was broken by the *Red Wing*'s steam whistle; a piercing sound reverberated across the water, echoing back from the cliffs on shore. The sound cut like a lance in Robert's ear.

The Indians answered the whistle with a shriek of terror and disappeared from their cliff as quickly as if swept away by the wind; quicker almost than the eye could see, they had run and hidden behind bushes at the foot of the cliff. The two boys had never seen human beings so swift of foot. The highly entertained passengers on the upper deck laughed heartily.

Arvid was much surprised: he had heard that the Indians were cruel and horrible as wolves. How could they be dangerous when that little boat whistle could scare them away? And now he knew what he would do if encountering wild Indians in the forest: he would whistle; then they would scatter like chickens from a hawk.

Robert thought that perhaps these Indians had never before seen a steamer. At home people said steamers were Satan himself traveling about on water in these latter days, spurting fire and smoke. The heathens out here could hardly be expected to have more sense than Christians in Sweden. Perhaps they thought the steamer was an evil monster risen from the depths of the river. They might be familiar with crocodiles, sea serpents, and other river creatures, but had they ever seen an animal spewing smoke, sparks, and fire? Were they accustomed to roaring river creatures, paddling along with wheel-feet, shrieking like a thousand pigs simultaneously stuck with sharp knives? Robert's own ears could not stand the sound of the whistle, and Arvid had said that his heart had stopped inside his breast for many minutes when he heard the whistle for the first time. Robert was sure that a sound like the steam whistle had never before been heard on God's earth.

And he thought it was an evil deed to let loose the whistle in order to

117

frighten the Indians and entertain the passengers. It was true that the Indians were heathen and unchristian, but there was no need to plague them unnecessarily.

Robert had read about the Indians shooting with poisoned arrows and killing people with dull wooden spears. He had even heard that they scalped people without sharpening their knives, a thought which made him shudder so that his hair stood on end. Such were the deeds of unchristian people who were neither baptized nor confirmed; heathens knew no better. This would change as soon as they became civilized and Christian. When the missionaries arrived among the Indians and baptized them and gave them the Lord's Supper, the one-time wild Indians would learn to use their enemies' breech-loading guns and scalp their victims with sharp knives.

The captain said: "The Indians are horrible people; they tie their captives to poles and burn them to death; they fry them the way Christian people fry pork."

And Robert appreciated this warning. He had now actually glimpsed the natives of this unknown wilderness where he and his group were about to build their homes. They would soon reach their destination; a new, strange life would soon begin. And the life awaiting them began to take shape in his imagination.

Each day Robert carefully observed the new country, its natives, plants, animals, general appearance. Sometime in the future, when he had leisure and writing implements, he intended to write a description of his surroundings according to his own observations. He possessed a small writing book, once given to him by Schoolmaster Rinaldo, in which he had put down the most unusual happenings so far.

With the arrival of evening, both river and shores flowed together in that impenetrable darkness of North America, the densest and thickest darkness of all the darknesses God had created. Then Robert could observe neither land nor water. But sometimes in the evenings or during the nights, flames could be seen from the invisible shores of the Mississippi. They looked like moving torches or tongues of fire; they were fires from Indian camps, glowing, flaming somewhere on land. The Indians were there—they weren't visible, but they were there, they lurked somewhere in the forest, somewhere in the bottomless darkness—the most horrible people the old Mississippi captain had ever seen.

And Robert watched these fires with deep apprehension; they indicated to him the presence of the cruel redskins; they were all around him here, they were close. And this very country was to be his home, in the midst of these heathens he would have to live, among Indians he would pass the rest of his life.

He felt a great fear, and a still greater foreboding.

ON THE LAST DAY of July, 1850, the immigrants from Ljuder stepped ashore in the town of Stillwater, on the St. Croix River, a tributary of the Mississippi, in Washington County, Territory of Minnesota.

They arrived at a time of year most inconvenient for farmers: the summer was by now so far advanced that it was too late to sow or plant anything. They were peasants who had lost a year's crops, and they knew what this meant.

# PART TWO

# The Settling

# XI

## "Will No One Help Me?"

THE PLACE SMELLED of the forest products and forest debris—green, lately milled lumber, pitch, sawdust, boards at seasoning. Along the river ran a fairly broad street covered with pine needles, bark, sawdust, sand—truly a lumber-town street. The riverbank was piled high with boards and logs for blocks, and on the river floated logs in such numbers that the surface seemed one vast, cobbled floor. Both earth and water smelled of pitch and pine. The travelers had arrived in a forest region.

Karl Oskar and Robert wandered up the street, to where the newly built houses clustered; they walked leisurely, trying to read the shop signs and other inscriptions: *Oxen for Sale Cheap for Cash; William Simpson, Druggist; Shoemaker and Watch Repairing; The House That Jack Built.* They passed a number of stores where tools and implements of many kinds were displayed in the windows. The largest inscription was painted on the side of a house: *Stillwater Lumber Company.* They had seen the same sign near the pier as they landed.

It had been late afternoon when they disembarked from the *Red Wing;* they must find lodging before nightfall. For two weeks Robert had practiced this one important sentence from his language book: *Please show me to a lodging house.* He was now completely familiar with every part of this sentence, even though he had not as yet used it. But now two more important and urgent questions confronted the immigrants: How were they to manage with all their belongings? How would they find their way to their place of destination?

Captain Berger had informed them a few days earlier that the *Red Wing* would be unable to carry them all the way up river to Taylors Falls. The Mississippi steamers turned back at Stillwater as the St. Croix was not navigable beyond this point for larger craft; the current was too strong and there were several rapids. Consequently, he was forced to land them some distance short of their destination. At the same time Captain Berger had warned them not to remain in this region, which was ravaged by cholera; he had pointed out many places along the river where houses and huts stood empty. Immigrants from his homeland had built them but had already been forced to move—not away from the district, but six feet down into it, to final decay. The survivors in these Norwegian settlements were impoverished, almost starved to death, existing in utmost misery. It was so bad, Captain Berger wasn't sure which immigrants were better off, those in the ground or those above it.

Such information was not encouraging to the newcomers, and they had felt downhearted and filled with concern as they left the steamer. Captain Berger had promised to ask someone to help them find their way after landing, but he had fallen ill that morning, and when they landed, he lay in high fever in his cabin; they had not seen him again. And as the *Red Wing* departed they were left alone on the pier, completely dependent upon themselves in this unknown place. There they sat down among their chests, sacks, bundles, and baskets, without knowing in which direction to go, or how to transport their possessions.

While the rest of the group remained at the pier to watch over their belongings, Karl Oskar and Robert went to seek information. Besides the question concerning lodgings, Robert had learned two sentences from the chapter entitled "The Journey": *Respected Sir, how can we reach Taylors Falls? Who will take care of our baggage?* The name Taylors Falls he had added himself, but he did not know how to pronounce it. He meant to put these questions to someone in the street who looked kind and helpful and seemed to have plenty of time; he was particularly on the lookout for older persons.

But they met only young people on the street of this new lumber town. And all were in a great hurry, passing them by quickly. Robert hoped to address someone who was walking slowly. But they met no limping old men or women. Few women were in sight on the street. Three times, Robert spoke to older men; each one stopped, shook his head at the questions, and muttered some incomprehensible answer. He spoke to a couple of middle-aged women sitting on the steps in front of a house, but they, too, shook their heads.

Karl Oskar was growing impatient: "I don't think they understand you!"

Robert had asserted that by now his English was so good he could lend his mouth for the use of all, and Karl Oskar was reminded again that he could not always rely on his brother.

Robert had followed the instructions in his book: *Practice the Speech Exercises! Become familiar with the words and phrases most frequently used!* He replied to Karl Oskar: The Americans undoubtedly understood what he said. But they spoke their own language so rapidly that he couldn't understand their answers.

He tried his questions on a few more passers-by but without success, and then Karl Oskar said they had better go back to the pier.

Their fellow travelers were still sitting among their possessions, all together, but helpless and at a loss as to what to do next.

Jonas Petter said it looked as though the inhabitants might be afraid of them; they had been left entirely alone on the pier; did people think a gang of robbers had arrived on the steamer?

Fina-Kajsa sat with her skirt tucked up, her broken iron pot on her knees. She sighed: "Oh me, oh my! We'll never get there! Oh me, oh my!"

All were hungry, and someone suggested opening the food baskets. But

Karl Oskar said it would soon be dark, they must find quarters before they did anything else; they couldn't remain on the pier all night.

Ulrika spoke up: "That was supposed to be your job, as I recall."

"*You* go and try!" Karl Oskar retorted tartly.

He was in low spirits and this affected the others. Even the Glad One, who usually encountered trouble with indifference, was now upset and irritable, and as it suddenly began to rain, she poured forth bad language on this new misfortune.

It was a cloudburst—apparently, all rains in America were cloudbursts. It splashed and thundered over the river, the heavy rain soaked the immigrants' clothing, it struck like knives, penetrating to their very marrow. After a few minutes they were all as wet as if they had been dipped in the river. The children yelled and refused to be comforted.

Everyone in the group was hungry, tired, and wet through and through; night was upon them, and they did not know where to find shelter. One after the other they felt despair overtake them. The company from Ljuder had never before during their whole journey felt so helpless, lost, and forsaken.

Robert went over and over his recent attempt to find his way with the new language—his hopelessly miscarried attempt! It was easy enough to remember and repeat the sentences to himself. But when he wanted to say them to strangers he grew nervous and confused, then he began to stutter, he hemmed and hawed. He couldn't understand it: not one of the three sentences he had learned had been of any use today. And he began to practice a fourth, which he would repeat until he was successful: *Will no one help me?*

—2—

HENRY O. JACKSON, Baptist minister in Stillwater, was busy sawing firewood outside his cabin near the river. Only a few steps separated the sawhorse from the water, and he kept his foothold precariously on the sloping ground. Pastor Jackson was a short, rather fat man of about forty, dressed in well-worn brown cotton trousers and a not-too-clean flannel shirt. He worked bareheaded, and tufts of thin hair fluttered in rhythm with the movement of the saw as it dug its way through the dry pine bough on the sawhorse. The handle of his saw, cut from a crooked limb, chafed his hands after a while; the pine log was tough and resistant, the saw teeth, dull from lack of sharpening, rasped slowly through the wood. The work was hard, and after cutting each piece, the minister rested a moment, drying the sweat from his forehead with a great linen handkerchief that hung on a peg of the sawhorse and flapped in the wind like a flag.

The St. Croix River, separating the new state of Wisconsin from the

Minnesota Territory, made a large bend as it flowed by Stillwater. Right here near the town the current was slow, almost imperceptible, and the river expanded into a small lake, on which all the timber floated down from above had been gathered; here on the west bank it would be hauled up and milled. A little farther to the west the ground rose in high hills, and the town of Stillwater had been built between these hills and the river. The community had an advantageous position, protected from winds by the forested hills at its back, and with the river flowing at its feet. Within a short space its population had grown to more than five hundred inhabitants; next to St. Paul, it was at this time the largest settlement in the territory. A year before, Stillwater had been made the county seat of the newly formed Washington County.

On the east shore of the St. Croix, directly across from Pastor Jackson's cabin, steep cliffs of red-brown sandstone obstructed the view of the countryside: there lay Wisconsin, which two years ago had become a state of the Union.

Jackson had been pastor in Stillwater ever since the Lord had founded his parish in the town. Up till now he had lived in a log cabin belonging to a fur trapper who spent most of his time in the forests, but a more comfortable abode was being built by his parishioners near his church and would be ready this fall. Most of the members of his congregation were generous, helpful people. Practically all gained their living from the lumber activities in the region or from farming. Many of the timbermen in the logging camps and the laborers at the mills in Stillwater were worldly and unregenerate, but the farmers moving into the district were nearly all good Christians. Some fifty homesteaders had moved into Washington County in recent years and these new settlers often had errands in Stillwater: Sundays they came to hear Pastor Jackson preach; weekdays they came to sell their grain, potatoes, pork, or mutton.

The minister's cabin stood only a few hundred yards from the pier where the *Red Wing* of St. Louis—well known in Stillwater—was unloading her cargo of beef, pork, and flour barrels. Soon the sound of her steam whistle drowned the saw's screeching and announced to Pastor Jackson that the side-wheeler had returned down the river toward the Mississippi. But before he had time to lay a new log on his sawhorse, a dark cloud suddenly came up from the Wisconsin side. During the heavy downpour he sought shelter in his cabin. The street outside quickly became empty of people, everyone running inside. But through his window he now noticed on the steamship pier a small group of people who had not sought shelter from the violent shower. They must be newcomers, passengers from the *Red Wing*. The minister guessed they were immigrants. And no one had been there to help them—all were afraid of the cholera which new arrivals might bring with them.

Last spring German immigrants had brought the cholera to Minnesota, and during the whole summer the pestilence had raged in the settlements farther south. Along the St. Croix, enormous graves had been dug and filled with the bodies of immigrants. In Stillwater a score of deaths had taken place, and the inhabitants were stricken by fear of this pestilence. Careful watch was kept over newcomers, and the city council had removed a great number of them and placed them on an island in a forest lake some ten miles to the west. Here they had been left to live, separated from other people, until free from contagion.

But Pastor Jackson never avoided strangers, he felt no fear of the dreadful disease: Whither in this world may man flee, that death shall not o'ertake him?

As soon as he saw the group on the pier, he made his way toward them. The violent rain was barely over. Huddled among the bundles and chests sat grownups and children. Shawls and coats had been tucked around the children to protect them from the rain; babies cried in the women's arms.

He saw at once he had come to people who needed him. He recognized that they had come from far away, they were immigrants from Europe. Both men and women were light complexioned, tall and sturdy, and he guessed they were from Germany, like so many other recent immigrants. He spoke German passably and made an attempt to address the strangers in that language: He was a Baptist minister. Wouldn't they come with him to his cabin?

He repeated his question but received no answer; all stared at him without comprehension. Then German was not their mother tongue.

As Pastor Jackson looked at the group more carefully he saw that nearly all were pale and starved-looking. Immigrant Germans, both men and women, usually arrived well fed, their cheeks blooming. He concluded these immigrants might be Irish—though why did they not know English?

A tall, gangly youth with a light down on his upper lip spoke a few sentences in a language Pastor Jackson recognized: immigrant English. Pastor Jackson was familiar with newcomers' first attempts to use the language of their new land, and he smiled encouragingly at the speaker, listened carefully, and did not interrupt him. And at last he understood. The youth wanted to tell him that he was a stranger in America and wondered if anyone here would help him.

The American asked where the immigrants came from, and in the answer he seemed to recognize the name *Sweden*.

Pastor Jackson had gathered much information about the various countries of the immigrants, and he knew that Sweden was a county of Norway. A Norwegian family in Marine belonged to his congregation. The newcomers on the pier must be countrymen of the Norwegian people in Marine, who were good, religious people. A Norwegian also lived here in Stillwater—Mr. Thomassen, a shoemaker who had resoled his shoes and made a good job of it. Thomassen lived some distance away, on the other side of the church. He would send a message to him to come and meet a group of his newly arrived countrymen.

And the minister turned again to the youth and spoke to him in English; he spoke as slowly and clearly as he could and tried to extend his message to the whole group. The people here were friendly and good people, but afraid of strangers who might bring the cholera. The newcomers need have no fears, he was a minister here in town; now they must come with him to his cabin and he would take care of their belongings and have them brought inside for the night.

The pale, gangly youth did not try to explain to the rest of them what Pastor Jackson had said. But he pulled from his pocket a small book, the leaves of which he turned eagerly as if searching for something. The minister turned to a young woman with a whimpering child on either knee and took the smallest child in his arms. It was a baby boy, and he held him as carefully as though baptizing him. The child was wrapped in a soaking-wet shawl, and water dripped from the shawl and wet the minister's clothing quite through.

Then Pastor Henry Jackson walked away with the child in his arms, and the whole group followed him. Last in the row came the youth he had spoken to, still searching in his book. He continued to turn the pages all the way until they reached the cabin, unable to find what he was looking for: *Conversation with a Minister*.

—3—

BEFORE KARL OSKAR stepped across the threshold of Pastor Jackson's cabin, he turned to Jonas Petter to seek his counsel: Was it advisable to believe this peculiar, bareheaded man? How could they know what he intended to do with them? Perhaps he was leading them to a lair of robbers and thieves? How could they know what kind of den they were stepping into?

"But he looks kind and helpful," Jonas Petter said.

"That's just it," Karl Oskar insisted. Didn't he know! The kinder and more helpful a stranger seemed in America, the more dangerous it was to go with him. He still carried on his body marks he could feel and see: a great scar on his chest and his left leg still aching. He did not believe in any stranger in North America.

"We need not be afraid. He is the minister in this town," Robert said, with respect in his voice.

"Minister? He? No! He lies!"

Karl Oskar's suspicions increased: this helper of theirs, going bareheaded outside, poorly dressed in worn trousers and a shirt that wasn't too clean—this man a minister? If this man was a minister then he, Karl Oskar, could stand in a pulpit!

Robert insisted that the man had said he was a *minister*, and that meant a preacher. They could see for themselves in his book. But Karl

Oskar thought Robert must have heard wrong. He had no confidence in his brother's knowledge of the English language. And he suspected that the stranger was luring them away from the pier so that he might steal their belongings.

But as the bareheaded man wasn't taking them so far away that they couldn't keep an eye on their movables, his suspicions were somewhat allayed, and he went inside the cabin. He whispered, however, to Kristina: They must not forget, the most seemingly helpful persons might be the most deceitful.

Pastor Jackson busied himself making a great fire in the stove so that his guests might dry their wet clothing. The women undressed to their petticoats and hung their skirts to dry in front of the fire; the children's wet garments were removed. The men weren't much concerned over their wet clothing as long as they felt warmth; they elbowed each other around the stove. Their host attended to all their needs: he acted as though they were his nearest relatives come to visit him. They weren't allowed to do a single chore—neither fetch water nor wood—he did everything himself, attended to them as if he were their servant.

He put a kettle on the stove and placed a sizable chunk of venison in it; fortunately, one of his church members had brought the gift to him this very day. He split some of his newly sawed logs and carried in dry pine wood and fed the stove until it was red hot. He put on a white apron and set his broad table with bread, milk, butter, sausage, cheese; he set out knives, forks, plates, and spoons as capably as a woman. He fussed over the children, warmed milk for them, found playthings for them. And during this whole time his guests sat wide-eyed and stared at him, struck dumb by all the work an unknown man in an unknown place was doing for them, and all the things offered them. He made his house their home.

And when they sat down to table, they discovered he was a cook worthy of a noble family; the venison was tender and juicy, melting in the mouth like butter. None among them had ever eaten such fare. Even Fina-Kajsa, with her single tooth, was able to chew this meat. And when they had eaten to their satisfaction, there was still a great deal of food left. As they sat there, sated and comfortable, they entirely forgot their miserable situation of a few hours earlier.

The women were still in their petticoats, but after the meal Ulrika took down her skirt, which had dried in front of the fire: "When I get my rump wet, I lose my good temper." So saying, she gave Pastor Jackson her broadest smile of honest appreciation.

He smiled back, full of understanding, not of her words, but of her need for dry clothing. And he behaved toward her and all of them as if concerned with only one thought: Did they have all the food they wanted and were they comfortable?

As they were dry again, they had indeed all they could wish for. And all were satisfied; since landing in America they had never eaten so well and enjoyed food so much as this evening, and yet all of it was a gift.

Now they knew the bareheaded man who had met them on the pier; now all realized who he was. They didn't understand what he said, but they understood what he did, and this was sufficient for them. Robert had asked if no one would help them, and this man was the answer: he helped them all.

After enjoying the food, the immigrants were also to enjoy rest. Pastor Jackson made up beds for his visitors. For his fifteen guests, big and little, he made beds over the entire floor of his cabin. He brought out sacks and filled them with hay for mattresses, he produced animal skins for covers; he made such roomy and comfortable beds that he himself could find no place to sleep in his own house—he said good night to his guests and went to sleep with a neighbor.

And they were barely awake the following morning when he was back, busying himself at the stove, preparing the morning meal for them. He boiled a pot of potatoes and beans, he warmed yesterday's leftover venison.

Their benefactor told Robert he had sent for one of their countrymen as interpreter. And while they were still at their breakfast a small, touslehaired man with a broad nose entered the cabin; he had on a black cobbler's apron of skin which smelled of leather and wax. He greeted them all as if knowing them in advance: "I am Sigurd Thomassen. I am a *Nordman*."

He spoke to the Swedes as if expecting them to know who he was: shoemaker in Stillwater, the only Norwegian in town.

The man was not exactly a countryman of theirs; Robert had been mistaken. But the Swedish immigrants understood his language as well as they had understood Captain Berger on the *Red Wing*, and they learned from him that Robert had been right in saying their host was a minister.

Karl Oskar felt ashamed of his suspicions yesterday; and all beheld in deep wonder the man whose guests they were, this kind American, now busying himself with women's chores. A man of the clergy, called and ordained for the holy office of preaching the Gospel—yet here he was making beds, washing dishes, tidying up the house, sweeping, performing the chores of an ordinary maid. They could not comprehend it. They could not imagine this man in the white kitchen apron, standing in the pulpit in frock and collar, they couldn't understand this man who scoured pots and pans on weekdays and would stand at the altar Sundays, administering the Holy Sacraments. Why should a minister, able to preach, stoop so low as to perform menial kitchen chores?

"I have never seen a man so handy in the kitchen," Kristina said to Ulrika.

"He is the kindest man with the biggest heart I've ever met," replied the Glad One. "Who could ever have guessed he was a priest?"

"Is he married?" Kristina asked.

"He is a bachelor." Thomassen used the English word.

"I mean—does he have a wife?"

"No. He lives single." He used the English word *single*, which Kristina didn't understand. She thought, however, the minister in Stillwater must not yet have married.

The Norwegian told them that women were scarce in the Territory. Here in Stillwater there was hardly one woman to ten men, and in the countryside maybe one to twenty men. So the men went about as eager as Adam in Paradise before God created Eve.

"You are most welcome! The settlers have been waiting for you!" he told Kristina.

And he looked from one to the other of the three Swedish women. Kristina did not like his eyes; there was lust in them. When he looked at her, she felt as though he were in some way touching her intimately. This she was sure of—she needn't ask if shoemaker Thomassen was unmarried.

Karl Oskar questioned him concerning the road to Taylors Falls, and he showed the Norwegian the piece of paper he had carefully saved, the address of Fina-Kajsa's son:

Mister Anders Månsson
Taylors Falls Påst Offis
Minnesota Territory
North-America.

From Thomassen he now learned that Taylors Falls was a small settlement deep in the wilderness to the north. There were only a few settlers there and they would find Månsson without difficulty. Taylors Falls was on the banks of the St. Croix, but no passenger boats went there. The lumber company in Stillwater had cut a road for timber hauling with their ox teams some distance along the river—after that there were trails. They would have to go by foot to reach their destination. He was sure the lumber company could be persuaded to freight their belongings up the river in one of their barges. It was almost thirty miles to Taylors Falls, and if they were good walkers, they might manage it in two days, but the paths were overgrown, and as they had children with them they ought to figure on three days. But they would have no trouble finding their way: if they stayed close to the river, they couldn't miss it, for Taylors Falls lay right on the bank.

The weather now was pleasantly cool, and as they had already been much delayed it was decided that they should continue on their way immediately. Thirty miles sounded a formidable distance to walk on foot, but counting in Swedish miles it was only five. Often on a Sunday they

131

had walked the distance to Ljuder church and back, which made two Swedish miles. Having sat inactive so long on ships and steamboats, they felt they ought to have rested themselves sufficiently to walk the distance.

They asked the Norwegian if there might be any danger of wild Indians during the walk, but he did not think that the Redskins they might encounter on the road to Taylors Falls would be dangerous, if left alone. There were only Chippewa Indians living in the wilds to the north, and they were a docile and peace-loving tribe. The Sioux, who had their hunting ground to the south and who roamed in great packs through the forest this time of year, were much more fierce and warlike, and the settlers were afraid of them. But he was sure they would not meet any members of that tribe in the region they were to pass through.

The Swedes wondered if shoemaker Thomassen didn't minimize the dangers. Perhaps he only wanted to allay their fears.

"You may meet Chippewas, but they are friendly to the settlers," he insisted.

The youngest and the oldest in their group would cause most concern during a long walk—Fina-Kajsa and the babies. Karl Oskar asked Fina-Kajsa if she would be able to go with them; perhaps she had better stay here with the kind minister for the time being.

The old woman flared up in anger: "Who says I'm not able to walk? Who will recognize my son Anders if I don't come along?"

And she assured them with many oaths that they would never get there if she didn't go with them to find her son for them; they would never arrive without her aid. They would lose their way in the wilderness, and no one would help them, unless she was with them and brought them to Anders.

So they prepared to get under way. They brought along as much food as they thought would be needed, and clothing and bedding for sleeping in the open; they took their knapsacks and their bundles, as much as they thought they could carry. Pastor Jackson had taken charge of their heavy goods, and he was to send it on the lumber company's flat barges to Mister Anders Månsson at Taylors Falls.

As the immigrants parted from the goodhearted man who had made his cabin their home for a night and half a day, they were all very sad at not being able to say a single word of thanks in his tongue. None of their honest words of gratitude were comprehensible to him. But all shook him by the hand in such a way that they felt he must understand. And Robert tried to express in English how grateful they were: Pastor Jackson could rely on them to do him a favor in return as soon as they could. This sentence he had not taken from the language book and he was not sure the pastor understood him. Robert was particularly grateful to the Stillwater minister: he was the first American able to understand his English. Pastor Jackson had understood more of his sentences from the language book than anyone else, and of the English words Pastor Jackson spoke, Robert had understood many more than any other American's. Robert had used a sentence which he had long practiced: *Please speak a little more slowly, sir!* and after this the minister had spoken more slowly and clearly. Their conversation had progressed almost to his full satisfaction, even though he had been unable to find a chapter, *Conversation with a Minister*. This American had understood him from the very beginning, ever since his question: *Will no one help me?*

And they were still all fifteen together as, toward noon, they started northward from the logging camp where the Stillwater Lumber Company dominated everything with its great signs. Thomassen, anxious to talk to the women, accompanied them part of the way, admonishing them to keep close to the river on their right hand; then they could not miss Taylors Falls: "You couldn't miss it even if you tried to."

During their long journey, the group from Ljuder had traveled on wheels and keels, they had ridden on flat-wagons and steam wagons, on sailing ships and steamships, on side-wheelers and stern-wheelers. They thought they had used all the vehicles in existence to transport a person from one place to another in this world. But for the last stretch of their long journey they must resort to the means of the old Apostles—the last part of their thousand-mile road they had to walk.

# XII

## At Home in a Foreign Forest

THE IMMIGRANTS had now seen a part of the new continent in its immense expanse; its size was inconceivable to them. Yet during their journey through this vast land they had lacked space in which to move about; in crowded railway wagons and ships' holds they had been penned up in coops or shut in stalls. The country was large, but the space it had offered for their use had until now been very small. At last they were liberated from the shackles of conveyances: here they had great space around them and nothing but God's high heaven above them.

They had felt lost in the towns through which they had passed, fumbling, awkward, irresolute. Mingling with great crowds of unknown people, unable to communicate with them, they had felt downhearted, worried, completely bewildered. But here they had at last come back to the earth and its trees, bushes, and grass. The immigrants now walked into a great and foreign forest, into untilled wilderness. But something marvelous happened to them here: For the first time in North America they felt at home in their surroundings.

They walked through a wilderness, and here they had elbowroom, a feeling of space in which to move freely. The path they followed resembled the cattle paths at home, but this path was not made by domestic animals, it was trodden by wild animals and wild people. They followed the paths of Indians and deer, of hunters and beasts. They were on the hunting trails which had been followed for thousands and thousands of years. But they were homeless wanderers without weapons, not looking for game or following animals' footprints. They only followed a trail that would, they hoped, lead them to new homes.

Their path was along a winding ridge of sandstone, and this ridge followed the river. On their left extended a valley, on their right flowed the river that was to guide them. At the beginning of their walk, the forest near the river had been cut down in great sections and these seemed to them like graveyards, with their high, carelessly cut stumps resembling tombstones. But after a few hours they reached sandy plains with tall, straight, branchless trees, topped with lush dark-green crowns. Here each tree was a mast tree, capable of carrying sails across the world's greatest oceans. On the foothills to their left were groves of leaf-trees, like a woof through which broke the darker warp of the pine forest. Here they discovered all the trees which each spring budded anew in Sweden: oaks and birches side by side, trembling aspens, elms, and lindens intertwined their branches with maples and ash trees; here and there they also espied the hazel bush. Of smaller trees, crouching under the tall ones, they recognized willow branches stretching above bushes of sloeberries, blackberries, and wild roses. Here lay fertile ground overgrown with underbrush of innumerable varieties whose branches, leaves, and clinging vines were intertwined, making one heavy impenetrable thicket, a living wall of greenery.

In these extensive thickets they discovered many thorny bushes that were new to them. They stopped now and then to inspect more closely some tree or bush which they didn't recognize. They would scratch the bark, or break off a small branch, or gather a handful of leaves, and try to guess the kind of tree or bush to which these might be related.

As far as they could judge, here grew everything in God's creation: trees for all their needs: for house timbers, floor planks and roof, for benches and tables, for implements of all kinds, and for firewood. The dead trees rotted in the places where they had fallen, never had a stump been removed, never had a dead tree been cut. All old bare trees remained standing, an unattractive sight with their naked, bark-shedding limbs in this healthy, living forest. Indeed, there were enough dead pines here for firewood for a thousand fireplaces for a thousand winters through. The forest was uncared-for, neglected, but it had cared for itself while living and covering the ground: it had died and lived again, completing its cycle: undisturbed and unmarked by man's edged tools, it had fallen with its loosened roots decaying on the ground and disintegrating among grass and moss, returning again to the earth from which it had sprung.

The farther into the wilderness the immigrants pushed their way the denser grew the oaks. In one day they had seen more oaks on root than

134

in their whole lives before. At home the oak was the royal tree—King and Crown had from old claimed the first right to it, while the peasants had to be satisfied with poorer and less sturdy trees. At home the noble oak tree was nursed like a thoroughbred colt. Here they walked through an oak forest that stretched for miles. And when their trail brought them atop a knoll, they saw across the western valley a whole sea of oak crowns, wreathed together until they appeared like one many-miles-wide crown of rich foliage. Here was a whole region—wide as a county at home—entirely filled with royal trees. In their fertile valley the oaks had for countless centuries grown straight and proud through their youth and maturity and quietly rotted in their old age. No Crown-sheriffs had disturbed them with marking axes, no despotic king had exacted timber for his fortifications and men-of-war. In this heathen land the royal tree had remained untouched and unviolated, here it displayed its mane of thick foliage, the lion among trees.

The landscape changed often and quickly, with hills and dales on both sides. They came to an open glade with still more fertile ground: here herbs and grass prevailed rather than trees and bushes. Here grew crab apple and wild plum, the heavy fruit bending the overladen boughs. Between thickets of berry bushes the ground was covered with wild roses, honeysuckle, sweet fern and many flowers. Here throve in abundance a lower growth of fruit and berry plants: blueberries, raspberries, currant bushes, black as well as red. And the berry vine did not crawl retarded along the ground in thread-thin runners as in the forests at home; here it rose on thick stems covered with healthy leaves, thriving as though planted in a well-fertilized cabbage bed. The blueberry bushes were flourishing with berries as large as the end of one's thumb, as easy to pick as gooseberries.

They would cross a meadow with fodder-rich grass reaching to their waists. Here the ground lay as smooth and even as a floor in a royal palace. No stone was visible, no scythe had ever cut this grass; since the time of creation this hay meadow had been waiting for the harvesters.

They climbed over brooks and streams where fallen trunks lay like bridges, they saw a tarn into which branches and other debris had fallen in such great quantity that it filled the lake completely, rising above the surface, a picture of death-haunted desolation. They walked by small lakes with tall grass all around the edges, the water bubbling and boiling with wriggling fins. They stopped and looked at the fish playing. The water was so clear they could see to the bottom where the sand glittered in the sun like gold. And they mused over this clear blue lake water, seemingly taking its color from the skies above.

In one opening they came upon a herd of grazing deer, sleek-antlered animals with light-red fur and short white tails. Fleet-footed, the deer fled softly, their tails tipping up and down. The immigrants had already tasted their meat, they knew how tender and delicious it was. Now and again a long-eared rabbit disappeared into the grass directly at their feet. Known and unknown forest birds took flight along their path, on the lakes swam flocks of ducks, undisturbed by their passing, and several times they heard the potent, whizzing sound of many wings in flight: flocks of bluish doves flew over their heads.

In this wilderness there was plenty of game; in the water, on the ground, and in the air there was meat, fowl, and fish. Many a meal had run past them into the forest, swum away into the depths of the lakes, flown away into the air.

The immigrants had reached a lush country, fertile and rich earth, a land well suited for settling. Here people could find their sustenance if anywhere on earth. Yet nowhere did they see tilled fields, nowhere a furrow turned, nowhere a prepared building site. No trees had been blazed to mark a settler's claim. This was a country for people to settle in, but as yet few settlers had come.

The group from Sweden walked along an unknown path in an unknown region, with no guide except the river; but they felt less insecure and put down their feet with more confidence than at any time before in the new country. They were walking in accustomed ways through old-country landscapes. They walked through a forest, they tramped on tree roots, moss, and grass, they moved among pungent foliage, soft leaves, herbs, among growing things on earth, its running and flying game, and they began to feel at home.

The travelers from Ljuder were in a foreign forest, yet they had arrived home: No longer were they the lost ones of this world.

—2—

AT FIRST the group of immigrants walked with good speed along the path on the ridge, but as the day wore on their burdens grew heavier and their steps slowed. All grownups had something to carry: of the children, only Danjel's two sons were able to walk the whole distance; he had to carry his four-year-old daughter Fina. Karl Oskar held Lill-Märta on one arm, extra clothing over his shoulder, and the knapsack in one hand. Kristina carried Harald, and this was considered sufficient, as she also carried another child within her. The food basket was entrusted to Robert. Johan could walk short distances, but his little legs soon tired and he too wanted to be carried. Karl Oskar stooped down and let the boy climb onto his back with his arms around the father's neck. Karl Oskar was no longer a fast walker.

Jonas Petter walked ahead of the others to locate the trail, which sometimes seemed to disappear in dense thickets filled with mosquitoes. It was his duty to see that they never lost sight of the river. As they pro-

136

gressed the thickets became more prevalent, and those with heavy burdens had to walk with care through the thorny bushes.

They had feared Fina-Kajsa would delay their progress but the old woman had a surprisingly tough body, and in spite of her emaciated condition, she kept well ahead of the younger walkers. She trotted along quite briskly, holding onto her iron pot, which she dared not leave behind with the minister in Stillwater, fearing it might be lost, as the grindstone was in New York. She had walked many miles during her lifetime, going to church at home on Öland every Sunday for fifty years, a distance of fifteen miles back and forth. Altogether, this would make enough miles to cover the distance from Sweden to Minnesota many times; indeed, she would easily manage the short distance left to reach her son's home, if it were true that they were now so close to him. And she described again the fine house he had built himself in the wilderness. He had written many letters to his parents about it—there was no place on Öland that compared with his home, his extensive fields, and possessions. He had asked his parents to come and see it, then they would be well pleased with their son. And Fina-Kajsa was convinced her son had changed into an industrious, capable man here in America, or he wouldn't have been able to acquire such a home. It had been well for him to get out in the world.

A west wind was blowing, cooling their perspiring brows; the air no longer felt oppressive.

By midafternoon they sat down to rest under a great oak that stood all by itself in an open, pleasing meadow. Now their communal food basket was brought out; during the last weeks of their journey they had become one big household; it seemed unnecessary to divide themselves into two families at meals, leaving Jonas Petter to sit alone. It was easier to keep all the food together; what one missed someone else had, one had bread but no meat, someone else meat but no bread.

After the meal, the immigrants stretched out on the ground under the giant oak; it was comfortable in the shade, and they all felt well and rested contentedly. But the children played in the tall grass of the meadow; they had already eaten their fill of raspberries, blueberries, currants, and wild plums. Many unfamiliar berries also grew hereabouts but parents forbade the children to taste these, fearing they might be poisonous. On little trees almost like bushes grew clusters of berries resembling over-large blueberries, and Robert insisted these were wild grapes. From them wine could be pressed, the drink of noble people at home, which ordinary people got a taste of once a month at communion. They tasted the grapes cautiously, they seemed sweet and good, but they dared not eat more than a handful lest they get drunk from these sweet berries that made wine: it was written in the Bible that one could get drunk from sweet wine.

Elin filled her little basket with great, juicy dark-red raspberries, which

137

she showed proudly to her mother. The girl's fingers were stained blood red from the overripe berries.

"Here in America we can have beautiful rosy cheeks," Ulrika said. "We can wash our faces in raspberry juice."

Kristina's eyes never left her children. They mustn't go too far away, no one knew where snakes might lie hidden in the thick grass which was indeed a good hiding place for all kinds of dangerous creeping things. Jonas Petter had already killed two green-striped snakes, but they were no larger than the snakes at home. Danger was by now such a persistent companion that Kristina considered it omnipresent: its shape might alter but it was always at hand in some guise. She had once and for all accepted danger, and consequently she met it with less worry than before.

Here in the forest only the venomous mosquitoes annoyed her and all of them; they swarmed about constantly and bit every exposed part of the body. The delicate skin of the children was attacked most fiercely, and their faces showed welts from the bites. They had never encountered such disgusting gnats before. Everything was different in America, day and night, weather and animals: the warmth was warmer, the darkness darker, the rain wetter than at home—and the mosquitoes were a thousand times worse.

Kristina's eyes had come to rest on the men sprawling in the grass, and suddenly she burst out laughing: "Ulrika—look at those shaggy-bearded, long-haired men! Don't they look worse than scarecrows?"

Unmarried Ulrika of Västergöhl joined in the laughter. None of the men had had scissors or razors near their heads since leaving Sweden, and now their hair hung down on their shoulders. Danjel had always worn a beard, but Karl Oskar and Jonas Petter, accustomed to shave at home, had left their beards unattended—it had been difficult to use razors on the journey. Arvid had a thin growth of beard and seldom needed a shave, and Robert had not yet begun to shave, but their hair had grown long. Gathered together in a group, all the men seemed equally shaggy and rough. On the journey, Kristina had not paid much attention to their appearance, but alone here in the forest she was suddenly conscious of their uncombed hair and beards: they seemed like a group of wild highway robbers. And she said, if this had been the first time she had laid eyes on Karl Oskar, meeting him like this in the forest, she would have been scared to death of the man and would have run away to hide as fast as her legs would carry her.

"Hmm," said Jonas Petter. "The worst part is, my beard itches like a louse nest."

"Our poor men are pale and skinny," Ulrika said. "That's what makes them look so frightful."

Yes, Jonas Petter thought he had lost about fifty pounds from heat and diarrhea, his trousers hung loose around his waist as though fastened to a fence post. Their bodies were only skeletons covered by sun-parched skin. But all American men were thin; they were Americans now—and by and by they would also be rich.

Ulrika admitted that the men in America were skinny. But she insisted they were courteous and well behaved and kind and considerate toward women. She had never before seen a man like that priest they lodged with last night—he had even grabbed the pail out of her hand when she wanted to fetch water and had gone to the well himself. A minister in America fetching water for Ulrika of Västergöhl—what would people in Ljuder say if they had seen that!

Ulrika kept an eye on her daughter, who was now busy picking flowers.

Elin called to Robert: "Come and see! Such beautiful cowslips!"

Robert hurried to her side; he looked on the ground between the lush bushes but could see neither cowslips nor any other flowers. "Where are they?"

"They flew away!" the girl exclaimed in surprise.

"The flowers flew away?"

"Yes! Look, they are flying up there!" Elin was staring wide-eyed at a great many butterflies, beautiful yellow ones, sailing about above their heads. "I thought at first they were flowers."

She had mistaken butterflies for flowers. And Robert thought perhaps she hadn't been so much mistaken. After all the strange animals and plants they had seen in this country, he would not have been in the least surprised had he suddenly found flying flowers. Hadn't they seen a flying squirrel today—a squirrel that flew between two trees and used his tail for a rudder! If squirrels in North America could fly, why not flowers also? "Anything might take flight!" Robert said.

They sat down near a raspberry bush and ate the juicy red berries.

Robert and Elin had made peace again, they had agreed they had nothing to quarrel about. She ought not to have been so talkative in New York, she ought to have kept to herself what he had confided about the captain's slave trade. She had not asked Robert to forgive her for this treachery, but he had forgiven her in his heart. Besides, she had admitted to him that he had spoken the truth when, before leaving the ship, he had insisted that the Åkians would be unable to speak English when they stepped ashore, even though they were convinced they had been given the tongues of apostles. The only English words Elin knew, she had learned from Robert and not from the Holy Ghost.

And after she had promised not to divulge to a living soul what he was about to tell her, he related what had happened to Arvid and himself on Broadway Street in New York: He had saved Arvid's life. An enormous, sinister-looking man had rushed toward them with a long knife in his hand, ready to stick it into Arvid and steal his nickel watch. He had been one of the fifty thousand murderers who lived in New York and who every day except Sunday commit at least one murder. The murderer had managed to get the watch away from Arvid and was aiming the knife at his

139

heart, already piercing the cloth of his vest, when Robert had rushed up and given the man such a hard blow with his fist, right on the man's temple, that he had immediately fallen backward and fainted. Then Robert had pulled the knife from the murderer's hand and recovered Arvid's watch. Police had arrived and had jailed the fallen bandit, and Robert had understood enough of their English to realize that they had lauded him profoundly: Thanks to his coolheaded interference, one crime less than usual had been committed that day. If he had wanted to, he could easily have stayed in New York and joined the police force.

But Elin must promise not to whisper a word to anyone about his saving Arvid's life: he was not one to brag about his deeds; if he were able to do a favor for a friend, he liked to keep it to himself. Nor must she mention it to Arvid, who might feel embarrassed about the incident.

Elin listened to Robert in great admiration and gave him her promise of silence. In turn, she wanted to confide something to him: She was not going to remain with Danjel when they arrived in Taylors Falls, she intended to find employment with some upper-class American family. And he promised to help her with this, now that he could speak English with ministers and other learned Americans. As a matter of fact, he himself had no intention of working for Karl Oskar. He had other prospects of getting rich.

"What are you going to do?" the girl asked.

"I'm not going to work as a farm servant all my life. I remember *Angelica.*"

"What does that mean?" she asked curiously.

"It is the name of a woman, but it means much more than a woman ever could mean."

And he was about to tell her of the clipper ship with the gold diggers and the red pennant which he had seen in the New York Harbor, when he suddenly lowered his voice and then stopped speaking: someone was approaching them from the other side of the bush. It was Arvid, picking raspberries. He did not notice them, although they could see him through the bush. Elin whispered: Arvid still had the hole in his vest, right over his heart. Yes, Robert said, that was the tear slashed by a murderer's knife, on the most beautiful street in the world. Now she could see for herself that Robert always spoke the truth.

The others were ready to resume their walk, and the youth and the girl, their hunger lessened by forest raspberries, rose to join them. Arvid caught up with them and complained to Robert that he had just torn his vest on these darned big thorns on the bushes here; he must have it mended at once or he might lose his watch. Robert glanced around rather nervously to make sure Elin had not heard.

The travelers now felt rested and well pleased. Evil and good fortune shifted quickly for them: yesterday they had been lost, hungry, and wet; today the weather was pleasant and they rested in fresh grass under a shady oak and ate fresh fruit. They were pleased with the land they saw about them; it gave good promise: this was the land where they would settle. They felt almost repaid for the arduous journey and its great inconveniences.

"Fair is the country hereabouts," Danjel Andreasson said. "The Lord has led us to a blessed land."

All agreed with these sentiments. Danjel had just finished his table prayer and now he took out his Bible: before he rose from his first meal-rest on the ground of the new land he would like to bend his knees and thank the Lord God who so far had led and aided them.

He knelt near the great oak and read from the Bible the Lord's words to his servant Joshua, who, with the tribes of Israel, was ready to ford the river Jordan to dwell in the promised land after the many years of wandering in the wilderness: "Be strong and of good courage: for unto this people shalt thou divide for an inheritance the land which I sware unto their fathers to give them."

The playing children were silenced and all the grownups rose and stood in a circle around Danjel; the men removed their hats, and men as well as women folded their hands and bent their heads. The little group of wanderers stood immobile and silent under the great tree. Danjel Andreasson knelt and bowed his head toward the sturdy trunk of the oak, now his altar, folded his hands over his breast, and uttered his prayer of thanks:

"A strange land has kindly opened its portals to us, and we have come to live here peacefully and seek our sustenance. But we would have been like newborn lambs, let out to perish among the heathens in this wilderness, hadst not Thou, Lord, sustained us. Hunger would have ravaged us, pestilence stricken us, wild animals devoured us, if Thy fingers of mercy were not upon us. We have journeyed thousands of miles, over land and water, and Thou hast saved our lives and all our limbs. Be strong and of good courage! So Thou spakest to Thy good servant and to his folk. Thou hast promised to give us this land and we want to be Thy servants. Aid us in this foreign and wild land, as Thou hast helped us until now. We have here eaten our meager fare in Thy forest, and we call on Thee from this ground which Thou created on the First Day. We are gathered in this church which Thou Thyself builded and whose roof is raised taller than any other church—Thy heaven is its roof. O Lord, here in Thy creation, in Thy tall temple, we wish to praise Thee and sing to Thy glory as well as we may with our singing tongues! Turn Thine ear to us and listen, O Lord!"

Then slowly and haltingly Danjel Andreasson, still kneeling under the oak, began to sing a psalm. He sang in a weak and trembling voice. The group around him joined in, one after another, as they recognized the hymn:

Eternal Father in Whose hand,
From age to age, from land to land,
All mortals comfort seek,
Ere mountains were, or man, or field,
Ere pastures gave their season's yield,
You were, and are, forever. . . .

The wind had died down and the voices echoed through the forest—weak voices and strong, rough voices and sweet, husky and clear, trembling and steady, men's and women's voices. And the chorus rose for each verse higher and higher under the lush ceiling of branches and leaves of the wide tree; a hymn in a foreign language, by a little group from far away, a song never before heard in this wilderness:

The lilies bloom with morning's breath,
Yet eventide beholds their death,
So Man must also meet his doom,
A flower, a mere withering bloom. . . .

When the song to the Creator's glory had rung out to an end, the immigrants again loaded their burdens on their backs and resumed their walk with increased confidence. And over their resting place with its downtrodden grass stillness and silence again reigned, disturbed only by a faint whispering in the thick foliage of the oak.

—3—

THEY KNEW HOW QUICKLY dusk could fall in this country, and a good while before sunset they began to look for a place to camp. They chose a pine grove where the ground was covered with thick moss. They collected fallen branches in a great pile, and so dry was this excellent fuel that the very first match ignited it. Karl Oskar, Danjel, and Jonas Petter each had a box of matches brought from Sweden, which they used sparingly, each box being used in turn for fairness. The women cooked their evening meal in Fina-Kajsa's limping iron pot; they fetched water from a running brook and to the water they added various leftovers to make a stew: Kristina donated a piece of pork, a few bread heels, and a pinch of salt, Ulrika scraped together a few spoonfuls of flour from the bottom of Danjel's food basket, and Jonas Petter contributed a dozen large potatoes, which he had got from one of the cooks on the *Red Wing* in exchange for some snuff.

This stew was eaten by all in the company with such great appetite that none noticed how it tasted. Then Kristina offered as dessert one of the last things she had left in her Swedish food basket: a small jar of honey, which they spread on their bread. Each of the grownups got a small slice, each child a large slice.

After supper they gathered more faggots for the fire, which they had to keep burning, less for the sake of warmth than to keep off the swarms of mosquitoes. Nothing except smoke seemed to drive them away. Jonas Petter expressed the opinion that the North American mosquitoes were far more dangerous than the Indians, whom they hadn't seen a sign of today; no heathens or cannibals could be so thirsty for Christian blood as were these bloodsucking insects, flying about everywhere with stingers sharp as needles. All complained about this new plague, and Fina-Kajsa most of all: she had been able to escape the scurvy and the tempests at sea, the fire in the steam wagon, the cholera on the steamboat—was she now to be eaten by these hellish gnats before she reached her son and had a chance to see his beautiful home? No, God wouldn't allow this to come to pass. He ought to give her credit for the thousands of miles she had walked in her life to hear His word every Sunday. If God had any sense of justice He undoubtedly had written down in His book the many miles she had walked to church.

They gathered moss to sleep on and covered themselves with warm clothing and a few blankets. The children went to sleep the minute they lay down. All were tired from the day's walk and their heavy burdens; they would sleep soundly in this camp during the night. But they didn't forget that evil people and dangerous beasts might be in their neighborhood. The four men each in turn kept a two-hour watch; they must tend the fire, guard the sleepers, and rouse them in case of danger.

Robert was too young to keep watch, but he couldn't go to sleep. He lay under a pine tree with his head toward the trunk. He had gathered enough moss to make a soft bed, but he felt as though his body were broken to pieces. Every muscle ached. And the forest had so many sounds to keep him awake. The leaves rustled, bushes and grass stirred, he wondered what kind of reptiles might lurk in the thickets. Buzzing insects swarmed in the air, the mosquitoes hovered over him with their eternal plaintive humming. There were sounds everywhere—hissing, whizzing, chirping. But the most persistent sound of all came from some small animal in the grass, it screeched and squeaked like an ungreased wagon wheel. It reminded him of a cricket, but it was louder and more intense, and it hurt his ears. He looked for the animal but could not find it; how was it possible that an animal could be so small and yet make such an infernal noise?

From his *Description of the United States of North America* Robert remembered all the wild beasts of the American forests; all of them might now lurk quite close to him in the dark, waiting their moment: the bear and the wolf to bite his throat, the rattlesnake to wreathe its body around him, the crocodile . . . But Captain Berger had said there were no crocodiles in the northern part of the country. Wild Indians, however, were

143

here in the forest, even though they hadn't yet encountered them, and Indians could move without the slightest sound: before he knew it, without the least warning, he might lie here with his scalp cut off, wounded and bleeding to death. An Indian could cut off a scalp as easily as a white, Christian person could cut a slice of bread.

As herdboy at home Robert had never been afraid, but here he lay on his bed of moss and scared himself until he felt clammy with perspiration. Arvid slept only a few feet away from him, snoring loudly; he did not hear any sounds, not even the ones he made himself. And Robert could see Karl Oskar, who had taken the first watch—he moved like a big shadow near the campfire, now and then poking the embers with a branch, making the sparks fly into the air until they died high up among the treetops. His brother was not afraid: Karl Oskar and the others didn't know enough to be afraid, they didn't realize how dangerous it was to lie here and sleep. Had they possessed all the knowledge Robert had concerning lurking dangers during the night in Minnesota Territorial forests—if they only knew what he knew about the unbelievably sharp knives the Indians carried, and with what complete silence they could sneak up—then they wouldn't enjoy a moment's sleep.

Each time Robert was about ready to go to sleep he was disturbed by the screeching noise like an ungreased wheel from the small animal in the grass. And his injured ear began to hum and throb as it often did when he lay still. What kind of a sound could it be in his ear, never ceasing? Sometimes he wondered if some buzzing insect hadn't managed to get in there. And as this noise had continued he had grown to hear less and less with his left ear. For two years now the sound had pursued him; it had followed him from the Old World to the new one. Perhaps it would stay with him and annoy him for the rest of his life, perhaps he would suffer from it until he died, and by then there would be small joy in losing it. And all because of that hard box on the ear which his master, Aron of Nybacken, had given him when he served as hired hand in Sweden; all this a hired hand suffered undeservedly because of the master. He had secretly shed many tears at the memory: How had God allowed this injustice to befall him?

Now he lay listening to his ear until the noise sounded like a warning: Don't go to sleep! You may never awaken again! Or you may wake up with a knife cutting through your scalp! You will cry out and feel with your fingers and find warm, dripping blood. . . . Better not go to sleep! Listen to what your ear says!

But Robert slept at last, and slept soundly, awakening only when Karl Oskar shook him by the shoulders: It was full daylight, they must resume their walk while it still was cool—they would rest again later in the day when the sun was high.

The pot was on the fire again, the food baskets open. Blinking, still with sleep in their eyes, the immigrants sat down to their morning meal and scratched their mosquito bites. The men keeping watch had not once had to warn the sleepers. Several times during the night Karl Oskar had heard a howl in the distance—it might have been wolves but it could also have come from human throats, for it had sounded almost like singing, and he didn't think wolves could sing. During Jonas Petter's watch a sly, hairy animal had sneaked to the food basket and attempted to scratch it open. It looked like a young fox, it had a sharp nose, a long bushy tail, and was yellow-gray in color. He had shooed away the creature with a stake and hung the basket in a tree, to be on the safe side. But the beast had scared the devil out of Jonas Petter later—it had come back and climbed the tree to get to the food basket! He had had to throw a fire brand at the animal before he could get rid of it. He hoped he had burned the beast good and well—in fact, he was sure he had—he had smelled the singed hair for quite a while afterward.

It couldn't have been a fox or a wolf since those beasts didn't climb trees. Jonas Petter thought perhaps their night visitor had been an ape or large wildcat: the animal was long but short legged, and moved as quickly as a monkey.

Fina-Kajsa had her own opinion: "You say he was hairy? Then it must have been Satan himself. He must have tried to fetch you when you were awake alone!"

"If that was the devil, then I'm not afraid of him any longer," retorted Jonas Petter. "If he is so badly off that he must snoop about nights and try to steal our poor fare, he must be near his end."

But Fina-Kajsa knew that the devil was afraid of fire only, and if the brand hadn't been thrown after him, Jonas Petter would have been missing for sure when they awoke.

"Did you hear the screech hoppers?" Ulrika asked. "I thought at first it must be ghosts or goblins. I couldn't see a sign of them."

All had heard the continuous screeching noise, but no one had seen the animal producing it. Kristina said that crickets and grasshoppers were, of course, also different in North America—perhaps they were invisible here.

Their walk was continued, but today the immigrants moved at a slower pace than yesterday, their legs weren't so limber. Karl Oskar was footsore from his heavy boots, and his left leg gave him trouble intermittently. Johan, riding on his shoulders, grew heavier and heavier and he tried to persuade the boy to walk on his own legs. But after a few steps he wanted to ride on his father's back again: "You carried me before, Father."

"But don't you understand, dear child, your father is worn out," said Kristina.

"He wasn't worn out before. . . ."

Arvid had a strong back and could carry more than his allotted burden —he relieved Karl Oskar and carried the boy now and again. Karl Oskar was more heavily laden than the others, and Kristina felt sorry for him;

145

she could hear him puff and pant as their trail led uphill, and she knew that his left leg wasn't quite well yet. He didn't complain, not one single word, but she wondered where his thoughts might be: Hadn't their troubles and inconveniences been greater than he had anticipated when deciding to emigrate? Here he lumbered along like a beast of burden—had he ever expected to haul his children on his back miles and miles through wilderness in America? She was sure he hadn't. Yet he would never admit this, he would never admit anything was more difficult that he had thought it would be.

"It's too much for you to carry two children," she said.

"You also carry two," he reminded her.

They kept up their walk during the morning hours when the weather was cool, rested for a while during the noon heat, and continued in the afternoon as the sun grew lower. During the second day they did not meet a single person, either red or white. This did not surprise them. The forests were vast, yet sparsely settled. But as long as they were able to manage by themselves, they were just as pleased to find the forest empty of people—strangers weren't always trustworthy.

The ridge with the trail wound its way through ravines and clefts in the rocks. The terrain was hilly, the soil poor, and for long distances the ground was bare, with no signs of the trail. Then they walked where the going was easiest and kept close to the river that was to show them the way to Taylors Falls.

The second night they made camp in a cleavage of the ridge. This night no furry animals came to sniff their food boxes, and they were disturbed by no living creature except the mosquitoes.

They had been told they would arrive about evening of the third day. During the afternoon they began to look for the village in the forest where Anders Månsson, Fina-Kajsa's son, had his home. As yet they had seen no sign of human habitation, no sign of people.

According to her son's letters, insisted Fina-Kajsa, his home was situated near a river with great cliffs along its shores and many falls and rapids. One place was called The Devil's Kettle because it was the entrance to Hell. Now they could see how steep the cliffs were along the shore of the St. Croix River. All stopped to look at the rapid current as it came rushing along down the cliffs with a terrific roar. This could well be the region Anders Månsson had described in his letters. But there wasn't the slightest sign of people living near by.

They walked on a little farther, and Fina-Kajsa was now sure they had lost their way. A farm like the one he had described could not possibly be located in this region—her son couldn't live near here. She suspected that the little Norwegian who directed their way from Stillwater had been false and unreliable: he had undoubtedly led them astray on purpose. By now the old woman was completely exhausted, dragging her

146

feet, stumbling and falling into holes in the trail, she had to be helped up several times.

"Oh my, oh me! We'll never get there! Oh my, oh me!" said Fina-Kajsa.

They had only a few hours until darkness would fall and their third day would come to an end. They must again prepare to sleep in the open. And their food was running low, they would hardly have enough for the evening meal. They had eaten a lot of berries during their walk, but berries did not satisfy hunger.

The men were talking about what to do, and all walked with slower, wearier steps as the sun sank lower. Should they make camp or go a little farther? Then they came into an opening in the forest and suddenly discovered a clearing where every pine had been cut down. They stopped short in surprise.

"These trees were only recently cut down!" Karl Oskar exclaimed.

The stumps were new, and branches and logs were strewn about. The stumps were three feet high—yes, those lazy bastards had stood straight backed while felling the trees.

"And there they have left the ax," said Arvid, and pointed to a tall stump. Karl Oskar quickly stepped up to the ax and loosened it, not only because he wanted to inspect an American tool but for a much more important reason: If a pregnant woman let her eyes fall on an ax stuck in a stump or chopping block, then her child would be born with a harelip, and this was an incurable defect. Karl Oskar hoped that Kristina had not noticed the broad-bladed ax.

Jonas Petter, who was a bit ahead of them, now called out in great happiness: "Folks live back there!"

A few gunshots to the left of their trail, the clearing ended in a green meadow where a cabin could be seen against a stand of leaf trees.

It took only a few minutes to reach the newly built shake-roofed log cabin. A small field near by had growing crops, and two cows grazed in the meadow, fine, fat animals with full udders.

This was a settler's farm, here they could buy milk; cows with such splendid udders must give many gallons at each milking. They all sat down in the grass outside the cabin, and Karl Oskar brought out his stoup from the knapsack; then he went up to the door and knocked.

A middle-aged, scrawny woman with heavy men's boots on her feet opened the door. She looked curiously at the group outside. There was fear in her eyes as she turned them on Karl Oskar. Seeing her look of fright, he remembered what Kristina had said about his unkempt beard and hair. Not wishing to be mistaken for a robber he tried to look as friendly as possible and greeted her pleasantly in Swedish. The few English words he had learned he could never remember at such a time, but he talked with his hands and held out his stoup, then he moved it to his lips as if drinking. He tried in this way to tell her that he wanted

147

to buy milk. The woman in the doorway said something incomprehensible and then she just stared at him. He opened his mouth still wider and acted as if gulping gallons from his vessel, at the same time pointing to the cows—the woman must understand what he wanted.

But she looked still more frightened and stared at him as if he might be insane. Perhaps she thought he was making fun of her. He was unable to make himself understood and he had little confidence in Robert after their experience on the street in Stillwater.

However, just as the woman prepared to shut the door, Robert stepped up and said clearly in English: "We want to buy milk."

She looked searchingly at the English-speaking youth who was beardless, but long haired, and they realized she understood him. He repeated his request a second and a third time, and each time she nodded in comprehension. Then she left them and disappeared into the house, returning in a few moments with a large wooden pail filled almost to the brim with milk.

Both Kristina and Ulrika spoke heartfelt Swedish words of thanks to the woman, and all gathered with their mugs around the milk pail.

Kristina turned to Robert and said: "We have you to thank for this milk!"

At last Robert had shown that he could lend his mouth as a help to all, explain in the foreign language what they wished, and obtain what they needed. This time he had prepared himself well: he had repeated the words to himself many times before he used them: *We want to buy milk*. This was the way he must do it—chew the words many times, as he chewed his food.

Robert grew courageous from his success, and as the kind woman was returning to the cabin he followed her and said: "Respected Sir, how can we reach Taylors Falls?"

He asked Karl Oskar to show her the piece of paper with Anders Månsson's address. But she did not look at it or answer him—instead she hurried inside and closed the door. When Robert tried to open it he found it bolted. The woman had given them a pail of milk and then she had locked herself in the cabin, without even waiting to be paid! That was peculiar.

The immigrants eagerly emptied the milk pail; the children were given as much milk as they could drink, and there was still plenty for the grownups. The milk was cream-thick, the cows hereabouts must get good grass; all felt refreshed by this unexpected refreshment.

But the American woman had not waited to be paid. She had locked herself in the cabin. She was afraid to let them come inside, this much they understood.

They put the empty pail at the door and waited for her to reappear. Robert was still determined to find out where Anders Månsson lived. And he began to practice a new sentence: *I want to expose you this*

148

*paper with an address* . . . when suddenly a dog's bark was heard quite near them, and two men with guns in their hands approached across the clearing.

The men who headed toward them were apparently hunters. They wore broad-brimmed hats and skin jackets on which the fur still clung at the seams. They were unkempt, fully bearded, and were accompanied by two fierce curs whose hair stood on end. As they neared the Swedish immigrants they lifted their guns threateningly. The dogs barked furiously, and the frightened children began to yell.

A commotion of indescribable fear broke out among the travelers at the strangers' unexpected behavior. The women pressed their children to them and huddled together, the men looked irresolutely from one to the other, feeling for their knives. The strangers acted and spoke roughly, and although the immigrants couldn't understand their words, they understood their guns: the men ordered them not to move and seemed ready to lay hands on them. Karl Oskar and Jonas Petter fingered their knives —their guns were still in their chests in Stillwater—and wondered what kind of ruffians they had encountered. What did the men want? If they were hunters, they ought to pursue their game and let peaceful folk alone. This Karl Oskar and Jonas Petter told them in Swedish.

A third man was now approaching across the clearing. He was shorter than the other two, but he too had a gun and was dressed like them. His trousers had great patches over the knees. He carried two rabbits by their hind legs, blood dripping from their headless bodies. He looked more threatening than either of the other two hunters.

The unarmed group of men, women, and children was now surrounded by three men with guns, apparently hunters of peaceful human beings. Now they were indeed in danger and they huddled close together like a herd of game, stalked and encircled by hounds. What could they do?

The dogs rushed to the third hunter and licked the blood dripping from his rabbits. Then, suddenly, one of the immigrant women rushed after the dogs, calling in fury at the top of her old voice: "You bastard! Don't you know how to behave?"

It was Fina-Kajsa, the oldest and most decrepit of the women. She rushed forward in an insane rage as if threatening the ruffian. But suddenly she stopped and stared at the man, and the hunter with the rabbits pushed back his broad-brimmed hat; he too stopped and stared; his chin fell, leaving his mouth open.

Fina-Kajsa took a few steps forward: "Shoot your paltry rabbits, but leave peaceful folk alone! Have you no shame at all, boy? To meet your old mother with a gun!"

The hunter's chin fell another inch. He dropped his rabbits on the ground.

"Throw down your shooting iron too," Fina-Kajsa ordered him.

"Mother!"

149

"I had expected you to greet me like a decent man. And here you and your pack of friends aim guns. . . ."

"Mother—I didn't expect you!"

"I thought I would never get here. But here you see me as I am, Anders my son."

"Mother—you're here!"

"I thought America had no end!"

"Where's Father?"

"He lies on the bottom of the sea."

"Is Father *dead?*"

"As dead as the rest on the bottom of the sea! And the grindstone he had brought for you lies there too."

"Did Father bring me a grindstone?"

"The stones are cheap on Öland. Here is our old iron pot! Here, right in my hand! They broke one leg. . . . Anders . . . if you don't recognize your mother you at least remember our old pot!"

"Yes, yes! You bring our old *gryta!* Yes, yes. . . . Welcome, Mother!"

Mother and son had found each other, and the group around them listened in silence.

—4—

THEY HAD REACHED Taylors Falls; they were only a short distance from Anders Månsson's home.

He told them he had been out with his two neighbors to shoot some rabbits for supper. And now they also heard the explanation for the strange behavior of the woman and the other two hunters: The settlers here were afraid of cholera, and all newcomers were met and questioned before they were allowed to enter the settlement. If anyone arrived from a contaminated region he was put into a shed near the falls where he was fumigated with sulphur and tar for a few days before he was let out. Weak people could not stand the ordeal of being smoked like hams, some only lasted a day before fainting. But it was a fact that in this manner they had so far avoided the sickness in Taylors Falls.

Fina-Kajsa pointed out to the group what might have happened to them if she hadn't been along to recognize Anders. And turning to her son she asked: "But what kind of sickness ails you? Your face blooms like a red rose!"

"It's the heat, Mother."

Anders Månsson greatly resembled his father, whom they all remembered from the beginning of their journey, and whom they had helped bury in the North Sea. Anders was a thickset man with broad, somewhat stooping shoulders. He was almost bald, his complexion was red, his

150

nut-brown eyes restless, avoiding a direct look at them. At first he had looked threatening, but now they discovered he was shy to a fault.

Twilight was upon them, they had arrived none too soon. They walked down a slope, through a grove of green trees, and arrived at a level, low-lying piece of ground. They could see water, a lagoon or small tarn, bordered by tall grass. Near the water was tilled ground, they saw a yellowed stubble field with some rye shocks. These were Anders Månsson's fields which he himself had cleared. By now it was too dark to see how far the fields extended. A cabin stood in the flat meadow, with a few lindens and elms around it. There were other cabins across the rye field.

Anders Månsson approached the small cabin of roughly hewn logs; it was situated like a hay barn in the meadow.

"So this is your hay shed," said Fina-Kajsa.

"Hay shed?" the son repeated, as if not remembering what the Swedish word meant.

Anders opened the door, and Fina-Kajsa stuck in her head to inspect the hay crop in her son's shed.

"Did you get much hay this summer?" she asked. She couldn't see any hay at all, but in the dim light she espied pieces of furniture; clothing and tools hung on pegs around the walls: "You keep your hay shed empty!"

"Yes—no— You see, Mother, I have no hay in this house—"

"Do you have people living in the barn?"

"I live here myself."

"Isn't this your hay barn?"

"No, Mother. It is my house."

"But why do you live in the barn? Where's your main house?"

"I have built this cabin for my own use. Welcome to my home, Mother! We must boil these rabbits for supper."

And Anders Månsson took out his hunting knife and began to skin and clean his game.

Fina-Kajsa turned to her Swedish traveling companions: "My son is the same! Here he stands lying to my face. He won't show us his home. He's telling stories. All of you can see this is nothing but a barn. A small barn."

The rest of the immigrants had at first, like the old woman, taken this cabin for a hay barn, since it sat in the middle of a field. Also it was rather small, not more than fifteen or sixteen feet square. And the door, cut through the logs without a jamb, was as low as a barn door. Kristina whispered to Karl Oskar: This house was exactly like their meadow barn which had burned down when lightning struck it.

But by and by they all understood that Anders Månsson had led them to his main house; this barn was his home. All understood this, but none mentioned it—none except his mother.

151

"Anders! Don't fool me any longer! Show me your house!" she commanded.

"This is my house, Mother! Come into my house, all you *Svenskar*! I'll fix you a good supper tonight."

And the immigrants obeyed him and entered his humble abode; fatigue had overcome them to the very marrow of their bones, and they climbed with great contentment over the log serving as threshold, happy and pleased to be in a house, under a roof, having reached a shelter where they could rest.

But old Fina-Kajsa sat down on her pot outside the cabin, she remained there, repeating more and more severely, "Take me to your house!"

While all the others gathered in the cabin, and darkness fell, she remained there, sitting on her iron pot. At length Anders went outside and half carried, half dragged his mother over the threshold.

The group from Ljuder had now reached the end of their long journey. All but the widow Fina-Kajsa Andersdotter from Öland. She had not yet arrived: she had not yet seen the home her son had described in his letters. It had come to pass as she had predicted so often during the journey: she would never arrive.

# XIII

## Distant Fields Look Greenest

THE ARRIVAL of the Swedish immigrants in Taylors Falls was a momentous occurrence. The whole population of the village consisted of only thirty-odd people, and with the fifteen new arrivals it was increased in one day by half. Until now there had been only four women in the settlement; with the arrival of Fina-Kajsa, Kristina, Ulrika, and Elin their number had doubled. Previously there had been only three families, the rest were single men.

Taylors Falls had been named for an American, Jesse Taylor, who was the first white man to settle here, twelve years earlier; he had built a sawmill at the falls. He had since died, but the mill was operated by an old Irishman named Stephen Bolles who had also started a flour mill. A German couple, the Fischers, had recently opened a combined inn and store, consisting of two log cabins connected by a roofed passage. Mr. and Mrs. Fischer also kept a bull to serve the settlers' cows. A general store was owned and operated by a Scot, Mr. Abbott, who was the postmaster as well, with the post office located in the store. The largest building in the settlement was occupied by the Stillwater Lumber Company.

Besides Fina-Kajsa's son, two other Swedes lived in Taylors Falls, one man and one woman—Samuel Nöjd and Anna Johansdotter, the latter known as *Svenska Anna,* or Swedish Anna. Samuel Nöjd was a fur hunter by trade, and Swedish Anna was cook in a logging camp a few miles north of the village. With fifteen newcomers the Swedish population in this part of the St. Croix River Valley increased six-fold at once.

Anders Månsson offered the use of his cabin to his homeless countrymen until they could build living quarters for themselves or for as long as they wished to stay. Helping them thus he was only repaying a debt: "You have cared for my mother," he said.

And should they feel too cramped in his cabin, they might sleep at German Fischer's inn; lodging there would cost only. ten cents a night for each person; they would, of course, have to sleep with other people, but never more than four in the same bed; and the host was quite strict and let no one wear his boots in bed. The Fischers were particular and cleanly people and maintained good order at their inn.

There were now sixteen persons living in Anders Månsson's small cabin; but they had become accustomed to close quarters during their voyages; indeed, they had been more cramped in the holds. Here they could let their children run outside in the daytime and could themselves go out whenever they wished, so they need not jostle each other in the house all the time. Since Anders Månsson was kind enough to let them use his house, they accepted gratefully. In this way they saved a dollar and fifty cents a day, the amount it would have cost them if all had been forced to sleep at the inn. And Fina-Kajsa's son felt proud that they considered his cabin good enough; he was well pleased with it himself. During his first winter in Taylors Falls he had lived with thirteen other people in a cabin half as large as this one. He said it was only nine feet square, and only six feet from the ground to the roof, and it had no flooring.

The travelers could now rest for a few days until their belongings arrived. The men helped Anders Månsson harvest his crop. His fields were smaller than they had realized; he had broken barely eight acres. He owned a team of oxen and two cows as well. But he would only keep one cow for the winter; he intended to butcher the other one, for she was too old to breed. Each time he milked his cows all four women came to watch him: they had never before seen a man do the milking.

As soon as the news spread of the arrival of guests at Anders Månsson's, the two other Swedes in the settlement came to visit the immigrants from their homeland. Samuel Nöjd, the fur hunter, was a friendly, talkative man of about fifty, but he mixed so many English words with the Swedish that they understood only half of what he said. He had been in North America more than ten years, he had moved from place to place, and soon he would move away from this river valley: desirable fur-bearing animals were getting scarce hereabouts. He advised his countrymen to take land on the prairies instead of here.

Swedish Anna was in her forties, a buxom woman with big arms and a voluminous bosom. She was the picture of health, capable and unafraid, as a woman cooking for men in a logging camp should be. She showed also a tender, motherly side: she was much concerned over the small Swedish children and was surprised that the babies could have survived the long journey in such good health. Swedish Anna was a widow who had emigrated alone from Östergötland; Samuel Nöjd came from Dalecarlia.

Counting the new arrivals, there were now immigrants from four Swedish provinces in this valley; and the Smålanders, of course, were in the majority.

The newcomers were eager for information and at every opportunity questioned those who had arrived earlier: How was life for settlers in this St. Croix Valley, and how should they go about the business of getting settled? Anders Månsson, himself a homesteader, could best advise them; but he was a man of few words; much probing was required to learn anything from him. This much they discovered: The Territory was almost as large as all of Sweden, yet hardly more than two hundred settlers had taken up land and begun tilling it. Most of these lived to the south in Washington County. The Territory was as yet surveyed only along the rivers. To the west and southwest the whole country was still unsurveyed and unclaimed—it lay there free and open to the first claimant.

There was indeed space for all, land in abundance. But many of the inhabitants of the river valley took land only for the timber, said Anders Månsson. They did not clear fields, they cut down the forest and sold the lumber for a high profit. They left the soil untouched and grew rich from the forest. Most of the newcomers had only one desire: to get rich quickly.

The farmers from Ljuder said they had not come for that purpose. They were merely seeking to earn a living, they intended to break land, build houses, settle down: they had come to live on their land as settlers of this country, where they hoped in time to better their condition.

But they must begin from the very beginning and find everything a farmer needed, ground and house, chattel and cattle. And they were filled with concern at learning how much livestock cost: a cow, thirty dollars, a yoke of oxen, one hundred dollars. Hogs and poultry also fetched sky-high prices; Anders Månsson had only recently bought a laying hen in St. Paul for five dollars, but she had died of loneliness, and so he was unable to treat them to eggs. The exorbitant prices were explained in this way: domestic animals were also immigrants into the Territory, and as rare as the settlers themselves.

One evening, as all were gathered together in Anders Månsson's cabin, Karl Oskar asked his advice: What should a man in his predicament do? He had sold his farm in Sweden, but most of the money had been spent on the journey, and he was now practically a pauper. He had only ninety dollars left in cash. A farmer needed first of all a team of oxen, and he didn't even have enough money for that! And how could he buy land with the small sum he had left?

"You don't pay for the land before it's put on the market," Anders Månsson explained. "To begin with, you must sit down on the claim as a squatter."

And he explained what the word *squatter* meant—a settler who built his house on land that had not yet been surveyed or sold. That was why he needn't pay anything for the claim to begin with. Later, when the land had been surveyed, the government would put it up at auction and he would have priority because he had been there first. Anyone wanting to take a claim as squatter need only locate and mark the place he wanted and report it to the land office in Stillwater. Then he could remain in security on the land until it was offered for public sale. It might be several years before he need begin paying for the land.

This arrangement sounded generous to Swedish peasant ears—no one could ask for better conditions.

"I came here as a squatter myself," said Fina-Kajsa's son. "To squat means to sit on one's haunches."

"Skvatter . . . skvatter . . ." Karl Oskar attempted to pronounce the word, but its sound had something degrading in it, it sounded like a reproach to his poverty. "Yes, I guess I too must be such a one. An impoverished farmer, arriving in America . . ."

The other two farmers were better off than he; Danjel had four hundred dollars left from the sale of his farm Kärragärde, and Jonas Petter had about two hundred and fifty dollars left of his traveling money. Karl Oskar had the least for a new start. But Anders Månsson advised all three to take squatters' claims on unsurveyed land, then they could use their cash for livestock and implements. Each settler could claim a hundred and sixty acres, the American acre being a little less than the Swedish acre.

Karl Oskar thought: The manor at Kråkesjö at home had only seventy-five acres of tilled fields. If all the land he could take here were tillable, he would have fields for two manors!

Anders Månsson also told them the price they would have to pay when the land went on sale: one dollar and twenty-five cents for each acre. This sounded like a most reasonable price for such rich and fertile land as they had seen on their walk from Stillwater. A farmer would undoubtedly be able to manage and prosper here as soon as he got started.

Anders Månsson continued: All products from the fields commanded high prices: bread, butter, pork, milk, eggs, cheese. Consequently, broken ground was highly valuable. If they were able to clear and plant the fields, and hold on to them, they would soon be well off. He himself had experienced great adversity during the four years after his arrival; the first summer his crop had suffered from drought, the second year a forest fire had spread to his fields and part of his rye had burned while in the

155

shocks; last year it was the grasshoppers, which appeared in such swarms that they darkened the sun and left nothing but bare ground behind them. Each fifth year was a hopper year, when every green blade was eaten, and last summer they had even devoured his jacket and the scythe handle which he happened to leave in the field; he could only be grateful they hadn't eaten him too.

Karl Oskar had closely inspected Månsson's fields and he did not think the Ölander was an industrious farmer; he had suffered adversity, yes— but why hadn't he broken more land in four years? All he had to do was to plow this stone-free ground. Nor had he built a threshing barn as yet, in spite of all the lumber around him. Månsson threshed his crops in wintertime on the ice of the small lake. But that was a poor way to handle grain. Karl Oskar thought something must be wrong with Fina-Kajsa's son, he seemed to lack energy and an enterprising spirit.

"The first years are hard ones for settlers," Anders Månsson assured them. He continued: There were no roads anywhere out here in the wilderness, and it was not until last year that he had been able to buy a yoke of oxen in St. Paul. Before he got the team his chores had been endless; he himself had carried or pulled everything that had to be moved. A settler without a team had to use his own back, be his own beast of burden.

Fina-Kajsa looked searchingly at her son: "You've grown hunchbacked here in America, Anders. Have you carried something that was too heavy?"

"No longer, Mother. I carry nothing more now."

He straightened his bent shoulders. Then he sat silent a while and replied only in monosyllables as they tried to glean more information about his four settler years. He seemed to avoid their questions and said at last, in an effort to clarify everything to them: He had had his difficulties at times, but he had managed, one way or another.

Jonas Petter questioned him to the very point: "Do you regret your emigration?"

"Oh no, *nej*! Never! I don't mean that!" he assured them eagerly. "I have no such thoughts any longer."

"I think you have been ailing, you look so old," Fina-Kajsa said.

"The weather here is hard on one's health," the son exclaimed quickly. "If you intend to stay long in Minnesota Territory, it is well to take care of your health from the very beginning. I was sick the two first summers because I hadn't taken care of myself."

The first year he had felt lonely in America, and his thoughts had returned to Sweden at times. But the second year he had begun to like the country, and the third year he actually felt at home, and ever since, he had liked it more and more; in every respect the new country was better than the old.

And now he would soon get his American papers and become a "sitter." "Sitter" was Anders Månsson's word for citizen.

156

"I have already got my first *najonal-paper.*"

From his Swedish chest Anders Månsson produced a large paper, which he proudly showed his guests, but as it was printed in English, only Robert was able to glean some of its contents. They would all in due time get such papers, and then they too would become "sitters" in North America.

Anders Månsson's house guests understood plainly that he was unwilling to tell all of what had happened to him out here. He was a taciturn man and seemed to have a secret, something that weighed on his mind.

The newcomers hoped to profit by the experience of those who had come before them. Already they were aware that their own problems would be greater because they had arrived at this inopportune season; it would be a whole year before they could harvest anything from the earth. Somehow they must sustain life during this long year of waiting; above all, they must manage to live through the winter.

–2–

IN TIME their belongings arrived at Taylors Falls, having been freighted by the lumber company's barge; but they were dismayed at the great cost: thirty dollars! Karl Oskar, Danjel, and Jonas Petter must pay ten dollars each.

"Those dirty dogs!" exclaimed Karl Oskar, but aside from voicing his disgust he could do nothing about the price.

Anders Månsson was of the opinion that the lumber company took advantage of settlers as often as possible. A barrel of flour cost ten dollars in Stillwater, and fifteen in Taylors Falls, because the company charged five dollars for freight.

But the settlers had waited impatiently for their goods; now they had their own tools and needn't wait another day to go out and find land; without delay they must seek out their places for settling.

The clothes chests from Sweden were opened. Karl Oskar first of all dug up his axes from the bottom of his chest.

"You have two axes!" Anders Månsson exclaimed in surprise. "Then you are not poor."

Karl Oskar had only brought along one heavy ax and one hand ax. He still had no felling ax.

"If you have an ax all your own you are ahead of the rest of us."

The settlers often owned an ax together, using it in turn, every second day, or every second week, according to agreement. Sometimes three might own one ax together. Anders Månsson knew a settler who had owned no tools except a knife and one-half of an ax when he arrived. Seeing all the tools Karl Oskar had brought from Sweden, he said with respect in his voice: A well-off man has arrived here.

157

Fina-Kajsa's son had promised to go with them and point out places suitable to settle on. It was decided that Arvid and Robert should remain at home with the women and children while the men were away looking for land. Following their guide's advice, they now made themselves ready for the expedition: they took food for three days, and each carried a copper container of water, as it was said they might get chills and fever from the stagnant water in the forest. Besides axes, they took their guns. In these regions no one went far from home without a weapon of some kind, and a settler was as much dependent on his loaded gun as a limping man is on his staff.

They were to walk through regions where Indians had their favorite hunting grounds; as yet their fall hunt hadn't begun, but they moved their wigwams constantly and had no permanent camp. Anders Månsson had never been annoyed by the Chippewas, the tribe roaming in the forests near Taylors Falls; during the winter, Indians often came into his cabin to warm themselves, and they sat hours on end by the fire without saying a single word. Many times they had brought him venison. But the savages were never to be relied on; no one knew what they might do, or when they had murder on their minds. A trader, James Godfrey by name, living alone in his cabin not far from Taylors Falls, had been scalped by the Indians one night last winter as he lay in bed. It was thought that the trader had taken advantage of the Indians in some deal and that they had murdered him in revenge. The Chippewas never disturbed anyone unless they themselves had been disturbed or cheated.

So one morning at dawn the Swedish farmers set out to find new homes.

Smålanders had always looked down on Ölanders, yet here walked three Smålanders guided by an Ölander. They headed southwest down the broad valley. Their guide told them that if they continued in this direction they would find the most fertile soil in the whole river valley. A road had been begun from Taylors Falls, and they followed this clearing as far as it ran, then they had to find their own way, using their axes to cut through the worst thickets. The farther away from the river they walked, the fewer pine trees and more leafy wood they found. The birches here were mostly river birch, growing near water. The newcomers asked their guide the names of the trees that were unknown to them. He pointed out cedars and walnut trees, and they tried to remember the color of the bark and the shape of leaves and trunks. In a bog they discovered larches which they at first assumed to be some kind of pine tree. But the needles were softer, and they were told that these trees lost their needles in winter and made fine lumber. The deeper they penetrated into the lush valley, the larger and more numerous grew the sugar maples, from which sap was tapped in spring. From the rich, sweet maple sap sugar and sirup were made.

The three Småland farmers missed only one leaf-tree in this new forest—the alder tree, which supplied them with material for wooden shoes at home. And when they were told that no alders grew here, they wondered which one of the other trees might supply them with wood suitable for shoes. Their leather shoes would soon be worn out, and they would be forced to use the same kind of footgear they had worn in Sweden.

The land-seekers walked leisurely through the fertile valley, they did not walk straight ahead, they turned off to left or right, they made side trips, they observed everything they saw, particularly evaluating the soil. They walked as their forefathers once had walked through their homeland, countless thousands of years ago; they sought what their forebears had sought before a single turf had been turned in that parish where later generations had cultivated their fields. And they compared the American forest with the one at home and felt proud when they discovered that this enormously rich growth lacked one tree which was found in the forest of the land they had left.

They saw game frequently: rabbit ears stuck up in the grass, big fat squirrels scampered about and jabbered like magpies, near streams and lakelets they saw flocks of wild geese. Gnawed saplings indicated the presence of elk. Once a furred animal ran up a tree, and Jonas Petter recognized the hairy thief who had tried to steal their food the night they camped in the forest. He was told it was a raccoon, a harmless little animal that abounded in that country.

The forest shone luminously green, the grass stood tall in open places, an abundance of wild fruit and berries weighed down the branches of trees and bushes this beautiful August day.

"The Lord's sun has never shone on a more pleasing countryside," said Danjel Andreasson.

And where the land-seekers wandered now they had only to choose: they could stop wherever they wished and each stake out one hundred and sixty acres of land.

From time to time, Karl Oskar measured the depth of the topsoil with a small shovel he had brought along. Black mold lay on clay bottom; red clay on hard ground, blue clay on low-lying ground. In a few places he found sand mixed with the clay. But in practically every place he dug, he found topsoil to a depth of two feet, sometimes nearly three feet.

"More likely earth can't be found in the whole of creation," Jonas Petter said.

But they were also looking for clean drinking water; they had been warned that some of the stagnant pools and tarns were full of insects and small animals which caused dangerous sicknesses. If they were unable to locate a spring or running stream near their place of settling, they would have to dig wells for drinking water, and Anders Månsson maintained that this would be a heavy, long-drawn-out undertaking: once he had had to dig a well twenty-five feet deep.

He showed them all the lakes he was familiar with. The greatest lake in this region lay farther to the southwest and was called Ki-Chi-Saga; it was an Indian name, said to mean "Great and Beautiful Lake." Anders Månsson himself had never roamed the forest as far as Ki-Chi-Saga, but he knew a Swede, Johannes Nordberg, who had reached the big lake last autumn. Nordberg was a farmer from Helsingland who had embraced Erik Janson's new religion and had accompanied him to Illinois. Later he had fallen away from that sect and had left the colony on the prairie to look for a new place in which to settle in the north. He was said to be the first white man ever to see Lake Ki-Chi-Saga, and he had told Månsson that the finest land and the richest soil he had ever seen in this valley lay around it. He had gone back to Illinois but had promised to return last spring with many of Janson's deserters to settle near the lake with the Indian name. As yet nothing had been heard of him.

However, added the guide, fine soil was obtainable much nearer. They needn't go so far to find good places for settling.

The immigrants made no haste in choosing a site, but inspected the land carefully as they walked along. The heat also forced them to move slowly; they breathed heavily in the muggy atmosphere. They sought to refresh themselves with the water they had brought with them, but it was already tepid in the copper containers and did not quench their thirst.

In the depth of the forest they suddenly came upon a strange mound, and their guide told them this was an old Indian grave. They stopped and looked in wonder: earth had been thrown up in a great pile, and grass had grown over it. The mound had oval sides, narrowing at the top, and resembled a giant beast whose legs had sunk into the ground, an animal stuck in the forest and unable to move for so long that grass had grown on its back. And inside this huge body rested the dead savages, in the midst of their forest hunting grounds; they had never known Christ or the Gospel, throughout life they had been heathens, and so after death were lost souls. But peaceful seemed their camp, lying here in the thickest part of the wild forest, green and thriving was the grass covering their grave.

The peasants from Sweden stood a long time gazing at this mound built by human hands, rising like a round, green-furred animal-body, and they sensed that they beheld something immeasurably ancient, something from the long-past time of witches, trolls, and sagas. In this barrow where the country's native hunters returned to dust, the immigrants sensed vaguely that inexplicable something which makes women and children shudder in the dark. Before encountering these savage people in life, they had come upon them in death, they had met the dead before the living.

The strangers from faraway Sweden knew nothing of the answer the Chippewa chief had given the whites when they had asked the price of the tribal hunting grounds: "Fill this valley with gold until it lies even with the hills! Yet we will not take your gold for the graves of our fathers. Wait still a little longer, until all my people are dead. Then you may take our whole valley, and all our graves, and keep your gold as well."

The men who had traveled thousands of miles to take over the Chippewas' land, and who measured the topsoil of the Indians' hunting grounds, gazed in wonder at the grave in the forest; they stood there timidly, glancing about suspiciously, as though listening to the oldest saga of all sagas in the world.

—3—

THE LAND-SEEKERS rested in the shade of some maples and ate from their knapsacks: bread and cold rabbit. They took off their shirts, wet and clammy with perspiration, and spread them to dry on the bushes. But as they sat with their upper bodies bare, the mosquitoes attacked them in great swarms and bit them furiously. They made a fire to drive away the plague, but Anders Månsson said the best way to protect oneself was to cover the whole body with mud; while sleeping in the forest one could in this way rest peacefully.

Anders Månsson had been a homesteader for some time, he seemed to have much useful information. Jonas Petter asked him how it went with men in these womanless regions. He remembered the little shoemaker in Stillwater who had looked with such longing at the women in their company. There was only one woman to each twenty men in the American wilderness; what did the men here do?

Jonas Petter put this question to Anders Månsson, but he looked away and answered only with an embarrassed grin. He was shy with people, especially with women; he had probably never touched a woman, Jonas Petter guessed. Fina-Kajsa had once asked her son, in the presence of all, why he hadn't married yet. Anders Månsson had said nothing and had only grown redder in the face than he usually was.

Jonas Petter went on. He almost wished he had been turned into a woman here in America, as they were the only ones who needn't sleep alone. Even Ulrika seemed to think she might get married out here; she had said she need only choose among the men ready for marriage.

"Well, why wouldn't a man marry Ulrika?" Anders Månsson asked. "She is healthy and well shaped. How long since her last husband died?"

Jonas Petter and Karl Oskar exchanged glances: unmarried Ulrika of Västergöhl was taken for a widow here, as she had arrived without a husband but with a daughter. And here people might think whatever they wished, let them think her husband was dead. Ulrika herself had said, when questioned by Swedish Anna if her menfolk had died: Yes, of course her menfolk had died, all her menfolk had passed away from her forever, none would return, she had none left. And people in Taylors Falls now believed that Ulrika had been married and widowed many times, and none of her group would tell the truth about her carryings-on at home; all had agreed that everything discreditable that had happened in the land of

161

Sweden, no matter whom it concerned, must be forgotten, buried, and lost in this new country.

Jonas Petter had almost let the cat out of the bag, but he saw Karl Oskar's warning glance, and hastened to explain: Concerning Ulrika's widowhood, he knew only what she herself had said—all her menfolk had left her forever, they were dead to her. And how long it was since the last one passed away, that Jonas Petter couldn't say. But this much he knew: Ulrika was free and open to marriage.

Thus Jonas Petter avoided the truth without telling a lie.

Anders Månsson nodded and seemed satisfied with this information. Such an elegant and handsome woman as Ulrika, he said, would soon be married here in Minnesota Territory.

—4—

LATER in the afternoon the four Swedes reached a small, longish lake with low shores overgrown with reeds and grass. Oaks, maples, lindens, and ash trees were scattered in this region, but the ground nearest the lake was even and ready to till, sloping gently toward the water.

"Here it's easy to break land," said their guide. "This is a fine place for homesteading."

They walked around the lake, a distance of only a few miles, and inspected the ground everywhere. Yes, the earth was easy to break; one need only turn it with the plow. The topsoil was two and a half feet deep in some places. Material for building grew everywhere close by.

Danjel and Jonas Petter were at once satisfied with the location and inclined to stake claims here. Karl Oskar admitted that the topsoil was excellent, but the ground nearest the lake was low and swampy, full of muddy pools and quagmires.

"It's a mosquito hole," he said.

Jonas Petter replied that the mosquitoes swarmed about every place and that they shouldn't let this factor influence their decision. And when they discovered a spring with clear, translucent water under a fallen tree near by, he and Danjel were in enthusiastic accord: At this little lake they had found all they wanted, here they wished to settle.

Anders Månsson advised neither one way nor another. The lake was about seven or eight miles as the crow flies from Taylors Falls, and he didn't think they would want to be farther away from people.

"It is far enough," Danjel said. "Let us all three take claims here. This is a good place for us to live."

They laid down their burdens at the edge of the forest and rested in the shade to talk it over. Danjel continued: As they had come from the same place at home, they oughtn't to separate now, they ought to stick together. If they settled here, close to each other, they could help each

162

other and enjoy each other's company. To begin with, they could even use each other's tools and teams.

Jonas Petter also wanted them to build close together, like a village at home; to live like villagers would be more enjoyable here in the wilderness than to live alone.

Then it was Karl Oskar's turn to voice his thoughts: Just because there was so much space out here, they must not settle on top of each other, elbow each other and build their homes corner to corner as farmers did in Sweden. He thought they should live a little apart. They could do as they pleased, but he wanted to settle in a place some distance from the others. He didn't, of course, mean to be so far away that they couldn't see each other and help each other when needed.

Danjel wanted them to remain one family, as they were at present; the first Christians whom he tried to imitate, had owned all things in common. But Karl Oskar wanted to think this over, and he would obey no head except his own. Even though Danjel well knew that his sister's daughter's husband never followed any advice, he now seriously tried to persuade him: "Don't seek any farther! Be satisfied with this fair land."

"I might find some more likely a little farther on."

"We should be satisfied when the Lord has shown us this."

Jonas Petter said: "Don't be a fuss-pot, Karl Oskar! This place is good enough!"

But Karl Oskar turned to Anders Månsson and asked him for more information about the region near the lake with the Indian name. That farmer from Helsingland who inspected the soil, hadn't he said that the richest farm land in this whole valley was beside that lake? Karl Oskar would like to see for himself if this were actually the truth before he chose his own land. How far from here would it be to the lake?

Anders Månsson didn't think it was more than two miles from where they now were to Lake Ki-Chi-Saga, but he couldn't say for sure. The country to the west and southwest had not yet been explored, no one except Indians and an occasional pelt trader had been farther. But streams ran in that direction, and if he followed one of these, he would undoubtedly reach Lake Ki-Chi-Saga.

Karl Oskar looked thoughtfully at the fields in front of him: he did not wish to appear displeased with what he saw, but he had once and for all made up his mind that he would have the best soil in North America, wherever it was to be found. And now it was said that the soil was even better at the other lake. Why be satisfied with the next best if the very best was within reach? Suppose he took a claim here—and then for the rest of his life had to regret not having gone a few miles farther. He couldn't know until he had seen the other place. He was to settle down for the rest of his life, he wanted to choose carefully, find a place that he liked so well he would never want to leave it. He had traveled many thousands of miles, all the way from Sweden. He had strength left to go a few miles farther.

163

The farmer from Korpamoen was so stubborn that nothing could change his mind once he got an idea in his head, and Danjel and Jonas Petter could only wish him good luck when he said he would go on farther by himself. They had firmly decided to settle down here as squatters.

"Cut marks in the trees," said Anders Månsson. "That means you have taken a claim."

Danjel and Jonas Petter each blazed a maple; then Anders Månsson carved in each blazed tree a ten-inch-high letter, C: this indicated that the land at the lake had been claimed, anyone coming later would see it.

But Karl Oskar picked up his pack again—there were still some hours before sunset, and if it were only a few miles to the lake with the peculiar name, he thought he might get there before dark. He would be back by tomorrow noon, if they cared to wait for him, but if he were delayed they had better return to Taylors Falls without him; he was sure he could find his way back alone.

As he disappeared among the thick tree trunks, Jonas Petter looked after him and said: The old proverb was right—distant fields look greenest. . . .

—5—

KARL OSKAR NILSSON walked alone through the wilderness. He continued directly southwest, and when the trees did not shade him, the sun shone right in his face, burning him like a flame. Progress became more difficult, he had to use his ax often to get through. He reached a swamp where he sank down to his boot tops, he circled giant trees, seemingly yards around the base, he climbed over fallen trees whose upturned roots towered house tall, he walked around deep black water holes like wells, he tore his way through tangles of ferns and bushes, he fought thorny thickets which clawed his hands and face until they bled. At times he walked on the bottom of the forest ocean with the sky barely visible, at other times— while craning his neck to look up at the tall trees—he was reminded of the church steeple at home, which, as a little boy, he had thought reached into the very heavens.

Karl Oskar mused to himself that probably he was the first white man ever to go through the forest at this place.

The ground had been tramped by hunters and game, by soft moccasins and light cloven hoofs, by the pursued and the pursuer. But now came a man, lumbering along in heavy boots, who was neither Indian nor deer, neither hunter nor hunted. Cautiously he took one step at a time, treading firmly on the unknown ground. He had entered this forest on a new mission, a mission that had brought no one here before: Karl Oskar Nilsson was the first one to enter here with a farmer's purpose of planting and harvesting.

In spite of the many obstacles hindering his progress, he felt in high spirits. During the whole journey from Sweden he had lived closed in with other people, forced to be part of a group. Here he had miles of space in every direction, he didn't hit his head on a ceiling, his elbows against walls, he didn't jostle anyone if he moved. Here he walked along as if the whole wide wilderness were his own, to do with as he pleased; wherever he wished, he could choose his land, blaze a trunk: "This earth is mine!" he thought.

He was in high spirits because he was the first one here, because he knew a freedom which none of those would have who came after him. He walked through the forest as if he had a claim to everything around him, as if he now were taking possession and would rule a whole kingdom. Here he would soon feel at home and know his way.

Now he was searching for Ki-Chi-Saga; the name was like a magic formula, like a word from an old tale about an ancient, primeval, moss-grown, troll-inhabited forest. He spelled the word and tried to pronounce the three syllables he had heard Anders Månsson utter; the foreign name had a magic lure; he would not return until he had seen this water.

He reached a rushing stream, which he followed; the creek, with all its turns, indicated the direction he must go. To make doubly sure of his way back, he blazed occasional trees with his ax as he had done all day.

Karl Oskar followed the brook until dusk began to fall. But he had not reached a lake, large or small. Fatigue from the long walk during the hot day overtook him, and he decided to find a place to camp for the night. In the morning he would continue his search for Ki-Chi-Saga. Perhaps the distance was greater than Månsson had guessed, perhaps the brook had led him astray—who knew for sure that it emptied into the lake? But he didn't think he had gone far since leaving his countrymen, he had walked slowly and been delayed by having to cut his way through thickets.

He sat down to rest on a fallen tree; he ate a slice of bread and some meat and drank water from his container, water he had taken from the spring where the other men were. The landscape was different here, it was now more undulating and open. Should he lie down and sleep under this tree trunk, or should he try to go on? His feet had gone to sleep in his boots, his injured leg ached. Another day would come tomorrow—the land around him would not run away if he rested here for the night.

A flock of birds, large and unfamiliar to him, flew overhead, their wings whizzing in the air. They were quite low, barely above the treetops—they slanted their wings and descended and he lost sight of them. He guessed they were water birds—the lake must be near by!

This action of the birds made him decide to go on. After a few hundred paces he reached a knoll with large hardwood trees amid much greenery, behind which daylight shone through. He hurried down a slope and was in an open meadow. Now he could see: the meadow with its tall, rich grass sloped gently toward glittering water; the lake lay in front of him.

At first glimpse he was disappointed: this was only a small lake, it was not the right one. But as he approached he discovered that it was only an arm of a lake. Through a narrow channel it connected with other arms and bays and farther on the water expanded into a vast lake with islands and promontories and channels as far as his eyes could see. He had arrived.

All that he saw agreed with what he had heard—this lake must be Ki-Chi-Saga. Staggering with fatigue, he walked down to inspect it. He must complete his mission before night fell.

The shores had solid banks without any swamps, and he could see sandy beaches. Here and there, the topsoil had clay in it. The stream, his guide, emptied into the west end of the arm, near a stand of tall, slender pines. To the east a tongue of land protruded, overgrown with heavy oaks. A vast field opened to the north between the lake and the forest's edge, open, fertile ground covered with grass. He went over to inspect the tongue of land with leaf-trees: besides the oaks there were sugar maples, lindens, elms, ash trees, aspens, walnut and hazel trees, and many other trees and bushes he did not recognize. The lake shores were low and easily accessible everywhere. Birds played on the surface of the water splashing, swimming in lines, wriggling about like immense feathered water snakes, and there were ripples and rings from whirling, swirling fins.

Karl Oskar measured the sloping meadow with his eyes. It must be about fifty acres. He supposed a great deal of this ground once had been under water, the lake had at one time been larger. The soil was the fattest mold on clay bottom, the finest earth in existence. He stuck his shovel into the ground—everywhere the topsoil was deep, and in one place he did not find the red clay bottom until he had dug almost three feet down.

Earlier in the day he had seen the next best; he had gone on a little farther, and now he had found the best. He had arrived.

He felt as though this soil had been lying here waiting just for him. It had been waiting for him while he, in another land, had broken stone and more stone, laid it in piles and built fences with it, broken his equipment on it; all the while this earth had waited for him, while he had wasted his strength on roots and stones; his father had labored to pile the stone heaps higher and higher, to build the fences longer and broader, had broken himself on the stones so that now he must hobble along crippled, on a pair of crutches for the rest of his life—while all this earth had been lying here waiting. While his father sacrificed his good healthy legs for the spindly blades that grew among the stones at home, this deep, fertile soil had nurtured wild grass, harvested by no one. It had been lying here useless, sustaining not a soul. This rich soil without a stone in it had lain here since the day it was created, waiting for its tiller.

Now he had arrived.

In the gathering dusk Karl Oskar Nilsson from Korpamoen appraised the location of the land: Northward lay the endless wilderness, a protection against winter winds; to the south the great lake; to the west the fine pine

166

forest; to the east the protruding tongue of land with the heavy oaks. And he himself stood in the open, even meadow, the grass reaching to his waist, hundreds of loads of hay growing about him, covering the finest and most fertile topsoil; he stood there gazing at the fairest piece of land he had seen in all of North America.

Now he needn't go a step farther. Here lay his fields, there grew the timber for his house, in front of him lay the water with game birds and fish. Here he had fields, forest, and lake in one place. Here things grew and throve and lived and moved in whatever direction he looked—on the ground, in trees and bushes, on land and water.

At last he had found the right spot: this was the place for a farmer's home. Here he must live. And he would be the first one to raise his house on the shores of Lake Ki-Chi-Saga.

He turned left to the stand of oaks and selected the biggest tree he saw. He cut wide marks with his ax; then he took out his red pencil, his timberman's pencil from home, and wrote on the wood: *K. O. Nilsson, Svensk.*

This would have to do; if it wasn't sufficient, he must do it over some other time. The red letters on the white blaze in the oak could be seen a long way and would tell anyone passing by that this place was claimed. Besides, he wasn't able to do more, not today. After the few cuts with the ax he suddenly felt tired, more tired than he had ever felt in his life. He sank down under the tree, heavily, and laid his pack beside him—his gun, ax, water keg, knapsack, all; he had forced himself to walk a long way, and now he had no more strength, he fell at last under the tree on which he had just printed his name.

He felt he couldn't move, couldn't do another thing this evening; he was too tired to make a fire, to gather moss for a bed, to take off his boots, open the knapsack, eat. He was too tired to do anything at all, even to chase away the mosquitoes—he no longer felt their smarting bites. He didn't care about anything now, he was insensible to everything except the need to rest his body: he stretched out full length on his back, on the ground under the big oak, with his coat as a pillow.

He was satisfied with his day; he had persevered and reached his destination before the end of the day. He had found what he so long had striven to find. And this evening he rested, unmindful of all the dangers of the wilderness—he rested with the assurance of having arrived home, protected by his own tree, on his own land: The farmer from the Stone Kingdom had arrived in the Earth Kingdom which he would possess.

He went to sleep at once, his weary body fell into the well of oblivion, peace, and renewal. Karl Oskar Nilsson slept heavily and well during his first night on the shore of Lake Ki-Chi-Saga, where he was to build a farmer's life from its very beginning.

167

# XIV

## A Småland Squatter

THE NEXT MORNING Karl Oskar returned to the small lake where the other three settlers awaited him, and before nightfall the four of them were back at Anders Månsson's cabin in Taylors Falls.

The following day the men began to stake out and cut a road through to their claims, so as to be able to move their belongings and whatever they might need for the settling. Their clearing work began where the logging road ended; they continued past the small lake where Danjel and Jonas Petter had decided to settle, all the way to Lake Ki-Chi-Saga. They were five menfolk. Five axes cut all day long, through thickets and groves, felling and chopping and clearing. They built a road, digging here, filling there, until wagon wheels could roll along over the ground. The distance from Taylors Falls to Lake Ki-Chi-Saga was estimated to be ten miles, and it took the five men ten days to make a passable clearing.

Then it took three days to haul boards from the Taylors Falls mill to their places of settling. With these boards they intended to raise huts in which to live while building their log houses. For the hauling they hired Anders Månsson's oxen, which moved so slowly on the newly cleared road that a whole day was required for each load.

Their almanac indicated to the Swedish settlers that the year had reached the last week of August. Only two months remained before winter would come to the St. Croix Valley; they were told that snow and cold weather would begin early in November. But the autumns were mild in the river valley—during all of September and most of October pleasant weather was said to prevail. For another two months people could live in huts and sheds without discomfort or danger from cold. And during this time they must build more permanent houses, able to withstand all weathers. They had not one day to lose if they were to have comfortable log houses before winter set in with its severe cold and blizzards.

First they must build a shanty on each claim. "Shanty" was Anders Månsson's name for a shed. Jonas Petter was an experienced carpenter and timberman, and in three days he had built his small hut on the shores of the little lake; then he helped Danjel and Arvid build a larger one for Danjel's family to move into. As soon as this was done they began felling timbers for their log houses.

Karl Oskar chose as the site for his first home the oak grove where he had slept during his first night at Lake Ki-Chi-Saga. With Robert as helper he soon raised a hut of rough boards, about nine feet square in size; he made the roof of young lindens, on top of which he laid bark and sod. This work took him and Robert four days. There were not sufficient boards left for flooring, and the two brothers stamped down the ground and covered it with a thick layer of hay, which they gathered from the meadow. They had left an opening to the south, facing the meadow, and now Karl Oskar hammered together a door, which he hung on hinges he had made of willow wattles; then he cut open a few holes to let in light. He did not bother with a fireplace, as it would be difficult to get rid of the smoke. Instead, he built a makeshift cooking place of clay, sand, and a few stones outside near the door. This could be used as long as the warm season lasted. But he had to search widely along the shores before he found enough stones. To search for stones was a new and unusual occupation for the farmer from Korpamoen!

The family's first home in North America was now ready, and they could move in under their own roof. Kristina and the children had remained with Anders Månsson and had not yet seen their new home. Karl Oskar prepared his wife cautiously: "It's only a simple weather break: soon I'll raise a sturdy log house."

She looked forward to being in her own home where she could have her own say; this had long been her fervent desire.

Karl Oskar borrowed the oxen from Anders Månsson for the moving, and their belongings made a big load. Besides their things from Sweden, they must bring a supply of foodstuffs, which Karl Oskar had bought from Mr. Abbott, the Scot, in Taylors Falls: one barrel of rye flour for bread, one sack of salt, a few pounds of sugar, and other necessities for the household; he had also bought various articles needed for the building of the main house. He had dug deep into his cash, spending almost twenty-five dollars. The barrel of flour would last a long time for bread baking, but he had bought no meat or pork: for more substantial food they must depend on game from the forest and fish from the lake.

It was a pleasant morning in early fall when the family from Korpamoen set out for Lake Ki-Chi-Saga. The weather was now cooler, with mild sunshine over the green forest wilderness; perfect weather for moving. Kristina and the children rode on the wagon, Karl Oskar and Robert walked on either side of the load, holding on to it now and then to prevent the wagon from turning over. Karl Oskar drove, holding the thongs in one hand and steadying the load with the other. The new road was rough and the wagon was no soft-rolling spring carriage: it was entirely made of wood.

The wheels of Anders Månsson's ox wagon consisted of four trundles sawed from a thick oak log. The axles fitted into holes in these rough blocks and had pins of wood on their ends, like the pins in a single-horse pull shaft. The front wheels were a little smaller than the back pair; the wagon tree connecting the two pairs had holes in it to lengthen or shorten the wagon, if required. The dry wooden axles groaned as the trundles turned, they squeaked loudly at the friction of wood against wood. And the clumsy wheels jolted and rolled heavily over hollows and stumps.

The children yelled in delight; they had not been on a wagon pulled by a team since leaving the horse wagons in Karlshamn last spring. But Kristina was not so well pleased to sit on this jouncing, shaking wooden vehicle. And was this clearing through the forest called a road? Even a person walking would find it difficult to get through between stumps and thickets. She wondered that the wheels were able to roll at all, she sympathized with the whining, whimpering wagon; if she had been a wagon she too would have complained about being forced through this wild woodland.

Karl Oskar explained that the wagon was not greased; Anders Månsson did not keep his implements in good order. Nor had he himself been able to find any fat—animal tallow, or such—to use this morning for greasing the axles. The wagon reminded him that iron was as scarce here as wood was abundant.

Kristina called the vehicle "The Whimpering Wagon," but the day they hauled the boards to the claim, Robert had already named it "The Screech Cart."

The riders on the big load were soundly shaken; the wagon jolted and bumped, almost worse than a ship on a stormy sea—it rolled and pitched more than the *Charlotta*. After a few miles Kristina felt sick: "No! I want no more swinging! Neither on water nor land!"

She stepped down from the load and walked. She was afraid of being badly shaken; it might injure the child she carried in her. Only ten or eleven weeks remained before she would be in childbed, and she might have a miscarriage if she weren't careful. She would rather walk than sit on a load that shook like a threshing floor, even though she had begun to be heavy of foot.

The ox wagon crept along the wretched road, squeaking and screeching. The load nearly turned over many times—only through the efforts of the two men was it kept upright. The oxen moved at a snail's pace, and Kristina walked on one side and kept an eye on her children.

The trail skirted a glen in the depths of the forest, and here stood a strange pole which the Indians had erected. The settlers stopped to let the oxen rest while they inspected it. Karl Oskar and Robert had seen this image before—now they wanted to show it to Kristina. The pole was made from a cedar tree and stood taller than a man. But it did not represent a man—it ended in a snarling wolf's head.

The wooden image in the midst of the forest seemed to Kristina a phantom, and she was afraid to go near it. Robert guessed it was some kind of god whom the Indians worshiped when they gathered here—remnants of huts were to be seen close by. Kristina knew that heathens lacked knowledge of even the first of God's Ten Commandments, she knew they worshiped images, but she couldn't understand how they could worship so horrible an image as this one—a wolf with ravenous jaws. She urged the group to continue their journey: the savages must revere their image; should they happen to arrive and find people gaping at the pole, they

170

might do harm. And since she had seen what horrible idols heathens made unto themselves, she thanked her Creator from the bottom of her heart for letting her be born in a Christian land.

The plodding ox team pushed on sluggishly, step after step, and the wooden wheels rolled along, turning slowly while the axles cried out. Robert said the noise hurt his ears, particularly the injured one. To Kristina, the four wooden wheels sang a song about impoverished wanderers: their long-drawn-out wail was to her a song of their own tribulations, of their eternal struggle, of loneliness in the wilderness. Long had their journey taken, long would it be before they had a home. As slowly as these wheels turned on their axles, keeping up their constant groans of complaint—so slowly would they manage to establish a home.

But Karl Oskar, walking beside the wagon and urging on the team, said many times: "If these were only my oxen and my wagon!"

The complaint of the ungreased wheels did not dishearten him. He was stimulated, in high spirits at being able again to drive a wagon, however much it groaned—but he drove someone else's team, someone else's wagon. A settler who owned a team had improved his situation. If this had been his own team and his own wagon, then the squeaking wheels would have been a beautiful tune. If he had been the owner of this team and this wagon, he would be walking along listening to a happy song—a song of persistence, tenacity, and reward—a song of comfort to the ears of a settler.

—2—

THEIR NEWLY BUILT ROAD made a circuitous turn to Jonas Petter's and Danjel's settlement, lengthening the distance to Lake Ki-Chi-Saga. Karl Oskar had cleared a short cut to his own land which he now followed, thus lessening the distance by one mile. From Taylors Falls to Ki-Chi-Saga the road was now only nine miles.

Therefore, they did not drive by the smaller lake where their companions from Sweden had settled. Kristina knew full well that Karl Oskar had taken his claim farthest away—she had known this a very long time, long before he knew it himself. She had known it before they left Sweden —she had guessed he would search for a settling place as far away as he could within America's borders.

How far away from people must they now settle down? She thought the road to their new home was long and tedious. But Karl Oskar explained to her, they hadn't actually driven very far; it was the oxen, they were so slow and lazy that it took a long time to reach the claim. That was all. They could have traveled this road faster by foot.

Kristina asked: Wouldn't they be there soon?

Karl Oskar answered: Only a little stretch farther.

171

Some time elapsed, and then she asked again: How much farther? . . . Oh, not very much; they would be there presently. . . . But when they had driven on some distance, her patience ran out: now she insisted that he must tell her exactly how much of the road was left.

He said he couldn't tell her exactly, he hadn't measured the road in yards, feet, and inches. Moreover, they were now supposed to count in American measurements, so he couldn't compute the distance.

Kristina flared up: "Don't try to make a fool of me! You'd better figure out that distance!"

He had jested with her about the road length only because she had asked so many times. He said, "Don't be angry, Kristina. I didn't mean anything."

"You might at least have talked it over with me before you went so far away for land!"

"But I had to make the decision alone. You couldn't have gone with us out here in the woodlands."

"How far do you intend to drag us? Speak up now!"

"I've told you before—I've selected the best earth there is hereabouts."

"But the road to it—it's eternal."

Karl Oskar assured her that when she arrived she would forget the tiresome journey to the wonderful land he had chosen. She must have confidence in his choice, she must rely on him here in America as she had done in Sweden.

But she was still vexed: he mustn't think she would always endure his whims. He never asked anyone's advice, he always thought he knew best. It was time for him to realize that he was nothing but a poor, wretched, fallible human; he too could make mistakes and wrong decisions.

"But I often ask your advice, Kristina. . . ."

"Maybe sometimes. But then you do as you please!"

His wife was touchy in her advanced pregnancy, she was easily upset, but he mustn't let this affect his temper, he must handle her carefully. She angered him at times, but when he controlled himself, she soon calmed down.

Suddenly he heard a cry from Kristina. He reined in the team with all his might. Little Harald had fallen off the wagon.

Robert picked up the boy before his mother reached him. Luckily the child had fallen into a mass of ferns, so soft that no damage was done. He cried only a few tears, caused more by fright than hurt. But now Kristina climbed onto the load in order to hold Harald in her arms the rest of the way. She was regretting her earlier outbreak: it was as if God had wished to give her a warning by letting her child fall off the wagon.

They now came onto more open, even ground, and Kristina no longer had to "ride a swing." She looked over the landscape and saw many flowers; the countryside was fair and pleasingly green; she caught herself comparing

172

it with the prettiest parts of her home village, Duvemåla in Algutsboda Parish.

In a moment the wagon rolled slightly down a wide meadow toward a lake. The ground sloped gently, and in no time they had reached the shore. The team came to a stop on an outjutting tongue of land.

Karl Oskar threw the thong across the back of the left ox: they had arrived. According to his watch, it had taken more than five hours to move their load from Taylors Falls. But that was because of the sluggish oxen; a good walker could cover the distance in three hours; their home here was not at the end of the world!

Kristina climbed down from the oxcart and looked about in all directions: this then was the lake with the strange name, Ki-Chi-Saga. The sky-blue water with the sun's golden glitter on its waves, the overflowing abundance of green growth around the shores, all the blossoms and various grasses in the wild meadow, the many lush leaf-trees, the oaks and the sugar maples, the many birds on the lake and in the air—this was a sight to cheer her. This was a good land.

"The ground is easy to break," Karl Oskar said. "There isn't any finer!"

He hoped she would forget the long road and feel better as she saw the place where they would build their new home.

"You've found a nice place, Karl Oskar. It looks almost as nice as home in Duvemåla."

Kristina had compared the shores of Lake Ki-Chi-Saga with the village where she was born and had grown up; it was the highest praise she could give. Looking at Karl Oskar she knew he had expected more, probably he had expected her, on seeing the land, to break out in loud praise and grateful joy as if they had arrived in the Garden of Eden. But all the while the thought would not leave her that here they must live like hermits in the midst of savages and wild beasts.

Karl Oskar pushed the whip handle into the ground and said the top-soil was as deep as the whip handle was long. He had measured all over—it was the same everywhere.

"Such pretty flowers in the meadow," she said.

She saw things above ground, while Karl Oskar was anxious to impress her with what was under the surface; the growth came from below, down in the black mold which they couldn't see, down there would grow the bread.

"There are only flowers and weeds now," he said. "Bread will grow here from now on. You can rely on that, Kristina!"

This was Karl Oskar's promise for the future, an earnest and binding promise to wife and children: here the earth would give life's sustenance to them all, and his was the responsibility of breaking the land whence it would come.

The ox wagon with their possessions had come to a stop in front of the newly built board shed, and Karl Oskar and Robert began to unload; soon they were struggling with the heavy America chest. Kristina stood at the open door which hung there on its willow hinges; the children hovered around her.

She knew now how people lived out here when they began with the earth from the very beginning. Like Anders Månsson's old mother, she too had taken his house for a meadow barn at first sight; it was so exactly like those rickety sheds on moors and meadows at home in which the summer hay was harvested. At first, she had been unable to accept that it was a farmer's house and home. But at least it had been a solid house, built of logs. Here she stood in front of a still smaller hut, roughly thrown together of unfinished boards; this could not even be called a barn, it looked more like a tool house or a woodshed.

But then—what had she expected? Kristina looked at the shanty Karl Oskar had built for them; she realized her husband had done the best he could with a few boards, as yet she couldn't expect anything better. Seeing how people lived out here, it would have been impossible to ask for anything better, to insist on a more comfortable house. No one could conjure forth a real home in a few days; she must be satisfied with a hut.

Karl Oskar looked at his wife, anxiously wondering what she might say about his cabin. Deep down he was a little ashamed not to be offering her a better home in the new country. They had traveled such a long way to come here—and at last they stood in front of a small board shed, hurriedly nailed together in a few days. She might not think it much of an achievement; even though he had prepared her in advance, he was afraid she might be disappointed:

"It's only a *shanty*, as they call it here," he said.

The very sound of the English word emphasized to Karl Oskar better than anything he could say in Swedish that this was a makeshift. He added, "The shanty will give us protection until the house is ready."

"It'll do as long as the weather is decent," said Kristina, and felt the walls. "You put it up fast," she added.

Karl Oskar had done carpentry work as a youth, helping his father, but he did not consider himself proficient. He could have built himself a hut of twigs and branches and saved the cost of the boards, but it would have been too wretched, he thought; and then the mosquitoes, they would have come in everywhere through the brush; boards were more of a protection in every way.

Now he was pleased Kristina had found no fault with his cabin; it was the first house he had made all by himself, however it had turned out. He himself knew how poor it was. But she had said not one belittling word about the shanty, however clumsy or crooked or warped it was. She had only praised him for his handiness and speed.

He said that in the beginning they must live like crofters, without flooring in their house, it couldn't be helped. But see all the land they had! They might live like cotters but they had better and larger fields than the biggest farmer in Ljuder; they had reason to be well satisfied.

"And next time, Kristina, just wait and see! Next time we shall timber a real house! A real home! Just wait and see. . . ."

And he waved his hands in the direction of the pine stand across the meadow where the lumber still stood—couldn't she just see their sturdy, well-timbered house! Back there grew the walls for it, it was rooted, it wouldn't run away from them, it was well anchored in their own ground—no one could take their future home away from them!

Karl Oskar had moved in as a squatter, a man possessing the land without having to pay for it as yet. A squatter was a man staying close to the ground, and he too would need to stay close to the ground in the beginning; but not for long! No longer than he absolutely had to! He guessed Anders Månsson had squatted so long on his land that it had made him stoop-shouldered. Karl Oskar would be careful to avoid this; he had decided, if health and strength remained his, that only a short time would elapse before he would begin to rise, rise up to his full stature; on his own land he could rise to a man's stature, to the proud independence of a free farmer.

So far, he had always kept his resolutions; as far as it depended on him, this one would be kept also.

For a time they would have to live in a board shed, without windows, without fireplace, the black earth for their floor. As Kristina now entered her new home she had to stoop to get through the door. Here they were now moving in with all their possessions, her children were already playing about in the hay inside, the hay for beds which all of them would sleep on; the children had great fun digging holes in the hay, tumbling about, screaming and laughing. They were already at home, acting as if they had lived here all their lives.

Johan called out to his mother, in jubilation: "Now we live in a house, Mother! Our house in America!"

Yes, she answered the boy, they were now living in a house, at last in their own house; no longer need they crowd in among others, they could at last be their own masters, do as they pleased in their own home. From today on they had a home of their own to live in. And for this they must be grateful to God.

But deep inside her Kristina was also grateful for something else: that no one at home, neither her parents, nor her sisters, nor any other person from the old country need ever see this shanty, her first home in North America.

# XV

## . . . To Survive with the Help of His Hands

IN THE WILDERNESS at Lake Ki-Chi-Saga in Minnesota Territory Karl Oskar and Kristina were to begin again as tillers of the soil; they must begin their lives anew.

During the journey their hands had rested. Often they had wished to have something to do. Now all at once the settler's innumerable chores crowded upon them; all were important, but all were not equally important; all could not be performed at one time, some must be put off. To find shelter, warmth, and food for the winter at hand—these were the most urgent tasks and took precedence over all others.

For the time being they settled in their shanty, much smaller than Anders Månsson's cabin, but now they were only six people instead of sixteen, and this hut was their own. In the center of the earth floor sat the large clothes chest, half as long as the shanty itself and occupying much of the space. At home it had been called the America chest, here it was called the Swedish chest. It was their one piece of furniture in their first American home. The chest bore the scars of its emigration adventure; it had been used roughly on the journey, in New York one corner had been smashed in, it was marred and scratched all over. But within its oaken planks, held together with heavy iron bands, it had protected its owner's indispensable belongings. Men who had had to handle the chest, lifting it by its clumsy iron handles, had been surprised by its weight, and cursed and complained about what it might contain.

The clothes chest contained exactly the articles which the owners could not be without if they were to survive in the wilderness—so thought Kristina as she now unpacked them all. How could they withstand the winter's cold without the woolen garments she now lifted from the chest? Camphor and lavender had protected them against moths and mildew; she found to her satisfaction that all the pieces of clothing were unharmed, though they had been packed this long time, from spring to autumn. Carefully Kristina handled woolen jackets, wadmal coats, linen sheets. She could have caressed the well-known pieces of clothing from home, in gratefulness that they had followed her out here, that they were ready for her now that she would need them. And it seemed almost incredible that they could be here with her in these foreign surroundings, so far away from home; they were like strangers here, they belonged to another home, in another country.

It was so long since she had packed the chest, she could not remember what was in it, and now she found objects she had not expected; she made

176

discoveries, many times she was pleasantly surprised: Did she pack *that?* Had she brought along *this* also? What luck!

She found her carding combs, her wool shears, her sewing basket with balls of yarn, knitting needles, tallow candles which she herself had dipped last Christmas, her tablecloth of whole linen, woven by herself as part of her dowry, the small bottle of Hoffman's Heart-Aiding Drops, children's playthings. All these came now as unexpected gifts, at a moment when she needed them. She was most pleased when she found the swingletree which Karl Oskar had decorated with red tulips—his betrothal gift to her: through this her youth was brought back to her, such a long time ago, she thought —her betrothal time.

In the Swedish chest were also Karl Oskar's carpenter tools; without them he could not have attempted to build a house for his family. Had he known how expensive tools were out here, he would have brought along much more edge iron: planes, augers, chisels, more axes. He also regretted not having more powder and shot, for it was costly to load a gun here. For once Robert had shown foresight—his hooks, fish traps, nets, and other fishing gear would come in handy for them, living as they did on the shores of a lake.

The odor of the camphor and lavender that had kept the packed clothing in good condition filled the shanty as the lid of the chest was thrown open. It was pleasing to Kristina—it smelled like *home.*

It had been in late March that she packed the America chest—it was in early September that she unpacked the Swedish chest. During all the months in between she had been moving; she had traveled from spring to autumn, and she had experienced so much during this time that it seemed more like years than months since she had left home. Was it only last spring that she had packed her possessions? To Kristina it seemed the packing had taken place in another life, in another world. And it was indeed true—they were living a new life, in a new world.

Many were the memories awakened in her as she unpacked the chest; every object was linked with some happening at home, some experience with people close to her, friends or relatives. The wool cards had been given her by her mother when she moved into her own home, the sewing basket she had bought at the fair the first spring she was married, the knitting needles had occupied her hands during winter evenings in company of friends around the fire. So many intimate things were here thrust upon her; from the old clothes chest she now unpacked Sweden.

And with these objects came many thoughts of little value to her— rather, they annoyed her. She knew that nothing could be more futile than to let her thoughts wander back and dwell on what once had been and never could be again. Her family must begin anew, they could not bury themselves in memories of the past. She had taken it as a warning when Karl Oskar had said: If their thoughts were too much on their old home-

177

land, on things they had once and for all given up, this would hinder their success in the new country.

From that point of view, it had been disturbing to open the lid of the America chest—now the Swedish chest: their old home and their life there had thrust itself upon her; yet, it was as distant as ever.

But the chest *was* the only piece of furniture in the hut. And now she used it as a table; she spread food on the lid, and it became the family's gathering place at every meal. And the old homeland odor remained; the chest occupied the center of the shanty and smelled of camphor and lavender—a lingering reminder of Sweden.

—2—

KARL OSKAR arranged his work according to the sun; he began early, before it was too warm, rested during the noon heat, and continued his work in the afternoon and into the cool evening as late as daylight would permit him. He was felling pines near the stream for house timbers. He felled the straightest and most suitable trees, stripping them of bark so the logs would dry while there was still warmth in the air. He cut young lindens, which he roughhewed for a roof and floor boards; he dug sod for the roof, he gathered and dried the birch and pine bark that was to hold the sod, he collected the stringy linden bark for ropes, he burned debris and cleared roads, he built a simple baking oven near the shanty, he dug a hole in the ground where they could keep food in a cool place and where it was protected from wild animals and insects, and he daily performed innumerable small chores. But even though he used the last reflected rays of the sun, the day was not long enough for him, he wished to do still more. And he complained because he had only two hands.

"Be satisfied with your two hands!" Kristina said. "You might have had only one."

So much of the work was new to him, he was constantly learning new ways, he was ever improving the knowledge of his hands. All that specially skilled workmen had done for him at home, he himself must do here as best he could. Necessity was the best teacher, his father had said, and necessity forced a settler to try his skill at all kinds of work.

Karl Oskar had always learned easily and quickly imitated others. Now everything depended on his hands' knowledge—unable to help himself with his hands, a settler would soon perish in this wilderness.

Kristina too must learn new ways: how to make beds without bedsteads, wash without proper soap, keep food without a cellar. And she was much concerned about their clothing, badly worn during the journey; some garments were completely worn out, all were soiled, all must be darned and patched, mended and washed. Her bridal quilt had fared ill in the hold of the *Charlotta*, it was spotted and torn and would never be the same;

178

Kristina took this very hard. The working clothes for every member of the family needed attention, they must last a long time; she must be careful of every single garment, as she thought it might be a long time before new things could be obtained to cover their bodies.

Their soft-soap jar from Sweden was empty, and Kristina could wash nothing clean. Karl Oskar tried to help her: he boiled a mixture of rabbit fat and ashes, he thought this might be strong enough to eat away the dirt. And most of the dirt did wash away in the soap he had invented.

Kristina's greatest concern was to keep dirt and vermin away, to keep grownups and children clean. During their journey cleanliness had been neglected, and this had troubled her. One evening as she sat outside the shanty and watched Karl Oskar and Robert, who busied themselves stacking firewood, the thought came to her that she should cut the hair of her unkempt menfolk; they looked uncivilized, bringing shame to all Sweden, should anyone happen to see them.

She went inside and fetched her wool shears: "Come here! Your heads need attention!"

"You—a woman—you can't cut men's hair!" exclaimed Robert scornfully.

"I used to shear the sheep at home."

"Hmm," grunted Karl Oskar. He took off his cap and sat down on the chopping block. "Better begin with the old ram, then."

"When I shear frisky rams I usually tie their legs. Shall I do the same with you?"

Kristina's wool shears mowed mercilessly through Karl Oskar's thick locks, which fell from his head and gathered in piles on the ground. She guessed he gave at least a pound of wool.

Karl Oskar hardly recognized his own head as he looked in a piece of mirror-glass; his hair was cut in steps, marking each shear bite, just the way sheep looked after the shearing. But he was well pleased to be rid of the thick mat of hair which had been uncomfortable in the heat.

Robert sorely felt the degradation of having his hair cut by a woman. But he insisted that Kristina cut his hair as short as she possibly could; this would save his scalp from the knives of the Indians. Samuel Nöjd, the pelt man in Taylors Falls, had related how some of his companions a few years earlier had been scalped by the savages; only one man in the group had escaped, and this because he was completely bald; the Indians thought he had already been scalped.

Robert's hair was cut according to his instructions, and his head looked something like a scraped and scalded hog; this would undoubtedly make the Indians believe he had no scalp. But he would not be secure for long, his hair soon would grow out again.

Kristina also cut Johan's and Harald's hair quite short, but this was less from fear of Indians than of head lice, which were thus discouraged from building their nests.

179

The children had improved so much since the journey's end, she was happy to see. Their little bodies and limbs were now quite firm, their eyes clear, and their pale cheeks had bloomed since arriving here. They spent most of their time in the open. Food at the moment was fresh and plentiful; wild fruit and berries grew in abundance near the shanty. The family fare had lately changed fundamentally: they had fresh meat at every meal, fish or game which they seldom had enjoyed in Sweden, except on rare occasions. The countryside abounded with rabbits, which supplied most of the meat, as well as fat for many uses. Robert learned to catch them by hand; he ran after the fat animals until they tired and crouched, when he grabbed them. In this way he saved powder and shot for larger game. Ducks and wild geese kept to the lake and could only be obtained through shooting; but it was child's play to catch fish in Lake Ki-Chi-Saga, where life bubbled below the surface. They would put a pot over the fire, go down to the lake, and return with the fish before the water was boiling. They caught pike and perch, but these were the only fish they recognized. The pike had black backs with yellow stripes, and a narrower body than those at home. The perch had enormous jaws and were less tasty than the Swedish variety. Among the unfamiliar fish suitable for food was one called whitefish, delicious either boiled or fried. Whitefish resembled roach in color, but had longish bodies like pike. The catfish was ugly, with long whiskers, and purred like a cat when pulled out of water. A short, fat fish, the color of perch but with blood-red eyes, was called bass, Anders Månsson told them.

One morning at daybreak as Karl Oskar stepped out of the shanty, his eyes fell on an unusually large stag with immense antlers drinking from the lake less than fifty yards from him. He picked up his gun—always near by and loaded with a bullet—and fired at the buck. The animal fell where it stood, shot through the heart. The fallen stag with the multipronged antlers was heavy, as much as Karl Oskar could handle by himself, but he managed to hang his prey by the hind legs to a pole between two trees. He skinned and drew the animal before Kristina was up; when she came out to prepare the morning meal, Karl Oskar surprised her by pointing to his morning kill—she had not even heard the shot! He cut a few slices from the carcass, which she fried for their breakfast.

The weather was still warm, and meat would not keep long; if only they had had vessels to salt it in, they could have had meat for the whole winter.

At Lake Ki-Chi-Saga there was little concern about meat at this time of year. But bread they must use sparingly. They had paid dearly for the flour in Taylors Falls. Kristina herself cut the loaf and divided the slices at each meal: the menfolk doing the heavy work rated two slices each, while she and the children had to be satisfied with one slice apiece. This made eight slices to a meal and left little of a loaf. The flour in the barrel shrank with alarming speed; here it was easier to find meat for the bread than bread for the meat.

Anders Månsson had given them a bushel of potatoes, and they had bespoken a barrel for their winter supply. Butter, cheese, and eggs they must do without, since they had no cows or chickens. And milk! As yet they had no milk. Always, it seemed, they missed the milk. The children often pleaded for it, for sweet milk, as they had during the long journey.

Kristina looked out over the vast, grassy meadow: there grew fodder for thirty cows! But they owned not one. If she had only one—one lone cow to milk mornings and evenings! In Sweden they had owned cows but were often short of fodder—here they had fodder but no cows. Why must this be so? And how could her children survive the winter in good health without milk?

Why hadn't Karl Oskar thought about this? He was the one who managed and decided for all of them. She spoke to him: "You must get a cow, to give us milk for the winter."

To her surprise, he didn't answer at once; he turned away, embarrassed.

"Why haven't you bought one already?"

"Kristina—I should have told you before. I am sorry. . . ."

He looked pained, as though pressed to admit something shameful. He looked away from her and spoke with obvious effort: "We have nothing to buy a cow with."

It wasn't easy for him, but now he had managed to say it; he should have told her before, since she would have to know sooner or later.

"Nothing to buy it with! Are things as bad for us as that?"

"Most of our money is already gone."

And he explained to her: When they arrived in Taylors Falls he had had ninety silver dollars in his belt. Ten dollars he had had to give the greedy wolves who freighted their goods from Stillwater; besides the barrel of flour and other foodstuff, he had bought a load of boards, some nails, a felling ax, and a few essentials for the building; these supplies had cost more than fifty dollars; now he had only thirty-eight dollars and a few cents left in his purse. Yes, they had had great expenses, everything they had bought was unchristian dear; and yet, Anders Månsson had not requested any payment for either their lodging with him or the loan of the oxen. He must repay him by doing favors in return, by and by. Yes, the money had gone awfully fast. But he had bought only essentials, things they couldn't do without.

It had originally been his intention to buy both oxen and cows as soon as they arrived. But he hadn't known the price of cattle; a good cow cost thirty dollars, almost as much as they had left. And he still had to buy a few essentials for the house-building if they expected to have shelter for the winter. And next spring he would have to buy seed grain. He

181

must lay aside money for the seed. If they had nothing to plant next spring, all their troubles in emigrating would have been in vain.

That was how things were with them. They had already spent so much that a cow was out of the question; and yet, he had been as careful as he could with his outlays.

"Have I bought anything unimportant, Kristina?"

"No—I can't say that you have. But a cow that gives milk is as important as anything else."

"Not as important as the house!"

"But a whole, long, milkless winter, Karl Oskar! How can the children live through the winter without a drop of milk?"

And she added: The children had lately gained in weight and strength, but without milk, there might be nothing left of their little bodies by spring. She had heard him say many times that above all they must keep healthy through the winter. To do this, they needed a cow. They had been poor at home, but they had always had a drop of milk for the children, all year round.

Karl Oskar repeated: First of all they must build a house; they could get along without a cow, but not without a house. If the children were given other food they would survive the winter without milk, but if they were forced to live in the shanty, they would freeze to death. And she mustn't forget that they awaited yet another tender life—that one, too, would need a warm shelter, that new life must be saved through the winter. They couldn't live in a shed with a newborn baby through the winter; they couldn't live in this hovel where daylight shone through the cracks, where it would be as cold inside as outside.

He was right; but she insisted that she too was right. They must save their lives, and the question was how best to do this. Timbered walls gave protection against cold, milk against hunger and illness. They needed the cow as well as the house, she was not going to give in on this point —they must have the indispensable cow. Couldn't he at least look about for one? Now that they had land, mightn't they be allowed some delay in payment, wouldn't people trust them?

He answered, as yet they had no paper on their claim; an impoverished squatter was not trusted for anything out here. The Scot in Taylors Falls wouldn't give him credit for a penny's worth. Moreover, how could they expect to be trusted, strangers as they were? No one knew what sort of people they were. Here in America a newcomer must show that he could help himself, before he could expect help from others.

Kristina thought this sounded uncharitable; a person unable to help himself needed help above all others.

"Isn't there *any* way we could get a cow?"

"It looks bad. I can't buy without money."

But she had made up her mind to have her own way, that he understood. She said, as a rule he made the decisions alone, but there were

182

times when he must listen to her. He had persuaded her to emigrate.—
She had never before reminded him of that, but he often reminded himself of it and felt the responsibility he had assumed. If she had wanted
to, she could have said: You never told me we would be without milk
out here! You never mentioned in advance that we must be without a
cow. Had you mentioned that fact the time you persuaded me, then perhaps I mightn't be here now.

Karl Oskar thought long over her words about the children and the
milkless winter. It could be a question of life or death. He handled their
money, he was the one who had to choose—and the choice stood between
two indispensables; there was no choice. How could he decide—when life
or death might depend on his decision?

—3—

ROBERT WAS NOT very deft with his hands, he had never learned anything
about carpentry, he had no feeling for working with wood. Karl Oskar
could rely on him for only the simplest chores. Together they had felled
the timbers and prepared the logs, and after this was finished Karl Oskar
told his brother to grub hoe the meadow. His feeling was that the two
of them, as brothers, ought to stick together, that Robert should remain
and help him until he was of age and could take a claim for himself;
he would pay his brother for this as soon as he could. Robert was now
eighteen, in a few years he could choose his own farm from the thousands
of acres that lay here waiting on the shores of Lake Ki-Chi-Saga.

"I'll never take land!" exclaimed Robert with conviction.

"What do you mean? Wouldn't you like to be on your own?"

"Yes! That is exactly what I want! Here in America everyone decides
for himself. That's why I wanted to come here."

Karl Oskar stared at his brother in surprise: Didn't Robert want to be
the owner of one hundred and sixty acres of this good earth? Was he so
shiftless that he wouldn't claim all the land he could on such favorable
conditions?

"If you don't take land before it's claimed, you'll regret it," Karl Oskar
insisted.

"Maybe. But I don't think so."

And Robert thought to himself as he said this: Karl Oskar was not
his guardian, he had never promised to serve as farm hand for his brother
here in America; he had paid for his emigration with his own inheritance,
which Karl Oskar had kept; he didn't owe his brother anything, he was
not bound to him in any way.

Yet here his brother put a hoe in his hand and asked him to break
land! He felt almost as though he were back home again, in his old
farm-hand service; he had cleared land many long days, back in Sweden

183

—now it was the same here. The tools he had thrown away in Sweden he had had to pick up again. And the American grub hoe Karl Oskar had bought was much heavier than the one at home. What advantage had there been in his emigration if everything was to be the same as before? To stoop all day long until his back ached in the evenings—this he had done enough of in Sweden. He had not emigrated to America in order to hoe.

Robert could not understand his brother's joy in squatting on a piece of land that required so much labor—a patch to plow, seed, and harvest, year after year, as long as he was able, all his life. A patch of soil he could never get rid of. Robert only wanted to do the kind of work that would liberate him from work. Only the rich man had no master, only the rich were free to do as they pleased; and no one would grow rich from hoeing the earth, even if he hoed to the end of eternity.

Never, never would Robert become a squatter. While he hoed for his brother he kept listening to his left ear: through that ear the Atlantic Ocean had called to him, and he had listened to the call and crossed the ocean. He had come here to get away from cruel masters, from the servant law, from drudgery with hoe and spade—and now he turned the clods and lived the same life he had fled from. Again he heard the humming call in his ear: *Come! Don't stay here!*

In New York Harbor he had seen a ship with a red banner, its soft-sounding girl-name beckoning him: *Angelica.* In his ear he could now hear that name again, the name of the speedy, copper-plated ship with her singing and dancing passengers. Why hadn't he stepped on board and joined them? Why hadn't he gone with the *Angelica?*

In the New World there were other fields than farmers' fields. And Robert listened so intently to his own ear that he didn't hear when Karl Oskar spoke to him; his brother had to repeat his words.

"Have you lost your hearing?"

"No. But I only hear in English."

The fact was that Robert would not admit his hearing was bad. He now explained to Karl Oskar that he tried to close his ears to the Swedish language, he wished he could listen to English only; in that way he would learn the language sooner.

Robert also wished to consult a doctor about his deafness, but he must wait until he could speak English fluently in order to explain the nature of his ear illness. In the language book there was not a single word about bad hearing under the heading: *Conversation with a Physician.* There was instruction about what to say when seeking a doctor for malaria: *I shiver and my head aches. I have vomited the whole night.* Another sentence concerned immigrants with sprained ankles; there was also one for those with irregular voiding, and lastly one for people who didn't know what was the matter with them, since they were sick in every way. For immigrants with other ailments there was no help to be found in the book; it was of no use to one who must say: *I don't hear well with my left ear.*

And a youth of barely eighteen would feel ashamed to go to a doctor and say: "My hearing is getting bad." At the height of his youth to admit that he was hard of hearing, like an old man of eighty!

He still hoped that the climate of North America would heal his ear. This he knew, however: the weather in Minnesota Territory was so far of little help. His ear alone told him so; in fact, it told him to leave! He must travel farther, farther west.

There were other fields in this new land where he now labored with his grub hoe—there were gold fields in the New World.

Why must he hoe turf here, when in another place he could hoe gold? What pleasure could he get from crops that might grow here? Why hadn't he sought the fields where a crop of gold could be harvested? A gold harvester need not work in the earth year after year. He would get rich from one single crop—he would become free.

And again and again Robert heard a song that had remained in his ear, a song he had heard sung in a foreign language by the deck hands on the Mississippi steamer while darkness fell over the broad river—a song about the winds of the earth and the waves of the sea. It was the song of promised freedom his ear had sung to him, long ago in Sweden; then the ocean's roar in his ear had called him to cross the sea: *Come!*

This time too he must obey that call.

## —4—

Now IN LATE SEPTEMBER the weather was cooler. The air no longer felt oppressive, it was easier to breathe. It was fine working weather.

But climatic changes were violent and sudden; without any warning a thunderstorm would blow up, booming and shaking the earth. The bolts blinded one's eyes, the rain fell, lashing the face like a whip, pouring from the heavens in barrelfuls; in no time at all, every hole and hollow would be filled with water, while the stream rose over its banks in its rush toward the lake. And when the wind blew, it swept across the ground as mercilessly as a giant broom with its handle in the heavens. No weather in America was just right; all was immoderate.

As autumn progressed the leaves of the trees changed color, making the forest seem more beautiful than ever. There stood the red mountain ash, surrounded by brown walnut trees, the green aspens among the golden-yellow lindens. The oak—the master tree of the forest—still kept its leaves green, as did the aspen and the poplar. Here grew white oak, black oak, red oak, and now they could recognize the different types. The white oak grew in Sweden also, its leaves turned brown in fall. The leaves of the other oaks now took on a dark-red sheen resembling blossoms; the settlers said that it looked as though these oaks bloomed in autumn.

The meadow grass remained as fresh and green as before. It bothered Karl Oskar that this splendid fodder would wither away to no use. He said to Kristina, if only they could send home a few loads to the poor cow his parents kept in Korpamoen!

It had been impressed upon him ever since childhood that the growth of the earth must be tended and gathered. Once, as a small boy, he had stepped on the head of a rye sheaf; his father had then unbuttoned his pants and switched him with a handful of birch twigs: he must learn to respect the earth's growth.

Now he made a handle for the scythe blade he had brought from Sweden and cut the grass on the plot he intended to hoe. Here he could mow as wide a sweep as his arms could reach, here he need not rake the straws together in swaths, the hay fell in one long thick swath behind him. In a few side swings, he had enough for one feeding of a full-grown cow; in a day, he could gather enough fodder to feed a cow through the winter. In Korpamoen, he had struggled with the hay harvest a whole month, picking the short thin blades from between the stones with the point of his scythe. He had labored from sunup to sundown, mowed and sharpened and cut against stones—yet he had gathered such a small amount of hay that he had been forced to half-starve his cattle.

As yet he had no cattle to feed, but he couldn't help saving some of this good fodder. It might be of some use. And he made a row of hay-stacks along the shore. It was good hay weather; what he cut one day, he turned the next, and stacked the third day. Stacked hay was not as good as barn hay, and he decided to build a shed later in the fall after the house was ready.

His work with the scythe over this even ground was a joy, and every day he felt more and more remorseful over the six years he had wasted on his stone acres in Korpamoen. He had left that farm poorer than when he took over; it had gone backward instead of ahead for him; he had put in thousands of days of futile labor on the paternal home: these were lost years. He had wasted his youthful strength in the land where he was born, and he realized that had he instead spent those six years of labor in this country, he would by now have been a well-to-do farmer.

However, at twenty-seven he still had his manhood years ahead of him, and his manhood strength he would give to the new country. Here he would earn something in return; here he worked with a greater zest than at home, because the reward was greater. He felt his ability to work had increased since settling here, his physical strength had grown. The very sight of the fertile land stimulated him and egged him on to work. Also, he enjoyed a sense of freedom that increased his endeavor to such a degree that he was surprised at himself when evening came

186

and he saw all he had done during the course of one single day: that much he had never managed in one day in Sweden!

However great the inconveniences out here, he felt vastly happier than he had in the old place. Here no one ruled him, no officials insisted that he bow to them, no one demanded that he obediently and humbly follow a given path, no one interfered with his doings, no one advised him, no one rebuked him for refusing advice. He had seen no one in authority, nobody had come to tell him what he must do; here he had met not a single person to whom he must defer; he was his own minister and sheriff and master.

At home, people struggled to get ahead of each other until they were full of evil wounds that never would heal; their minds grew morbid, festering boils corroded their souls; they went about bloated by grudges and jealousy. Most of them were afraid, bowing in cowardice to the great lords who sat on high and ruled as they saw fit. No one dared decide for himself, no one dared walk upright; it was too much of an effort, their backs were too weak. They dared not be free, were incapable of freedom. That required courage, entailed responsibility and worry as well; anyone trying to decide for himself in the old country was derided, mocked, slandered, pushed out. For the Swedish people could not endure someone who attempted what the rest of them dared not do, or were incapable of.

Here no one cared what he did, nor need he care what others did. Here he could move as he pleased, with his body and with his soul. Nowhere could he be freer than here. Here a farmer ruled himself— though in return, a demand was put on him that might scare many away: he must take care of himself—he must survive with only the help of his hands.

But a man unable to improve his situation, with such generous freedom, such fertile soil—such a man was good for nothing in the world.

# XVI

## At Home on Lake Ki-Chi-Saga

THE HOMESTEADER'S AX cut its way through the land—through trunk and timber, through beam and board, through shingle and shake, through branch and bramble. Clearing, splitting, shaping, it cut its way. There was the felling ax with the long handle and the thin blade, eating its way through the heart of the tree, leaving the stump heads even and smooth. There was the dressing ax with the short handle and the broad blade, shaving trunks and timbers while the chips flew in all directions; there was the splitting ax with the heavy hammer and the thick blade, forcing its blunt nose into the wood, splitting logs into planks and scantlings.

187

Then there was the short, light, hand ax, clearing the thickets, brambles, and bushes. Narrow axes and broad, thin and thick, light and heavy. From early morning to late evening the echo of the axes sounded over the shores of Lake Ki-Chi-Saga—a new sound, the sound of peaceful builders in the wilderness.

With the ax as foremost tool—with the ax first, with the ax last—the new home was raised.

Karl Oskar and Kristina had chosen the site for their log house among some large sugar maples at the edge of the forest on the upper meadow, the distance of a long gunshot from the lake shore. Here their home would be protected by the forest on three sides, while the fourth overlooked the bay of the lake. Their house was to be twenty feet long and twelve feet wide, and placed the same way as farmhouses in Sweden: the gables to east and west, the long sides to north and south. The back of the house would then be toward the forest and the cold north winds, while the front opened on the lake and the warm south sun.

Karl Oskar had promised to help Danjel and Jonas Petter, and they in turn would help him raise his house the second week in October. The green, peeled logs were too heavy for two men to handle; three or four would be needed. But Karl Oskar alone prepared all the timbers and laid a footing for his house. For the foundation, he selected the thickest pines he had cut, and with the aid of Anders Månsson's oxen, dragged the clumsy logs to the building site. For floor boards he used young linden trees which he split in two, to be laid with the flat side upward. He hewed and smoothed the edges of these to make them fit as tight as possible, in order to avoid big cracks in the floor. For roof boards he cut straight elms—there were enough trees to choose from in the forest, and he selected what he thought most suitable for each need. Oak logs would have lasted longer for house timbers, but they were hard to work with, and pine would last long enough. He had no intention of living in this house of peeled logs for all eternity.

He cut sod for the roofing—sod was used for roofing at home in Småland, and it took less time than to split shakes. Kristina said she was afraid the sod might not withstand the violent rains here—the earth might blow away in the merciless winds. Karl Oskar replied that he would put on shakes next summer if the roof did not withstand the weather. She must not worry, he would see to it that they did not sleep under a leaking roof.

He had to buy odds and ends for the building and carry them on his back from Taylors Falls. He bought everything in Mr. Abbott's store, except sash, which he ordered from Stillwater. Everything of iron was absurdly expensive; he paid a full dollar for a pair of hinges for the door. And the price of nails was equally high. But wood could substitute for iron in many instances, and he made pegs of ash—in Sweden used for rake teeth and handle wedges—to take the place of nails. Without cash, he was forced to be inventive. Each time he had to buy something he searched his mind: Couldn't he make it with his own hands?

October—the almanac's slaughter month—had arrived, but the only slaughter which took place at Lake Ki-Chi-Saga was the occasional killing of rabbits and deer. The days sped by, the weeks flew, only one month remained of the autumnal season of grace, with its mild weather, permitting them to live in the shanty. Winter was fast approaching, and Karl Oskar had promised his wife their new log house would be ready to move into in good time before her childbed.

The third week in November, Kristina's forty weeks would be up, if she had counted aright. It seemed to her as though this pregnancy had lasted longer than any of the previous ones; she had been through so much during this tedious year, her twenty-fifth. She had gone through the usual period of expectancy during a hard journey, carrying the child within her from Sweden to the new land. Perhaps this was why she felt the period had been longer this time than any of the others. And now she was as big as the time she had carried the twins; she wondered if she would again give birth to two lives. As things were with them at the moment, twins would be inconvenient; she had not even had time to prepare swaddling clothes for one baby.

Her movements became more cumbersome every day, every day she felt heavier. She could walk only short distances; her chores were confined to the shanty and its immediate vicinity. But she never let her children entirely out of sight. At home she had let them run free, but here she never knew what kind of snakes might hide in the thick, tall grass; what kind of biting, stinging, flying creatures infested the air. All around the cabin she saw hordes of creeping, crawling little animals she had never found at home, and as yet she could not distinguish between the dangerous ones and the harmless. In the meadow, the men had killed snakes with yellow and silver-gray stripes; these vipers lifted their egg-shaped heads from the ground, open mouthed, their blood-red stingers protruding exactly like those of the poisonous snakes at home. She tried to keep the children where the grass had been mowed and where they could watch where they stepped. A few times the children had been frightened by a gray, furry animal the size of a dog, with thick legs and a short tail, which they thought was a lynx or small wolf. Large, fat, gray-brown squirrels called gophers played around the shanty in great numbers, their heads sticking up everywhere in the grass; one could hardly avoid stepping on them, and they looked as if they might bite; they frightened the children, but they were harmless. There were flying squirrels, too, with skin stretched between their legs. They flew about in the trees, waving their long tails like sails. They came and ate out of one's hand, like tame animals; the children liked them.

The little creature who made the persistent screeching sound had at last been discovered, and they had been told its name—cricket. It was

189

gray-brown, smaller than a grasshopper, and difficult to see on the ground; its wings were so small it couldn't fly but jumped about like a grasshopper. This small thing screeched loudly all night through, and because of its noise they called it "the screechhopper." If a cricket happened to get into the shanty at night, Kristina had to find it and kill it before she could get a wink's sleep.

However small an animal might be in America, it always caused trouble. But the rodents, devouring Kristina's food, were the greatest nuisance of all. Rats and ratlike vermin were everywhere, running in and out of their holes, hiding underground. Kristina found it did little good to hide food in a hole in the ground, she still found rat dirt in it, and her heart ached when she had to throw away rat-eaten pieces of food. If only they could get hold of a cat to catch the rats. But Karl Oskar had no idea where they might find one. In Taylors Falls, he had seen only one cat; probably cats were as expensive as other animals; perhaps a cat would cost five dollars, like a hen. It would be a long time before they would have all the domestic animals they needed.

One day Johan came rushing into the shanty holding tight in his arms a small, black-furred animal: "Look Mother! I've found a cat!"

The boy held out the animal toward Kristina. The long-haired creature had a white streak along its back, and it was the size of a common cat.

"Is it a wildcat?" Kristina asked.

The little furry beast fretted and sputtered, Johan had great difficulty holding it. He said he had found it in a hole outside the cottage.

"You wanted a cat, Mother! But we have no milk for it."

His prey stared at him, its eyes glittering with fury.

"Be careful! He might scratch you!" Then Kristina sniffed the air: a horrible smell overwhelmed her.

"Have you done something in your pants, boy?"

"No!"

"Then you must have stepped in something."

She inspected the clothing and shoes of the boy but could see nothing to explain the smell.

"Is it the cat?"

"No, he isn't dirty either."

And she could see that its coat was clean. Johan looked at the paws, but these too were clean.

"No, he hasn't stepped in anything either."

Kristina put her nose to the little animal. Such a disgusting smell overcame her that she jumped backward, almost suffocating. The cat was alive, yet it smelled as if it had been dead a long time. She held her nostrils with her thumb and forefinger, crying: "Throw the beast out!"

"But it's a cat!" Johan wailed.

"Throw it out this minute!"

"But he will catch the rats. . . ."

She grabbed the boy by the arms and pushed him and his pet out through the door. Johan loosened his hold, and the animal jumped to the ground and disappeared around the corner of the shanty.

Johan looked at his empty hands and began to cry; the beautiful cat with a white stripe on its back and tail, he had caught it for his mother and now it was gone and he couldn't catch it again.

Kristina was rid of the nasty-smelling animal, but the evil stench remained in the hut. And little Johan smelled as bad as the cat! She told him to stay outside until the smell was gone.

When Karl Oskar came home he stopped in the door, sniffing: "What smells so bad in here?"

"Johan dragged in some creature."

She described the animal, and guessed it must be a wildcat.

"Disgusting the way cats smell in America!" she said. "You can't have them in the house here."

"It must have been a baby skunk," Karl Oskar said. "Their piss stinks, I have heard. I guess it pissed on him."

And he pinched the boy on the ear: hadn't he told him not to touch any animals or try to catch them? He must leave them alone, big or little, however tame they seemed.

He turned to Kristina: "Now we have to wash the child's clothes or we'll never get rid of the stink."

Kristina undressed the boy to his bare skin. Then she wrapped him in one of his father's coats, which hung all the way to the ground and made him stumble when he walked. His own clothes were boiled in ash lye. They had to boil them a long time before the smell of skunk disappeared. But in the shanty the odor remained. The baby skunk had left behind him such a strong smell that for weeks it lingered; it drove the settlers outside, and for many days they ate in the open, near the fire where the food was prepared.

All this trouble had been caused by a little cat that was no cat at all. If the animals hereabouts didn't bite with their teeth or scratch with their claws, Kristina said, they smelled so bad that they drove people from their homes. They must all be doubly careful in the future.

Indeed, they must be on their guard about everything in North America.

—2—

IT WAS about one hour's walk from Lake Ki-Chi-Saga to the settlement of Danjel and Jonas Petter. When settling down, Danjel Andreasson had said he did not wish to live in a nameless place, nor in a place with a heathenish name. He had therefore named his home New Kärragärde, after the old family farm in Sweden, and it was his belief that through the revival of this name his old family homestead would blossom to new

191

life in the New World. The little lake near his home he called Lake Gennesaret, a reminder of the Holy Land; the shores of Lake Gennesaret in the Biblical land had once carried the imprint of Jesus' footsteps; the Lord had wandered about there, preaching the Gospel, and His disciples had enjoyed good fishing in its water. The lake near Danjel's house resembled the Biblical Gennesaret in that it was blessed with many fish. A brook emptying into the lake he called Chidron.

The men had many errands back and forth, and often walked the road between the two settlements, but the women seldom met after they had settled on different claims. It was dangerous for a woman to walk alone through the wilderness; besides, Kristina was unable to walk any distance at this time. Week after week passed and no one came. No callers arrived at the hut on Lake Ki-Chi-Saga. The young wife missed people, she looked for callers and awaited guests, without exactly knowing whom she looked for or might expect

One day Swedish Anna came to visit them; she accompanied Karl Oskar, who had been in Taylors Falls, and she stayed overnight. Kristina had met her only once—the woman from Östergötland was practically unknown to her, and yet she felt she had known her for years: someone had come to whom she could talk. Swedish Anna brought a coat she had made for little Harald; she was fond of children, she had had two of her own in Sweden, but they were both dead, she said. Kristina was touched to the bottom of her heart by the gift, and she wished her guest could have remained several days, even though she could offer her only a poor sleeping place in a shed. When Anna had left, Kristina thought how kind God had been in creating some people in such a way that they could speak the same language.

She missed her countrymen who now lived at a distance—and most of all, she found, she missed Ulrika. She wondered about this: she actually felt lonesome for the Glad One! How could this be? Now she realized she had enjoyed Ulrika's company. There was something stimulating about her, she was never downhearted; many times during the journey Kristina had felt Ulrika's presence as a help: she realized it now. And during the final weeks they had grown quite intimate, Ulrika had confided to her all she had had to go through in life, ever since that day when, as a four-year-old orphan, she had been sold at auction to the rich peasant of Alarum, called the King of Alarum. He had been known in the village as her kind, good foster father. When she was fourteen years old, he had raped her, and for years afterward, as often as he felt inclined. Each time she had received two pennies from the "King," but when she had saved enough for a daler, her foster mother had taken the money away from her, saying she had stolen it and ought to be put in prison.

And she *had* been put in prison: the honored and worthy farmer had taught her how to sell her body, she had become the parish whore, banished from church and Sacrament, and at last imprisoned for unlawful communion. But the King of Alarum—who had raped a child and used her for his aging body's lust—when he died, he had been given the grandest funeral ever seen in Ljuder Parish.

Kristina could remember how as a little girl she had been to the church when this funeral took place. The church had been filled to the last pew, people standing in the aisles, the organ had played long and feelingly, the coffin had been decked with the finest wreaths, and the dean himself had stood at the altar, lauding the dead one and extolling his good deeds in life. The memory of the "King" still was held in respect at home, and his tombstone was the tallest one in the whole churchyard.

Then the truth about him had been revealed to Kristina. And Ulrika said that she was only one of his victims, he had seduced and ruined many girls before they were of age. But the mighty ones could do whatever they wanted to in that hellhole, Sweden. Two of the jurors at her trial ought to have been in prison themselves, they had stolen money entrusted to them as guardians of orphans; and one owed her four daler for having committed what was known as whoring, not punishable in men. This she had told the judge and had pointed out that the law ought to be the same for all. But he gave her fourteen days extra on bread and water for having insulted the jury. And she had never received the four daler.

Ulrika was straightforward and said whatever came to her mind to whomsoever she met, even mighty lords. She could not help it, she was made that way. But in Sweden such honesty brought only misery; if you told the truth there, you were put in prison.

Having believed that justice ruled in her homeland, Kristina was deeply disturbed by Ulrika's confidence. How rash and unjust her condemnation of Ulrika had been! She had listened to what other women said about the Glad One. No woman had a right to judge Ulrika and hold her in contempt unless she herself had been sold at auction as a four-year-old, and raped at fourteen. Kristina felt she could no longer rebuke Ulrika for her adultery before coming to live with Danjel. Vanity and self-righteousness were as sinful as whoring, and she had committed these sins many times. But that day in the steam wagon, when she had shared her food with the onetime parish harlot and her daughter, then her eyes had been opened: she had approached Ulrika, and Ulrika had approached her. When at last she had accepted Ulrika—something she felt now she should have done from the very beginning—she had discovered that this so-called bad woman was honest and could be a good friend.

Ulrika had changed, too, since people had changed their behavior toward her. Here she was no longer the parish whore. Here she was honored and treated like other women. Kristina was still bothered by the ugly words Ulrika liked to use, but now she knew they belonged to her old way of talking. The ugliest names invented for parts of men's and women's

193

bodies, and for their conjugal acts, were part of the life she had led. The King of Alarum had taught them to her. But from Ulrika, Kristina learned that a person's way of speaking had nothing to do with that person's heart.

Now at Lake Ki-Chi-Saga, she discovered that she longed for Ulrika to come and visit her in her loneliness.

To the north lived the people who spoke her language, but in the other three directions there were no people of her own color. Their nearest neighbors were copper colored. The Indians had recently gathered in great numbers to make camp on one of the islands in Lake Ki-Chi-Saga, and every evening after dark she could see their fires. On that island now lived her nearest neighbors.

These Indians were said to be docile and peaceful, they would never commit atrocities against white people—but they were also said to be treacherous and unreliable, always watching their chance to scalp and kill the whites! Thus, the varying reports: They were kind, gave the settlers food, and helped them in need; they were bloodthirsty and cruel and blinded the eyes of their prisoners with spears before burning them in their campfires. They were as innocent as children, yet they murdered the settlers' wives and babies. How could a newcomer know which was the truth?

From time to time they could hear piercing, long-drawn-out yells from the Indian camp. Only wild beasts yelled like that. But these were not wolf howls, these were human sounds, and as such they were terrifying. These yells through the night would frighten the most courageous, and lying there in the shanty listening to them, the settlers were inclined to believe the evil things they had heard of the brown skins.

The immigrants on Lake Ki-Chi-Saga had met and escaped so many dangers on their journey that they could scarcely imagine any worse in store for them. Yet now it seemed that their settling here might be as calamitous as their journey. The wild, heathenish people in the neighborhood filled them with insecurity.

Almost every day Karl Oskar met Indians in the forest, but they had not spoken to him or annoyed him; they only seemed curious, stopping and staring at him. He guessed the Indians were inquisitive. One day, some of their women came to look at the shanty. They carried children in pouches on their backs. One old woman looked hideous, with a face like gray-brown, cracked clay; the mosquitoes hung in droves on her wrinkled face. All the women were thin and looked wretched. Kristina felt sorry for them and wondered if the Indian men tortured them. Comparing her situation with theirs, she felt fortunate in her poverty. These poor creatures lived in the lowliest hovels, under matting hung on a few raised poles; next to their pitiable shelters, her own hut was like a castle. She did not understand how they could survive the winters in such dwellings.

Karl Oskar felt it unwise to mingle with the Indians in this vast wilderness, and he did not intend to get too close to them. Probably they considered him an intruder. But he had not come here as a thief, he intended to obtain his land honestly from the government of the country, who in turn had bought it from the brown skins. The Indians were too lazy to cultivate the ground. The whites here called them lazy men. And since they did not wish to till the land themselves, they could hardly object if others came and did so. The tiller of the soil had a right to it above all others; it would be a cruel injustice to hungry people if this fertile land—capable of feeding so many—should be allowed to lie fallow, producing only wild grass.

In the end, the family decided, all they heard of the heathens indicated that they could not be trusted. Though now they left the settlers in peace, there was no assurance of future safety. Karl Oskar always carried his gun when he went into the forest, and he kept it at hand when working near the shanty.

The building of Danjel's house had begun, and now Karl Oskar went there to help, as Danjel would help him in return. One day while he was away, and Kristina was alone in the shanty, she suddenly was frightened into immobility: a face had appeared in the opening at the back of the shanty! At first she didn't realize it was a human face: it looked like a furry animal skin. She saw a black, thick, stringy mat of hair, a dark oily skin splotched with red streaks. But when she discovered something moving under the mat of hair—a pair of coal-black eyes peering at her—then she realized it was a human face looking in through the opening. Human eyes were looking at her. She fled outside with such a loud outcry that she frightened herself.

Robert heard her, in spite of his deafness, and came running from the clearing. As they looked through the shanty door, the face in the opening disappeared. Turning around, they saw an Indian running into the woods.

That evening, when Kristina told Karl Oskar about the Indian, he said he would send Robert to work on Danjel's house tomorrow. Now that he knew the savages were sneaking about their house, he wanted to stay close by; he dared not leave his family alone with the Indian camp so near.

It could be that the savages had no evil intentions, that they were only curious about the strangers who had moved in on their land—though no one could know for sure what they had in mind. But as Kristina listened to the outlandish yells from the camp on the island, she was filled with a deep sense of compassion. The Indians frightened her, but they were, after all, unchristian, they did not know their Creator, they did not know the difference between good and evil, they lived in darkness, according to their own limited knowledge—who could blame the poor creatures for anything? She herself could not condemn them. She was only grateful she had not been born one of them.

Here among the savages she could only trust to God's protection.

195

UNEXPECTEDLY they had a change in the weather. One morning they awakened in their hut shivering—frozen through and through by a cold wind. An icy northwester was sweeping through their shanty, they felt as though the walls had fallen down during the night, as if they were lying in the open. The merciless wind seemed to strip them naked, it penetrated their thick woolen clothing, pinched their skin until it hurt, clawed with sharp talons, and blew right into their bodies.

When they looked out through the door at this weather, it seemed as if the crust of the earth might blow away. The grass lay flat to the ground like water-combed hair on a head. At the edge of the forest great trees were blown over, the exposed roots stretching heavenward like so many arms. All the haystacks in the meadow had blown over. They wondered that their little shanty still stood.

Now they could not use their fireplace, which lay to windward of the storm; but they managed to make a fire on the lee side of an enormous oak trunk. When they walked against the wind, they had to stoop in order to move. The unrelenting northwester swept away anything not tied to the earth.

Kristina said that none among them had ever known what a wind was, until they came to North America.

The children were blue-red from the cold; Lill-Märta and Harald coughed, and the noses of all three were running. Kristina put an extra pair of woolen stockings on each of them and wrapped them in woolen garments; she herself bundled up as much as she could, until she felt wide as a barrel; she was now in her last month. But clothes did not help against this ferocious wind, big and little shivered and shook; nothing helped. In the daytime they could get some warmth from the fire behind the oak, but how were they to keep warm inside the shanty during the nights if this weather continued?

"Has the winter come so soon?" Kristina wondered.

"It couldn't come so suddenly," Karl Oskar said anxiously. "It would be too bad for us—the house not yet ready. . . ."

They had heard of the unexpected changes in temperature hereabouts, and that the thermometer could fall forty degrees in one minute (but American degrees were said to be shorter than Swedish ones). Now the sudden cold and wind had come upon them while the timbers for the house still lay and waited. The men would come as soon as they had put the roof on Danjel's house. It was expected to be ready in a week or so. Now Karl Oskar tightened the shanty as best he could; he nailed extra pieces of boards to the windward side and closed all cracks and holes with moss and wet clay. Inside, he laid a ring of stones for a fireplace and cut a hole in the roof for the smoke; now they could heat their hut. During the second night they were able to keep a fire alive, and they covered themselves with every piece of clothing they had, but the cold still penetrated—they froze miserably. The children whined and whimpered in their sleep like kittens. Many times during the night Kristina rose and put a kettle on the fire and boiled a meat soup, which they drank to warm their insides—though nothing could help their outsides.

In the morning the hurricane died down a little, but toward evening it increased again, with heavy showers of hail. Inch-long pieces of ice, hard as stones, fell and remained in drifts on the ground. But on the third morning the wind abated, and by evening the storm had spent itself.

After the three days' frightful weather the sun warmed them again. The hail drifts melted away, the air was so still that not the smallest leaf moved, and the grass that had been combed flat rose again. Mild, late-fall weather reigned once more.

But the new settlers in the shanty on Lake Ki-Chi-Saga had experienced the touch of the blizzard on their bodies, they felt as if they had been saved from death. The winter had discharged a warning shot to show what miserable shelter they had against the cold north winds; to survive, they would need a tighter, better house, and soon.

And early one Monday morning their helpers arrived and began to raise the house. They were three carpenters—Karl Oskar, Danjel, and Jonas Petter—with two helpers, Robert and Arvid. Now there were rushed days for Kristina, who must prepare food for all of them over a fire in the open, while she kept an eye on the children. But the break in their loneliness was welcome, now there was life on their place with the menfolk building, and new strength came into her as she saw their house rise on the foundation timbers. Back there, under the great sugar maples, the walls of their new home grew, higher for each meal she prepared for the builders. Often she walked back to watch them and felt as if she herself were participating in the building.

The house was to be eight feet high at the eaves. The timbers were roughhewn, and now the men smoothed the upper and under sides of the logs to make them lie close together. Karl Oskar would later fill the cracks with moss, which he intended to cover with a mixture of clay and sand. The timberman's most complicated task was the fitting of the logs together at each corner. "When a corner you can lay, you get a timberman's pay" was an old saying at home, often quoted to a carpenter's helper. Karl Oskar had learned building from his father, but he did not feel he was a master; working now as a timberman, he was glad his house had only four corners.

The long, heavy logs were hoisted into place on the wall by the combined strength of all five men; each log was fastened to the underlying timber by means of thick pegs driven into the lower log and fitted into auger holes in the next one above. There was a racket all day long from

197

three ax hammers; three axes were busy, three timbermen timbered. And the sound of axes against wood was no languid, depressing sound, it was bold, fresh, stimulating—it was a promise, an assurance of security. Here something took place of lasting import—not for a day, or a year, but for future times; here a human abode was raised. And the echo from the timbermen's axes rang out over the forest in the clear autumn air, it was thrown from tree to tree—the axes cut and hammered, and the echo returned from the other side of the lake.

Jonas Petter was the master among the three timbermen; his ax corrected and finished where the others had begun. And in rhythm with his ax blows against the timbers, he sang "The Timberman's Song," which his father and grandfather before him had sung at house-building in the homeland, a song that had been sung through centuries when walls were raised for Swedish peasant houses, a song always sung to the music of ax and hammer—a song stimulating to the timberman, suitable for singing at his work, and now for the first time sung in Minnesota Territory:

> What's your daughter doing tonight?
> What's your daughter doing tonight?
> What's your timberman's daughter doing tonight?
> Timberrim, timberram, timberammaram—
> What's your daughter doing tonight?
>
> Your daughter is making a bed,
> Your daughter is making a bed,
> Your daughter is making a timberman's bed—
> Timberrim, timberram, timberammaram—
> Your daughter is making a bed.
>
> Who shall sleep in your daughter's bed?
> Who shall sleep in your daughter's bed?
> Who shall sleep in your daughter's timberman's bed?
> Timberrim, timberram, timberammaram—
> Who shall sleep in your daughter's bed?
>
> I and your daughter, that's who
> I and your daughter, that's who
> I and your timberman's daughter that's who. . . .

"The Timberman's Song" was fully ten verses long; Jonas Petter knew only three verses and part of the fourth; his father had sung the song to him when they worked as timbermen together, and he had managed to sing it from beginning to end while he set one log in place. The verses Jonas Petter had forgotten described the occupation in the timberman's bed; but he couldn't for the life of him remember how it went, except that in the timberman's bed was made a timberman's tyke, by a timberman's "stud." But, asked Jonas Petter, could there be anything easier

198

than to be a stud, when you had the bed and the woman? He thought it might be more difficult not to.

The three men timbered up the house walls in five days, and on the sixth they put on the rafters and laid the roofing. Robert and Arvid handed up the turf, each piece fastened to a long pole, and the three men laid the sod over a layer of bark. So the house was ready with four walls and a roof.

The timbermen's work was done, a house had been built in the same number of days as God had required in the beginning for the Creation. The seventh day arrived, and the almanac indicated it was a Sunday; and the timbermen kept the Sabbath and rested on the seventh day, while they inspected their handiwork; they found it good, strong, suitable for human habitation. A new home had been built, a solid, sturdy log house on secure footing, not to be felled by wrestling winds. It had been built to stand, by men who had built houses for farmers in Sweden, who had timbered the way their forebears had timbered through the centuries. A new house, of ancient construction, was built in a new land, on the shore of Lake Ki-Chi-Saga. His helpers had done their part, but the long, tedious work of completion remained for Karl Oskar before they could move in. First he laid the flooring; he placed the split linden trunks with the flat side up and fastened them to the joist logs with a wooden peg in each end. The planks were smooth hewn, and the floor turned out as even as it could be from hand-hewn boards. Through the front wall he cut a hole for a door, three feet wide and six and a half feet high; he wanted to be able to step over his threshold into his new home in America without having to bend his neck. He made the door of oak, heavy and clumsy as a church door; it would be a chore for the smaller children to open. He hung it by the strong, expensive hinges— the ones that had cost a whole dollar. Then he made a simple wooden latch for the outside, but on the inside he fitted heavy timbers for bolts, so that they could lock themselves in securely against their brown neigh- borfolk, if need be. He cut three holes for windows—one larger one, to the right of the door at the front, and a small one in each gable; the glazed sash, sent for from Stillwater, was fitted into these. He would have liked to let more of God's clear daylight into his house, but he could not afford any more of the expensive glass.

Next in turn was the fireplace where the food was to be prepared; it would also be the source of heat and of light at night. He had lately worked as carpenter, timberman, and roofer, now he must also do a mason's work, and this worried him. He asked Jonas Petter to help him, and with his skillful neighbor's aid, he built a fireplace and chimney of stone, clay, and sand. Later, with less urgency, he would build a bake oven beside the fireplace.

The fireplace took up one corner of the house; in each one of the three remaining corners, Karl Oskar built a bedstead: one for Kristina and himself, one for the children, and one for Robert. Six feet from each gable and five feet from the side walls, he fastened posts to the floor on which he placed timbers long enough to be secured to the gable walls; this made the bed frames. Crossing these timbers and fitting between the wall logs he laid thinner scantlings for the bed bottom. He had seen beds built this way in an American settler's house in Taylors Falls and he liked them; they were easy to make, yet ingenious and practical. During the coming winter he would make such furniture as they absolutely needed when he was forced to sit inside by the fire.

Karl Oskar brought Kristina over to their new house for a tour of inspection, to show her all he had done. He explained that everything was on the rough side—walls, windows, floor, door, and ceiling. There were no perfectly smooth surfaces—but he had done the best he could. And nothing was intended for looks, anyway, all was done to keep out rain, wind, cold. It could not be helped if the walls were a little rough, if the floor wasn't quite even, if the door hung askew. Yes, the door did hang somewhat crooked, but she must remember the old saying: "Out of plumb is dumb, but a little lean cannot be seen." Many planks might be poorly fitted, for he had used mostly pegs, he hadn't driven a hundred nails into the whole house; the price of nails had worried him so much that he had thought a long while before using one.

Their new house was built roughly, but he was sure it would provide them with comfort and shelter.

Kristina said that this house was like a castle, it was heaven compared to the shanty! And she was well pleased with all she saw, especially their new beds; these were the most comfortable sleeping places they had since leaving home.

Karl Oskar assured her he would make the house still more comfortable for her. On the long back wall, between the beds, he intended to place an oak log, which would make an excellent sofa; next to the fireplace he intended to build shelves, he would drive pegs into the logs to hang clothes on, and as soon as he had time he would make her a table, surely before Christmas. By and by they would be quite comfortable in this house.

Kristina was aware of the rough timbers in the cabin, the unfinished walls; she saw better than her husband all that was crooked and out of line, but she had been deeply worried that the house would not be finished before winter came. How glad she was now that she could move into it! They had wandered about so long and had to change shelter and sleeping places so often—how wonderful it would be to settle down under a real roof, be within four solid walls, live in a house where they could stay!

Yes, Kristina was satisfied with their house of roughhewn logs, even though Karl Oskar said: "Wait till next time! Next time I'll build a real . . ."

Even before they had moved into their new house he was planning the next one: This forest had timber enough for real mansions; as soon as he had improved his condition, he would build something larger and finer than any farmhouse in all Ljuder Parish! It would be at least two stories high, of the finest timber, elegantly finished.

Yes, he assured his wife, she could rely on him; their next house would be well finished, both inside and outside.

—4—

KARL OSKAR made a cross in the almanac on the twenty-eighth of October —that was the day they moved into the new log house.

They invited their countrymen at the other settlement for a housewarming, and Anders Månsson and his mother were also asked. All the guests came in Anders Månsson's ox wagon—the ungreased wooden wheels, ever moaning and squeaking, announced their arrival half an hour before the wagon emerged from the forest. Now the new house was filled with people jostling for seats. Karl Oskar had made a few chairs from sawed-off oak blocks, leaving a back rest sticking up, somewhat rounded to fit the back of a full-grown person. These made solid seats, but for the party he had to roll in ordinary blocks as well, and still some of the guests had to sit on the beds.

So they were again together, sixteen of them, all born in the same land, all speaking the same language. They had settled in different places, made up separate households, and had no possessions in common except their language, and this united them and held them together in their new country. They felt almost like close relatives. However kind and friendly people may be, if they are unable to speak a common language, they remain strangers. Today, no strangers had come to visit Karl Oskar and Kristina; their visitors seemed like blood relations.

Kristina had prepared a venison dinner; she had peeled the potatoes before boiling them, as was the custom at parties at home. She had boiled a whole kettle of cranberries; these berries were now ripening in great quantities in the bogs hereabouts, and they had a pleasing sour-fresh taste. To a housewarming the guests were supposed to bring gifts of food, and Ulrika had cooked the moving-in porridge, made of rice; she came with a large earthen bowl full of it. Jonas Petter had brought a keg of American brännvin. There were not as many dishes or as much of everything as was customary at housewarmings in Sweden, but all felt that they were sitting down to a great feast.

Karl Oskar and Kristina had invited their guests before they had a table; the food was served on top of their Swedish chest, around which they all sat down. Their guests said they too were still using their chest lids for food boards.

Ulrika had not been stingy when she cooked the housewarming porridge, it was sugar-sweet and won praise from all; before they knew it they had reached the bottom of the earthen bowl. As a young girl, Ulrika had occasionally worked as cook's helper at Kråkesjö manor; she had learned cooking well and was handy at both stove and oven, when she had anything to cook with.

Today, for once, the settlers felt entitled to many dishes at the same meal, and they ate steadily and solemnly. At last the coffeepot was taken down from its hook over the fire, and a delicious odor of coffee spread through the cabin. Robert proudly showed the coffee grinder he had made for Kristina: he had hollowed out a stone to make a mortar with another stone for pestle, to crush the coffee beans. He had seen the Indians use such mills—their coffee now was ground Indian-wise.

All ate to their full satisfaction, and when Ulrika wanted to rise, the chair clung to her behind. She had eaten so much that she couldn't get out of the chair, she blamed Karl Oskar who had made the seat too narrow for a grown woman; he ought to be old enough to know that women were broader across the behind than men; God had created them that way in order to make them lie steady on their backs those times when they obeyed His commandment to increase and replenish the earth.

Jonas Petter poured the American brännvin, and all drank—even the children were given a few drops each. Anders Månsson said the whisky was stronger than Swedish brännvin; at first it burned the tongue a little, but later it felt good in the stomach. Some people had a hard time getting accustomed to the taste of whisky, some had to keep at it persistently, it might take years; he himself had already become accustomed to it. The whisky was made from Indian corn, "Lazyman's Grain" as it was called. He had planted this corn for the first time last spring.

"At home the brännvin is white, why is it brown here?" Kristina asked.

"They haven't strained it carefully," said Ulrika. "There's mash in it."

Jonas Petter had his own opinion: "It's the color of cow piss but it tastes mighty good!"

Kristina and Ulrika both thought Swedish brännvin was sweeter and milder; this tasted pungent. But old Fina-Kajsa liked American brännvin better than Swedish: "Brännvin should be felt in the throat! It mustn't slip down like communion wine!"

Anders Månsson's mother had changed much since she had found her son; at times she sat silently by herself, staring straight ahead for hours, hardly hearing if she were spoken to. At other times she seemed to have lost her memory. Believing herself still on the journey, she kept mumbling, downhearted and confused: "Oh me, oh my! We'll never get there! Oh me, oh my!"

She could forget everything around her to such an extent that she wasn't aware she had reached her son three months ago. The long journey seemed to have been too much for her head. But at other times she pulled herself together and worked all day long like a young woman, running her son's house and cooking for him the delicious Öland dumplings which he had been without so long in America. Since he now could get the dumplings here, Anders Månsson said, there was nothing left in Sweden to go back to.

After their feast, the settlers grouped themselves around the hearth where a great fire of dry pine boughs was burning. And sitting there, to let the "food die in the stomach," they began to talk of Sweden and of people in their home community: It was now the servants' "Free Week" at home, all crops were in, the potatoes picked, the fields plowed. The bread for the winter was in the bins, the cattle in the byre. Those at home lived in an old and settled land, they had their food for the winter. And they could not help but compare their own situation: they were farmers without crops, without grain bins, without pork barrels, without livestock. And ahead of them lay the earth's long resting season, when the ground gave nothing.

But Sweden had already begun to fade into the vague distance; it seemed far away in time and space. Heaven seemed closer than Sweden. Their old homes had taken on an aspect of unreality, as does everything at a great distance.

They began speaking of the loneliness of the great wilderness, and Jonas Petter said: "Is there one among us who regrets the emigration?"

The question caught them unaware, and a spell of silence fell over the group. A puzzling question had been asked—a poser—which required a great deal of thought before they could answer it; it was like a riddle to be solved. Do I regret my emigration? It was an intrusive question, forcing itself upon them, knocking at each one's closed door: a demand to open and show what was hidden inside.

Ulrika was the first to answer. She stared at Jonas Petter, almost in fury: "Regret it! Are you making fun of me? Should I regret having moved to a country where I'm accepted as a human being? I'd rather be chopped to sausage filling than go back to Sweden!"

"It was to be," Danjel Andreasson said. "We were chosen to move here. We shall harbor neither regret nor fear."

"I regret one thing!" spoke up Karl Oskar. "I regret I didn't emigrate six years ago, when I first came of age."

"You are not yet of age—your Guardian still lives in Heaven," Danjel said. "His will has been done."

"But the Lord's servant—the dean—advised against my emigration."

"Then it was an evil spirit that spake through him," Danjel retorted calmly.

"Well—I'm here! And no one can get me away from here! As surely as I sit on this chopping block!" Karl Oskar spoke with great emphasis.

He was settled now, he and his family had moved into their house, furnished with sturdy beds and seats he had made. Beginning this very day, he felt settled and at home in North America.

Jonas Petter said: Life in the wilderness had its drawbacks, but things would improve by and by, as they improved themselves. It had been well for them to travel about and see how great the earth was, how vast its seas and countries. At home, people thought Sweden made up the whole world; that was why folk there were so conceited.

"They should read geography books," interrupted Robert.

"That they should, instead of poking their noses into everyone else's business," agreed Jonas Petter. If anyone hiccoughed in Sweden, folk picked it up and ran with it until it was heard throughout the whole county. His father knew an old morning hymn which all should follow:

> Peaceful walk and do thy bit,
> Obey thy Lord, on others spit!

This psalm Jonas Petter's father used to sing every morning before he began his day, and if they obeyed it, they would be happy through all their days, and at last pass to the beyond in contentment.

Judging from the replies to Jonas Petter's question, no one regretted his emigration. And the settlers began to talk of work to be finished before winter set in. Karl Oskar intended to dig a well before the frost got into the earth; he had not been able to find a spring in the vicinity, they had been using brook water, which didn't seem to hurt them; it was running water, but it wasn't quite clear in color or taste.

The talk around the fire was suddenly interrupted by Kristina, who was seized by a fit of weeping. This happened unexpectedly and without forewarning. No one had said a word to hurt or upset her. She herself had been silent a long time. She had not joined in their talk about Sweden, but she had listened. Karl Oskar now asked in consternation if she was in pain. But she only shook her head—he mustn't pay any attention to her. And she continued to cry and sob, she put both her hands to her face and wept without saying why. No one could comfort her, as no one knew what ailed her. They asked many times if she were ill: No, she was not ill. . . .

Karl Oskar felt embarrassed and didn't know what to say to the guests; but they would understand she was sensitive now. . . .

"You're worn out, I guess?" he said kindly.

Danjel patted his niece on the shoulder: "Lie down and rest, Kristina. We too must seek the comfort of our homes."

"I am acting like a fool. Forgive me, all of you. . . ."

Fearing that the guests were departing because of her behavior, Kristina pleaded with them to remain, trying to swallow her sobs: "To blubber like this . . . I don't understand it. Pay no heed to it; it will soon be over."

But their guests must start on their homeward road to be back before dark. Anders Månsson did not wish to drive the new road after nightfall; he went out and yoked the team to the wagon, while Ulrika washed the dishes and picked up her empty earthen bowl; Jonas Petter left his keg with at least half a quart still splashing in it.

Karl Oskar accompanied his guests a bit of the way, walking up the slope. The housewarming had ended on an unhappy note, too suddenly. And he was worried over Kristina's peculiar behavior; if she wasn't sick, she must be crying for some other reason, and this reason she had kept secret from him. He must know what it was, she must tell him what ailed her.

When he returned to the house, Kristina had dried her tears. She began to speak of her own will: "I couldn't help it, Karl Oskar."

"I guess not."

"I assure you, it was nothing. . . ."

"One can be sad and weep. But why did you have to weep just this day?"

"It irks me terribly—with all the guests . . ."

Karl Oskar wondered if after all she wasn't a little disappointed with the log house. Had she expected their new home to be different—better and roomier? He tried to comfort her by telling her about the house he intended to build next time: "You wait and see our next house, Kristina! Next housewarming you won't cry!"

"Karl Oskar—I didn't cry because of . . ."

No, he mustn't think she shed tears because their house wasn't fine enough! He mustn't think she was so ungrateful! That would have been sinful of her. No, the house was good, she had told him she was pleased with their new home. And she hadn't complained before, when there might have been reason—she hadn't said a word when they shivered and froze in the shed. Why should she be dissatisfied now when they had moved into a warm, timbered house? No, she had everything she could want, this last year she had learned to be without; before they managed to get under this roof, she had learned to value a home; she had thanked God Who had let them move in here, well and healthy and all of them alive, after the dangers they had gone through.

But she couldn't help it—something had come over her today, making her cry. Before she knew it the tears had come to her eyes, as if forced out. She didn't know what it was—she only felt it was overpowering. And she couldn't tell him how much it disturbed her that this had happened at their housewarming, on that longed-for day when they moved in. . . .

Karl Oskar was satisfied with her explanation: no wonder she was a little sensitive, unable to keep her tears, the condition she was in. She needed comforting words and he went on talking of their next housewarming: "Just wait and see our next house! Then we'll be really at home here on Lake Ki-Chi-Saga!"

205

WHEN KRISTINA went to bed the first evening in the log house, the first time in the new, comfortable bed, with her husband beside her, she remained awake a long while: Had she lied to him today? Didn't she know what had come over her and made her cry? It had come over her many times before, although never so overpoweringly as today. It used to come when she had nothing to busy herself with, nothing to occupy her mind. Usually it soon passed, but it came back, it always came back. And of course it would come back today, with all the others sitting there talking about it! Indeed, they forced it to come. They sat and reminisced about the old country and the people at home, they made everything come to life so vividly, everything she had given up with a bleeding heart to follow her husband.

Now they were at last settled, now they would stay here forever, *at home* on Lake Ki-Chi-Saga, as Karl Oskar put it. So strange it sounded, to have her home linked to that name. She was to be at home here for the rest of her life—but she wasn't at home. This house was her home, but it was so far away. . . .

Here was *away* for Kristina—Sweden was *home*. It ought to be just the opposite: the two places should change position. She had moved, but she could not make the two countries move, the countries lay where they had lain before—one had always to her been *away*, the other would always remain *home*.

And she knew for sure now, she had to admit it to herself: in her heart she felt she was still on a journey; she had gone away but hoped one day to return.

*Home*—to Kristina, this encompassed all that she was never to see again.

# XVII

## Guests in the Log House

THE SETTLERS at Lake Gennesaret had moved into their log house a few weeks before their countrymen on Lake Ki-Chi-Saga. Jonas Petter would build his house next summer, and in the meantime he lived with Danjel. He had begun to fell timbers to let them season for his building, and Robert helped him with the felling; he was doing exchange work for his brother. To avoid the hour-long walk from Ki-Chi-Saga and back, he stayed in Danjel's house during the week and went home only Saturdays.

One Saturday afternoon Robert arrived at his brother's settlement leading a cow behind him with one of Karl Oskar's linden-fiber ropes. He tied the cow to the sugar maple at the door and called Kristina.

She came out, looked at the cow, and rubbed her eyes. "What kind of creature is that? Did you run across a stray cow in the forest?"

"No. I've led her from Taylors Falls."

Kristina inspected the animal more closely: It was one of Anders Månsson's cows, the one that wouldn't get with calf, which he intended to butcher.

Karl Oskar also came out and stood there by Kristina laughing to himself: Was she surprised? She could thank Fina-Kajsa for this, the old woman had suggested lending her son's cow for the winter; the cow had once more been taken to German Fischer's bull in Taylors Falls, and as it now appeared she was with calf, it would be a shame to butcher her. Anders Månsson and his mother had enough milk from the other cow, and as Karl Oskar had gathered plenty of hay to feed her, he could keep her through the winter; he was to bring her back to the owner at calving time next spring. The cow still gave a couple of quarts of milk a day and would not go dry for several months.

"The animal is old, of course," he concluded.

The cow was badly saddle-backed and had an enormous stomach; she must have borne fifteen calves at least in her day. But Kristina threw her arms around the neck of the animal: she had a milch cow, even though it was only borrowed, and they would have milk for the children during most of the winter. And she patted the cow, caressed her, felt above the udder for the milk arteries, and said they were good, for an old cow: she could easily increase her milk if she were fed and cared for.

Karl Oskar was as pleased as Kristina with the cow. He thought that this time his wife had enforced her will in spite of him.

Here in Minnesota people had miserable shelters for their cattle; the Swedish settlers thought it a wonder they didn't freeze to death during the winters. Karl Oskar led his borrowed cow to the lately vacated shanty. The cow moved into the house they themselves had occupied until a few days before. Their old home was turned into a byre! They would let the cow graze in the meadow until the snow began to fly, but they would be careful to put her in the shanty every night.

Anders Månsson was the owner of one young and one old cow. Both had American names—the young one was called Girl and this one was called Lady, which was supposed to be a title like Mrs. in America. Large-bellied Lady was a calm, easygoing, friendly animal, grazing peacefully and contentedly, never trying to run off to the woods. She became a pleasant companion to Kristina and the children in their isolation; it seemed almost that they had acquired a new member of the family, and this member contributed to the family sustenance. Lady was always called by name, like a human being, a respected woman of noble lineage. And Robert pointed out that women were scarce out here and a noble name for a cow showed how highly men valued women in North America.

207

THE NIGHT FROSTS had begun. The grass stood silvery in the mornings; winter was lurking outside their timbered house.

One late afternoon, at twilight, Kristina was alone inside their log house with Lill-Märta and Harald. Karl Oskar had gone to the lake to examine some willow snares he had placed in the shore reeds near a point where the pike often played, and Johan had run after him; the boy was always at the heels of his father. Kristina poured water into a pot and hung it over the fire, as Karl Oskar would soon be back with the fish for their evening meal. She hoped he would find pike in the snares, pike tasted better than any other fish in the lake; whitefish and perch were good too, but the catfish with its round head and long beard was so ugly that the sight of it did not whet the appetite.

Lill-Märta was playing on the floor and Harald was still taking his nap in the children's bed. Kristina was busy at the hearth with her back to the door when the girl suddenly began to scream.

"What's the matter with you, Lill-Märta?"

The child answered with another yell, still louder.

"Did you hurt yourself, child dear?"

The girl was sitting on the floor, staring wide-eyed toward the door. Kristina turned quickly. The door was open and two figures stood inside the threshold. She could barely see them in the dim light, and at first she couldn't determine whether they were men or women; she saw only two skin-covered bodies which had somehow got inside. But how had they opened the door? She hadn't heard it open, nor had there been any other noise, or sound of steps.

The startling sight near the door made her back up so quickly that she almost stepped into the fire. Then she rushed to pick up the child on the floor—her heart stopped beating and felt cramped in her breast, and fear spread over her whole trembling body, as if it had been drenched with ice water.

The two figures at the door peered at her with black-currant eyes, set deep under low foreheads. And now she recognized who the guests were: their nearest neighbors had come to pay a call.

But what did they want here? Why had they come to her?

She called to them: "Go outside!"

The two Indians remained immobile inside the threshold. In her fear, she had forgotten they couldn't understand a word she said.

Harald awoke and sat up in his bed, rubbing the sleep from his eyes. With the girl in her arms Kristina cautiously stole back to the children's bed in the corner, she walked slowly backward, she dared not turn her back to the Indians. With one child in her arms she stood protectingly in front of the other.

"What do you want? Please go outside!"

Uncomprehending, the Indians remained, and again she remembered that she spoke to deaf ears: What use was there in talking to savages who didn't understand her?

"Karl Oskar! Karl Oskar! Come quick!"

She kept on calling, she yelled as loud as she could, she must yell loud enough for him to hear her down at the lake. Karl Oskar wasn't far away, perhaps he was already on his way back, he ought to hear her calls. . . .

Then she stopped calling; she might anger them by yelling, it might be better to keep quiet and pretend she wasn't afraid of them. If she only knew their errand. What could they want of her?

The unwelcome guests did not leave, they moved from the door toward the hearth, and in the light of the fire Kristina had a good look at them.

The Indians were dressed in soft brown-red skins, and their feet were shod in the same kind of hides. Their faces were deceptively alike, except that one had a flat nose. Their cheeks were beardless. On their cheekbones were painted red, bloodlike streaks, and black hair hung in tufts from their heads, gleaming as if greased with fat. Both Indians had red animal tails dangling from the backs of their necks, they looked as if they had live squirrels sitting behind their ears. From their squirrel tails to their moccasins, they looked furry and ragged; they hardly resembled human beings. And they had sneaked into the house on soft paws like wild beasts.

The Indians looked around the cabin, they inspected the pot over the fire, the chest, the clothes hanging on the wall. Meanwhile they spoke in low voices to each other; their words sounded like short, guttural grunts.

She could not take her eyes off their red-streaked faces. Their eyes burned like black coals under their brows, they looked cruel and treacherous. Long knives hung at their sides; they might stick their knives into her and the children, any moment. The Indian with the pushed-in nose seemed to her the more dangerous of the two.

Kristina kept silent now, she no longer called for help, no use frightening her children. She stood at the corner of the bed, as far from the intruders as possible, with her two little ones pressed close to her. The children too kept silent, their round eyes staring at the strange, uncouth creatures.

They had left the door open; could she pick up Harald and the girl and escape through the door? Would she dare run past the two savages?

The flat-nosed Indian pointed to Karl Oskar's gun which hung on the gable wall above the clothes chest; now both Indians stood looking at the gun with their backs toward Kristina. Now she must run by them out of the house! She gathered her strength, took a firm hold of her children, measured the distance with her eyes . . . it was only a few steps. . . .

But suddenly the Indians turned toward her again. They had managed to lift Karl Oskar's muzzle-loader off the pegs; both held the gun, one had the butt, the other the barrel.

What did they want with the gun? It was loaded. What were they about to do, did they want to steal it? Why didn't Karl Oskar come? What was he doing all this time?

Now the flat-nosed Indian alone held the shooting piece; he lifted the weapon to firing position, level with his shoulder; he stood with his back to the gable end of the house and aimed toward Kristina!

He intended to fire—he was going to shoot her and the children! She was looking right into the gun barrel, and there was no place to flee now; she pushed against the logs but she couldn't creep through the wall. She stood petrified, a target.

"No! No!" she screamed.

She wanted to tell them they could have the gun, if only they wouldn't shoot her and the children. The children! Quickly she pushed them behind her; now she protected them with her own body, now the bullet must first go through her. If she only could have called to them: Don't shoot! Let us live! Don't kill us here now!

But they wouldn't understand her.

The flat-nosed Indian again held the butt, while the other one held up the barrel, helping his friend to aim the heavy weapon. It was clear they wanted to try the gun by firing a shot; the flat-nosed Indian was fingering the hammer, trying to cock it.

Pressed against the wall, Kristina crouched over her children, she couldn't move any farther, she was trembling and weak with fright. The poor children—she couldn't ask the savages to spare them, they wouldn't understand. But Someone else understood and would listen to her; she stammered forth a prayer: "Dear God! If I die now, what will become of my children? My little, innocent children? Dear God, help me!"

Lill-Märta and Harald, squeezed between her body and the wall, began to whimper. But the visitors paid no attention to Kristina and the children, they were busy with the gun. Now both of them were fingering the hammer. The gun had a hard action. Kristina followed their motions with wide-open, frozen eyes. And she saw they had managed to cock the gun. Then she didn't see anything more.

Black and red clouds covered her eyes. She closed them, her whole body numb with terror. Karl Oskar! What *are* you doing out there? Why don't you come?

Karl Oskar! Perhaps he had encountered the Indians before they came in! Could they have done him any harm? Was that why he didn't come? Suppose he were lying out there . . .

"Dear sweet God! Help him! Help us!"

Kristina closed her eyes and waited. She waited for the shot, she waited for the lead bullet. . . . She must die. This was the end for her on earth. And she prayed incoherently and silently that her merciful Father would receive her, wretched, sinful creature that she was, and let her children live unharmed in this world: the poor children . . . dear God, let them live, my poor children. . . .

Her trembling lips moved, but she kept her eyes closed and waited, waited through an eternity. It was silent in the house. She heard nothing. As yet no shot had been fired from the gun. It remained silent.

Kristina kept her eyes closed and waited. . . . Until a child's voice said: "Open your eyes, Mother! Why do you keep your eyes shut?"

Then she opened her eyes and looked about her, all around the cabin, as if awakening from a long, bad dream. Lill-Märta sat on the floor with her playthings as before, and little Harald stood in the open door and looked out. No one else was in sight. She was alone in the house with her children. The callers had gone: the two Indians had gone their way with the gun. They had come into the house soundlessly, they had left in equal silence—stolen away on their soft moccasins like animals slinking back into the forest. They had not fired a shot. . . .

But when she tried to walk, she felt the floor sway under her: the planks sank steeply under her feet, she took one step into a depth—she fell full length to the floor and knew nothing more.

—3—

KARL OSKAR came in, Johan at his heels; he carried a few pike strung through the gills on a branch; he threw the fish on the floor in front of the hearth. It was cold inside the cabin and he wondered why the door had been left open. Then he discovered Kristina, stretched out on the floor at the other end of the room.

He hurriedly soaked a towel in the water pail and laid it on his wife's forehead. In a few minutes she opened her eyes and sat up, confused and questioning: What was it? Why was she on the floor?

"You fainted," Karl Oskar said.

She still felt dizzy, she put her hand to her forehead and began to remember: Karl Oskar had returned—at last!

"What were you doing? Why did you stay away so long?"

"So long? I was only gone a short while."

He looked at his watch: he had examined the snares and moved them a bit, but he hadn't been gone a half hour.

"A half hour?" Kristina was surprised. In that time she had suffered death, spent time in eternity. "I called you." Her dulled senses were clearing: "The Indians came. Two awful ones! They took your gun."

Karl Oskar looked at the wall—the gun was still there where he had hung it. As Kristina noticed this, she said: "I was so confused—I thought they stole the gun. But they cocked it."

Karl Oskar took down his muzzle-loader and examined it; he couldn't see that anyone had touched it.

211

"Did they handle it?"

"They aimed it."

"At you? Oh Lord in Heaven!"

"I thought they would shoot me and the children."

"God, they must have frightened you! No wonder you fainted!"

She related what had taken place in the cabin the few minutes he was gone. And as Karl Oskar listened, a cold perspiration broke out on his forehead. While he had been gone less than half an hour, the greatest disaster he could imagine had nearly befallen him: he might have returned to find wife and children dead on the cabin floor.

"Oh Lord my God! What an escape!"

Kristina said: First she had called him. Then she had prayed God to help her, and He had listened to her prayer and sent the savages away from their house without harming her or the children. Never before in her life had she realized so fully as today how all of them were under the protection of their Creator.

"They left the gun. I don't understand it. What did they want in here?"

Karl Oskar suggested that the Indians were curious: they hadn't come to murder anyone, they only wanted to see how the new settlers lived. But they handled shooting irons like children—the gun might easily have gone off and killed her!

"This must never happen again," he said.

They had had a serious warning today. She must bolt the door carefully whenever he was out, even if only for a short time. And they must rig up a loud bell so she could call him when there was danger.

"I hope you didn't hurt yourself?"

"No. I feel perfectly well again."

She had looked very pale when he saw her lying on the floor, but now her color had come back. She busied herself with her chores, they must have their evening meal at last. She stirred up the fire under the pot and Karl Oskar went outside for more wood.

She sat down to clean the fish. But as she stuck the knife into the first pike belly, she felt a jerking convulsion grip her: an intense pain began in the small of her back and spread through her whole lower body. It felt as if she had stuck the knife into her own belly instead of into the fish.

When Karl Oskar came back with the wood, he saw she had grown pale again, her very lips were bluish. And her hand with the knife trembled as she cut the entrails from the pike.

"Is something wrong?"

"Nothing much. It'll soon be over."

"But you've pain?"

"It will soon pass."

She went on cleaning the fish, she cleaned all the pike, and the pain abated. She had told Karl Oskar the truth—the pain had passed.

But what she hadn't said was that it would soon be upon her again; she had recognized the pain.

And it did come back—an hour later, when they sat around the chest lid eating their supper. The same pain returned, radiating from the small of her back, shooting and cutting through her lower body. This time it lasted longer than before. Her appetite was gone, but she forced herself to swallow a few bites of the boiled fish.

Karl Oskar looked uneasily at his wife: "How do you feel, Kristina?"

"I don't feel so well, after the fainting spell."

"Eat! That will bring back your strength."

She tried for a moment to persuade herself that it was only the after-effect of fainting. And the pain eased, but in a little while it came again for a third time, and now it seized her so violently that she had to let a few moans escape her lips. She panted and drew in her breath with difficulty.

"Take some drops!" Karl Oskar urged.

He found the bottle of Hoffman's Heart-Aiding Drops, which Kristina had hidden with great care; he poured a tablespoonful and gave it to her. She swallowed the drops without a word. But by now she knew: no drops would help her, this would not pass, this would come back many times, and more intense each time it came—until it was over. She remembered it well; after all, she had experienced it four times before. And she regretted immediately having taken the heart-aiding drops, they couldn't help her in any way; those drops had been wasted on her; they might better have been used for the children, when they ailed. Foolish of her. . . . Why had she believed something would help? The first time might have been a mistake—but now. . . . Why didn't she tell Karl Oskar the truth?

"It's my time, Karl Oskar."

"Do you think so?"

"Yes. It couldn't be anything else."

He looked at her in foolish surprise. "But—isn't it too soon?"

"Fourteen days too soon."

"Yes, that's what I thought. . . . Then we must get someone right away!"

He had just finished pulling off his boots, now he pulled them on again quickly. Where could he find a woman to help? Who out here could act as midwife? At home she had had both her mother and mother-in-law at her childbeds. But here—a married woman, a settler woman who spoke their language—there was hardly a one. An unmarried woman who had never borne children would not be good for much. He had had it in mind to suggest to Kristina—as long as she herself hadn't mentioned it—that they ought to bespeak a woman to help her in childbed, before it was too late. Fina-Kajsa was too old, her hands trembled, and her head wasn't

213

always clear. He had thought of Swedish Anna, who was a widow and had reached ripe age—she should be able to help a life into the world.

But it was a long way to fetch her from Taylors Falls—a three-hour walk by daylight. And would she come with him through the wilderness tonight? This had happened so suddenly, night was falling, and this too was bad luck.

"I had better get Swedish Anna. But it will take a few hours."

"You needn't go so far," Kristina said. "Get Ulrika."

"What? Ulrika of Västergöhl?"

"Yes. I asked her at the housewarming."

"You want the Glad One to be with you?"

"She promised me."

Karl Oskar was stamping on his right boot, and he stopped, perplexed: The Glad One was considered as good as anyone here, no one spoke ill of her now. Both he and Kristina had made friends with her, had accepted her in their company. But he had not imagined that his wife would call for Ulrika of Västergöhl to be with her at childbed, he had not thought she would want her so close. Yet she had already bespoken her—the woman she had wanted to exclude as a companion on their journey. She would never have done this at home; there a decent wife would never have allowed the public whore to attend her at childbirth.

Kristina rose and began preparing the bed: "Don't you think Ulrika can manage?"

"Yes! Yes, of course! I only thought . . ."

But he never said what his thought was. It was this: he had accepted Ulrika, but hardly more. He could not forget that, after all, she had been the parish whore in Ljuder, and he was surprised that Kristina seemed to have forgotten. Perhaps it was as well, perhaps it was fortunate that she was within call when a midwife was needed. She should know the requirements at such a function, she had borne four children of her own, she should know what took place at childbirth. Ulrika had health and strength, she was cleanly. She would probably make a good midwife. She could help a wedded woman, even though all her own children had been born out of wedlock. What wouldn't do at home would have to do here; here each one did as best he could, and they must rely on someone capable, regardless of her previous life.

Karl Oskar now was surprised at himself for not having thought of Ulrika. "I shall fetch her as fast as I can run."

"It's already dark. It won't be easy for you."

He said he could find the road to their neighbors' settlement, he had walked it often enough. But it was too bad that Robert was staying with Danjel, or he could have sent him instead. Now he must leave Kristina and the children alone—and just after they had been frightened by the Indians. She must bolt herself in, to be safe. Would she be able to push in the bolts after he left? It would be almost two hours before he could get back.

"Can you hold out till I get back?"

"I think I can. But be sure to bring Ulrika with you."

Karl Oskar cut a large slice of bread for each of the children, to give them something to gnaw on while he was gone. He stopped a moment outside the door while Kristina bolted it, and then he took off.

Outside it was pitch-dark. Karl Oskar had made himself a small hand lantern out of pieces of glass he had found in Taylors Falls: he had fitted these into a framework of wood. But the tiny tallow candle inside burned with so weak a flame that the lantern helped him but little. Later there might be a moon, but at the moment the heavens were cloaked in dark clouds, not letting through a ray. He must hurry, he hadn't time to look for obstacles, he strode along fast, stumbled on roots, slipped into hollows; thorns stung him and branches hit him in the face; he was drenched with perspiration before he was halfway to Danjel's. A few times he had to stop to get his breath. It was difficult to hurry in his heavy boots.

Karl Oskar was panting and puffing like a dog in midsummer when at last he espied the light from Danjel's cabin; he had never before covered the distance between the two settlements in so short a time.

He arrived as the Lake Gennesaret people were preparing for bed. Danjel, shirt-clad only, opened the door for him. Looking at Karl Oskar's face he guessed the caller's errand: "It's Kristina? She must be ready."

"Yes."

Ulrika of Västergöhl was sitting on the hearth corner darning socks in the light from the fire. She stood up: "How far has it gone?"

"I don't know. The pains came right after dusk."

"Had the birth-water come?"

"I don't know."

"It's probably just begun."

"It came on somewhat suddenly. Two Indians came in and frightened her. That might have brought it on."

"It's always sudden," Ulrika told him.

She gathered up the worn socks and put them away; then she threw a woolen shawl over her shoulders and was ready. Danjel handed her a bottle of camphor drops and a large linen towel.

Robert asked if he should go with them, but Ulrika said: "There's no need for any more menfolk." She glanced at Karl Oskar, who stood there anxious and pale: "No—no more chickenhearted males!"

And out into the darkness went Karl Oskar in Ulrika's company; he went ahead through the forest and tried to light their way with his lantern. Now he couldn't walk fast, partly because he was tired, partly because of Ulrika.

Soon the moon broke through the clouds, and the moonlight was of more help than the lantern.

215

Ulrika talked almost incessantly: Yes, menfolk were soft at a woman's childbirth; they used as excuse that they couldn't bear to see a poor woman suffer. . . . Hmm. . . . The truth was, probably, they suffered from bad conscience—those who had a conscience; they themselves had put the woman in childbirth pain.

Karl Oskar answered her in monosyllables, mostly he listened. Whatever was said of Ulrika in Västergöhl she was a fearless and plucky woman. This was well—such a one was needed at a childbed.

Ulrika continued: She herself had been delivered four times, but at her childbeds no man had needed to see her suffer; least of all the fathers of the children, for they had kept themselves far, far away. They had kept away at the birth and after; indeed, she had never heard from them again. It was best for them, of course; they were wise; they wanted to partake of the sweet tickling, but not of the sour suffering. Men were always quick to be on their way; and she had been too proud to ask their whereabouts. No one could ever accuse her of having run after men. It was the menfolk who had never left her in peace, they had tempted and promised and lured her in every way; and that poor excuse for a man who didn't do the right thing of his own will was not worth running after.

Yes, Ulrika knew the menfolk; the only one who might know them better was God the Father Himself, Who had made them. She had been with many; she knew what cowards they were toward women, how they tried to shirk their responsibility for what they had done, how they lied and accused others, how they wriggled and squirmed—those men. She knew how they shammed concern and acted the hypocrite, their tongues sweet and soft until they got a woman on her back, and how afterward —having been let in to enjoy the feast—they grew cheap and penurious and unkind: turned back into the useless cowards they actually were.

There might be a few real men; the best that could happen to a woman in this world was to be married to a real man, one she could rely on when she needed him.

"You are a man with a will, Karl Oskar. And you take care of your brats as well as your woman," said Ulrika.

The man who received this praise felt somewhat embarrassed.

The Glad One went on: Kristina was a fine, honest woman, she did not begrudge her a good man. She, Ulrika, had accommodated many married men who were in need of her, but she would never go to bed with Kristina's husband, no, not even for a whole barrel of gold.

This annoyed Karl Oskar and he rebuffed her tartly: "I've never asked you, have I?"

"You were pretty hot on me at sea. You can't deny that. No one fools me about such things."

Karl Oskar felt his cheeks burn; even his ears smarted: once on the ship he had used Ulrika—in his dreams. But no one could help what he dreamed. And even if there had been times when he felt himself tempted

216

by the Glad One's attractive body, he was too proud to go where other men had been before. Better not pay any attention to what she was saying, it wasn't a penny's worth. It was just like Ulrika to talk of bed play when they were on their way to a woman in childbirth. His own wife to boot! He would not be dragged into a quarrel with the woman he had fetched to help. . . .

Ulrika went on heedlessly. She nudged Karl Oskar in the side and told him it was nothing to be ashamed of that he was hot on women, particularly as he had been forced to go without for such a long time—his wife had been ill, and pregnant, these were long-drawn-out obstacles, trying his patience. But any man of Kristina's she, Ulrika, would never help, however badly in need he might be.

What she said was true; it struck him to the quick. But he did not answer. He had a sense of relief as the surface of Lake Ki-Chi-Saga glittered in the moonlight ahead of them.

A hundred yards from the cabin they stopped short at the sound of a scream. Both listened intently; it wasn't a bird on the lake, it was a human voice, a voice Karl Oskar recognized: "It's Kristina!"

He ran ahead as fast as his legs could carry him. He hammered with his fists on the door, which was bolted from the inside; he could hear his wife's shrieks, she was in her bed, unable to open the door. How would he get in?

"Kristina! Can you hear me?"

Ulrika came up to his side, panting: "Have you locked her in?"

"Yes. And I don't think she is able to open . . ."

"Break a window."

Karl Oskar picked up a piece of firewood and was ready to break the nearest window when he heard Johan inside: the boy was trying to open the heavy bolts. The father directed the boy, told him how to lean against the door while he pulled the bolts, and he and Ulrika tried to pull the door toward them. After a few eternity-long minutes, the door swung open on its hinges.

Kristina was lying on her side in the bed, her body twisting as she shrieked and moaned.

"Kristina! How is it?"

"It's bad. Where is Ulrika? I've been waiting so . . ."

"We hurried as much as we could." Karl Oskar took hold of his wife's hand: it was clammy with perspiration; her eyes were wide open, she turned them slowly to her husband: "Isn't Ulrika with you?"

Ulrika had thrown off her shawl and now stepped up to the bed, pushing Karl Oskar aside: "Here I am. Good evening, Kristina. Now we'll help each other."

"Ulrika! God bless you for coming."

"How far along are you? Any pushing pains yet?"

217

"Only the warning pains, I think. But—oh, my dear, sweet Ulrika! Why did you take so long?"

The fire in the corner had died down, Lill-Märta and Harald were huddled on their bed with their clothes on, asleep, but Johan was up and about, his eyes wide open, full of terror: "Why does Mother cry so?"

"She has pain."

"Is her nose going to bleed again, as on the ship?"

"You can see for yourself—her nose doesn't bleed."

There had been one night on the *Charlotta* which Johan never would forget. "Will Mother die?"

"No—she won't die. Go to bed and be a good boy."

"Father—is it true? Mother won't die tonight?"

"She is just a little sick. She'll be well again tomorrow morning when you wake up."

Ulrika pulled down the blanket and felt Kristina's body with her hands, lightly touching her lower abdomen; then she asked: Had the birth-water come, and how long between the last pains? While Karl Oskar undressed the children and tucked them in, and rekindled the fire, the two women spoke together: they understood each other with few words, they had gone through the same number of childbeds, four each; they were united and close through their like experience.

"It feels large," said Ulrika after the examination.

"I have thought—perhaps it's twins."

"Haven't you had twins before?"

"Lill-Märta's twin brother was taken from us when he was fourteen days old."

"It runs in the family. Karl Oskar. Get me some light. Heat water over the fire. Be of some use!"

Ulrika assumed command in the cabin, and Karl Oskar speedily performed as he was told to do. It was not his custom to take orders, but tonight at his wife's childbed he was glad someone told him what to do.

From dry pine wood he made such a roaring fire that it lighted the bed where Kristina lay, comforted by her helping-woman in between the pains. She had not had time to sew anything for the child, not the slightest little garment; she had had so many other things to do this fall. And she had thought it would be another two weeks yet; it came too early according to her figuring; no, not a single diaper—and suppose she had twins!

"No devil can figure out the time," said Ulrika. "A brat will creep out whenever God wants him to."

Kristina had hoped it would happen in warm daylight; then she could have sent her children out to play. Now they had to stay inside and listen to her moans; but she couldn't help that.

The next pain came and she let out piercing screams, filling the small

218

cabin with her cries. Johan began to sob; the father took him on his knee and tried to comfort him. Karl Oskar had never before been present at childbirth; at home the women had taken care of everything and never let him inside until all was over. He didn't feel too much for other people —sometimes his insensibility made him feel guilty—but his wife's cries of agony cut right through him, he could scarcely stand it.

"You look pale as a curd, Karl Oskar," said Ulrika. "Go outside for a while. You're of no use here. I'll put the boy to bed."

He obeyed her and went out. It was now about midnight. He went down to the shanty near the lake and gave Lady her night fodder. Then he remained in the shanty with the cow, who stood there so calm and undisturbed, enjoying her own pleasant cow-warmth. The closeness of the animal in some way comforted him. And he didn't feel cold here— Lady warmed him too. The cow chewed her good hay peacefully and rhythmically, and he scratched her head and spoke to her as if she were a human. He confided his thoughts to Lady, it eased him somehow to talk: Yes, little cow, things are strange in this world. The Glad One is inside helping Kristina . . . and I stand here . . . I can't help her. How many times I've wished to be rid of Ulrika! And Kristina herself thought she would bring disaster. Instead, she is our great comfort. Yes, little cow, we never know our blessings. It happens, this way or that, strange things, one never could have dreamed of at home. One can't explain it.

Karl Oskar Nilsson spent most of the night in the byre, lost and baffled, talking to his borrowed cow; he felt he had been sent to "stand in the corner," he didn't know what to do with himself. He had been told to go out—he was driven out of his own house and home. The Ljuder Parish whore was master in his house tonight.

—4—

AFTER A FEW HOURS he went to inquire how the birth was progressing. Kristina lay silent, her eyes closed. Ulrika sat by the bed, she whispered to him: He must walk quietly, she had just gone through another killing pain. Things went slowly, the brat did not seem to move at all. The real birth-water hadn't come yet, and the pushing pains had not yet set in. This birth didn't go according to rule, not as it should; something was wrong. Perhaps she had been frightened too much by the Indians, perhaps the fright had dislodged something inside her. The birth had come on too suddenly—the body was not yet ready for delivery, it did not help itself the way it should when all was in order. This appeared to be a "fright-birth," and in that case it would take a long time. But there was no use explaining to him; he wouldn't understand anyway.

"I wonder how long . . ."

No one could say how long it would take; maybe very long; Kristina might not be delivered tonight. And Ulrika told him to go to bed. There was no need for his roaming about outside, like a spook.

Johan had at last fallen asleep. Karl Oskar stretched out in Robert's bed; he didn't lie down to sleep, he lay down because he had nothing else to do. He had been sitting up late for several evenings, writing a letter to Sweden, but he couldn't work on that tonight.

Kristina had dozed off between the pains; she moaned at intervals: "Ulrika . . . Are you here?"

"Yes. I'm here. You want something to drink?"

Ulrika gave her a mug of warm milk into which she had mixed a spoonful of sugar.

Kristina dozed again when the pains abated. She had always had easy births—what she went through this night surpassed all the pain she had ever experienced in her young life. But she felt succor and comfort close by now: a little while ago she had been lying here alone in the dark, alone in the whole world, alone with her pains, no one to talk to—no one except her whimpering children. Now she had Ulrika, a compassionate woman, a sister, a blessed helper.

There was so much she wanted to tell Ulrika, but she didn't have the strength now, not tonight. She had lived with Ulrika in bitter enmity —she remembered that time when Ulrika had called her a "proud piece." Ulrika had been right. She had been proud. Many times, at home, she'd met unmarried Ulrika of Västergöhl on the roads without greeting her. She was the younger of the two, she should have greeted her first with a curtsy. Instead she had stared straight ahead as if not seeing a soul. She had behaved like all the other women, she had learned from them to detest and avoid the Glad One. She had acted the way all honorable, decent women acted toward Ulrika. But when she had met the King of Alarum, she had greeted him and curtsied deeply, for so did all honorable women. One must discriminate between good and evil people.

Yes, all this she must tell Ulrika—some other time—when she was able to, when this agony was over. Oh, why didn't it pass? Wouldn't she soon be delivered? Wouldn't God spare her? It went on so long . . . so long. . . . "Oh, help! Ulrika, help!"

The pains were upon her; she felt as if she were bursting into pieces, splitting in halves lengthwise. A wild beast was tearing her with its claws, tearing her insides, digging into her, digging and twisting. . . .

Ulrika was near, bending over her. The young wife threw herself from side to side in the bed, her hands fumbling for holds. "Oh! Dear God! Dear God!"

"The pushing pains are beginning," Ulrika said encouragingly. "Then it'll soon be over."

"Dear sweet, hold me! Give me something to hold on to!"

Kristina let out piercing cries, without being aware of it. The billowing pains rose within her—and would rise still higher, before they began

220

to subside. In immeasurable pain she grasped the older woman. She held Ulrika around the waist with both arms and pressed her head into the full bosom. And she was received with kind, gentle arms.

Kristina and Ulrika embraced like two devoted sisters. They were back at humanity's beginning here tonight, at the childbed in the North American forest. They were only two women, one to give life and one to help her; one to suffer and one to comfort; one seeking help in her pain, one in compassion sharing the pain which, ever since the beginning of time, has been woman's fate.

—5—

"It will be over soon now. Come and hold her."

Ulrika was shaking Karl Oskar by the shoulder; he had dozed off for a while. The night was far gone, daylight was creeping in through the windows.

The midwife was calling the father—now she would see what use he could make of his hands.

Kristina's body was now helping in the labor, Ulrika said. Her pushing muscles were working, she was about to be delivered. But this last part was no play-work for her; Karl Oskar might imagine how it would hurt her when the child kicked itself out of her, tearing her flesh to pieces, breaking her in two. While this took place it would lessen her struggle if she could hold on to him, as she, Ulrika, had to receive the baby and couldn't very well be in two places at the same time.

Karl Oskar went up to the head of the bed and took a firm hold around his wife's shoulders.

"Karl Oskar—" Kristina's mouth was wide open, her eyes glazed. She tossed her head back and forth on the pillow. She stretched her arms toward her husband and got hold of his body, pressing herself ever closer to him, seeking a solid stronghold.

"Hold on to me. . . ." The words died in a long, moaning sigh.

"The head is coming! Hold her firmly. I'll take the brat." Ulrika's hands were busy. "A great big devil! If it isn't two!"

Karl Oskar noticed something moving, something furry, with black, shining, drenched hair. And he saw a streak of dark-red blood.

The birth-giving wife clung convulsively to her husband, seeking his embrace in her deepest agony. Severe, slow tremblings shook her body, not unlike those moments when her body was joined with his—and from moments of lust had grown moments of agony.

While the mates this time embraced, their child came into the world.

A hair-covered crown appeared, a brow, a nose, a chin—the face of a human being: Ulrika held in her hands a living, kicking, red-skinned little creature.

221

But the newcomer was still tied to his mother.

"The navel cord!" Ulrika called out. "Where did I put the wool shears?"

For safety's sake she had rinsed Kristina's wool shears in warm water in advance; they had seemed a little dirty and rusty, and one was supposed to wash everything that touched the mother's body during childbirth. Oh, yes, now she remembered—she had laid the shears to dry near the fire.

"On the hearth! Hand me the wool shears, Karl Oskar!"

With the old, rusty wool shears Ulrika cut the blood-red cord which still united mother and child.

Then she made that most important inspection of the newborn: "He is shaped like his father. It's a boy!"

Kristina had given life to a son, a sturdy boy. His skin was bright red, he fluttered his arms and legs, and let out his first complaining sounds. From the warm mother-womb the child had helterskelter arrived in a cold, alien world. The mother's cries had died down, the child's began.

Ulrika wrapped the newborn in the towel Danjel had sent with her: "A hell of a big chunk! Hold him and feel, Karl Oskar!"

She handed the child to the father; they had no steelyard here, but she guessed he weighed at least twelve pounds. Ulrika herself had borne one that weighed thirteen and a half. She knew; the poor woman who had to squeeze out such a lump did not have an easy time. Ulrika had prayed to God to save her—an unmarried woman—from bearing such big brats; the Lord ought to reserve that honor for married women, it was easier for them to increase mankind with sturdy plants. And the Lord had gracefully heard her prayer— He had taken the child to Him before he was three months old.

Thus for the first time Karl Oskar had been present at childbed—at the birth of his third son—his fourth, counting the twin who had died.

Yes, Ulrika was right, his son weighed enough. But he lacked everything else in this world: they hadn't a piece of cloth to swaddle him in; his little son was wrapped at birth in a borrowed towel.

Ulrika warmed some bath water for the newborn, then she held him in the pot and splashed water over his body while he yelled. And her eyes took in the child with satisfaction all the while—she felt as if he had been her own handiwork.

She said: "The boy was made in Sweden, but we must pray God this will have no ill effect on him."

Kristina had lain quiet after her delivery. Now she asked Karl Oskar to put on the coffeepot.

She had put aside a few handfuls of coffee beans for her childbed; Ulrika had neither drunk nor eaten since her arrival last evening, they must now treat her to coffee.

"Haven't you got anything stronger, Karl Oskar?" Ulrika asked.

"Kristina must have her delivery schnapps. She has earned it this evil night."

The delivery schnapps was part of the ritual, Karl Oskar remembered; he had given it to Kristina at her previous childbeds. And this time she needed it more than ever. There were a few swallows left in the keg of American brännvin Jonas Petter had brought to the housewarming.

"I think you could stand a drink yourself," Ulrika said to Karl Oskar.

She finished washing the baby and handed him to the impatient mother. Meanwhile Karl Oskar prepared the coffee and served it on top of an oak-stump chair at Kristina's bedside. He offered a mug to Ulrika, and the three of them enjoyed the warming drink. The whisky in the keg was also divided three ways—to the mother, the midwife, and the child's father. And the father drank as much as the two women together, and he could not remember that brännvin had ever tasted so good as this morning.

While the birth had taken place inside the log house, a new day had dawned outside. It was a frosty November morning with a clear sun shining from a cloudless sky over the white, silver-strewn grass on the shore of Lake Ki-Chi-Saga.

The newly arrived Swedes in the St. Croix Valley had increased their number by one—the first one to be a citizen in their new country.

# XVIII
## Mother and Child

THE CHILD is handed to the mother—it had left her and it has come back.

All is over, all is quiet, all is well.

Kristina lies with her newborn son at her breast. She lies calm and silent, she is delivered, she has changed worlds, she is in the newly delivered woman's blissful world. It is the Glad One—the public whore of the home parish—her intimate friend, who has delivered her. But it is the child—in leaving her womb—who has delivered her from the agony; the child is her joy, and her joy is back with her, is here at her breast.

Mother and child are with each other.

The mother tries to help the child's groping lips find a hold on her breast. The child feels with its mouth aimlessly, rubs its nose like a kitten; how wonderfully soft is its nose against the mother's breast; as yet it seeks blindly. But when the nipple presses in between its lips, its mouth closes around it; the child sucks awkwardly and slowly. Gradually the movements of the tiny lips grow stronger—it answers her with its lips: it answers the mother's tenderness and at the same time satisfies its own desires.

The mother lies joyful and content. The newborn has relieved her of all her old concerns, as he himself now has become all her concern. Now it is he who causes her anxiety: she hasn't a single garment ready to swaddle his naked body, not even a piece of cloth, not the smallest rag. What can she use for swaddling clothes?

A child could not arrive in a poorer home than this, where nothing is ready for it, it could not be given to a poorer mother. Wretched creature! Arriving stark naked, to such impoverished parents, in a log house in the wilderness, in a foreign land! Wretched little creature. . . .

But a child could never come to a happier mother than Kristina, and therefore its security is the greatest in the world.

At her breast lies a little human seedling, entrusted to her in its helplessness and defenselessness. It depends on her if it shall grow up or wither down, if it shall live or die. And at this thought a tenderness grows inside her heart, so strong that tears come to her eyes. But they are not tears of sorrow, they are only the proof of a mother's strong, sure feeling for her newborn child.

When God gave her this child in her poverty, He showed that He could trust her. And if the Creator trusted her, then she could wholeheartedly trust Him in return. From this conviction springs the sense of security and comfort which the child instills in the mother.

Poor little one—happy little one! Why does she worry? Why is she concerned about him? She *has* something fine to swaddle him in! Why hadn't she thought of it before? She should have remembered at once: her white petticoat, the one she never uses, because it is a piece of finery. Her petticoat of thick, fine linen, woven by herself, her bridal petticoat! As yet she has used it only once—at her wedding. And for what can she use it here in the forest? Here she'll never go to weddings, here she'll never be so much dressed up as to need such a petticoat. She can cut it to pieces and sew diapers from it; it is large, voluminous, it will make many diapers. And she must use it because she has nothing else. But isn't it the best thing she could ever find for protection of her child, that delicate little body, with its soft, tender skin? Her own bridal petticoat!

How happy the woman who can cut up her best petticoat for her child.

So much for the clothing. Food for the child the mother has herself. Milk for the child runs slowly as yet, only a few white drops trickling. And Kristina aids the newborn's blindly seeking mouth, pushes her nipple into blindly seeking lips which do not yet quite know how to hold and close and suck, to receive the mother's first gift.

All is well, all is over, all is quiet. Now mother and child rest in mutual security.

# XIX

## The Letter to Sweden

North America at Taylors Falls Postofice in
Minnesota Teritory, November 15, Anno 1850

Dearly Beloved Parents,

May all be well with you is my Daily wish.

I will now let you know how Our Journey progressed, we were freighted on Steam wagon to Buffalo and by Steam ship further over large Lakes and Rivers, we had an honest interpreter. On the river boat Danjel Andreasson lost his youngest daughter in that terrible pest the Cholera. The girl could not live through it. But the rest of us are in good health and well fed. Nothing happened on the journey and in August we arrived at our place of settling.

We live here in a Great Broad valley, I have claimed and marked 160 American acres, that is about 130 Swedish acres and I will have *delasjon* with the payment until the Land is offered for Sale. It is all fertile Soil. We shall clear the Land and can harvest as much Hay as we want. We live at a fair Lake, full of fish and my whole farm is overgrown with Oak, Pine, Sugar Maples, Lindens, Walnuts, Elms and other kinds whose names I do not know.

I have timbered up a good house for us. Danjel and his Family settled near us in the valley, also Jonas Petter. Danjel no longer preaches Ake Svensson's teaching, nor is he making noise about his religion, he is pious and quiet and is left in peace by Ministers and Sheriffs. Danjel calls his place New Kärragärde.

Our beloved children are in good health and live well, I will also inform you that we have a new little son who made his first entry into this world the seventh of this November, at very daybreak. He is already a *sitter* as are all who are born here. We shall in time carry him to Baptism but here are ministers of many Religions and we dare not take the Lord's Supper for fear it is the wrong faith. Here is no Religious Law but all have their free will.

Scarcely any people live in this Valley, rich soil is empty on all sides of us for many miles which is a great shame and Sin. We have no trouble with the indians, the savages are curious about new people but harm no one. They have brown skin and live like cattle without houses or anything. They eat snakes and grasshoppers but the whites drive away the indians as they come.

There is a great difference between Sweden and America in food and clothing. Here people eat substantial fare and wheat bread to every meal. Newcomers get hard bowels from their food but the Americans are honest and helpful to their acquaintances and snub no one if ever so poor. Wooden shoes are not used, it is too simple for the Americans. They honor all work, menfolk milk cows and wash the floor. Both farmers and

Ministers perform woman-work without shame. In a town called Stillwater we were given quarters with a priest who did his own chores.

I have nothing of importance to write about. Nothing unusual has happened to us since my last letter. Things go well for us and if health remains with us we shall surely improve our situation even though the country is unknown to us. I don't complain of anything, Kristina was a little sad in the beginning but she has now forgotten it.

We hope soon to get a letter from you but letters are much delayed on the long way. Winter has begun in the Valley and the mail can not get through because of the ice on the river. I greet you dear parents, also from my wife and children, and Sister Lydia is heartily greeted by her Brother. My Brother Robert will write himself, he fools with writing easier than I. Kristina sends her greetings to her kind parents in Duvemåla. Nothing is lacking her here in our new settlement.

The year is soon over and we are one year nearer Eternity, I hope these lines will find you in good health.

Written down hastily by your devoted son
Karl Oskar Nilsson

# PART THREE

# To Keep Alive Through the Winter

# XX

## The Indian in the Treetop

SOME DISTANCE WEST of the creek which emptied into Lake Ki-Chi-Saga a sandstone cliff rose high above the forest pines. The cliff had the copper-brown color of the Indians, and its shape strongly resembled the head of an Indian. Seen from below, a broad, smooth, stone brow could easily be recognized. Under the forehead lay two black eye holes, well protected by the formidable forehead boulders. Between the eyes a protruding cliff indicated a handsome Indian nose. The upper lip was formed by a ledge, and under it opened a broad indentation; this was the mouth, a dark gap. Below the mouth opening was a chin ledge. Even the neck of the Indian could be discerned below the chin and on top of the head grew maple saplings and elderberry bushes which the Indian in summer carried like a green wreath on his head.

This cliff in the forest was visible from afar and served as a landmark. The Swedish settlers at Lake Ki-Chi-Saga soon referred to it as the Indian-head.

In the caves and holes of the rock, animals found protection and hiding places, and those forest creatures which sought refuge in rain and storm within the Indian's jaws could rest there in comfort. But on the deer path below could be seen great boulders, which from time to time had fallen from the cliff. And near some of these blocks were whitened, disintegrating bones, remnants of animal skeletons; perhaps, as a forest beast had run by below, the Indian had spit out a stone from his mouth and crushed it.

This Indian was of stone, and as dead as a stone, but the white bones indicated that he could be trusted as little as a living Indian.

When Robert passed the Indian-head he trod lightly and stole quickly by, lest a boulder be loosed by his step and come crashing down on him. No one knew when the Indian might hurl a stone at a passer-by, human or beast.

In the beginning, Robert was as much afraid of the Indians as he was curious about them. But as time went by his curiosity increased and his fear diminished. The Indians seemed so friendly that they might in time become a nuisance. They frightened people sometimes with their terrifying appearance, they liked to deck themselves in all kinds of animal parts, but as yet they had done no harm to the Swedish settlers.

Karl Oskar despised the Indians for their laziness and called them useless creatures. Kristina pitied them because they were so thin and lived in such wretched hovels; and both she and Karl Oskar were grateful not to have been created Indians.

No one knew what the copperskins thought of their white neighbors, for no one understood their language. Robert guessed they considered their pale brethren fools to waste their time in work. He had begun to wonder which one of the two peoples could be considered wiser, the whites or the browns, the Christians or the heathens. The Indians were lazy, they did not till the earth, and what work they did was done without effort. He had watched them fell trees: they did not cut down the tree with an ax, they made a fire around it and burned it off at the root. The Christian hewed and labored and sweated before he got his tree down. But the heathen sat and rested and smoked his pipe until the fire burned through and the tree fell by itself, without a single ax blow.

The Indians did not waste their strength in work; they spared their bodies for better use, they saved their strength for enjoyment. At their feasts they danced for three weeks at a stretch—it was just as well they had rested beforehand. But Karl Oskar and the other peasants in Småland had accustomed themselves to tiresome labor and drudgery every day, they would not have been able to dance for even one week, so worn out were they. The heathens wisely economized their body strength so that they were capable of more endurance than the Christians.

The Indians were vain, they decorated themselves with buffalo horns, they greased their hair with bear fat, they smeared red clay over their faces. At times they painted their whole bodies so red they resembled blood-stained butchers; in such things they were childish. But in other ways they were so clever one might take them for magicians; their bows were simple and useless looking—only a piece of skin stretched between the two ends of a broken-off branch—yet their arrows killed game in its tracks; Robert had once seen an Indian shoot a big buck with his bow and arrow. The brownskins' flint arrows were short, but they sharpened them against a peculiar stone called Indian-stone until their points grew so sharp they would penetrate hide and flesh and shatter bone.

The Indians were childish in another way—they believed dead people could eat and drink; they carried food and drink to the graves of their relatives.

But in one way they were much wiser than the whites: they did not hoe the earth.

Robert had once seen the picture of an Indian girl in a book; she was so beautiful he would have liked to make her his wife, could he have found her. But the young women he had seen here among the Chippewas were almost all ugly: they had short legs, clumsy bodies, broad, square faces with thick noses. The older women had such rough skin that they were almost repulsive. Yet white menfolk were said to desire Indian women. Samuel Nöjd, the fur trapper, had related that in the old days there were French trappers so burning with lust they couldn't pass a female in the forest. They had raped every Indian woman they had encountered, however ugly or old she might be. And this caused them no more concern than shooting an animal.

However, Nöjd said, the trappers had grown less eager to attack Indian women after the Sioux had taken a gruesome revenge on one white man. They had tied him to a pole, and for a whole night they sharpened their knives in front of him, now and then calling out to him: "You may live until our knives are sharp!" At intervals they tested their knives by cutting off a piece of his skin. At daybreak the knives were sharp—and the trapper insane. Then the Indians stuck their well-honed knives into his breast, cutting loose his heart, as slowly as they could, and the man lived a long while with his heart dangling outside him like a big red blossom. This had taken place near the Indian cliff. Later the savages had buried the trapper in the cave called the mouth of the Indian-head. Every day at dawn the trapper's agonized cries could still be heard, Samuel Nöjd concluded.

The Sioux, who from time to time roamed through these regions, were much more cruel than the Chippewas. But Robert did not avoid the Indians because of their cruelty or their heathenish ways; rather, he admired and esteemed them for their wisdom and their easy way of living. Had he himself been given brown skin instead of white, he would not have been forced either to cut timber in the forest or grub hoe the earth.

—2—

THE NIGHT FROST grew sharper; each morning the meadow resembled a field of glittering white lilies. An intense storm had in a single day shaken the leaves from the trees, carrying them into the air like clouds of driven snow; afterward the surface of Lake Ki-Chi-Saga shone golden yellow with all the floating leaves from the naked forest on its shores. After the storm came the cold, and land and water were soon frozen hard. On the lake the mirror-clear ice crust thickened each night, and in the ground the frost dug deeper, not to release its hold until spring.

No one could work frozen ground, and Robert put away his grub hoe for the winter. He must now help his brother cut fence rails; in the spring Karl Oskar would fence the part of his land he intended to cultivate, and thousands of rails were needed.

Robert and Arvid visited each other every Sunday; either Robert would walk over to the settlement at Lake Gennesaret, or Arvid would come to Ki-Chi-Saga. Usually they went down to the lake shore, where they made a fire; here the two friends from Sweden could sit undisturbed in intimate talk.

Robert had told Arvid when he first decided to leave his Swedish service and emigrate to North America. Now he again had a secret of a similar nature, and Arvid was the only one he confided in. One frosty

Sunday, as they sat feeding their fire on the lake shore, he began: "Can you keep your mouth shut?"

"I never say anything. You can rely on me."

"I carry a great secret—no one knows it; I'm going to run away from here as soon as I can."

Arvid was astonished: "What's that you say? You want to leave your brother?"

"Karl Oskar is not my master."

"I thought you two brothers would stay together."

"I shall travel far away and dig gold."

"Dig up gold? The hell you will! And you haven't told anyone?"

"Such a plan must be kept secret."

Robert explained: It wasn't that his brother treated him badly, Karl Oskar neither kicked nor hit him; but the work was no different from the drudgery he had endured while a hired hand in Sweden; it was equally depressing and heavy; the days dragged along with the same monotony. He could not stand it much longer, he had never wanted to be a day laborer, he knew a shorter way to riches, and here in America no one could stop him from traveling wherever he wished.

"Do you know where the gold lies?" Arvid asked.

"Yes. In California. Farthest away to the west."

"Is California a—a broad land?"

"Broader than Minnesota."

"Do you know the exact place? I mean, where the gold lies?"

"No. I'll have to look and ask my way, I guess."

"Is the gold spread all over? Or is it in one place?"

"It's spread all over."

Arvid thought about this for a while, then he said: Gold was supposed to glitter, it should be easy to see it, if one looked sharp. But if California was bigger than Minnesota, and if the gold was spread all over that broad country, then Robert might have a troublesome, long-drawn-out journey before he found it; he would have to walk over the whole country and look everywhere.

Robert realized that Arvid did not know anything about the gold land; he had only heard the name. He must explain to his friend about that country, since he wished to share his plans for the future with Arvid.

And so Robert began a simple explanation of California. He told Arvid all he had read and heard, besides much he had neither read nor heard but which he knew must be so, without exactly knowing how he knew it. And perhaps the things he knew in this way were the most important.

In California the valuable metal called gold was almost as common as wood in Minnesota. Gold was used for all kinds of tools, implements, and furniture, because it was cheaper than iron or wood. Rich people used gold chamber pots. The gold grew in that country on fields called gold fields. It grew quite near the surface. Only a light hoe was needed to

232

reach it, not a heavy ten-pound grub hoe such as he labored with here. In some places no hoe at all was required—there were those who had dug up as much as fifty thousand dollars' worth of gold with a tablespoon. The only tool needed was a wooden bowl in which to wash the gold to remove the dirt. And if you couldn't afford a bowl, you might wash the gold in your hat; an old, worn-out hat was all one needed to gather a fortune. And when the gold had been washed clean of earth and other dirt, until it shone and glittered according to its nature, one had only to put it in a skin pouch and carry it to the bank, and then return to withdraw the interest each month. All gold pickers with good sense did this; the others squandered their gold in gambling dens, or ruined themselves with whores.

One needn't pick up a great deal of gold in order to get rich. About a hundred pounds would be right, or as much as one could carry on one's back; about two bushels would be right.

"How big might the gold clods be?" Arvid asked.

"They are of different weights."

The gold grew in pieces of all sizes, from about half a pound to twenty-five pounds weight, Robert explained. There were chunks as large as a human head, while others were tiny as dove eggs. There was also a still smaller kind, about the size of hazelnuts, and these lumps were most prevalent and easiest to find. But they were such a nuisance to pick that he did not intend to bother with them; for himself he would choose the larger chunks, then he wouldn't have to bend his back too often; by picking the twenty-five-pound pieces one could save one's strength in the gold fields.

Nor would Robert gather such a great fortune that it would be a burden to him. He wanted a medium-sized fortune that would be easy to look after and not bring him eternal damnation; he did not intend to build himself a castle, or buy expensive riding horses, or marry some extravagant woman with a desire for diamonds and pearls. He only wished to gain enough of a fortune to live for the rest of his life without drudgery, or labor, or masters.

Robert wanted to weigh up for himself a hundred pounds of the California gold; then he would return completely satisfied. Perhaps he might even return to Sweden and buy himself a manor house. He had heard of two farm hands from Småland who had dug gold in California and then returned home and bought great estates. They had each brought home a sack of gold, which they had exchanged for Swedish coin. But Robert thought he would be satisfied with a smaller estate, about two hundred acres or so; the larger ones required too much attention and could easily become a burden to their owners. Robert would get himself an overseer; and he would pay his hands well—a thousand daler a year, and they would be let off work at six o'clock, Saturdays at five.

"You are good to them," said Arvid.

"Having served as farm hand myself I know what they deserve," said Robert modestly.

"And . . . was it your thought to travel alone to California?"

"No. That's what I wanted to tell you: the two of us should go together."

There should be two, because the road was so awfully long. And two would find the gold much more easily than one. True enough—gold glittered and shone, but four eyes could see twice as much as two; and two would be safer against robbers and thieves.

"Are you coming with me, Arvid?"

It was the same question Robert had once before asked his friend, one night long ago in a stable room in their homeland. Then it had concerned North America, and so great had been Arvid's surprise at Robert's daring and ingenuity that he had been speechless for a long moment. Now the question concerned a journey to the land of gold in North America, and that land also lay so far away that the sun needed extra hours to reach it in the mornings.

Robert repeated his question: "Are you coming with me, Arvid?"

"I want to—that you must know. But I'm in Danjel's service."

"He cannot keep you here! Not in America."

"But I owe my master for the journey here."

Danjel Andreasson had paid the expense for his servant's emigration, and Arvid felt it would be dishonest to leave him before he had repaid Danjel through his work. But he too knew full well that no master could keep him longer than he wanted to stay; no servant law was in force here, no sheriff fetched runaway farm hands.

"You can pay Danjel what you owe him when you come back from California!" said Robert. "You can just hand him a chunk of gold."

Yes, returning from the gold fields Arvid would be so well-to-do that he need never again lift his hand in work, neither with ax, hoe, nor any other tool. He had only to carry his gold to the bank and each month withdraw sufficient interest to pay his expenses; there would be plenty of money to pay Danjel.

Moreover, the two youths had once and for all promised each other to stick together in America.

"I haven't forgotten that promise," said Arvid, deeply moved. "I want to follow you, that you must know. But I must talk to Danjel before I shake your hand on it."

Robert already felt sure he could persuade Arvid to go with him to California.

"You mustn't whisper a word to anyone! I don't intend to tell Karl Oskar until the day before I leave!"

He had already figured out the way to take: They would board the *Red Wing* next time the packet steamer came to Stillwater, then the boat would carry them down the Mississippi to St. Louis, the same way they had traveled last summer. By helping to load wood and wash dishes, they would not have to pay a cent for their transportation on the *Red Wing*. From St. Louis they could walk dryshod all the way to California, following the great highways that led to the West.

"Isn't there any—any ocean in between?" Arvid asked with some concern.

Robert assured him there was not; only solid land, mostly dry, sandy stretches where they could walk comfortably to the home of the gold in the New World.

Robert had long been listening to his left ear, its persistent humming and ringing urging him on: *Come! Come!* A new land far away called him again, and having obtained his friend's promise of company, he would soon follow the call.

But the winter was to interfere with his plans; the frost grew in intensity, soon the whole St. Croix River was covered with solid ice. The *Red Wing*'s bell no longer was heard in Stillwater; indeed, no craft would be seen on the river until next spring when the ice had broken up; the inhabitants of the St. Croix Valley were separated from the outside world by the frozen river.

For the rest of the winter Robert was shut up in Minnesota Territory.

—3—

EARLY ONE SUNDAY MORNING, Robert picked up his brother's gun and went into the forest. New-fallen snow, three or four inches deep, covered the ground; it was fine hunting weather. Not far from the cabin he came on the tracks of an elk, and hunting fever seized him. The elk could not be very far away—Karl Oskar had not yet shot an elk—think if he could shoot this big animal and be the first one to bring home all the meat!

The elk tracks led past the Indian-head, and Robert stopped a moment to look up at the cliff. The stone Indian stared back at him with his unchanging, black eye holes. As long as this cliff had existed—for thousands of years—those deep, inscrutable eyes had looked out over the forest; the Indian stood guard for his brown-skinned people, an eternal watchman over the hunting grounds hereabouts. But his green wreath was now withered, the bushes on top of his head had lost their leaves, the wind whipped the naked, dry branches; only above the Indian's left ear some limbs still carried their leaves—like eagle feathers stuck behind his ear.

Every time Robert looked at the enormous face of this cliff, a strange sensation of uneasiness stole over him; there was something threatening in the stone Indian's eternal immobility; he felt like a sneaking intruder on the age-old hunting grounds of the savages.

235

Suddenly he crouched, holding his breath: he had discovered a living Indian close by.

Below the cliff, hardly a gunshot from where he stood, a human figure huddled in the top of a small birch. His face was turned away from Robert, but he could see skinny legs, partly covered by tattered skins which fluttered in the wind. And near his hands Robert could clearly see a bent branch—the Indian's bow!

For a long minute he grew cold and hot in quick succession. An Indian lurking in the tree, with his bow and sharp arrows! Whom could this sly brownskin be waiting for? White intruders who trespassed on his hunting grounds? Was he waiting for Robert? Was that why he had climbed the birch? The Indians were said to surprise their prey from tree-tops. . . .

Robert held on to his gun butt with trembling fingers. Apparently he had discovered the Indian before being seen himself; why not fire first? But if he missed? An Indian could shoot a score of arrows in a minute. And already Robert could feel them penetrate his body—twenty arrows all over his body! Hadn't he seen one single Indian arrow kill a huge buck? If he should miss—he could see himself dead.

But perhaps the Indian too was after elk. Perhaps he too had seen the fresh tracks? If he were waiting for game, then Robert might be able to sneak away before being seen. As yet there had been no threatening move.

Robert threw himself down in the snow and began hitching himself away on his elbows, his gun above his head. In this way he moved some twenty yards until he reached a thicket, behind which he crouched cautiously; now the man in the tree could not see him. He wasn't sure if an arrow had pursued him—a bow did not give a report like a gun, and he didn't hear too well.

He waited a few minutes but nothing happened. Carefully he separated the branches to peek through: the Indian was still sitting in the tree, he didn't seem to have moved the least bit, he still held his bow in the same position. Indians could sit for hours in a tree, as immobile as stones; he must still be waiting, watching the trail below the cliff.

Robert was now sure the Indian had not yet seen him, and if he could get away a little farther he would be beyond reach of an arrow.

As he began to steal away he heard a rustle in the thicket. He listened. Was it the wind? Or a rabbit? Or was it an arrow? He heard the sound again; some branches moved close by his head where he lay on the ground. It must have been an arrow striking in the thicket, the Indian must have discovered him when he peeked through a moment before.

For a third time there was a rustle in the bush, the branches quivered; now he could clearly hear the whizz of an arrow through the air!

He grew panicky; his heartbeats throbbed in his ears, he felt choked. He aimed the gun in the general direction of the Indian and fired. The report echoed loudly against the cliff, the shot must have been heard for miles. It was so loud that it deafened him and echoed inside his eardrums. What had he done? He had fired the gun in fright, without exactly knowing why. Now all the Indians in the vicinity would be warned, now they would all come after him!

Seized by an overwhelming fear, Robert took to his heels. He ran as if the devil were after him. He ran toward the cabin the shortest way he knew, he slunk between the trunks of a thick stand of timbers; he was conscious of leaving tracks behind for his pursuers to follow, but he was too scared to look back; the Indians could run twice as fast as white men, and they had fresh snow tracks to follow. But Robert dared not look to find out if they followed him; he did not stop to consider that if an Indian had pursued him he would immediately have been overtaken.

He didn't even slow down as he reached the lake shore and saw the cabin, he rushed panting in through the door and sank down on his bed. It was some time before he recovered his breath sufficiently to speak, and Karl Oskar and Kristina watched him and wondered what had happened.

Robert had brought back no game. But Karl Oskar knew that he often missed with his shots and as he now looked at the gun he could see that it had been fired; a little annoyed at this waste of powder and bullet, he asked: "What have you been shooting at?"

"I shot—an Indian."

"You lie!"

"No. No. But he shot at me first."

And by and by Robert breathed easier and could stammer out his story: He had almost been shot to death, near the Indian cliff. A brownskin had been sitting in wait for him in a tree. Robert had sought protection behind some bushes, but the Indian had shot several arrows at him. He had had to defend himself and he had fired a shot at the Indian. Then he had run home as fast as he could.

"Did no one come after you?"

"Not as far as I could see. That's why I'm sure I shot him."

Karl Oskar grew more concerned. But he controlled himself, he didn't want to say anything that might frighten Kristina. He took Robert outside and questioned him in detail about everything that had taken place below the cliff.

Since the Indian had not pursued him, Robert was sure his bullet had hit him, he had seen him fall down from the tree like a fat woodcock.

"Did you really see him fall?" asked Karl Oskar.

"Well—I ran as fast as I could. . . ."

"But you don't know for sure if you hit him? I hope to God you didn't!"

And Karl Oskar told his brother what he had not wanted to say in

237

Kristina's presence: If he had shot an Indian, he had brought disaster on all of them.

He had many times admonished Robert to avoid the Indians and never in any way to disturb them. All had been well so far, they had lived in peace with the Chippewas. If it was true that Robert had been waylaid and attacked with arrows, and had defended himself, then he was within his rights. But if he had wounded or killed a peaceful Indian, then revenge-hungry tribe members would make them all pay for it; then their copper-colored neighbors would soon come and call on them.

"I only hope you missed him!" Karl Oskar repeated.

The next few days Karl Oskar went in constant fear that the Indians would appear at the cabin for revenge. He tried to figure out how he might summon help in time. He had heard of Fort Snelling, near St. Paul, where the Americans kept a company of soldiers to protect the whites. But it was thirty miles to the fort, and long before a message could reach there the Indians would have had time to murder them and burn down their house. There was this about the savages, they could never be relied on; no one could predict what they would do.

But then one day something happened to allay his fears: The Indians on the island in Lake Ki-Chi-Saga broke up their camp and moved away; brownskins no longer lived in their vicinity. It was the custom of the Chippewas to live in winter quarters some forty or fifty miles to the south.

—4—

SOME WEEKS went by, and Karl Oskar had almost forgotten about Robert's encounter with the Indian in the tree. Then one day, having picked up his gun to follow some forest birds, he happened to pass the Indian cliff. Snowdrifts had now piled on the Indian-head, giving him wintry eyebrows, and a crown of glittering snow. In summer this Indian had a green wreath, in winter a white crown. But Karl Oskar's alert eyes espied something else: A birch tree grew below the cliff, and something was fastened to the top of the birch.

He walked toward it to investigate; someone was hanging in the treetop, a human being, an Indian. This Indian could not move, however, he was frozen stiff. The wind had swept away the snow, but no odor tainted the air—the frost was protecting the corpse from decay.

Robert's Indian was still hanging in his tree. He had hung there for weeks; he was stone dead. The shot had hit him then, the calamity Karl Oskar feared had taken place. But the rest of the tribe must not have discovered what had happened to one of their members, they must not have found his body. Or why hadn't they come for revenge?

Then he discovered something else in the treetop, something he couldn't understand at first. He walked around the tree, looking up; he climbed a stone to see better, and suddenly the mystery was solved; now he knew why they had been spared a visit from revengeful neighbors: *The Indian in the tree had been hung there!* His neck was pierced through by the top of the birch, which had been sharpened and stuck through the neck like a spear. The top of the young tree was bent like a bow, the Indian was strung up through his neck, like a dead fish on a forked stick.

And now Karl Oskar remembered what he had heard about the Indians, how they preserved the bodies of their dead in wintertime, when the digging of a grave in the frozen ground was too hard work. They strung up the corpses in trees, high enough above ground to be safe from beasts. The dead one had been placed there by his own tribe!

He left the Indian in the tree and walked home; he had no desire to disturb the body, he did not wish to interfere with the doings of the Indians. But now he knew the truth about his brother's adventure: Robert had been attacked by an Indian who was strung up in a tree, he had run for his life from a dead Indian.

Walking home, Karl Oskar recalled Robert's story on the *Charlotta* about the captain's slave trade. That time he had greatly doubted his brother's veracity; this time he knew that Robert had invented the story, he had proof that his brother was a liar.

As soon as he reached home he called Robert aside: "Did you say the Indian in the tree shot an arrow at you?"

"Yes! He shot several arrows, right into the bush where I hid!" Robert assured him.

"Did any of the arrows hit you?"

"No. Luckily enough, the bush protected me."

"Yes, I understand. I guess the Indian had poor aim. And I don't wonder—you see, he was dead. He's still hanging dead in the tree. The top is stuck right through his neck!"

Karl Oskar took Robert with him to the tree with the Indian. This was his proof, and he turned to Robert, sterner than ever: "You're a damned liar! The Indian never shot a single arrow at you!"

"But I could hear them rustle in the bush!"

"I think it was the wind."

"It was arrows! I'm sure! I could hear them!"

"You don't hear very well. And you invent lies! You spin yarns! Now I want you to tell me the truth."

"But it is the truth! I swear it, Karl Oskar."

To Robert, his story of the Indian in the treetop was irrevocably the truth. The brownskin had shot at least three arrows at him, with his own ears he had heard them whizz through the thicket. And how could Karl Oskar know that the Indian wasn't alive when he shot at Robert? Moreover, he couldn't remember if the Indian had been sitting in exactly that tree; perhaps it was another Indian, in another tree. He, Robert, had seen a living Indian, with a bow, he could not alter his story in the least, for he had told the truth.

Robert's behavior angered and worried Karl Oskar; not only did the boy lie, he was so thoroughly dishonest that he stubbornly insisted his lies were true. He insisted he had been attacked by the Indian and that he had run for his life.

Now Karl Oskar spoke sternly, with fatherly concern: Was Robert so hardened that he believed his own fabrications? Didn't he know the difference between truth and lies? If he continued to invent and tell tales like this, people would soon believe not a single word he said, no one would have confidence in him. And if no one could rely on him, he would have a hard time getting along in America. He must be careful about what he said, or disaster might follow.

He must realize that Karl Oskar felt responsible for him as an older brother, now that he was in a foreign country without his parents to look after him. Didn't he think his own brother was concerned for his welfare? Why couldn't he admit that he had lied, and promise never to do it again? He ought to do it for his own sake, for his own good!

But Robert admitted nothing. His ear had heard the Indian's whizzing arrows in the bush; at least three times his ear had heard them, and this remained the truth to him.

Karl Oskar could get nowhere. Robert had a weak character, and no persistence in work or effort. He hadn't a farmer's feeling for the earth, he did what he was told, but unwillingly, without joy or pleasure. At work he often acted as if he neither saw nor heard, as if walking in his sleep in full daylight. Karl Oskar had long been aware of these shortcomings in his brother, but he had hoped they would disappear as he grew older and his common sense increased. A settler in this new land needed a sturdy character, persistence, clear vision; he couldn't walk about in his sleep. . . . To these faults, Robert had lately added this infernal habit of lying, more dangerous than all the rest—it might bring him to utter ruin.

After this happening, Karl Oskar's concern about Robert increased; he thought it might have been better if his brother had remained in Sweden.

# XXI

## The Swedish Settlers' Almanac

NOVEMBER PASSED with changing weather—cold days followed milder ones. Little snow fell. But in early December the first blizzard broke, beating the cabin walls for four days.

All living creatures sought their lairs for shelter against the fierce north wind. The snow did not fall on the ground, it was driven down violently, flung by the forceful sling of the storm. Man and beast trying to move against this wind must crouch, almost creep along. And the north wind brought in its wake a cold that penetrated bone and marrow, that made the blood stop in its course.

During this blizzard no one ventured outside unless forced by necessity. It was an undertaking even to open the door. Karl Oskar had to go to the shanty morning, noon, and evening, to give Lady water and fodder. It was hardly more than a hundred steps between the cabin and the small stable, yet the first day of the blizzard he almost lost his way. The snow beat into his eyes so that he could not see, everything around him was snow, hurled, whirling snow; he walked in a thick, gyrating snow cloud, fumbling about like a blind person. He could not see one step ahead of him, he lost his sense of direction, and wandered about a long time before he found the cabin.

In the raging blizzards of this country he could lose his way a few steps from his house. And should he get lost on his way between cabin and stable there was the danger of freezing to death in the snow.

Karl Oskar felt the need of something to guide him between his two houses, and from the linden bark he had saved he now twisted a rope, fastening one end to the cabin and the other to the shanty. While walking the short distance he never let go of the rope; each time he opened the door and faced the blizzard he felt like a diver descending to the bottom of the sea and holding to a guide rope—without it he might have been lost.

During the blizzard Karl Oskar milked Lady every day. The cow still gave little at each milking—only one quart—but this was sufficient for the children; the grownups had to do without. He had never before sat on a milking stool, and now he learned a chore which in this country was usually performed by the menfolk. Strong hands were needed to squeeze the milk from the teats, and he wondered why milking had always been considered woman's work.

Now that the feared winter had come Kristina spent most of her time within the house; she had regained her strength and resumed her household tasks but she dared not go outside. She said the snow, like everything else, was different here: at home the snowflakes fell soft as wool on one's face, here they were hard and sharp and pricked like awl points.

Karl Oskar had made sure they need not freeze in the house this winter; outside the door he had stacked firewood in high piles, logs from dry pines long dead on root, excellent wood that gave much heat. As long as the fire was kept burning it was warm in the house. He had also split pitch wood in great quantity to be used for lighting the cabin; these splinters were stuck in the wall between the logs and used as candles, but they had to be watched carefully to avoid setting fire to the house.

Their home was now taking on the appearance of a carpenter shop. Karl Oskar spent much time making furniture and tools—chairs, food vessels, snow shovels, hay forks, rakes. He busied himself long after the others had gone to bed. Being handy with wood, he could use it for many purposes; a settler beginning from the very beginning had to use it for almost everything.

He had already worked as lumberman, carpenter, mason, roofer, rope maker—now he attempted a new handicraft: that of shoemaker. Their leather shoes were wearing out and they couldn't buy new ones; he must make wooden shoes for his family. No alder trees grew in this forest so he decided to use elm; the American elm was softer than the Swedish and easy to work with. But wooden shoes could not be made comfortable and light without years of experience. He had neither experience nor the proper tools; the shoes that came from his hands were clumsy and ill fitting though they could be worn. He made one pair of wooden shoes for each member of his family except the baby, who would not need shoes until he could walk. For his newborn son he made a cradle—a dug-out log which he fastened to rockers.

Then he began to make a table. He had made up his mind to have a fine table, solid and well made, a durable piece of furniture, a table he could ask visitors to sit down to without feeling ashamed. And he worked long and carefully on this piece of furniture. He cut a block from the thickest oak he could find and made a table top; to this he fastened a smaller log for footing. He planed the top until it shone; now they would not get splinters in their fingers when eating. The leg logs also caused him great labor, the table must stand evenly on the floor without leaning or limping.

And he took his time with the table, time hung heavily upon him during these winter days and long evenings. And when he rested he got into the habit of fingering the three books they had brought from Sweden: the Bible, the psalmbook, and the almanac. Two thick books and one thin; the thick ones contained spiritual fare, they were the soul's guide to eternity; the thin book was their guide in this transitory world. Karl Oskar had used the almanac most often, and now in the last month of the year it was badly worn and soiled. Each Sunday he or Kristina read the text in the psalmbook, and each Sunday Karl Oskar also looked in the almanac to determine where they were in the calendar year. He had marked the days of this year which they must remember: April 6, when they left their home; April 14, when they said farewell to their homeland in Karlshamn; June 23, when they arrived in North America; and July 31, when they reached Minnesota Territory. After their arrival here he had put a cross in the almanac on the day they moved into their house, the day when his third son was born, and the day Lady had been taken to the bull at Fischer's, the German's.

The year 1850 was nearing its end, and when the old year ended, the almanac too would come to an end. They could not obtain a new Swedish almanac, and they could not read an American one. Karl Oskar wondered how they would manage to keep track of days and weeks and months in the year to come. He must invent some means. To make an almanac that would last a single year was harder than to make a table that would last for generations. But without the almanac he would feel lost in time.

—2—

YULETIDE WAS NEAR—a strange Yule for Kristina, a Christmas in another world, a Christmas without Yule chores. No pig to butcher, no ale to brew, no great-bake to bake. But they must nevertheless celebrate the holiday and honor the Saviour's birth like Christian people. She said to Karl Oskar, this year they must not think of the outside—food, drink, and material things. They must celebrate Christmas in their hearts; this year must be a Christmas for their souls.

She scoured the cabin floor until it was shining white, she washed their underclothes in ash lye, so that all could change for the holiday, she hung fresh pine boughs on the walls and decked the cabin inside as best she could. Of a pine top with upright branches Karl Oskar made a five-armed candlestick, an ingenuity which his wife praised greatly. He had promised they would celebrate Christmas at a table, and he kept his promise: on Christmas Eve itself he gave the table the last finishing touches with his plane. He was proud of his handicraft, the first piece of real furniture he had ever made, particularly when, at the final inspection, Kristina said: This sturdy oak table would undoubtedly last so long that not only they themselves but their children and grandchildren as well could eat their meals at it throughout their whole lives.

While they had eaten their meals at the chest lid Karl Oskar had felt like a pauper sitting in a corner of someone else's house, eating handed-out food. Now, as he put his feet under his own table, his self-confidence increased: Now he had settled down, now he had become his own master in the new land.

They used their new table for the first time at the Christmas Eve dinner. And Kristina too was pleased—to gather for a feast around a table was something quite different from sitting down to a meal at the old chest lid. The five-armed candleholder was put in the center of the table; they had saved only three candles for Christmas, so two arms were left empty, but the three burning candles spread Yule light in their house. They had bought a pound of rice for the Christmas porridge, and with it they used sweet milk. It was their only Christmas dish, but they ate it with a deep sense of holiday spirit. Its smell and taste brought to their minds recollections of this Holy Eve's celebration at home. Long-ago Christmases now entered their cabin, Christmas Eves with the whole family gathered; and their thoughts lingered on those who at other Yuletides had sat down at table with them. Relatives at home in Sweden tonight

243

seemed more alive than ever, and they spoke of the letter from Sweden which they had been waiting for so long. How much longer before they would hear from parents and relatives? The expected mail from Sweden had not had time to arrive before the river froze and the packets stopped coming for the winter. Now it could not arrive until spring, and that was a long time to wait.

Tonight Karl Oskar remembered his parents as he had seen them that last morning—when he had looked back from the wagon seat for a final glimpse of them as he left the old home: father and mother, looking after the departing ones, standing on the stoop close together, immobile as two statues. To him they would always remain in that position; they could not move or walk away; they stood there, looking after their departing sons; they stood like two dead objects, hewn in stone. His parents could never again resume life in his mind's eye. Perhaps this was because deep within him he knew he would never again meet them on this earth.

A thought came to him—it remained a thought only, which he would not utter: his father and mother might already be dead and buried, without his knowledge. . . .

After the meal Kristina opened the Bible and read the second chapter from St. Luke which in her home had always been read by her father on Christmas Eve in commemoration of the Saviour's birth:

"And so it was, that, while they were there, the days were accomplished that she should be delivered.

"And she brought forth her first-born son, and wrapped him in swaddling clothes, and laid him in a manger; because there was no room for them in the inn. . . ."

Kristina read the Christmas Gospel for all of them, but after a few verses she felt as though she were reading it for herself only: it concerned her above all, it concerned her more than the listeners. Mary's delivery in the stable in Bethlehem reminded her of the childbed she had but recently gone through. It seemed that Mary's time too had come suddenly and unprepared for, even though her days were accomplished: Mary had been on a journey, and perhaps they had been delayed, unable to reach home in time. And Mary had been poor, even more impoverished than she herself. Kristina had borne her child in a human abode, in a well-timbered house—Mary had lain on straw in an animal shelter, in a stall. Kristina had enjoyed the comfort of a kind and helpful midwife, but the Bible said not one word about any help-woman for Mary in the stable. And she wondered whence the Saviour's mother had obtained the swaddling clothes she wrapped about her child before she placed it in the manger. Had she prepared them in advance and brought them along on the journey to Bethlehem? The Bible was so sparing with details that she often wondered and questioned while reading. She guessed Mary must have had as much concern about the clothing of her first born as she

244

herself had had for her child. Perhaps Mary too had been forced to cut up her petticoat to prepare the swaddling clothes for Jesus.

For the first time in twenty years Kristina slept on Christmas morning; ever since early childhood she had gone with her parents on this morning to the early service, which took place hours before daylight, the church illuminated with many candles. But here also they would revere Christmas Day, and Second Christmas Day: all work in the house ceased. They had carried in enough firewood before the holiday, all they had to do was to tend the fire and prepare food.

On Third Christmas Day they had unexpected guests. Swedish Anna and Samuel Nöjd came driving a team of oxen and a dray which they had borrowed from the lumber company; holidays were the time for visits among their countrymen, and they were eager to see the first child born to Swedish settlers in the St. Croix Valley. The boy was now seven weeks old, he was in splendid health, he nursed heartily and cried for more. The mother had enough milk for him, and he was hungry—both facts made Kristina's heart glad. What more could she ask? Suppose she had been without milk, or the child without appetite?

Swedish Anna looked at the tender child as if beholding a miracle of God; she wanted to hold the baby in her arms the whole time she was there. And for luck each of the guests gave the child a coin—a whole silver dollar each!

The parents were in great perplexity about having their last born baptized; so far as they knew, there was not a single Swedish minister in the whole Territory. Karl Oskar wished Danjel Andreasson to conduct the baptism: he was experienced in religious matters, he lived as piously as any minister. In Sweden Dean Brusander had once forbidden them to invite Danjel to be godfather to Harald, because Danjel had been excluded from the church; but the dean had no power over them here, and they ought to compensate Danjel for this insult—they ought to ask him to perform the Sacrament of Holy Baptism for their last-born son.

Kristina was much devoted to her uncle and thought as highly of him as Karl Oskar, but she worried about his earlier heresy and wondered if he weren't still a little confused in religious matters. And she had always felt that the rites of Holy Baptism should be performed by an ordained minister in frock and collar.

Karl Oskar argued: If Danjel read the ritual according to their own Swedish psalmbook, following every word, then it must be valid; they themselves had been baptized in accordance with these instructions.

Kristina asked if a baptism by an American minister wouldn't have the same effect as a baptism by the Swedish clergy. She had thought of Pastor Jackson in Stillwater, who had been so kind to them last summer when they landed from the steamboat. She turned to Swedish Anna: Was there anything wrong in having a child baptized in English?

245

Wouldn't Jesus accept it equally well? Weren't all tongues the same to the Lord?

Swedish Anna looked at her in consternation: "You must be out of your mind! Do you want your child to be a Baptist?"

"Baptist?"

"Pastor Jackson is a Baptist! I thought you knew!"

"No, I didn't know that. But Anna—are you sure?"

"Ask anyone in Taylors Falls!"

Yes, it was true, insisted Swedish Anna: Pastor Jackson was minister of the Baptist Church in Stillwater. He was a sectarian, an Anabaptist, a heretic, an Antichrist preacher. Of all sectarians, the Baptists were the most dangerous, because they rebaptized grown people and robbed them of their Christian grace, bringing them eternal damnation.

And Swedish Anna paled in terror, hovering over the cradle of the unbaptized baby as if trying to protect him against evil powers. "If you let Pastor Jackson baptize the child, you hand him over to the devil instead of to Jesus!"

By now Kristina's concern was as great as Swedish Anna's. But she was also confused: How could the pastor in Stillwater be a false teacher, baptizing people to eternal damnation, eternal fire? Of all the Americans she had met he was the kindest and most helpful; there had been no end to his thoughtfulness for their comfort last summer. And now she related how good he had been to her and the children and all of them. How could he be an evil person, an Anabaptist, sent by Satan?

"That is exactly what he is!" Swedish Anna assured her with inflexible determination. "All Baptists are tools of the devil!"

And this Kristina ought to have realized: That time last summer, he had only tried to snare the newcomers with his false religion, so that he might baptize them and snatch them from Jesus. *That* was why he had given them food and lodging! That was why he had pretended kindness, while the devil sat in his heart and roared with laughter at the easily lured Swedish souls. That was how the Baptists gained their adherents—through deceit and falsity! And Kristina ought to know that devilish evil powers always decked themselves in sheep's clothing while stealing souls! Had she looked closer, she might have seen the cloven hoof of Pastor Jackson, hidden in his boot!

Swedish Anna picked up the unbaptized child from its crib and held it firmly and protectingly in her arms: Before this child were turned over to a false priest, she herself would steal it from the parents!

Moreover, the Baptists only baptized grown people.

Still Kristina could not entirely understand; she grew more confused. She felt in her heart that she had not heard the whole truth about the minister in Stillwater, even if it were true he preached a false religion: he too might have been led astray; perhaps in his honest simplicity he believed what he taught.

246

After this there was no further talk between Karl Oskar and Kristina about taking their son to Stillwater. But they were not concerned only about the child—it was high time they found a minister for themselves as well; their souls needed a nourishing sermon. And Kristina ought to be churched after childbirth; she felt the need of entering a temple to thank God for His grace in giving her a child; she needed His blessing, His comfort, she wished to seek Him in His temple. When a woman was touched by the minister's hand, she was cleansed and purified after her childbed. And all of them needed the Sacrament of Communion after the long journey from the home church. She tried to tell herself that the Lord would overlook their delay and not consider it an unforgivable sin, since they were settled in this wilderness and unable to reach His table— but often, nevertheless, she prayed for forgiveness, worrying over their inability to partake of the Sacrament: though God must look kindly on her, she sometimes said to herself, else He wouldn't have entrusted a new life to her care.

The boy was now so old the parents could no longer keep him unbaptized with a clear conscience. It was their duty to give the child to their Lord and Saviour. They therefore agreed to let Danjel perform the ritual in their home on New Year's Eve. Kristina wished to invite Ulrika of Västergöhl as godmother, to hold the child at the baptism. After some hesitation, Karl Oskar gave his consent.

The father made a neat little bowl of ash wood for the baptismal water. The christening robe Kristina sewed from leftover pieces of her bridal petticoat, which she washed and starched in potato water until it shone. A child should wear a snow-white robe when the Saviour received him at baptism.

They had never before had a christening performed at home, and now they felt as though they were going to church in their own house. They dressed themselves in their best clothes. The floor was swept and the cabin put in order. They could not afford a feast this time; no guests were invited except the officiant and the godmother. Besides, it was difficult now in the middle of the winter to get from one house to another. This time they would have only a simple christening ale; the important thing was that the child be baptized according to the clear Lutheran confession.

And on New Year's Eve in late afternoon the christening took place in the log house. Parents, christening officiant, and godmother stood gathered around the new table, on which was spread their only linen cloth, brought from their old home. Before the holy act Kristina had given the breast to the baby; she held him a long while and let him suck out every drop of milk she had so that he would keep silent while receiving the Sacrament. He was now satisfied and content as she handed him to the godmother, and he lay goodnaturedly in Ulrika's comfortable arms.

Ulrika herself realized fully the importance of her function here; she stood solemn and silent and let Danjel do the talking today.

Kristina had asked her uncle to perform the christening word for word as it was printed in the psalmbook on the page *About Baptism*. And Danjel did as he had been asked to do—he used only the printed words of the book, not a single one of his own. He read *Our Father* and the Christian doctrine into which the child was to be baptized, he read every one of the Tenets of the Faith, from beginning to end. And with his hand laid gently on the little one's head, he asked according to the book: "Child! Do you wish to be baptized in this faith?"

The babe in Ulrika's arms was so filled with his mother's milk that part of his last meal began to run out of his mouth in little runnels. Down his chin it dripped—he spluttered all over his godmother's blouse. And to the officiant's question he answered only with a satisfied belching.

But Ulrika answered for the baby in the psalmbook's own words, which she had learned by heart in advance: Yes, he wanted to be baptized in this faith! Then Danjel Andreasson picked up the boy from the godmother, three times he dipped his hand into the water in the wooden bowl and sprinkled it over the downy head: He was baptizing a human soul in the name of the Holy Trinity.

The child suddenly began to yell, annoyed at this wetting, even though Kristina had been careful to warm the water so it would be neither too hot nor too cold for his delicate scalp. But Ulrika, with motherly care, stuck her thumb into the baby's mouth and the little one sucked and kept his silence.

According to the ritual, Danjel now turned to Ulrika: In case of the parents' inability or absence, it was the godmother's duty to watch over the child, to see that it faithfully kept the promise it had today given in baptism. And she answered her "Yes" in a loud voice and promised to obey all God asked of her. And the parents observed all was performed to the very last word as was written in the psalmbook. Everything at this baptism was done right.

Thus the christening was accomplished: the pure Evangelical-Lutheran Church had one more adherent in the St. Croix Valley.

The budding American citizen in the settlement on Lake Ki-Chi-Saga had been given the name Nils Oskar Danjel. He was to be called Danjel. He had one name from his father, one from his grandfather, and one from the man who had baptized him. All three were good Swedish names. Ulrika had wished to add a fourth, an American name, because he was born in America; but the parents thought they would wait to use such a name until they had another child to christen. The boy, after all, had had his beginning in Sweden.

After the Sacrament was over, the godmother prayed a silent prayer to the Lord of Heaven for her foster son: Would the Almighty ever keep His hands over him, so that no disadvantage might come to him and no evil befall him, even though he was begotten in Sweden.

So ended the year of our Lord 1850. It had been the most unusual year yet in the lives of the immigrants.

—3—

THE NEW YEAR 1851 opened with blizzards, followed by heavy snow-falls over the Territory. The snow piled so high around the cabin that they could not see through the windows; it reached to the eaves. Karl Oskar Nilsson's log cabin lay there at the edge of the forest like a tall snowdrift, little resembling a human habitation. Inside, the cabin's owners lived as in a mine, deep in the ground.

They had heard the story of one settler who had hung his cabin door swinging outward; after a heavy snowfall he had been unable to open it; for three weeks he had been locked inside his house and had almost starved to death before the snow melted and he managed to get out. At home all entrance doors swung inward; the locked-in settler could not have been a Swede.

After the heavy snowfall the men had a new chore—to shovel the snow from the door, make paths to the shanty, the lake, the water hole at the brook. They also cleared away the snow from the windows, but the tall drifts against the walls were left undisturbed, as they were a protection against winds and helped to keep the warmth inside.

After the blizzards followed a time of even, strong winter. The air was crystal clear and like hoarfrost to breathe. The cold dug and tore with its sharp frost claws; the hard snow crust, strong enough to carry full-grown men on its glittering back, now made the wilderness easily accessible. During the stillness of the nights, cracking sounds could be heard as the frost sharpened under a starlit sky.

They must ever be on guard against freezing to death. In the cabin the fire was kept alive day and night. If the embers should die down for a few hours toward morning they would feel the cold when awakening. The children were not very anxious to crawl out of their beds until the fire was burning brightly. All of them—big and little—huddled around the hearth with its blessed fire.

Outside, all animals had sought invisible hideouts. The lake birds had long ago disappeared, and so had the rabbits, the squirrels, and the gophers. The crickets no longer drove their ungreased wagon wheels; the screechhopper had been heard in the grass until late in November but now at last it was silenced. And the settlers at Lake Ki-Chi-Saga wondered how any of the delicate forest creatures could survive such a winter, such unmerciful cold; here even able-bodied people found it hard to survive.

249

THE ALMANAC had come to an end with the old year, and with it Swedish time had ended for the immigrants. They had no guide for days and weeks, nothing to indicate name days and holidays.

Now an idea came to Robert: He could take the old almanac for 1850 and from this figure the days of the new year. He could write a new almanac for the whole year 1851. In Sweden it was forbidden by law to use any almanac except the one printed and sold by the government, but North America had a friendly government; here people could live according to their own almanac, free from persecution or punishment. And once Robert had written one almanac he might make copies of it and sell them to other Swedes who might be equally lost in time.

Karl Oskar gave his brother a few sheets of paper which he had bought when he wrote the last letter to Sweden. Robert folded each sheet twice, cut it up and sewed the pages together into a small book about the size of the old almanac. Then he filled each page with his writing in ink; this work helped him while away the long winter evenings.

Within a week Robert had his almanac ready, an almanac that would last for a whole year. He labored long on the letters of the front page to make them look like those of the old almanac.

All almanacs were prefaced with a chapter on some subject of interest to the reader; for Anno 1850, this chapter was entitled: "Watering of Meadows and Fertilizing Same." Robert also began his almanac with a chapter of general interest and information; he wrote a description of North America which he had long had in mind and for which he had gathered notes. In his description he had changed and corrected all earlier, false descriptions of the New World.

ALMANAC
FOR THE YEAR
AFTER OUR LORD'S BIRTH
1851

Which Year is Considered to be the Fivethousandeighthundredfiftythird from the Creation.

At Stockholm Horizon
59 degr. 20½ min Lat.
*Without*
His Royal Maj.'s Permission or Instruction
Written, issued and sewn together
by
Axel Robert Nilsson from Sweden.
In the Year 1850 Emigrated to
N. America

In Accordance with His Majesty's Pleasure and Decree of August 10, 1819, the small Almanacs are hereafter to be sold, cut and bound, for 4 Skilling Banco apiece, which in American money is 3 cents Silver; whosoever dares increase this price or whosoever at the sale of almanacs offers them uncut or unbound at 4 Sk. apiece, will be fined 33 Riksdaler 16 Skilling Banco for each offence.

---

### A New Description of the United States of North America

Truthfully written down after personal inspection on the spot. Begun during a Steamship Journey on the Mississippi July 27, 1850.

#### First Part

A skipper named Christoffer Columbus was the first white man to discover the United States of North America. Columbus arrived in the Northamerican Republic almost four hundred years before me, and he showed other Immigrants and Skippers the way here. He was later put into prison and severely punished.

North America is a very large and spacious land. If the whole Kingdom of Sweden were moved over here, it would hardly be noticed. Here the sun sets each evening six hours later than in Sweden, which is caused by all clocks and watches being six hours late. But the country is so large and broad that the sun hasn't time to set everywhere at the same hour; far to the west in North America it does not set until many hours after dark.

The inhabitants of North America all speak English, due to the fact that they made themselves free of England's tyranny by melting the lead of the English King's statue in New York and making bullets of him. The English tongue is also called the language of the stutterers, because a stuttering person can speak it most easily. Most of the words are very short, and if they are too long they are bitten off in speech, and a stutterer will easier remember to bite off a word at the right moment.

Watercourses are in many places full of diseases, and the summers are often warm and unhealthy. It is better to take land in the forest, where the lakes are full of fish, than to settle on the prairies, where the rivers are full of fevers and chills. One can buy a horse and wagon and travel comfortably through North America, but this is expensive and takes a long time, for the country is large. Instead one can without danger to life ride on the Steam Wagon. Then one does not need a guide, for the Steam Wagon follows the road without concern to the rider. Two ruts are in North America called a road. Steamships move on all rivers faster than the current. They are also called Packets because they freight packets of mail. During the winter, ice lies on top of the running water, closing all passage of ships.

The rumors concerning white immigrants being sold as slaves in North America and sent to the Infidel Turk are without foundation. This I have been able to ascertain on the spot. Black people are offered for sale at their full price, but whites are not in demand and without value.

## Second Part

The oldest Americans in this country are savages and called Indians. They do not have red skins as so falsely has been written before; they are brown. Because they are of a different color than the white Americans, they do not wish to live orderly or work. When the browns are killed they sometimes make great objections and attack white settlers. The tame Indians go about free everywhere with gray blankets over their heads.

The Indians are heathens but do not eat people as heathens are accustomed to, in their simple-mindedness, but live on wild seed called rice which grows among the reeds of the lakes. The grains are small and consequently it takes a long time to eat one's sufficiency. For solid fare the Indians use the same food as John the Baptist in the desert: fried grasshoppers and wild honey and other larger and smaller animals. But when they meet a dangerous rattlesnake in the forest they say to him in all friendliness: Go your way and I will go mine! Him they do not kill.

The Indians live from hunting and such tilling as does not require work. On small patches they grow a grain which has no heads but a kind of rootstock, because this grain saves labor and requires no threshing with flail. The Indians paint their axes in all colors. But they do not use the axes for cutting trees or wood, only for smashing skulls of people and animals. When the Indian sees an enemy near by, he immediately cuts off the scalp and hangs it with the hair to dry outside his tent when the weather is fine. The one who hangs out the greatest number of scalps is highest in the tribe. Scalps without hair are without value and are not counted. Bald people are not scalped but allowed to run about.

The Indians are very clever at shooting with arrows. Even when they have climbed a tree and had their neck pierced through with the tree top they are able to shoot many arrows. In such cases, however, they seldom hit their aim. The men are the wisest and most intelligent among the Indians. The women do all the work.

## Third Part

All people in North America call each other *you*, regardless of position, riches, or situation. The word is the same as the Swedish *du* (thou) and is pronounced like the Swedish *jo* (yes); this word can be used to anyone without danger. It is not forbidden to remove one's hat in greeting but it is degrading in the North American Republic and not used.

In this country it is not—as in Sweden—considered distinguished or fine to show one's great fortune in a round and fat body; in North America a skinny person is considered and honored as much as a fat one.

The livestock of North America enjoy so much good grazing that their horns sometimes are invisible in the tall grass. All cattle are big, beautiful, and very expensive. Even the women of North America are scarce and of high value.

Examinations in the Catechism are not held in the North American Republic. This I have ascertained after investigations on the spot. Authorities in America are not like in Sweden—eternal and mighty. This is so because it is not as in Sweden—put in its place by God. Government exists maybe but is not seen. Those in Power do not use the Catechism to keep the populace in obedience. No one need obey another unless he murders or steals. If anyone obeys anyone else in North America then it is because he is still too much Swedish.

The way from Sweden to North America is one-fourth the circumference of the globe, which prevents most Swedes from moving here.

Not in one word have I departed from the truth in this my Description of North America in the Almanac of Anno 1851.

### 1851 JANIARIUS 1851

Give, Oh Lord, Success and Joy!

| Days | Moon | Weather | G. St. |
|------|------|---------|--------|
| | Christ's Circumcision Luke:2. | | |
| 1. Friday New Year | 9.0 .) | First qu. | 20 |
| 2. Saturday, Abel | 10.28 | | |

# XXII
## "Mother, I Want Bread!"

ONE OF THE SWEDISH HOMESTEADS had been given a name—New Kärragärde—and Danjel suggested that Karl Oskar ought to follow his example and call his farm New Korpamoen, after his childhood home in Sweden. But Karl Oskar answered: Korpamoen was the last name he would wish to give his new home; he had no desire to be thus constantly reminded of the six years he had thrown away among the stone piles in Sweden. He did not wish for a new Korpamoen in America, he had had enough of the old one; they would find a more suitable name for their home in due time—the christening of a piece of land was not so urgent as the christening of a baby; it was, after all, only a patch of earth, not a human soul.

Danjel also felt they ought to change the name of Ki-Chi-Saga. How could they live near a lake with such an outlandish heathen name? Couldn't they think of some pious Swedish word which a Christian could take in his mouth without distaste? Karl Oskar replied that as he lived on a small arm of the lake, he felt it would be presumptuous for him to change the name of the whole lake. As yet he was the only settler here; when he had neighbors on the shores, they would all think of a new name for Lake Ki-Chi-Saga.

The winter had made it easier for the Swedish settlers to visit back and forth. The frozen snow made a firm road, and they gave each other a hand whenever needed. Ulrika came frequently to the log house at Ki-Chi-Saga to see how her godson fared after his christening. Once

253

she was accompanied by Swedish Anna, and the two women had a violent dispute about sectarians and heretics. Swedish Anna began: "I'm ever thankful to the Lord for saving the child from that Anabaptist in Stillwater!"

Ulrika flared up and threatened dire happenings if Swedish Anna dared say ill of Pastor Jackson. No one could have anything but good to say about that man; he was so helpful, kind, merciful, that it was hard to believe he was a minister; he had even taken the pail from her hands and fetched water himself. It was nobody's business what religion he preached, Lutheran or Baptist, Methodist or Jansonist. When a man like Jackson preached, any religion became the right one. Swedish Anna need not bring up the subject again. Ulrika herself had been a sectarian ever since she came to live with Danjel; she would have been happy to have her godson baptized by Jackson in Stillwater, nay, she wouldn't hesitate for a moment to have such a minister baptize her too!

Swedish Anna started in horror: Ulrika had been led astray from the true Lutheran religion, had been snared already by the Evil One in his heresies! Didn't she know that only the Lutherans had the right religion and lived according to the Ten Commandments of the stone tablets?

How did the Lutherans live in Sweden! exclaimed Ulrika. God's commandments were only for paupers and simple folk! The ministers never dared say one word against the nobles, or correct them in any way. If the high and mighty lords broke every one of God's commandments a hundred times a day, they would never be rebuked from the pulpit. And if the Bishop from Vaxio on his visits to the parishes raped every parsonage maid until the bottom fell out of the bed, not one priest in the whole chapter would object. Yes, if the Swedish King himself should break God's commandments, and if besides this he were degenerate and committed vices against nature, all the priests would still bow to him, as low as ever, and praise him, and pray for him every Sunday according to the words of the prayer book—even though they knew the truth, for it was the King who gave them the parishes. Such were the Lutheran clergy in Sweden, Ulrika stated, and such they would remain.

But Swedish Anna was a strict Lutheran; the two women could not be friends.

During the Christmas holidays Jonas Petter had gossiped to Kristina that Anders Månsson intended to marry Ulrika of Västergöhl. Next time Ulrika came to visit, Kristina asked her if this were true.

"It's true. Månsson wants to marry me."

"May I congratulate you on your luck, Ulrika?"

"No!" exclaimed the Glad One. "I have no intention of marrying Månsson!"

"But he is a good and kind man," insisted Kristina.

"He's good and kind. But he isn't a man. No, he's not for me."

Kristina felt sorry in some way for Fina-Kajsa's son; he had lived alone

254

for so long in this wilderness; and he was sparing with his words, close-mouthed, as if carrying a great sorrow. Perhaps he regretted his emigration even though he wouldn't admit it. Karl Oskar had many times remarked that something must be wrong with Anders Månsson, he had done so little to improve his homestead. He barely managed—this winter he had borrowed thirty dollars from Danjel; having been here almost five years, Månsson ought to have reached a stage when borrowing no longer was necessary—if he had the right stuff in him. There must be some secret about Anders Månsson, Karl Oskar had said, but he was unable to guess what it was.

Ulrika admitted that Fina-Kajsa's son had been good to all of them when they arrived last summer without a roof over their heads; he was a kindhearted man; and he had a home to offer her. But each time she shook his hand she felt he wasn't exactly the way men should be. Something was missing, either in his head, or in his spine, or between his legs; something was missing that a man should have. Ulrika said this was only her feeling, but she usually felt aright: she had learned to know menfolk inside and out. Moreover, here in America there were so many men to choose from she needn't take the first suitor to approach her. She had not been here long, she wanted time to think it over before she chose her man. God would surely help her find the right one when the time came to stand as bride.

But Ulrika had consoled Anders Månsson to the best of her ability. Thus, she had promised never to divulge his rejected proposal, and she had held to her promise—she was not the sort of low person who would brag about being in demand. But Anders Månsson had made the mistake of asking Jonas Petter to intercede for him, and that loosemouthed gossip had of course not been able to keep it to himself. Jonas Petter also would undoubtedly have proposed to her, if he hadn't already had a wife in Sweden; she could feel that he was much in need of a woman. Ulrika knew menfolk, she knew them all right. . . .

While the snow crust still held, Karl Oskar, Danjel, and Jonas Petter walked through the forest to Stillwater to register their claims of land. The Swedish settlers used the few English words they had picked up when they reported to the land office that they were squatters within the Minnesota Territory; they were also able to tell in a general way where their claims were located. A man in the office told them that next summer a surveyor would be sent to their part of the forest.

While in Stillwater they also bespoke and paid for seed grain for the coming spring. Karl Oskar spent the last of his cash for rye, barley, and potatoes; the last of the money he got from the sale of his farm and live-stock in Sweden was now spent for spring seed, from which he hoped to reap a fall harvest to feed them next winter.

From Stillwater, Danjel and Jonas Petter continued south to St. Paul in order to buy in partnership a yoke of oxen, while Karl Oskar, now without funds, returned home. Five days later his neighbors came back with a pair of young oxen, measuring eleven and a half hands, which they had bought for seventy-five dollars. The animals had been part of a herd, driven from Illinois to St. Paul. They were unbroken and could not yet be used for hauling. Karl Oskar was promised the loan of the team for the spring plowing.

During the walk from St. Paul in the intense cold, Jonas Petter's nose became frostbitten, and he had had to stay over in Stillwater for a few days to seek a doctor.

The winter was far gone, and the food supply was running low for the settlers at Lake Ki-Chi-Saga. They were near the bottom of the flour barrel, and Kristina reduced their bread rations to one thin slice apiece at every meal. They were now on their last bushel of potatoes, and these too had to be rationed. They still had some frozen venison, and this was not yet rationed. Fresh meat was seldom on the table—the game seemed to have disappeared in the dead of winter. Indians used dogs to hunt, but without a dog a hunter usually returned without game. And Lady, their borrowed cow, had almost gone dry; she gave only half a quart a day.

Fishing, too, had become difficult after the snow had piled high on the lake ice. Earlier in the winter they had caught a great many pike without any fishing gear, using only an ax. They would walk over the clear ice until they espied fish, and then hit the ice above them with the ax hammer; the pike were stunned, turning up their white bellies, and it was easy to break the ice and pull them out. After the snow covered the lake several feet deep, Karl Oskar and Robert had to cut holes through the ice for fishing. It was mostly catfish they caught this way, standing at the holes with their fingers stiff from cold. Catfish had an unpleasant, oily taste, and no one liked them as well as the other lake fish. Robert detested them, with their round, catlike heads, actually purring like cats; after an evening meal of catfish he complained about being unable to sleep—the cat kept purring in his stomach the whole night through!

"Better to have a fish purr in you than to have your stomach purr from emptiness," answered Karl Oskar.

Kristina boiled the catfish, she fried it, salted it, dried it, made soup from it, she tried in all ways to make it taste good. They ate catfish at almost every meal, it was their only fresh winter food, and when the venison was gone, it would be their only animal food. The fish was ugly to look at, its taste was not appetizing, but Kristina said it would be ungrateful to speak ill of this creature, which had the same Creator as they themselves; hungry people ought to eat without complaint whatever they could find. And the catfish was faithful to them; when everything else on land and in the water failed them, they always had the bearded, purring fish. It came as a gift from God and helped them sustain life through the winter.

256

Robert's almanac indicated they were now in February. And each day the settlers asked themselves the same question: How long would it be before the ground grew green? When would the ice break up? How long before spring came?

They had put this question to Anders Månsson, he had spent several years here, he ought to know. He had answered: Spring varied from year to year, it might vary by many weeks. He remembered one spring when the frost had gone out of the ground the last week in March, another year he had not started his plowing until the second week of April. The ice on the St. Croix River usually broke up toward the end of March, and spring in the St. Croix Valley was counted from the day when the river flowed free.

So they must fight the winter, perhaps another two months.

The settlers in the log cabin at Ki-Chi-Saga kept their house warm with their constant fire, they were well protected against the winter weather, no longer were they afraid of the cold; but they began to fear hunger.

—2—

KRISTINA KNEW from experience: it was always harder to satisfy a hungry family in winter than in summer. All were hungrier and ate more in winter. During the cold part of the year a human body needed rich, nourishing food to keep the blood active and warm in the body. And as the food grew scarce, her family grew hungrier than any winter before. She too—her stomach ached all day long, she wakened during the nights with the pain. And she was in charge of their food—before she herself ate she must see to it that the others had something on their plates.

At meals she left the table a little before the others or she might be tempted to eat so much that the children would have too little. She was so careful of the flour she hardly dared use a few pinches for gravy; it must be saved for bread. But however she skimped and saved, she could not make the barrel deeper than it was. The time came when she swept the barrel bottom clean to have sufficient flour for a baking. And the moment arrived when the loaves from this baking were eaten. Now she had nothing more to bake with. Now they were breadless.

That day when they sat down at table there was no bread. No one said a word about it, no one asked about the missing bread. How could questions help them? The men had long dreaded the day when bread would be missing—it was no surprise to them. Nevertheless, Karl Oskar and Robert glanced from time to time at the empty place on the board where the bread used to lie. Did they think it would suddenly appear?

At the next meal little Johan began to complain: "Mother! I want bread! Where's the bread?"

"There is no bread, child," said the mother.

"Mother, you must bake," Johan told her. "I want bread."

None of the others at the table said a word, but the boy kept repeating: "Mother! Why don't you bake?"

No other food satisfies a human stomach like bread, no food will keep hunger away like bread. Nothing can take the place of bread for grownups or children, but a growing child-body suffers most from the lack of it.

And a mother suffers when she must deny her own child who hangs on to her skirts and cries persistently: "Mother, I want bread!"

It was the same at every meal. No one said anything except the child, but it was almost more than Kristina could endure. She knew only too well how things were with them; they had used all their money. At length she had to speak to Karl Oskar: Their children must have bread to stay healthy until spring; growing children needed bread. Couldn't he manage to get hold of a small sack of flour—only a very small sack?

This problem had been ever in his mind since the bread had been missing from the table; one sack of flour. . . . But their last money had been spent for seed grain which Karl Oskar had ordered for spring. The seed grain was more important to them than anything else—it was next year's crop. If they had spent the seed money for this winter's food, they would starve to death next winter.

Kristina argued: It did not matter which winter they starved to death —this one or next. What help would their spring seed be to them if they couldn't survive until spring? How could they put the seeds in the ground if they themselves were already under the ground?

Karl Oskar said he would go to Danjel and ask for a loan. This was the only way out. He would not be trusted by anyone else. Here everyone asked for cash. If he wanted to buy a penny's worth in a store, the owner would first ask if he had cash. *Cash* was an American word he now understood quite well, he had learned what it meant. Cash! Cash! Cheap for cash! How many times he had heard it! It began to sound like the rustle of paper bills. He could hear the same rustle in the voice of Mr. Abbott, the Scots storekeeper in Taylors Falls: "Do you have cash, Mr. Nilsson?" A settler's life—or death—depended on *cash*.

He was embarrassed to borrow from Danjel again; he still owed his wife's uncle one hundred daler for the mortgage interest on Korpamoen; his lost years at home still weighed him down. And now Danjel wasn't much better off than he was himself; Danjel too had a large family to feed, he had bought a half share in the ox team, he had lent thirty dollars to Anders Månsson, he was very generous to Ulrika and her daughter, he helped people without being asked. He had been extravagant with the cash he had on arrival, he too would soon be impoverished.

But Karl Oskar went to Danjel, and came back with five shining coins in his hand: five silver dollars: "Now we can buy a sack of flour!"

Kristina said: As long as there was one single human being who felt for his neighbor, the world was not lost.

The settlers in Taylors Falls had bought their winter supplies in early autumn, and Mr. Abbott had run out of flour long before Christmas; new supplies would not arrive until the river opened. Karl Oskar must therefore go to Stillwater for his sack of flour. This would not be so long a trip as the settlers' first walk to Taylors Falls. After all, Karl Oskar and his family now lived nine miles nearer Stillwater. Besides, the walk through the forest was shorter than the wandering way by the river; still, it was at least six miles longer than the walk to Taylors Falls. He had already carried home many burdens from Mr. Abbott's store, both on his back and in his hands. During the last half year he had struggled with more burdens than in his whole previous life. But the road northeast through the forest to Taylors Falls was only nine miles; southeast to Stillwater it was fifteen; and to walk that distance back and forth in one day, and carry a sack of flour on his return walk, would be a hard day's work. And he must start out early enough to reach home while it was still daylight.

The following morning, one hour before daybreak, Karl Oskar set off with an empty sack under his arm. Johan woke up and called happily to his father in the door: "Buy flour, Father! Then Mother can bake!"

"Be careful of your nose," admonished Kristina. "Remember what happened to Jonas Petter in this cold winter."

But the weather was now mild, had been for almost a week; the snow had thinned down, it was hardly more than a foot deep; the cold was not noticeable, the sky was hazy, with a flurry of snow now and then. Karl Oskar had walked through the forest to Stillwater only once before, but he had taken notice of landmarks and was sure he would find his way. He followed the east shore of Lake Ki-Chi-Saga, almost in a southerly direction; he passed by places he recognized—a fallen giant trunk over a brook, a deserted wigwam, an oak hill with an Indian pole, a mound like a bread loaf. Having crossed the brook, he followed an Indian trail until he reached the logging road used by the Stillwater lumber company, and from there on he could not lose his way.

The walk to Stillwater was easy; his whole burden was an empty sack, he walked with good speed and arrived before noon. He went to visit Pastor Jackson, the kind minister, as he had done last time he was in town. Pastor Jackson had now moved into a comfortable new house near the little whitewashed wooden church where he preached. But Jackson's door was locked, and no one opened for him. The minister must be on one of his many preaching journeys through the Territory.

Karl Oskar walked around and inspected the Baptist church. This was the first non-Lutheran church he had been close to. It was a simple building of wood, made of timbers faced with boards—it was the smallest God's House he had ever seen. He sat down on a bench outside the church and ate what he had brought with him—a piece of venison and a few boiled potatoes, which he gulped down without feeling satisfied. Then he walked the street at the river's edge and looked at the signs and tried to read the inscriptions: *Pierre's Tavern; Abraham Smith, Barber and Druggist; James Clark, Hardware—Tools.* Outside some houses horses stood hitched—the farmers near Stillwater were already so well off that they used horses.

He studied particularly one large sign in front of a ramshackle shed:

### CHRISTOPHER CALDWELL

### PHYSICIAN AND HOUSE-BUILDER

### CARPENTER AND BLACKSMITH

Caldwell was the name of the doctor who had taken care of Jonas Petter's frostbitten nose; this must be his house. Jonas Petter had said that the doctor had built his own house. He was a very learned doctor who could heal all kinds of ailments, he was also a carpenter and a capable smith. He had been busy shoeing a horse when Jonas Petter arrived, and after attending to the horse's hoofs he had cared for Jonas Petter's frostbitten nose. He administered equally well to the needs of people and livestock. Such learned and capable doctors were not available in Sweden. Karl Oskar thought he must remember the doctor's name; in case any of his family should be sick he would seek Dr. Caldwell.

But he must attend to his errand in town, he must buy his sack of flour and get on his way homeward.

He entered the finest and largest store he saw: Harrington's General Store. He knew that *store* was the American name for a shop, but he could not understand the meaning of the word *general*. In Swedish, general meant a high military man; perhaps the owner had been a general in the army.

Behind the long, high counter of Harrington's General Store stood two clerks dressed exactly alike: they wore gray cotton shirts, white aprons, and bowlers; the clerks in America kept their hats on inside; apparently they did not stand on ceremony with the customers.

While the two clerks waited on some fat men in skin jackets, Karl Oskar looked around the store. He espied a small wooden barrel with an inscription: *Kentucky Straight Whisky Pure 14 G.* Karl Oskar had learned the American measurements for both fluid and solid goods and he understood that the barrel contained fourteen gallons of the strong American brännvin. But in this country he could not afford brännvin; at home in Sweden he had distilled his own spirits.

Many articles of food were displayed in the store; on the counter lay heaps of fat sausages, dried and smoked; large, shining, yellow cheeses were piled on top of each other, breads of many sizes and colors were displayed. Over the counter hung hams and pieces of meat, whole sides of pork, short ribs; a steelyard in its chain hung near the meat, as if calling out: "I'll weigh up all of this for you!"

On the floor stood boxes full of eggs and fish in wooden buckets; in a corner were sacks full of flour, rice, peas, beans; in smaller boxes were stick candy, nuts, dried berries, and fruit; on the shelves lay bundles of all kinds of fabrics in all colors, rows of earthenware and china vessels. On small shelves in the window were jars and bottles of all shapes and sizes, round, flat, oblong, and square, containing salves, drops, and other medicines. From the ceiling hung pots and pans, pails and baskets, saddles and yokes, wheels, saws, guns, hats, boots, skin jackets; on the floor stood plows, churns, fire pokes, axes, hoes, spades, shovels. Karl Oskar felt that if he looked carefully in all the corners of this store he wouldn't find lacking a single object a person would need or wish for in this world; his eyes lingered on tobacco pouches and pipes, snuff boxes, powder horns, books as large as Bibles and as small as almanacs, hymnbooks, playing cards, dice. The store offered for sale everything a beginner might want in the wilderness for his spiritual and bodily needs.

In this store there was ten times as much as in Mr. Abbott's store in Taylors Falls, and Karl Oskar sighed as he beheld all the accumulated fortune; a feeling of hunger came over him: his eyes saw and his nose smelled all the tempting food—the fresh bread, the smoked hams and sausages, the fat cheeses. The people in Stillwater had sold their forests and grown rich from all the lumber, they could afford to buy anything they wanted in this store. . . . It must be an old general or some other very high person who owned this store and all it contained.

But Karl Oskar was only a poor squatter—the multitude of good things was not for him. He had come to buy a sack of flour which he must carry fifteen miles on his back; he was an impoverished settler without bread.

One of the clerks came up to him and Karl Oskar held up his empty sack, pointed toward the rye flour in the corner, and said: "Five dollar!"

He held out the five fingers of his right hand. The clerk kept up a constant flow of talk, the words spilling from his mouth with such speed that Karl Oskar was unable to understand a thing he said. He could explain his needs to Mr. Abbott in Taylors Falls, they understood each other's language. But each time he met a new American the same thing happened to him: he could neither understand nor be understood. It was as though he had to learn English anew whenever he met a stranger; he felt each time equally foolish and annoyed, standing there tongue-tied. As yet, however, he had not met a single American who poked fun at a newcomer because of his language difficulties. Instead, all were eager to help him, trying to guess what he wanted to say.

261

The clerk filled a wooden measure twice and emptied the rye flour into Karl Oskar's sack: "Five dollars' worth," he said.

Karl Oskar lifted the sack—it weighed about a hundred pounds, was probably about two bushels. He had hoped to get another twenty-five pounds for his five silver dollars. He tried two English words: "No more?"

The clerk shook his head. "No! This is cheap because of cash."

Karl Oskar could only comfort himself with the thought that the sack would be easier to carry; he should be able to manage only two bushels. He swung the sack onto his back.

"Too heavy to carry! Have you oxen outside?" asked the clerk.

Karl Oskar heard the word oxen, the clerk must think he had a team outside; he shook his head, "No, no—farväl!" In his confusion, he said good-by to the clerk in Swedish.

Karl Oskar Nilsson started on his way home from Stillwater with a hundred pounds of flour on his back. Now the weather was clear and colder. There was no wind, the snow crunched and squeaked under his booted feet, all indications were for strong frost tonight.

He stopped to pull on his woolen mittens. As always here, the change in weather had come on suddenly; no one could have guessed in the morning that it would freeze before night. He had left his thick wadmal coat at home and wore only his short sheepskin jacket, as it was easier to walk when dressed lightly. Now he regretted not having brought the heavy coat as well.

In the store he had handled the flour sack like a light burden, swinging it onto his back with the greatest of ease. And during the first part of his return walk he was little aware of its weight. But after a few miles the sack began to sag down his back, he felt it against his thighs; time and again he stopped to shove it up onto his shoulder. The sack grew heavier the longer he walked; the flour seemed to increase in weight the farther he got from the store.

He had carried sacks twice as heavy in Sweden, but never such a long distance; the more he thought about it, the more he realized that this was rather a heavy burden for such a long road. Apparently he must pay twice for his flour—first in money, then in backache.

The crooked sled tracks showed him the way through the forest; here and there on the glittering snow lay fresh ox dung, like dark loaves of bread on a white platter, and here and there were yellow stains from ox urine; axes could be heard at a distance, a logging camp must be close by.

The sack grew heavier, his right boot chafed his heel, the cold increased. But Karl Oskar gave himself no time to sit down and rest, he tramped on; he must not lose time, he hurried his steps to cover the stretch between the end of the logging road and Lake Ki-Chi-Saga before dusk; once at the lake he could follow the shore all the way home, but he had several miles yet to walk through deep wilderness, and he would have trouble finding his way after dark.

The logging road came to an end. From here on he had only his own tracks of the morning to follow. Some snow must have fallen in the forenoon, in places his tracks were filled up.

Mostly he kept his eyes on his own boot prints but he found familiar landmarks—he passed a deserted wigwam; as soon as he reached the brook with the wind-fallen oak trunk over it, he would be close to the lake.

Karl Oskar walked on, his boots crunching in the snow; he struggled with his sack up steep hills, down inclines, he forced his way through thorny thickets, he bent low under trees and branches, with the sack on his back. Dusk fell sooner than he had expected, and he found it more and more difficult to follow the tracks which showed him the way. The frost sharpened, his fingers went numb inside the thick mittens; his boot still chafed his heel, and the sack sagged all the way down to his legs. The sack would not follow him docilely any longer, it crept down below his waist, down the back of his legs, it wanted to get down on the ground. He felt the sack on his shoulders, on his back, against his legs, his knees, in his feet, in his hands.

After a few hours' walk the flour weighed two hundred pounds—had they given him four bushels instead of two? And he had yet a long way to go—his burden would grow heavier still.

The cloak of darkness spread quickly among the trees, it soon grew so dense that he could not see the marks of his steps from the morning. The snow shone white; otherwise everything in the forest was black, dark as the inside of a barrel with the lid on. No longer did Karl Oskar waste his time in looking for his earlier tracks; he followed his nose, he tried to walk northward; to the north lay the lake, and at the lake lay his home.

But he hadn't yet come to the brook with the tree trunk over it, and this began to worry him; he had crossed the brook quite a stretch after leaving the lake shore. What had happened to the brook? It was frozen over so he couldn't hear it.

Now he walked more slowly, plodding along among the trees. In the dark he could not see the low-hanging branches which hindered his path, snatching at the flour sack on his back like so many evil arms. He held on to his burden with stiff, mittened fingers; time and again he tore his face on twigs and thorns, he could not see in front of him. There would be a moon later, the stars already shone brightly, twinkling through the tall treetops. But nothing lighted his way except the snow, and the snow no longer showed him the way by his morning footprints—not even with the stars out.

The wanderer struggled through the dark with the flour on his bent back. But he did not reach a lake, he did not find a brook, and the forest grew thicker around him. He had not brought his watch—he never

263

brought it along on walks in the forest for fear he might lose it—and he did not know how much time he had spent on the homeward trek. But many hours must have elapsed since he had left the logging road; if he had followed the right path he ought to have reached Lake Ki-Chi-Saga long ago.

At each step he hoped to see the forest come to an end, he hoped to see a white field—the snow-covered lake surface. As soon as this happened he would only have to follow a shore line until he reached a newly built log cabin where his wife and children were waiting for him. But instead he seemed to go deeper and deeper into the forest.

He repeated to himself, over and over: If I walk straight ahead, I must come to the lake. I'm walking straight forward, I'm on the right road! But the hours went by and the thick forest around him testified to his mistake.

At last the stiff fingers inside the mittens lost their hold: Karl Oskar let his sack drop onto the snow and sat down on it. The truth had now been forced upon him: he was wandering aimlessly, he did not know in what direction home was—he was lost.

—3—

HE RESTED A WHILE, sitting on his sack, his legs trembling with fatigue and cold. He was worn out from the many hours' struggle with the flour: he had weakened sooner than he had expected because his stomach was empty. Hunger smarted his stomach, in his limbs and back was an ache of fatigue, but most terrible was the pain of cold after he had sat a while. The cold embraced his body from head to heel, crept like icy snakes up his legs, penetrated his groin, dug into chest and throat, pinched his ears, nose, and cheeks. But he remained sitting, letting it overtake him; he was forced to rest.

He had told Kristina he would return well before bedtime. She would be sure to sit up and wait for him, darning stockings or patching clothes. She was waiting, not only for him but also for the flour—she would surely wish to set the dough this very evening, so she could bake tomorrow.

And here he sat on their flour and didn't know in which direction he should carry it.

He had wandered about in a black forest like a child playing blindman's buff. Perhaps he had strayed too much to the left, or to the right; when he thought he had been walking northward, he might have walked southward; hoping to get nearer to his home, he had perhaps gone farther and farther away from it.

There was only one thing to do: He must walk on! He couldn't camp in the forest, the cold was too intense. He couldn't make a fire, he had

264

brought no matches. If he lay down to sleep it would surely be his eternal sleep.

Walk on! He must warm himself by moving. Sitting on the sack, his whole body shivered and shook with cold. He rose, stamped his feet, rubbed his nose, ears, and cheeks; he was not going to endure the cold that came with immobility any longer—he must move on.

Karl Oskar resumed his walk at random; he must walk in some direction, and one way was as good as another. Damned bad luck! If only he had been able to reach the lake before dark. He had walked as fast as he could, but that damned sack—it had sagged and delayed him. But now what was he doing? Cursing the sack with their bread flour—the bread that was missing from their table, the bread that would satisfy the hunger of their children! He must be out of his mind, he must be crazy from fatigue and hunger.

"Father is buying flour—Mother will bake bread!"

Put the sack under a tree and walk unhindered? But it would not be easier to find his way without his burden. And he might never again find his flour. Better carry it as far as he was able. . . . But his back felt broken, and his legs wobbled. He had carried it for many hours, an eternal road. He staggered; again and again the burden on his back sagged down, down to his thighs, to his legs, again and again his hold on the sack loosened, his fingers straightened out; his back wanted to throw off the burden, his fingers wanted to let it go.

Karl Oskar no longer walked; he reeled, tottering among the tree trunks. But he dared not sit down to rest in this cold; he dared not remain still because of the frost—yet he could not walk because of exhaustion. Which must he do—sit down, or go on? One he dared not, the other he was barely able to do.

He struggled along at random, stumbling, fumbling, stooping with his burden. He bumped against the trees, he could not see where he was going. He found no landmarks, no lake, no brook; perhaps he had crossed the brook without knowing it? A few times the forest opened up and he walked across a glade—then he was instantly in deep forest again.

Suddenly he hit his head against something hard. He lost hold of the sack and tumbled backward.

Very slowly he struggled to his feet in the snow; above him he vaguely saw an animal, a head appeared a few yards away. A bear, a wolf, or could it be a lynx? The beast was snapping at him with enormous jaws, below fiery red eyes. It was quite close—Karl Oskar crouched backward and pulled out his knife.

He crept a few more steps backward; the beast did not come after him, it did not move. He could discern the upright ears, the sharp nose, the neck—it must be a wolf—the eyes glittered in the dark. He expected a leap, he crouched and held his breath. But the wolf too remained immobile.

265

He yelled, hoping to frighten the beast: "Go to hell, you devil!"

But the beast did not make the slightest move, it seemed petrified in one position, its ears upright, its eyes peering. And a suspicion rose within Karl Oskar; he approached the animal cautiously. Now he was close enough to touch it—and it wasn't furry or soft, it was cold and hard: it was a wolf image on a pole.

His body sagged after the tension: an Indian pole, an image with glittering eyes and toothy jaws; it could startle anyone in the dark. Or—was he so far gone from struggling that he could be frightened by wooden poles?

His head ached; he felt a bump on his forehead from the encounter with the post; blood was oozing from his face and hands, torn by branches and thorns. He took off his mittens and licked the blood from his fingers; it felt warm in his mouth. He needed something warm this bitterly cold night.

With great effort he managed to get the sack onto his back again and continued his walk, lurching, stumbling. It had lightened a little in the forest, more stars had come out. High above the snowy forest and the lost settler with his burden glittered a magnificent, starry heaven. The firmament this night seemed like a dark canopy of soft felt spread by God above the frozen earth, and sprinkled with silvery sparks.

The wanderer below walked with bent head, stooped under his sack; he did not look up toward the heavenly lights. He carried the heavy fruit of the earth on his back. His steps were stumbling and tottering, he did not know where they would lead him. Home—in which direction lay the house where wife and children waited for him? Was he carrying their bread home—or away from home?

Suddenly he came upon large boot prints in the snow. They were his own! He felt his heart beat in his throat: then he had walked here in the early morning. He inspected the tracks more closely—and discovered they were quite fresh. He had been here only a short while ago. . . .

He was walking in a circle, in his own tracks. He wasn't carrying the bread away from his family, neither was he carrying it home.

But he must keep going, no matter where, to escape freezing. He staggered on. His foot caught in something—a root, a windfall, a stump—and he fell again, forward this time, with the hundred-pound sack on top of him. He lay heavily in the snow, sunk down, slumped, like a bundle of rags. After a few minutes he tried to remove the sack. Slowly, with endless effort, he managed to roll it off his back. In a sweet sensation of deliverance he stretched out full length in the snow, with the flour sack for a pillow.

266

THE FRUIT OF THE EARTH is good and sustaining, the fruit of the earth is indispensable, but heavy to carry on one's back.

How comfortable to lie on it, instead. Better to lie upon flour than kill oneself by carrying it . . . when one doesn't know where to carry it. And it has grown overpoweringly heavy, five hundred pounds. There is lead in the sack, five hundred pounds of lead—too much for one's back—better lie here and rest on the sack . . . better than to carry it . . . when one doesn't even know the way home. . . .

The cold is dangerous and evil, the cold has sharp teeth, digging like wolf's fangs into flesh and bone, the cold has tongs that pinch and tear and pierce. The skin burns like fire. But it is good to rest . . . better to be cold a little than struggle with the burden. . . . Don't be afraid of a little cold! Nothing is worse than to be afraid, Father used to say. Nothing is dangerous to him who is fearless. No, he isn't afraid. A settler needs courage, good health, good mind. . . . Father didn't say that—he has learned that himself—he has learned it now. . . .

Father has grown a great deal since he last saw him—that time on the stoop, with Mother. He is six feet tall, entirely straight; the way he stands here, he isn't a cripple any longer, he must have thrown away his crutches—no, he still has one crutch, but he doesn't lean on it, he shakes it at his oldest son: ". . . and you take your children with you! You not only take your children, you take my grandchildren, and my grandchildren's children! You drag the whole family out of the country! You are as stubborn as your nose is long, it will lead you to destruction!"

The sack—that damned flour sack! Here . . . here it is, under . . . how soft it is. Rye flour is the best pillow. With a whole sack of rye flour . . . sustain life until spring . . . not die this winter. Where is the loaf? Why isn't it on the table?

"Mother! Bake some bread!"

Now Father is speaking sternly, shaking his crutch: What kind of fool are you, Karl Oskar? Why do you wander about here in the forest with such a sack of flour on your back? You have a team of oxen in Korpamoen, why don't you drive to the mill, like other farmers? Sit up and ride, the way sensible people do, rest on your flour sack the whole way. Wouldn't that be better than carrying flour miles through the forest? No one can call you a wise farmer, Karl Oskar! Here you struggle like a wretched crofter! You have no sense about providing food for your family. A hell of a fool is what you are! Never satisfied at home, hmm—you must emigrate. . . . People should see you now, lying in a snowdrift! What would they say? No—don't show yourself to anyone, Karl Oskar. Crawl into the snow, hide yourself in the drift! Hide well. Let no one in the whole parish see you. . . .

"Be careful of your nose in this cold," Kristina says. She is concerned, she is a good wife. She is thinking of his nose because Jonas Petter's became frostbitten. But she means: Be careful of your life! Watch out against freezing to death. Don't stop too long. Don't lie down in the snow, whatever you do—don't lie down in the snow! I'm going to bake, this evening, as soon as you get home. I need the flour. . . .

"You've come at last!" she says. "Then I'll set the dough, knead it tonight. We'll heat the oven tomorrow morning, rake out the coals, put in the bread; you made a good oven for me, even though it doesn't give quite enough top-heat. . . . A hundred pounds, two bushels, three bushels? It'll last till spring. But the sack! Where is the sack? Did you forget the sack? You come home without flour?"

"The sack lies back there in the woods, but I know where I hid it— I buried it in the snow. How could I do anything so silly? I must go back at once and find it."

"Go at once and get the sack. Hurry, Karl Oskar! Hurry before it's too late!"

"It's already too late for you," says Father, and now he leans on both of his crutches; now he is a helpless cripple again, a wizened, dried-up old man. And he complains: "It's too late, Karl Oskar. You won't have time, you won't find the sack, you've lost it! How could you forget the sack in the snow, far out in the woods? Don't you know your children are in it? Don't you know they are all bundled up in there? How could you take your children to North America and carry them in a sack on your back? You must have known that such a burden would be too heavy. You must have realized you could never get home. That long road. . . . I told you you couldn't manage. And then you dropped them in the snow. Now it's too late to find them. They must be frozen to death, starved to death by now. . . . Didn't I tell you things would go ill with you in North America? But you wouldn't listen to my warning, you wouldn't listen to your parents. You were always stubborn and headstrong."

No! No! He must defend himself, he must tell Father the truth: It was because of the children he had emigrated—above all for their sake. He had brought his wife and three children with him, but he had also brought with him a pair of worn-out little shoes that had belonged to a fourth child. Didn't Father remember Anna? She died. She was hungry too long. Of her he had only the little shoes left, and he had taken them with him from Korpamoen; they would always remind him of his child, they would make him remember the hunger that snatched her away from him. Father must know, he must remember: the famine year, the famine bread, the poor beggars, all those who starved to death? If not, he would show Father Anna's shoes. They are here in the sack! I put them into the sack. There isn't another thing in the sack. . . .

When he lost his little girl he had been in despair. Father must remember how he had searched for knot-free boards for the coffin. It was lowered into the earth, but her shoes were left. At times he picks them

268

up, holds them in his hands: her small feet have been in them, her little feet have romped about in them, she has taken many steps in them, up and down, a thousand times. Anna's feet. . . . *Father, it hurts to die. Don't let God come and take me! I want to stay here with you.* . . . No, it mustn't happen again, it mustn't happen to his other children, he must take them away from the tormenting hunger—out here. And now he is here with his sack; and it has grown heavier and heavier, until he has fallen with it. He is crawling on his knees in the snow, with the burden on his back. But it's burning hot in the snow, it smarts, smarts. . . .

And his own father is also here in America—he hasn't written a letter, although he learned to write while sitting inside as a cripple. He has come here himself and speaks severe words to his eldest son: "I warned you, your mother warned you, friends and neighbors warned you. But you had to do it. You were self-willed, stubborn, listened to no one. Therefore things went as they did; now you lie here. . . . You dragged away my children, my grandchildren. Where are your own children? Where do you keep them? Have you taken care of them? Have you found them yet? Do you remember the place where you buried them in the snow? Be careful of your nose in this cold!"

Father will buy flour, Mother will bake bread. . . . Where is the bread? . . . It's *my* son! But you are my son. And things have come to pass as you wanted them to. Karl Oskar, are you looking for bread on your own table? You're as stubborn as your nose is long. You couldn't rest until you got to North America. You wanted to get here to fetch that sack of flour, to wander about with the sack. . . . It wasn't much to travel so far for—not much for one who wanted to improve things for himself. . . . But I told you it was a long way to travel, that you never would find your way, wouldn't be able to carry it all the distance, it's too heavy . . . and what a cold night! Not even a beggar would be out in this weather. . . .

I'll succeed! I'll improve myself! And Karl Oskar swings the sack onto his back again and waves good-by to his father and mother, who stand on the stoop looking after him. He walks lightly with his burden, through the narrow gate, onto the road, and then he looks back: Father and Mother stand there. He calls to them but they do not answer. They remain standing on the stoop, deaf, dumb, lame. Never more in his life will they move. They will remain standing there for ever, looking after him, the son who walked out through the gate, who emigrated. For all time they will stand there; they do not hear when he calls, but he must tell them, he must call louder: "It wasn't because I was stubborn and wouldn't listen to you, nor was I dissatisfied. That you must remember! I didn't emigrate because of this, do you hear me, Father and Mother? *I didn't want to make any more coffins.* No coffins for my little ones. Remember that! That was why I emigrated."

But Father and Mother do not listen, they do not hear. And they cannot move. They are only wooden images, put up by the Indians. The red eyes staring at him aren't human eyes; the Indians have put animal heads on Father's and Mother's bodies! They have cut off the heads of his parents and have replaced them with wolf heads! That's why they stand immobile without hearing him when he shouts at them: "Can you hear me?"

He shouts and yells, he has to, he can no longer endure the intense smarting from the fire, he shrieks as he lies there among the scorching firebrands of the bitter-cold snow. . . .

—5—

KARL OSKAR NILSSON sat up and felt his face with his hand: Where was he? Was he at home with his father, defending his emigration? Or had his father come here? Was he in two countries at the same time? Wasn't he walking homeward with a—*the sack*!

His befuddled mind cleared: He had gone to sleep on his sack in the snow. But the cold had bitten him badly, and he had shouted himself awake. He jumped to his feet, violently, as if attacked by a swarm of hornets; he was like a madman—he jumped about, kicking, stamping the ground. He flailed his arms, slapped his hands and face, beat his body with his fists. For several minutes he pummeled himself—and his blood pumped faster, his body heat was returning.

He must have dozed off for a little while; he might never have awakened! How could he have lain down this bitterly cold night? How could he have forgotten to guard against the treacherous temptation of rest?

He could not have been asleep long, yet he had had time to dream evil dreams, listen to many voices; they had told him things he probably had thought to himself, when alone; and all the while he had felt the smarting cold, burning his skin like firebrands. Thank God, he had not lost sensation—he was not frostbitten yet. But a few moments more, in that hole in the snow. . . . The ice-cold shroud of frost-death was down there —it would soon have soothed his pains, would soon have made him slumber forever!

But he was still alive. He loosened his stiff joints, he forced his body to move again. And once more he swung the flour sack onto his back. Fury boiled within him as he made ready to carry it farther; he gained strength from his seething anger, from adversity's bitterness. Many times before he had enjoyed the gift of strength from vexation, and this time it was more welcome than ever. Who said he wasn't able? Those spiteful neighbors in Sweden, how they would enjoy his misfortunes if they knew! He could just hear them say: Karl Oskar couldn't succeed! What did we tell you?

He was enraged. In a wild frenzy he began to kick the big stump that had tripped him. His feet felt like icicles in his boots. But suddenly he stopped and stood still: Who could have felled a great tree here in the wilderness? The stump was fresh and cut by an ax!

He dropped his sack, bent down, brushed away the snow and examined the stump carefully. It was a low stump, not cut by a straight-standing American. This stump was cut by a Swede! He recognized the stump— *he had felled this tree himself.* It was the great oak he had cut down here, their food table! And that oak had grown on a knoll close behind their house—only a few hundred yards from home. . . .

Now he would find his way; he was practically there.

But Karl Oskar walked the remaining distance slowly. He was exhausted; and he must have carried the sack much farther than fifteen miles, for he was approaching his house from the wrong direction! He could see the yellow light from a window greeting him between the trunks of the sugar maples. There stood his house, a fire burning on the hearth. With infinite slowness he dragged his feet the last steps. The sack's weight had increased again, this last stretch.

In a low voice Karl Oskar called Kristina's name. He heard her pull the bolt on the inside of the door. With great effort he managed to lift his feet over the high threshold and dump the sack onto the floor. He put down his burden for the last time, with a dull thud. And then he slumped down on a stump chair near the fire, limp, jointless, weak; he dropped a full sack on the floor and sank into the chair like a discarded, empty sack.

"You're late," said Kristina. "I've been worried about you."

"It was a long way."

"I guess so. And cold tonight. Did it bother you?"

"A little. The last stretch."

"You should have taken your other coat."

"But it was so mild when I left."

He was thawing out near the fire. He wondered how his feet had fared —perhaps his toes were frostbitten. He must go out and get a shovelful of snow, then he would melt some fat and rub his limbs, first with snow, then with fat.

Kristina had already opened the sack. She dipped into it for some flour which she strained between her fingers: "Good rye flour! You must have almost three bushels."

"Thereabouts, I guess."

"You had enough to carry!"

"About right for me."

"Now we'll have bread till spring. And we've been promised potatoes."

She related how Danjel had come to visit today and offered to lend them a bushel of potatoes, Jonas Petter too had promised them a bushel; they could pay back in the fall when they harvested their own.

271

"That's well," Karl Oskar said. "They are kind."

"It's hardest for us," Kristina said. "We're the poorest. Danjel wondered if we would survive the winter."

"We shall manage!"

Karl Oskar had taken off his boots and socks and sat with his bare feet near the fire: his toes itched and burned, feeling was returning. There was a spell of silence, and he thought: It could have happened that the next letter to reach Ljuder Parish, probably written by Danjel, would have said Karl Oskar Nilsson from Korpamoen had frozen to death in the forest a short distance from his house. One cold night February last. His body was found on a sack of flour which he had carried on his back from the store, many Swedish miles away. The exhausted man hadn't been able to reach home, he had lain down to rest in the severe cold, on his sack, had fallen asleep, and had never awakened.

But this piece of news would not reach Sweden now. It would not gladden those hearts who had predicted ill for him out here. What had happened to him this winter night in the wilderness would not happen again. Bread was necessary for life, but one mustn't give life to get it.

Kristina was putting food on the table for her husband; she would set the dough before they went to bed and she would get up early to heat the oven. . . .

Johan awakened in his bed in the corner; he yelled with delight as he saw his father sitting at the hearth: "Father is back!"

He jumped out of bed and ran to sit on Karl Oskar's knee: "Father has brought flour! Mother can bake bread!"

Karl Oskar sat silent, stroking his son's head clumsily with his frost-stiff fingers.

"You must be hungry, Karl Oskar," Kristina said. "It's all ready for you."

He sat down to his supper, and he ate quietly but he was satisfied in his silence; tomorrow the missing loaf of bread would again be in its place on their table.

# XXIII

## The Letter from Sweden

THIS WAS THE LONGEST of all winters for the settlers; they counted the days and waited for spring.

March had his cap full of snow, shaking it over the earth in a final blizzard. But after the snowstorm came mild weather with a south wind blowing day after day. The snow carpet thinned, the lake ice soon lay blueish bare. The night frost was still with them, but the sun warmed the air in daytime; no longer need they keep the hearth fire alive through the night.

One day Johan came rushing in from the meadow, calling out loudly before he reached the threshold. What had happened? In his hand the boy held a little flower, pulled up by its roots.

"Look Mother! A *sippa*! I've found a spring *sippa*!"

He had found the flower near the brook. All in the cabin crowded around to see it. It was a spindly little flower, hardly three inches tall, with liver-brown leaves and a blue crown on a thin stem. Below the crown was a circle of heart-shaped green leaves. It must be a *sippa*, but it was the smallest one any of them had ever seen. Kristina said the Swedish *sippa* had a wider crown, and this flower had no smell. Karl Oskar and Robert could not remember how it was with the *sippas* at home in that respect, but she insisted they had a fragrance: all flowers in the homeland were fragrant.

However small the flower was, it must be a *sippa*. In both Sweden and America the hepatica was the first flower to appear in spring, and this was a singular discovery for the settlers. The flower grew near a brook in Minnesota, just as in Småland. In some way it seemed to link the two countries, to bring home closer.

Kristina filled a cracked coffee cup with water and put the little bloom on the window ledge: the first message of spring had come to them.

Once more March shook his cap, but this time it was a wet snowfall, soon turning into heavy rain. For a few days the earth was washed with melting snow. The calls of water birds were heard from the lake: this was the second spring message.

The ground was bare, but ice still covered the St. Croix River. Robert went about in a dream, waiting. During the nights he lay awake in his bed, listening to the changing sounds in his left ear. He could hear one sound that impatiently called him away from here, he could hear the muffled roar of a mighty water which as yet ran under the winter's icy roof but soon would burst into open daylight and swell in its spring flow; it would bring a vessel with eagle feathers on the bow, a ship to carry him away. Soon he would travel downstream on that great water which was forever wandering on to the sea: Robert was waiting for the *Red Wing* of St. Louis.

Karl Oskar and Kristina were waiting for the same boat: they were waiting for a letter from Sweden.

A year would soon have passed since they had left the homeland, and as yet they had not heard one word from their parents and families.

Karl Oskar had written a letter to Sweden last summer, and another last fall, and now in spring they waited for an answer. During the fall Robert had written a letter for Kristina to her parents in Duvemåla, and she was now waiting for an answer. When she had learned to read in school, she ought to have asked to be instructed in writing also, then

273

she could now have written herself to her relatives and friends at home. But her father had been of the opinion that a female could make no use of the art of writing—it was always the menfolk who drew up sales contracts, wrote auction records and other important papers. She now deeply regretted having let her father decide for her. But how could she know when going to school as a little girl what she must go through in life? How could she then have imagined that one day she would emigrate to North America? At that time she didn't even know this land existed! It was only two years ago that she had first heard the name North America.

Karl Oskar was helping Jonas Petter cut fence rails, in order to earn a few dollars to enable him to buy food supplies from Mr. Abbott's store in Taylors Falls. He also helped his neighbors to break in their newly bought oxen, and to build a wagon of wood with oak trundles for wheels, a replica of Anders Månsson's ox wagon. Having no team, Karl Oskar needed no wagon, but by helping his neighbors he gathered knowledge that would be useful when he made his own.

Danjel's first journey with his new team and wagon was when he drove Ulrika and her daughter to Stillwater, where Elin was to seek work. He drove on a new road which the lumber company had cleared through the forest during the past winter. Ulrika returned to the settlement without her daughter, and a few days later she walked to Ki-Chi-Saga and related to Kristina what had taken place on their journey to Stillwater.

Elin had remained in town as maid to an upper-class American family. Pastor Jackson had found her a position with one of the richest men in his congregation, a high lord who ruled the lumber company. Elin was to receive eight dollars a month besides food and lodging, and all she had to do was wash dishes, scrub floors, and do laundry. She would not be called on to do a single outside chore, not even carry in water and wood. This was quite different from Sweden, where the maids had to do the menfolk's chores as well, and were paid one daler a month. Here not even half as much work was required—yet her wages were twenty times as high! For eight dollars made about twenty daler.

Ulrika praised God Who had helped her and her daughter to America, and next to the Lord she praised Pastor Jackson who had negotiated the position for Elin.

On this visit Ulrika had been able to speak with Pastor Jackson. She had understood about half of the words he said, and he had understood a little more than half of her words. For the rest they had guessed, and nearly always guessed right. The Glad One was quick-witted and learned easily, she had picked up so many English expressions that Kristina was surprised. She herself had learned hardly a single word yet.

But Ulrika was bold and resourceful, she talked to every American she met. She was often spoken to by American menfolk who—as menfolk will—let their eyes rest on an attractive woman. In this way she had

274

opportunity to practice the foreign tongue. Because of her shapely body she learned English faster than women who were spoken to less often. She told Kristina she was already dreaming in English, and in her dreams men spoke whole long sentences in English to her. But it still happened that she dreamed wrong about some words.

Jonas Petter had gossiped that unmarried Ulrika of Västergöhl had a new suitor, Samuel Nöjd, the fur trader from Dalcarlia. Kristina now asked if the gossip were true.

"Yes. Nöjd has proposed."

"He too! And you have answered him?"

"He got the same answer as Månsson. And the same comfort!"

Ulrika explained: She was just, she treated all her suitors alike. Here in America all people should be treated alike since there weren't four classes of people as there were in Sweden, but only one class, a human class. Samuel Nöjd had offered her a home in St. Paul, where he intended to open a store for meat—sausages, hams, steaks, and such. He was going to give up his fur trapping. But she had never liked the Dalcarlian, nothing was ever right for him, he complained wherever he lived, complained of the food and houses and people. That was why she had given a new name to the pelt hunter; in Swedish his name meant Samuel Satisfied, she called him Samuel Mis-Nöjd, Samuel Dissatisfied. If she married him, he would soon be dissatisfied and complain of her too. Nor did she think he was a desirable man for bed play. He acted like a man, but he liked to live in dirt, he didn't keep himself clean, he stank at a yard's distance. He stank of old slaughter, he smelled of fat, blood, and entrails. All his work had to do with slaughter, skinning animals, tanning their hides. She wouldn't mind working in his store in St. Paul—she had heard two thousand people lived in that city—and she would willingly sell his meat and sausage and ham at great profit. But she would not in her marriage bed have a husband who stank like an entrail slinger.

No, she would never become Mrs. Samuel Nöjd, she had thanked him and said no to the offer.

"I wonder who your next suitor will be," said Kristina.

"I've had one since Nöjd," Ulrika reported. "That Norwegian in Stillwater made a try for me."

Thomassen, the little Norwegian shoemaker whom they had met last summer, had dropped in at Pastor Jackson's last time she was there. He had asked if she were married, the man obviously meant business. Ulrika had never seen so lustful a man, he was so hot he had to walk stooped over. But he was such a little man, so spindly, she might have trouble finding him in bed. And before he had time to propose she had made it clear to him that she had no desire to become a shoemaker's wife in Stillwater. If she were to marry any man outside her own countrymen, then he must be an American. There were not many Swedes to choose

275

from in Minnesota, nearly all the unmarried ones had already proposed to her, so she guessed she would be forced to marry an American.

Jonas Petter had said to Kristina that Ulrika of Västergöhl was now the most sought-after woman in the whole St. Croix Valley. And Kristina answered that this was not surprising: Every unmarried man was looking for a wife, and Ulrika had the fortune to be shaped in such a way that she attracted and tempted menfolk. She was good-looking, still young, and looked younger than she was; she had a healthy, blooming appearance, and since arriving in America she had blossomed out in both soul and body. She was capable in all she did, she cooked good food, she was companionable, always in good temper and high spirits. No one had ever seen the Glad One weep. Those who knew her well could not imagine her shedding tears. Who wouldn't wish such a wife?

Jonas Petter predicted Ulrika would be married before full summer.

Kristina said to Ulrika: "I wonder who will finally get you?"

"I myself don't bother to wonder," replied Ulrika, full of confidence. "I leave everything to the Lord's decision."

—2—

BEFORE ELIN WENT TO Stillwater and accepted her position with the high American family, she and Robert had studied a chapter from his language book: "Advice for Swedish servant-folk in America." She must learn to understand the commands of the mistress, otherwise she would perform her duties wrongly and be driven from service the very first day. Together they read the most important sentences concerning her duties, they read them in English, over and over, until the servant-girl-to-be knew them by heart. The instructions began with the first day and went on for the whole week:

*Good morning, Missus! I am the new servant girl.—Welcome, change clothes and feel at home!—What time am I expected down in the morning?—You must get up at six o'clock. Clean out the ashes in the stove. Hand me the pot, I'll show you how to make oatmeal. Empty the slop bucket and tidy the maid's room. Eat your own breakfast. Leave no food on the dining-room table while you sweep and dust. Wash dishes and pots. Tomorrow is washday. Everything must be ironed Tuesday morning. After dinner on Sunday you may go to church. You must be back at half past nine. Wednesday you must clean upstairs. Now eat your own dinner. . . .*

They went through the whole week of a maid in an upper-class American family.

By now Elin had learned to move her lips less, and she kept her tongue far back in her mouth while speaking English. She had improved greatly

276

since her mother had been teaching her what she picked up in her conversations with American menfolk.

When Elin had served as nursemaid at home in Ljuder, the master had held morning prayers for all the maids and farm help every day. Each one had been required to repeat by heart the verses in the Catechism from Titus, Second Chapter, before they were allowed to eat breakfast: "Exhort servants to be obedient unto their own masters, and to please them well in all things; not answering again; not purloining, but shewing all fidelity; that they may adorn the doctrine of God our Saviour in all things."

Elin thought as an American maid she would now be required to read these verses and she wanted to learn them in English. But Robert told her: The Americans did not require their servants to obey the Catechism. Moreover, no one out here had to obey the authorities, who weren't put in their place by God. She herself could see from the book that servants were treated justly in America. The master and mistress bade them welcome! They asked servants to feel at home and gave them time off to go to church! Nay, the mistress was even so noble that she told her maid to eat! Both breakfast and dinner! Had anyone in Sweden ever heard a master or a mistress ask a servant to eat?

When Elin accepted the position in Stillwater, Robert stayed at home and waited. He waited for a secret message Elin had promised to send him. And one Saturday, the third week in March, it came: The ice had broken up on the St. Croix River, and in Stillwater they were looking for the first steamer.

The next day, Sunday, Robert walked to Danjel's and spoke to Arvid. They were ready, they had long been ready, they had been waiting. And when Robert came home in the evening he announced to Karl Oskar: "Tomorrow morning Arvid and I shall walk to Stillwater. We're taking the steamboat."

"The steamboat?"

"We shall journey to the gold fields in California."

"What are you talking about? What do you want to do there?"

"Dig gold, of course."

"Dig gold?" Karl Oskar thought that Robert had invented some tale to deceive him.

"We decided last fall. We were only waiting for the ice to melt."

"Are you serious?"

Robert assured him he was in earnest. Karl Oskar began to wonder if Robert and Arvid might have met an American who wanted to lure them away on some adventure; but as he listened to his brother he realized the gold-digging fancies had originated entirely with Robert. The boy had heard rumors about a land of gold far to the west, and he believed all he heard. He lived entirely in his imagination. And even though Arvid was a full-grown man, he was as credulous and gullible as Robert, and

277

equally childish. And these two intended to undertake a long journey in this vast, dangerous country. Karl Oskar could easily see the outcome of such a venture! He must avert his young brother's fancy.

"You couldn't manage alone, Robert! You're too young and too weak as yet."

"To dig gold isn't heavy work. It's easier than grub hoeing!"

"*If* you found some gold. *If* your fancies came through. But California lies far away, in the back end of America. How will you get there?"

"We'll work on the steamboat to St. Louis. Then we can walk the highway. I have a map and I know English. Don't worry about me, Karl Oskar."

Arvid was coming to Ki-Chi-Saga to meet Robert the following morning. Danjel had said he would not keep his servant against his will. Arvid had already worked for him a whole year, that was enough for the transportation from Sweden. Danjel was decent about everything, he let Arvid have his free will.

"This will come to a terrible end!" Karl Oskar almost shouted his words at Robert. If his brother had been strong and handy and tough! But Robert was a weak, inexperienced, timid boy. He ran from dead Indians and could hear the whizz of arrows that had never been shot. And his hearing was bad. He was filled with his own imagination; he was possessed by his own fancies. He was walking with open eyes into his own destruction!

Karl Oskar recalled that Robert had been odd as a boy at home: he was at least twelve years old before he stopped running after rainbows, trying to catch them with his hands. Robert was fascinated by the glittering colors and never realized that however far he ran the rainbow remained equally far away. Karl Oskar had never run to catch a rainbow.

It was pure folly for Robert to start out. And Karl Oskar pleaded with him and warned him. He was trying to talk him out of the gold-digging notion, not because he wanted Robert as a helper on the farm—he could take care of himself—it was for Robert's own sake. He could not with a clear conscience let his younger brother set out on so reckless, danger-fraught a journey. Here in a foreign country he felt in a father's place toward his brother. Had Robert thought of all the perils he and Arvid might encounter? They must travel through vast stretches of wilderness, they didn't know the roads, they could easily become lost; they didn't know people, they could be swindled and cheated; they might even be killed.

"You can't manage alone! Believe what I say. You're only eighteen!"

"You were only fourteen when you left home," retorted Robert.

"That's true. But that was at home, that was different."

"When you were fourteen you said to Father: 'I'll go! I've decided for myself!' And you left."

"Yes—but that was in Sweden."

278

"You went off on your own at fourteen. Haven't I the right to do the same at eighteen?"

Robert had put his older brother in a position where he was unable to answer. Ever since he was fourteen he *had* decided for himself, done as he pleased, traveled where he wished. He could not deny his brother the same right.

"You can't stop me, Karl Oskar," Robert said.

He had already gathered together his belongings. They were not many, they made only a small bundle. Persuasion and warning words were lost on him, no one could tie him down or tether him like an animal. And as Karl Oskar could not stop him by force, he could not stop him in any other way. From now on Robert must decide for himself and take the responsibility for his own life. Karl Oskar sought to ease his conscience—he had done all in his power, there was nothing more to do.

Kristina was as much disturbed as Karl Oskar but she agreed with him: they must let Robert do as he wanted. What else could they do?

Robert had saved five dollars; he had earned four of them as day laborer for Danjel, and one dollar had been his profit from the almanacs he had made at New Year and sold to the Swedish settlers in the St. Croix Valley. Of the eight dollars Karl Oskar had earned from rail splitting for Jonas Petter, he had only five left, and these he gave to Robert. It was the only help he could offer, the only cash he had to give when his brother left home. Kristina began to prepare a good-sized food basket for the boy; that was all she could do. He might be hungry many times and need many meals before he reached the California gold fields.

Robert said: He was going to California because he wanted to become rich while still young and able to enjoy his riches. But he would not forget Karl Oskar and Kristina when he returned from the gold fields. He would share his gold—first of all, he would give Karl Oskar money for a pair of oxen, a real draft team, then he wouldn't need to carry such heavy burdens long distances through the wilderness. And for Kristina he would buy cows, fine milch cows that would give milk enough for all of them. This family had been kind to him, he would remember them. This they could rely on: he would not keep all his fortune for himself, he was not like that—he would share.

Monday morning before daybreak Arvid arrived at the log house—he was ready to walk with Robert through the forest to Stillwater.

Robert had ten dollars in his pocket, his bundle of worldly possessions on his back, and food for ten days. As he shook hands with his brother in good-by, he said he had been lying awake during the night—his ear had bothered him—and he had made a decision: When he returned from California he would journey back to Sweden for a time and buy Kråkesjå Manor from Lieutenant Rudeborg and give this estate to his father and mother. They had such a little room, and their reserved rights in Korpamoen were very poor. It would be well for them in their old age to

279

live in a manor. They had earned this, he thought; they would have more room in a mansion. Yes, he would not forget father and mother at home, Karl Oskar could rely on that—this was the last thing he wanted to say before they parted.

Karl Oskar and Kristina stood outside the log house door and looked after Arvid and Robert. The two disappeared into the forest. Karl Oskar and Kristina asked the same question of themselves: Would they see the boys ever again?

—3—

THE RIVER WAS OPEN, its water flowed free—this was the final harbinger of spring in the St. Croix Valley.

In bays and inlets of Lake Ki-Chi-Saga the spawn-bellied pike began their play among belated, melting ice floes. Now the settlers again had fresh fish at every meal, good sustaining fare. And the rabbits emerged from their winter shelters and ate the green grass in the meadow; the rabbits were not so fat as last fall, but their meat tasted better. Food worry diminished each day. The weather was mild with a warming sun, the sap rose under the bark of the tree trunks. Karl Oskar took his auger and drilled holes in the sugar maples near the log house, and the running sap filled the containers he placed below the holes. From it they boiled a sweet sirup which they spread on bread instead of butter; the children were overjoyed with this delicious food. Useful trees grew around their house—with nourishment flowing under their bark.

People and animals came to life again, the shores of Lake Ki-Chi-Saga teemed with fresh, young growth. A new joy burst forth in all growing things—the joy of having kept alive through the winter.

Robert and Arvid had boarded the Red Wing, the spring's first steamer to Stillwater. The packet also brought the year's first mail to the Territory—it should include a letter from Sweden.

Kristina talked every day about this letter which they had been waiting for so long, and she begged Karl Oskar to go to the post office in Taylors Falls and ask about it. But the walk would require half a day, and now all his days were busy—the frost would soon be out of the earth, and he had begun to make a plow for the turning of the meadow. At last, however, he gave in to his impatient wife—early one morning he took off on the nine-mile walk to Taylors Falls to inquire in the Scotsman's store about the letter from Sweden.

There was always a paper nailed to the outside of the door of Mr. Abbott's store, a list of the names of people who had letters inside: Letters remaining at the Post Office in Taylors Falls, Walter H. Abbott, Postmaster.

How many times Karl Oskar had stopped on the steps of the store

280

and read through that list, searching for his own name! As yet it had never been there. He had read the name of every other inhabitant of Taylors Falls and thereabouts, but not his own, or Danjel's, or Jonas Petter's. He had read the names of other settlers until he learned to recognize them, but he had always missed his own name. Many times he had wondered how it would feel to find his own name written down, and be counted among the fortunate people who had letters inside in the custody of storekeeper and postmaster Walter H. Abbott.

And today his name was on the list! Indeed, it was the first one, it stood at the top of the list! He counted all the names, there were seventeen below his. It was as though his letter were the most important of all. For a moment he felt he was better than the others who had letters inside. His name was written in the Scot's firm hand, with large, round, clear letters, easy to read: *Mr. Karl Oskar Nilsson.* Here he was called *Mr.* like the others. That meant the same as *Lord* in Sweden. He was a lord here, like all Americans. But the Mr. before his name seemed strange to him. In some way it did not belong before a name like his, it belonged before Jackson and Abbott and other American names, but not before Karl Oskar Nilsson.

However, the letter from Sweden had arrived.

Karl Oskar opened the door and went inside. Mr. Abbott stood in his place behind the counter. He was a tall, scrawny man with sharp features and piercing eyes. He always wore the same serious look, his features were in some way incapable of change. And the strangest thing about him was that he could talk without seeming to move his lips. He was held among the settlers to be a good man, very exact in his business. He gave the customers full weight, though not an ounce more. He was an honest trader, but no one was ever granted delay in payment; in his store trading was done for cash only.

Karl Oskar had not come to buy anything, he was penniless since he had given Robert his last five dollars. That was one reason he had delayed going to the store—he could buy nothing to bring home. He could only fetch the letter.

Before he had time to ask for it, the postmaster-storekeeper behind the desk said to him: "I have a letter for you, Mister Nilsson."

Mr. Abbott pulled out a long drawer under the counter and looked through a stack of letters until he found a small, square, gray-blue envelope: "Here it is! Yes, Mr. Nilsson."

Karl Oskar's face lit up, he recognized the letter: it was the kind of envelope they used at home. He stretched out his hand for the letter.

"Fifteen cents." The tall Scot held the letter between his thumb and forefinger, but he did not give it to the Swede on the other side of the counter: "Fifteen cents, sir."

"What mean you, Mr. Abbott?" Karl Oskar spoke his halting English. Why didn't the postmaster hand over his letter? Did he want money

281

because he had held it so long? What was the meaning of this charge?

"You have to pay fifteen cents in postage due, Mr. Nilsson."

The postmaster of Taylors Falls still held the little gray-blue envelope between the thumb and forefinger of his right hand while he pointed with his left forefinger to some stamps on the letter. And Karl Oskar still stood with his hand outstretched for the letter from Sweden.

Then he thought he understood: the freight for the letter had not been paid. He must redeem it with fifteen cents. But he did not have even one cent.

"Yes, sir?" Mr. Abbott was waiting, expressionless. He held the letter firmly in his hand, as if afraid Karl Oskar might try to snatch it. Mr. Abbott was not a man to be taken by surprise.

"No—No—" The Swedish settler struggled with the language of the new land. "I can—can not today—no—have . . . not one cent!" Karl Oskar pulled out his pockets—empty!

A trace of pity was discernible in the postmaster's voice: "No cash, Mr. Nilsson? Sorry, I have to keep your letter." And he replaced it in the drawer under the counter.

Karl Oskar, who had stretched out his hand for the letter from Sweden, had to pull it back empty—he thrust it into his empty pocket.

The storekeeper at the other side of the counter scrutinized him sharply: Karl Oskar looked foolishly at the floor. He could not redeem the letter he had come to fetch. . . . "No cash, Mr. Nilsson?" He had heard those words so many times, he knew what they meant. Cash—the word still sounded to him like the rustle of paper money, the fingering of piles of dollar bills. It was one word in the foreign language which he did not like, he could not get by it, he always bumped against it like a stone wall—cash! It was the word of permanent hindrance, the word for the settler's greatest obstacle.

Mr. Abbott looked at Karl Oskar's feet, at his shoes. To save his boots, already quite worn, Karl Oskar now wore his wooden shoes even for walks to the village. People in Taylors Falls stared at his feet in the wooden shoes, they had never seen such footgear. They apparently thought that people who wore wooden shoes were impoverished and wretched, he could see in Mr. Abbott's eyes. The Scot pitied the woodenshod settler, the poor Swede who did not have even fifteen cents to pay for his letter from the homeland.

If there was one thing Karl Oskar detested above all else, it was to be pitied. "All right!" he said, as if the letter did not concern him. And he felt he pronounced those words like an American.

"Sorry," Mr. Abbott repeated. "But I have to keep the letter."

News from Sweden, the first in a year, again lay hidden in the postmaster's drawer. All that the settlers had wanted so long to know about their relatives at home—if they were well or ill, if all were alive, or if someone were dead—this long-awaited news was pushed back among the letters in the drawer. There it must remain until the fee was paid. Karl Oskar had nothing to reproach the postmaster with, it was not his fault if the addressee lacked the fifteen cents. The mail company granted no delay in payments. Mr. Abbott worked for the mail company, he did only his duty when he kept the letter.

Karl Oskar nodded a silent good-by and walked toward the door.

"Sorry!" Mr. Abbott said, for the third or fourth time.

His expression was still unchanged, but there was sadness in his voice. The postmaster was sorry for Karl Oskar, because he was unable to redeem his letter. Sorry, he heard that word often when Americans talked, it sounded as if they were constantly grieving for others. But he had sometimes heard the word uttered so lightly and unconcernedly that he wasn't sure real sorrow was always felt. This time, however, he believed Mr. Abbott was genuinely sorry he had had to leave without the letter.

The day had been almost wasted. A walk to Taylors Falls and back was tiresome, his wooden shoes were heavy and clumsy, his feet always felt sore after a long walk. Must he now walk back nine miles without the letter?

But Anders Månsson lived in the village only half a mile away; he could borrow the fifteen cents from him, go back to Mr. Abbott's post-office, and lay the money on the counter!

The Månsson fields lay deserted today, all was quiet. Fina-Kajsa sat in the sun outside the cabin, patching one of her son's skin coats. She sat slumped and her glassy eyes wandered listlessly as if following something far away in the forest. She did not look at the work in her hands, she stared in front of her as if in deep worry; perhaps she was still brooding over the journey of disappointment she had undertaken to her son's fine mansion in Minnesota; as yet she had not arrived.

Her cream-pitcher lips moved vaguely in answer as Karl Oskar greeted her and asked for Anders.

"He lies flat-back today."

"Flat-back?"

"Yes. He lies flat on his back inside."

Fina-Kajsa's voice sounded hollow. Karl Oskar looked at her in surprise. Did Anders Månsson lie in bed on a weekday for no reason, without working? Or had something happened to him? "Is he ailing? Is that why—"

The mother gave no answer, she only pointed to the door meaningfully: Go inside! And he entered the tiny cabin into which the whole group of Swedish newcomers had packed themselves last year.

A strong, sweet odor struck him as soon as he was over the threshold and in the stuffy air of the cabin. It was a work day, the middle of the day —but Anders Månsson lay in his shirt on his bed, stretched out on his back, sleeping and snoring. The door creaked loudly on its ungreased hinges, and Karl Oskar clumped noisily on his wooden shoes, but the

283

sleeper was not awakened by these sounds. Anders Månsson had not lain down for a light nap, he was sunk in deep slumber.

Karl Oskar went to the bed. As he leaned over the sleeper the rancid-sweet odor grew stronger. He discovered its source: his foot struck a wooden keg that lay overturned on the floor near the bed.

It was a whisky keg, rolling in a dark-brown wet spot on the floor, where some of the contents had run out. But not much had been wasted: Karl Oskar suspected that the keg had been practically empty when it was turned over. And the man who had emptied it now lay on the bed after his drinking bout, with open, gaping mouth, breathing noisily in deep jerky snores. His breath rattled in his throat, and his chest heaved slowly up and down. It seemed as if each new breath might choke him, stick in his throat, and be his last.

Anders Månsson was dead drunk today, a day in the middle of the week; he lay unconscious on his bed in full daylight, he lay flat-back as his mother had said. But his face bloomed red, his cheeks blossomed.

"Why are you so red in the face?" Fina-Kajsa had asked her son when they arrived last summer. And Karl Oskar remembered one time when he met Fina-Kajsa at Danjel's; he had asked about Anders, and she had answered: "He lies flat-back at home." He had wondered what she meant.

He looked at Anders Månsson with disgust and pity: he slept a drunkard's sleep and nothing would wake him now, nothing but time could stop that rattle in his throat. But his face looked healthy and red; "if you have red cheeks you are far from dead," the saying was. . . .

Karl Oskar walked slowly out of the cabin. The drunkard's mother was still sitting outside; he had nothing to say to her.

But she asked: "Was it something you wanted with Anders?"

"Nothing to speak of. Just wanted to look in as I passed by."

"He wakes up toward evening."

"Well . . . is that so? Does he often—"

"As often as he has money to buy drinks with." Old Fina-Kajsa spoke to the air in a low, hollow voice—without reproach or sorrow. "He got started on it when he lived alone."

"I suppose so."

"He ailed from lonesomeness."

"I see."

Karl Oskar felt embarrassed and ashamed, as though he had surprised her son during some natural but private occupation which concerned no one except himself and which usually is not performed in sight of others.

Fina-Kajsa continued: "Anders says he grew lonesome here. He says it can affect one's head, to emigrate and grow lonely. . . ."

Karl Oskar searched for words of comfort for the old one. But strangely, comforting words were far away when needed. He could not find a single one—he had nothing to say to Fina-Kajsa. He greeted her from Kristina,

284

and then went his way. The old woman remained sitting, her vacant eyes staring over the wilderness forest.

Her son who lay flat-back on his bed had grown lonesome . . . hmm. . . .

Now Karl Oskar knew why Anders Månsson had been unable to improve his circumstances during his years in the Territory—now he knew the secret of Fina-Kajsa's son.

–4–

KARL OSKAR could now go to Lake Gennesaret and borrow the fifteen cents from his neighbors, but then he would not have time for a second walk back to Mr. Abbott's store. He must let the letter from Sweden remain in the postoffice drawer for the time being; after all, it was not floating in the lake, Postmaster Abbott had it in safekeeping.

Karl Oskar walked straight back home. Kristina met him in the door: "Did you get the letter? What did it say? Are they well?" Three anxious questions, and she found time for a fourth before her husband had said a word: "Hasn't the letter come?"

"It has come. But it must be redeemed. It costs fifteen cents."

"You couldn't redeem it?"

"No."

"You walked all the way for nothing?"

"Yes."

Kristina had been waiting eagerly for his return, she was sure he would bring the letter from Sweden. Now she felt like a child who is chased away from the Christmas tree after waiting long at the door.

A silence fell between husband and wife. And Karl Oskar felt another question coming, but this one his wife need not utter. He said he had not wished to borrow from anyone in Taylors Falls, he was too proud to ask for a loan of fifteen cents; he did not wish to advertise his poverty among all the Swedes in the St. Croix Valley. Their letter was in good hands in the store, they need not worry, no one would take it away from them.

"Did you see the writing on the letter?"

"No, I wasn't that close."

"You don't know who wrote it?"

"No. It could be my father, or it might be yours. One or the other, I guess."

A few days passed. Spring had come to the valley. The ice on the river had broken up, the steamboat had come with the letter from Sweden; it now lay in a drawer in the post office in Taylors Falls and could be redeemed for fifteen cents. Kristina thought, what luck that the sun and the warmth came to people without having to be redeemed; had they been forced to pay fifteen cents for the spring, the winter would still be with them.

Karl Oskar and Kristina said nothing more about the letter, but their thoughts hovered around it. They could not get it off their minds, they wondered and mused: What was in the letter? A whole year had run away since they had climbed on the wagon for the drive to Karlshamn— how much might have happened in that time! And everything that had happened was written in that letter, and the letter had finally almost reached them, it was only a few miles away, yet as far away as ever. It cost fifteen cents!

Kristina thought it would have been better not to know about the letter. It would have been better if Karl Oskar had kept quiet about it. Now she was wrought up and worried about news from home. It was so close, yet not within her reach.

Karl Oskar was resigned to waiting patiently until the time he could redeem it, and he thought Kristina should do the same. He was busy all day long making his new breaking plow. He was making it entirely of wood, and he must have it ready when the frost left the ground. He had been promised he might borrow his neighbors' oxen and he was anxious to begin the plowing. A plow was far more important to him than a letter. He talked about it every time he came inside for a meal, it was on his mind early and late. It was the first time he had made a plow, the farmer's most important implement, and it required clever hands. He cut and carved, he chiseled and dug, he tried various kinds of wood, discarded and began anew, improved and finished each part from day to day. The blade must have the right curve, the pull tree the right turn, the shafts and handles the right angles. The plow body must be light, sensitive to the steering hands of the plower, it must cut its way easily through the sod. He would follow this plow in its furrow for a long time, he would follow it every day until the whole meadow was turned into a field. The new plow would give them the field for their bread to grow in.

But Kristina wished to hear no more of the plow he was making, she wanted to talk of the letter they must redeem.

Karl Oskar was too proud to borrow a mere fifteen cents from his neighbors. If a poor man could afford nothing else, at least he could afford his pride. This was a lesson he had learned in Sweden. But it might be that this lesson was neither good nor useful for an impoverished settler here in the wilderness. He could not live by his pride. And whence would he get the fifteen cents if he did not borrow it from Danjel or Jonas Petter?

A few more days went by and Karl Oskar kept busy at his plow. Then Kristina could wait no longer: Did he intend to get the letter soon? He replied that the letter was in good hands, Mr. Abbott would not give it to anyone else, she must not be impatient, the work on the plow was much more urgent.

Kristina made her own decision: She would go to her uncle and borrow fifteen cents.

Without Karl Oskar's knowledge she would set out early next morning through the forest to Danjel's settlement. She would show her stubborn husband that *she* could redeem the message from Sweden. His pride could not keep her letter from her any longer!

Strangers rarely came to the log house at Lake Ki-Chi-Saga. Occasionally a pelt trader might walk by. But the day Kristina had made her decision a stranger dropped in on them.

He was a man from the lumber company in Stillwater; he had walked through the forest staking out new roads and had lost his way. The stranger arrived at the new settlement as the family was sitting down to the noonday meal and he was asked to share their dinner: Would he be satisfied with their simple food?

Karl Oskar and the American could barely make each other understood, but he seemed a kind man. He thanked them for the dinner and before he left he patted Johan on the head and gave him a coin.

The stranger was hardly outside the door before Kristina turned to the boy and looked at the gift. It was a ten-cent piece.

She turned the thin coin in her hand, deeply disappointed. It was not enough, she was still five cents short. She would still have to borrow, and a five-cent loan would reveal their poverty more than a fifteen-cent one.

"That was close!"

"You mean . . . ?" Karl Oskar gave his wife a quick glance.

"You know what I mean!"

"But you wouldn't take the coin from the boy?"

Johan was pulling his mother's arm: "I want my money, Mother!"

"Give it to the boy," said the father. "It's the first coin he's ever had."

Kristina handed the child his coin: "But we could have borrowed it if it had been a fifteen-cent coin."

Johan meanwhile held the ten-cent piece tightly in his closed fist: "It's my money! He gave it to me!"

Karl Oskar said he would never have had the heart to rob the boy of the first money he had owned in his life.

Kristina flared up: "Then go and find fifteen cents! You're impossible! Wait and wait and wait! How long must we wait? When are you getting the letter? Shall we leave it there till Christmas?"

"I'll fetch it tomorrow morning."

"That I must see before I believe it! You're like a stubborn horse! My patience has come to an end!" Her cheeks flashed red from indignation, her eyes seemed to shoot sparks.

Karl Oskar let her anger spend itself and did nothing to interrupt her. When she had finished, he said calmly as before: Early tomorrow morning he would take the dried stag skin to Mr. Fischer in Taylors Falls. He had

287

thought they would use it for clothing but now they must sell it; they could not get along without cash any longer. He might get two dollars for the skin, he would have enough for both the letter and some groceries.

"Why didn't you sell the skin long ago? Why have you waited?"

She was interrupted by the door swinging open. The stranger who had given money to Johan was back. He stopped at the threshold and pointed to the lake shore, rolling a lump of tobacco in his hand while he talked.

Karl Oskar listened eagerly and tried to understand. He recognized the word hay. The stranger pointed to the haystacks in their meadow—three stacks were still left, Lady had been unable to eat all the hay before they returned her to Anders Månsson. The stranger had come back because he had discovered their hay—now Karl Oskar understood.

He accompanied the man to the meadow. Shortly, he returned to the house with three large silver coins in his hand: the lumber company in Stillwater was short of hay for their teams, and the man bought the three remaining haystacks for three dollars.

Never was a seller more satisfied with a transaction. "I felt it in my bones last fall when I cut the hay! I knew it would come in handy!" said Karl Oskar.

That very day he went to fetch the letter from Taylors Falls, and this time he carried it with him when he returned. He had recognized his father's big writing on the envelope but he carried it home with the seal unbroken, he wanted to break it in Kristina's presence, he wanted her to listen when he read it for the first time.

As soon as he was inside the door they sat down on either side of their table. It was the middle of the week, but both had a feeling of reverence, a Sunday mood. Karl Oskar picked up the bread knife, the sharpest one they had in the house and he cut the seal slowly and carefully so as not to harm the letter.

It was a small sheet, narrow and written full from top to bottom. The letters were stiff, crooked, and broken—they were reminders of the pain-stiffened, crooked fingers that had formed and written them.

The letter from Sweden brought the following message to the reader and the listener:

Dear Son, Daughter-in-Law and Children,
Our dearly loved Ones, May you be well is our constant Wish!

We have received your letter and its message that you have arrived alive and in health, Which is a great Joy to us. Now I will write to let you know how we are—we all have God's great gift of health and all is well.

Much evil and good has happened since we parted. The churchwarden in Åkerby fell off a wagon and was killed last summer near the hill at Åbro mill, Oldest Son took over home, on my Homestead all work and chores progress in due order, the farmer who supplies our Reserved Rights is penurious, but otherwise kind, this year has had fine weather and good crops.

288

Mother and I do not go to other places much, we keep busy at home, most the time I keep close to the fire as you know. You have had your free will and have deserted home, we hope you all have success, it must be un-Christian hard for you in the beginning in a new land. Mother wonders if you have any Minister to preach God's clear Word to you, your God is with you also in a foreign country. Turn to Him when your own strength fails.

Have no concern and do not worry for Us, We greet your little children and your good wife from Our Hearts. Her parents and Sisters in Duvemåla are well and wish the same to Kristina in North America. I have paid the freight for this letter, hope it is sufficient. You can afford it as little as I in a strange country.

You are every hour in our Thoughts, I invoke the Lord's blessing upon you, our dear ones in this world.

Written Down by your Father
Nils Jakob's Son
Korpamoen in Ljuder Parish October 9 in the
year of Our Lord 1850. Let no outsider see
my scribble.

# XXIV

## Unmarried Ulrika of Västergöhl Weeps

KARL OSKAR reread the letter from Sweden three times before Kristina was satisfied. Only after that did he have an opportunity to tell her the great news he had heard today in Taylors Falls: Ulrika of Västergöhl was going to enter into holy matrimony with Mr. Walter H. Abbott, she was to move to Taylors Falls as wife to the postmaster and storekeeper.

This he had heard and it had come from Swedish Anna, who was not one to spread untrue gossip. She herself would move to New Kärragärde as housekeeper for Danjel and Jonas Petter in Ulrika's place.

Mr. Abbott had often of late visited the Swedish settlement at Lake Gennesaret, according to Swedish Anna. And Ulrika had treated him to food—the most delicious food she could cook—sweet cheese, pork omelet, cheesecake. She had offered him all her choice dishes. And Mr. Abbott had been so taken by the Swedish fare that he wished for it on his table at every meal. In order to have the good food daily, he must keep the cook in his house, and so he had proposed to Ulrika. Swedish Anna had hinted that the impending marriage was some piece of witchery: Ulrika had be-witched Mr. Abbott with the food she had given him. She had taken advantage of a poor man who never before had known how food should taste. Ulrika could thank her Creator that the preparation of decent food was not as yet known in America.

289

Swedish Anna had spoken as though Ulrika had committed a heinous crime in offering Mr. Abbott her Swedish dishes.

The Taylors Falls postmaster and storekeeper was a well-to-do man, nothing in the way of worldly goods was missing from his house. There might be other women besides the Glad One who would have liked to be in charge of a store full of good wares. Karl Oskar suspected that Swedish Anna spoke in jealousy when she belittled Ulrika.

Kristina had seen Mr. Abbott behind his counter last summer. His head, on a lanky, loose-limbed body, almost reached the ceiling; she remembered his big hands, covered with black hair, his broad, flat feet. He was always dressed in a motley coat with long tails, his shirt neck open. Everyone said he was honest in his dealings. Kristina thought he had a hardened heart, denying the poor settlers credit for a single cent; but she would not call him stingy—many times he had given her sugar sticks for her children.

Kristina said to Karl Oskar: Next Sunday he must stay home alone and look after their offspring. She would go to Uncle Danjel's and wish Ulrika of Västergöhl well on her coming marriage.

—2—

SHE STARTED OUT on her walk early in the morning. It was the first time she had walked alone from Ki-Chi-Saga to the settlement at Lake Gennesaret. Karl Oskar had advised against it—but this time she wanted to go by herself through the clearing; sometime she must learn to walk alone, in a place where she would live for the rest of her life. She would feel like a penned-in animal if she could never leave her home without being followed and guarded like a herd beast. She could not lose her way—there only was one road to follow.

The Indians had returned and had been around the lake, but she tried to suppress her fear of the copperskins with this thought: If God protects me, I need not be afraid to walk alone through the forest. If God does not protect me, I would not be safe in the greatest company of people.

The forest had been washed clean by the mild spring rains, the grass was sprouting, the leaf-trees were budding, the air smelled fresh and good, of foliage and bark and buds, of earth and mold. Kristina stepped lightly over the wretched road, she breathed with an easy heart. For long stretches she could imagine she walked through the woodlands at home in Duvemåla. Here grew the same trees, though they were larger, more wild looking than at home. She was more at home with trees and bushes than with people, and did not feel lonely in her walk through the woods.

But she never forgot the dangers that might lurk in the forest. Any moment she might encounter something frightening. Last time Swedish Anna came to visit she had seen a cut-off human foot in the road. It was tied to a post stuck in the ground, a bloody foot with a brown skin—an Indian foot. It was a gruesome sign put there by the savages—Swedish Anna thought it meant war between the Chippewas and the Sioux.

Nor did Kristina forget the snakes which had come out of their holes in the spring sunshine and might lie in wait for her. But neither humans nor animals molested her on her Sunday walk, she saw neither snakes nor maimed human feet.

When she reached Danjel's house, she found Ulrika alone. Jonas Petter had made a small skiff, and he and Danjel had taken the children onto the lake; they hoped to catch some fish for dinner.

Ulrika had returned the evening before from a visit with her daughter in Stillwater. Elin was satisfied in her service, her duties were light and her American master and mistress were kind to their servants. Ulrika had also visited Pastor Jackson in his new house, and she had been to his church and heard him preach.

Kristina noticed at once that Ulrika was not herself today. She did not seem as lively or hearty as usual, she had a serious look on her face, her motions and bearing were different, there was something inscrutable about her. She had a new expression, a thoughtful, solemn look. Perhaps it was caused by the great change which her imminent marriage would bring her.

She took out her knapsack and began carefully folding garments and placing them in it. So she was already busy with her moving.

"I'm packing up a little," she said.

"Yes. I've already heard about it. You're moving to Taylors Falls to be the storekeeper's wife!"

Ulrika looked up quickly, with a strange, serious glance. She did not answer. Kristina wished her well in her marriage, she repeated her words twice. But Ulrika seemed not to appreciate this good wish, rather, it pained her. She did not acknowledge it, she did not say thank you. She seemed embarrassed and annoyed as she picked up a well-washed and newly ironed shift—Kristina guessed this shining white garment might be her bridal shift.

What was the matter with the Glad One today? Kristina scarcely recognized her. She was always jolly and in high spirits, and this was surely the time for rejoicing. Something must be wrong.

A worrying thought came to Kristina: Perhaps the marriage with Mr. Abbott was off? Had something come between them? Had the suitor regretted his proposal and taken it back? Something had happened. But Ulrika was packing her clothes—was she moving away from Danjel in any case? Kristina asked outright.

"Yes, I'm moving away," Ulrika said, as she spread her clean shift on the table. "But not to Taylors Falls! I am not going to be Storekeeper Abbott's wife."

"Then it isn't true?"

"It *was* the truth. Or almost the truth." Ulrika's voice trembled slightly in a way Kristina had never heard before. "It was as close to the truth as anything can be. I could have married Mr. Abbott. But now I've changed my mind."

"What in the world—"

"Everything has changed for me."

Kristina held her breath: Ulrika must mean that the suitor had changed his mind. Someone might have slandered Ulrika to Mr. Abbott, someone might have told him about her life in Sweden. It must be some Swede— who could it be? Who would be so cruel? Who had betrayed Ulrika?

"Has something come between you?"

"Yes, something came between."

Anger rose within Kristina. Never would she shake hands with the dastard who had ruined Ulrika's marriage plans. "Some wicked, jealous gossip has spoiled it?"

"No," said Ulrika. "It was not a human being."

"No human being?"

"It was God Himself."

"What do you mean?"

"God came between. He did not want me to marry Mr. Abbott."

Ulrika folded the sleeves of her shift. She turned toward Kristina, her full bosom heaving inside her tight bodice: "The Lord stepped in and averted the marriage."

Kristina was confused; Ulrika did not seem to feel she had lost a great opportunity; rather, the Glad One spoke as though a great disaster had nearly overtaken her, which at the last moment God had prevented.

Ulrika explained: Mr. Abbott was the American she had exchanged more English words with than anyone else; she understood him better than anyone, what she had learned of the new language she had learned from him. Ever since New Year's she had known that the postmaster wanted to marry her. Shortly before Christmas, when she went to shop in his store, he had walked part way back with her and helped carry her food basket. He did the same thing again and again, and one evening he had walked all the way to their house and stayed overnight. He had eaten with them, she had offered him the same fare she gave to Danjel and Jonas Petter, but never had she seen a man so grateful for food. He had said she was an expert at cooking, and a few weeks ago he had proposed. He said he needed a housekeeper, and she needed a home—if they married, both would have what they needed.

Abbott was a courteous and fine man, he acted toward her the way all American men acted toward women. How many pounds he had carried for her from Taylors Falls! Even a choosy woman could accept such a man. But she wasn't quite satisfied with the way he had proposed; he ought to have said: I need a human being in my home during the daytime, and a woman in my bed at night! But he hadn't said that. He had

292

only said he needed a housekeeper and cook. If he had proposed the other way, then she would have accepted him at once. Instead she asked for some time to think it over—and this she had done in such a way that he undoubtedly took it for half a promise to marry him.

She needed not only a home, she needed also a man, she hadn't slept with a man for more than three years. She was in her prime, her youthful blood still flowed warm in her body. And when she married, she wanted to marry a man who cared more for what a woman could give in bed than what she could offer at the table. She had long wished for a man who would rather starve at table than fail to appreciate what a woman could give with her soul and body. She wanted, too, a man to help her physically and spiritually, a man she could always rely on. She was afraid a marriage with Mr. Abbott would turn out badly.

That was why she had asked for time to think it over. And yesterday, as she came through Taylors Falls on her way from Stillwater, she had stopped in to see Mr. Abbott in his store and told him: She was honored by his proposal, but she could not accept, because the Lord Jesus would not give His sanction to their wedlock.

Kristina stared at Ulrika, more confused than before: Ulrika had declined to become a storekeeper's wife, she had refused the splendor of Mr. Abbott's store, she had rejected the kind man who had helped carry her burdens homeward!

"Are you serious?"

"I've never been more serious."

"But you're packing! Are you still moving away from Danjel?"

"Yes. I'm moving away. To Stillwater. A miracle has happened to me." She spoke the last sentence with great emphasis.

Something new lit up Ulrika's features, a light shone in her eyes, an unusual gravity was in her voice: "Listen to me, Kristina. You're the first to know: I'm going to be baptized. I'm going to be baptized by a Baptist."

"Oh . . . now I understand. You've changed your religion."

"No! I haven't changed. I've been on the right road. But only now have I come close to God. And for this I can thank Pastor Jackson."

"Ah . . . it's he who has made you a Baptist?"

"Yes. My husband-to-be will baptize me."

"What?"

"I'm marrying Pastor Jackson in Stillwater."

And Ulrika turned again to the table where her new-washed linen shift still lay spread.

Kristina was lost in astonishment. But not for long. Her surprise lessened as she thought the news over. She ought to have guessed from the very beginning, she should have foreseen, after all Ulrika's talks of Pastor Jackson and her visits with him, after all the praise Ulrika had lavished on the minister.

"Are you surprised?"

293

"No!" Kristina answered. "This is the best thing that could happen to you! A likelier man couldn't be found. With Pastor Jackson, I don't even need to wish you well!"

Yes, that was how things were; God had come between Ulrika and Mr. Abbott. And he had chosen another husband for her.

Ulrika was to be married in the Baptist Church in Stillwater this spring. But before she married Pastor Jackson she would be baptized at the great baptism which the church performed in the St. Croix River every spring.

"It's a God's miracle!" said the Glad One. "You don't even understand it, Kristina."

Her hand lightly touched the white shift on the table, slowly, tenderly, like a caress. Kristina had guessed right—it was her bridal shift.

Ulrika went on: Three years ago she had been converted by Danjel, but ever since that time she had felt something missing. She had shed her old body, but she had never felt quite at home in the new one. She had known something was missing from her rebirth in Christ. Since meeting Jackson she had spoken many times to Danjel about the Baptists and had asked him if a new baptism might give new comfort to her soul. Danjel no longer believed God had entrusted him with the care of any soul except his own. Since he had gone astray in self-righteousness, he felt he could lead no one else along the right road. And he had told her she had her own free will in religious matters. She knew best what God asked of her, he would not rebuke her if she turned Baptist and enjoyed a new christening.

Now Ulrika felt a rechristening was just what she needed. Only the Baptists were entirely reborn into this world. To rid herself completely of the old flesh-body, she must again go through baptism, which should never be undertaken until a person was full grown in mind and body. Now she felt old enough, her mind wasn't likely to grow any more, she was as wise as a woman in her position and of her age would ever be; the time had arrived for her rechristening into the Baptist faith. And the crown of the miracle was the fact that her husband-to-be would baptize her with his own hands.

The baptism would take place as soon as the river water grew warmer. Many other persons would be immersed at the same time as she. All would be fully dressed, but baptism for a rebirth required the whole body to be under water. They were to wade into the river until the water stood above their shoulders. Pastor Jackson would hold on to her neck and push down her head, while he read the baptismal prayer. It would take only a few moments with the head under water to make it binding, he had told her. Then the newly baptized must hurry home and put on dry clothes and drink warm milk or steaming coffee so as not to catch cold. But later in the spring the St. Croix River would be warmer, so there would be less risk of getting sick.

". . . but I can't explain it! I can't tell you any more! Oh, Kristina, I am chosen. I am."

And as Ulrika was talking in great exhilaration she suddenly stopped short—she rested her elbows against the table and broke out in loud weeping.

She slumped down onto a chair as if her legs had given way under her, she began to cry so violently that her whole body shook, she put her hands to her face, the tears dripped between her fingers and fell onto the shift on the table.

"Ulrika, my dear!" Kristina had never seen Ulrika of Västergöhl cry, no one had ever seen her shed a tear. No one had imagined she could weep, she was such a strong, fearless woman. Kristina realized that something profound had happened to her. "Ulrika! You never weep!"

Copiously Ulrika's tears ran while from trembling lips she stammered forth: She was not sad, she was happy. Her tears were tears of joy. She never cried when she was sad, only when she was happy. That was why she had never wept before, she had never been happy, never in all her life until now. What had there been for her to be happy over? Nothing—ever! Until now!

The Glad One wept. She soaked her wedding linen in tears.

Kristina sat silent and looked at her. Ulrika continued to sob. Long had she carried her tears, long had she saved them, now the moment had come when she spent her savings. It was as though all the tears she had kept back through all the years were now gathered in force, breaking through in one great torrent—as though she wished at one single time to weep tears for all the happiness which had been denied her throughout life.

At length she became aware of her tears dripping onto the white garment; then she put her apron to her eyes and wept into her apron. Her blooming cheeks were washed in her flood of tears, she wiped them away with the apron.

Kristina sat silent; one who weeps for joy needs no comfort. She was glad for Ulrika's sake, she would have liked to weep also, to show that she shared her happiness.

When the Glad One's tears at last began to give out and her tongue regained its former use, she told Kristina why she began to weep after these many years: It was because of God's all-forgiving love which she had experienced through her husband-to-be—through Henry. When he had asked her to be his wife—and he had spoken very slowly and clearly so that she would understand the English words—she had at once recognized who he was: he was the mate God had chosen and saved for her, and who had long been waiting for her here in North America. Then she had felt that she too must show him who she was—God demanded this of her, forced her to it. She had told him she was a great sinner, that she had lived in sin and shame in her homeland, that she had felt at home in her sin-body and enjoyed its pleasures. She was a sister of the Bible harlot who had been brought to Jesus for judgment. She had met a Lord's Apostle who had repeated Christ's words: Go, and sin no more! And for three years she had done repentance, for three years she had not let a single man near her.

Henry had told her that God had already informed him she had been a great sinner. But one forgiven by God had nothing to fear from mortals. Who was he to judge her? He himself was a great sinner, forgiven by God. They were alike, she and he. The old life was past, blotted out through the rebirth. And if some part of her old sin-body still clung to her, she would be cleansed in the baptism he would give her later in spring when the river water was a little warmer.

It was because of God's love, all-forgiving love, that Ulrika of Västergöhl now wet her bridal linen with her tears.

But only a person who knew what sin was could rightly understand her joy. Sin was like a wasp, a big, angry, buzzing hornet. Or like a bee. Sin had sweet honey in its mouth, and a sharp, piercing sting in its end. First it lured a mortal with its honey sweetness, then it stung with its stinger. Sin had led her astray with its delightful sweetness, but how bitterly it had then stung her! Nothing in this world could sting such deep wounds as sin!

But people too had hurt her. How much evil she had suffered from them! Ever since she had borne her first child she had been called *unmarried* Ulrika of Västergöhl. It was even written down in the church book. She had been born unmarried, she couldn't help it. God had created her unmarried, He had created her in such a way that she bore children easily, she couldn't help that either. And later she couldn't get married, later, when she had lost that which men required in a bridal bed. That too she couldn't help. She had never had a maidenhead to save, since it had been stolen from her as a little girl, before she was fully developed.

But now she had been sleeping alone in her bed so long, now she had spared her body so long that the old marks of sin must be obliterated. She had been with no man for such a long time, she had a feeling something had grown inside her, her maidenhead had at last had a chance to develop, to come back to her. She felt like a virgin, like an expectant and trembling virgin, now that she was to step into a bridal bed. And this too made her happy, this too was something to shed tears of joy over; this too was a miracle. She who was called the Glad One had never until now been glad.

Voices were heard outside the cabin, and Ulrika of Västergöhl rose quickly. "The men are coming with fish for dinner. I can't sit here and bawl!" She picked up her wedding shift and folded it quickly. "I must put on the potato pot!"

Hurriedly she dried the last tears with the corner of her apron. Now

296

she had wept and enjoyed it, she had wept to her heart's content. Now she had completed her joy-weeping over the passing of the old, the coming of the new.

—3—

KRISTINA started for home in the early afternoon; little Danjel must be waiting for her in his cradle. She had nursed her last born generously before leaving in the morning, but he must be howling with hunger by now, he was such a lusty child.

Her uncle Danjel had bought two cows this spring, and one had recently calved. As they were milkless at Ki-Chi-Saga, he now gave his niece a pail of milk. Kristina was overjoyed at the gift; she must save every drop for her children; she must walk carefully on the rutty road so the precious milk would not splash out.

Ulrika whispered to her that she had more confidences to share, she couldn't speak freely with Danjel and Jonas Petter listening, so she would accompany her a bit on the way and help her carry the milk pail.

Kristina told her she was much pleased that no one now could go to Pastor Jackson and slander his wife-to-be, no evil person could ruin this marriage. After all the sufferings Ulrika had gone through she had earned her happy lot as wife of the minister in Stillwater, and nothing should interfere.

Ulrika answered: She herself had always maintained that the best that could happen to a woman in this world was to marry a man she could rely on. Henry had a new house, he could offer her all she needed of worldly goods. With Mr. Abbott she would have had more than she needed, if she had been looking for things of this world only and wished to live in the flesh. Pastor Jackson earned his daily bread, but nothing more. Here in the Territory a minister earned no great sums for looking after souls. People spent most of their money on their bodies. Pastor Jackson was paid three pounds of pork for a very long sermon, a pat of butter for a wedding, a dozen eggs for a prayer for the sick. No one could get rich from such puny contributions. And he endured hardships and suffered want when he traveled about in this wilderness. He preached in the open, in log cabins and barns, in woodsheds and hovels, in logging camps and hunters' huts, in all sorts of dens and nests. He preached from morning to night, every hour of the day, the whole week through—it was only on Sundays he preached at home in his church. But that was the way an honest minister should preach, according to the words in the Acts: "The Lord of heaven and earth dwelleth not in temples made with hands."

But she would have an easy life as the minister's wife in Stillwater. Henry washed dishes and kept the house clean, scrubbed the floors, car-

297

ried in water and wood. All she need do was cook the food and run the house. The rest of the time she could stay inside and keep herself clean. The Americans wanted clean, neat wives, the men did all the chores to save their womenfolk from getting bent backs, crooked limbs, or wrinkled faces while still in their days of youth. Swedish menfolk could not ruin their women quickly enough, with slave labor and the roughest work—this gave them a good excuse when they later went to younger, better-looking women. . . .

"Are you coming to my wedding, Kristina?" asked Ulrika.

Kristina said she was sorry, but she couldn't leave the children long enough to journey all the way to Stillwater. Karl Oskar would stay home in her place if she asked him, but he couldn't give the little one the breast.

"I'll come to your first christening instead! Then I won't be nursing the baby any longer."

"You'll have to wait a long while. You'll have to wait till the child is grown. Then his father will baptize him in the river."

Since Ulrika had carried Kristina's child to baptism, she ought in turn to carry Ulrika's. But she had forgotten the parents' religion—their child would not be christened until full grown.

"Henry intends to ask the Lord for many children," said Ulrika of Västergöhl.

"You aren't too old yet."

"I should say not! I can bring forth brats another ten years!"

"And you give birth easily, you told me."

"Much more easily than you last time!"

Pastor Jackson did not hope for such a great blessing as Jacob—to father twelve tribes—but he would consider it a particular grace from God if he might be the father of half as many—six.

Ulrika went on: First of all she would pray to God for a son who could walk in his father's footsteps as minister. She herself could never become a priest, she felt women weren't good enough. Yet God allowed women to bear males for the holy priesthood. It wasn't forbidden women to take part in the making of priests, they were permitted to carry them inside their bodies for a whole nine months. And it was Ulrika's great desire to make use of that opportunity: She had never thought she would marry a priest, but she surely had wished to make one.

And if by the Highest One's Grace she were permitted to see the day when this took place, she would write a letter to Dean Brusander in Ljuder, who had excluded her from church and sacrament, and she would tell him: Great Lord's gifts were required in a minister, but now she had done something the Mr. Dean could not do—she had made a priest!

So she would write. And as Ulrika mused on this, walking at Kristina's side, helping to carry the milk pail through the forest, an expression of deep contentment and happy expectation lighted her face.

298

"There was something you wanted to tell me," Kristina reminded her.
"So there is! I'll tell you."

And after making Kristina promise to keep it to herself until after the wedding, Ulrika confided in her: *She had bought a hat.*

The transaction had taken place yesterday in Stillwater; for the time being she had hidden the hat under her bed in the log house. She had wanted to show it to Kristina, but the men had come, and she did not wish Jonas Petter to see it—he would poke fun at her. In Sweden everyone ridiculed a woman of the simple sort if she wore anything but a shawl on her head. The noble women could not bear it if anyone besides themselves wore a hat. But here in North America a woman was not denied a hat, here she could wear whatever she wanted without fear of heckling.

And so for her wedding she had bought a beautiful hat, with long plumes and blooms and ribbon bands. She would show it to Kristina another time. It was so elegant the imagination could not grasp it.

Ulrika would put on her hat the day she was married. And once she had her hat on, *unmarried* Ulrika of Västergöhl would be no more.

—4—

Spring found these changes among the new settlers in the St. Croix Valley: Robert's and Arvid's whereabouts were unknown, they were on their way to the far-off land of California; Ulrika and her daughter Elin had moved away from Danjel to Stillwater, and Swedish Anna moved to the Lake Gennesaret settlement in Ulrika's place, to run the household for Danjel and Jonas Petter.

It was a warm, sunny spring day when Ulrika was baptized in the St. Croix River. The following Saturday she was married in the little whitewashed wooden church in Stillwater and became Mrs. Reverend Henry O. Jackson.

She was the first Swedish bride in the St. Croix Valley. She was to be the mother of a flock of children, the founder of a fine new family; a strong, enduring family: One day her great-grandchildren would speak of their descent from the noble family of Västergöhl in Sweden, whence their female ancestor a hundred years earlier had emigrated.

# XXV

## "At Home" Here in America—"Back There" in Sweden

The sun's arc climbed, the days lengthened, but the evenings had not yet begun to lighten. The sun departed, darkness came in its place, but

299

no twilight under a pale heaven lingered over the earth. Kristina waited: Spring was as yet only beginning.

April came and brought sun-warm days to the shores of Lake Ki-Chi-Saga, but the evenings remained almost as dark as in winter. Kristina still waited.

And when at last she realized her waiting was futile, her thoughts wandered to a land where the evenings in spring were light.

After the many chores which each day fell to her with their unchanging sameness, her body was tired as she lay down on her bed in the evening. But her mind and soul would not rest, she lay awake with her thoughts. Outside the small log-house windows the night was dark, but she lay with her eyes wide open and gazed into the darkness where nothing could be seen.

As spring progressed, with darkness still prevailing, her sleepless hours increased. She still gazed through the darkness—toward that land where evenings were light in spring.

Memories reawakened, images stood clear. She and her sisters sat "twilighting" at the window; they used to delay lighting the candles, by the light of the spring evening they would sit talking in hushed voices to each other. They never spoke aloud at "twilighting"—the gathering dusk of an April evening called for whispered talk. Outside by the gable the great rosebush brushed against the window, with its tender green growth and swelling buds. Later in summer the roses would be out, and then the bush would cover the whole window with its fragrant blooms. Against the evening sky the young Astrachan apple tree stood out clearly —she had planted it herself as a companion for the lonely rosebush. Each autumn she had dug around the little tree; it had carried its first apples the last fall they were at home—big juicy apples with transparent skin; how many times she had gone out just to look at the apples; and how delicious they had been.

Would her apple tree bloom this spring? Would it bear apples in the fall? And would there be gooseberries on the bushes she had planted against the cellar wall? Those berries were as big as thumbs, and dark red when ripe; their taste was sweet as sugar.

A year had passed since the April evening she had said good-by to her parents and sisters at the gate of her childhood home. She—the departing one—had stood outside the gate, they—whom she would part from—had stood inside. Her mother had said: "Don't forget, our dear daughter, we want to meet you with God." Her father had stood bent against the gatepost, he said nothing, he stood with his face turned away, holding on to the post as if seeking support.

She had left, and they had remained; never more in this world would she see them.

That evening had been light, one whole long twilight that still lit her way home on sleepless nights. . . . It had rained during the day, but

300

cleared toward evening. There had been a spring fragrance over black fields and green meadows as she walked away from the farm where she was born.

And since that evening a year had completed its cycle, the year's great wheel had made a complete turn and carried her far away in the world, thousands of miles away. She had emigrated and now she lived so far away that only her thoughts could carry her back. Here she lay in her bed, next to her husband, in her new home, and peered into the darkness, looking for the land where the evenings were light in spring.

She traveled the way back, she traversed the great waters and the immense stretches of land. She retraced the road that separated her from her old home. She could see that road in her mind, bit by bit, mile by mile. And the mile she remembered at home was a long mile, six times as long as the American mile, it took her two or three hours to walk it. And as she gazed into the dark outside the cabin window she felt the distance increase a thousand times. She measured mile after mile, she counted as she traveled, ten, twenty, thirty . . . until she tired of her journey, and yet she had retraveled so small a part. Her thoughts would never reach the thousand-mile mark, her journey must end, the immense distance stifled her imagination. And after a while she grew dizzy, her tired eyes vainly penetrating the darkness—she was unable to fathom the road that separated her from her homeland.

That road she would never again travel.

Longing for home gripped Kristina in its vise more forcibly as spring came with no twilight. And the evening hours when she lay awake became the time of day she most feared.


—2—


WHAT WAS THE MATTER with Kristina? What did she long for? Didn't she live here, have her home here—wasn't she at home? How could she long for home when she was already at home?

Karl Oskar had said, "*Here at home* on Lake Ki-Chi-Saga I'll build a large house next time!" *Here at home*—but she felt as though she were away, as though she were in a foreign place. She always said, "*Away here in America—back home in Sweden.*" So she thought, so she spoke. But this was not right, and her saying it wasn't right, when her home would be here forever. She should say just the opposite, exchange the countries: This was home, Sweden was away.

And she tried, she tried to think and say the opposite. She said to herself: At home here in America—back there in Sweden. She repeated this, again and again. Her mouth learned to say it, but her heart wouldn't accept it. Next time, she forgot herself, again she used the words *back home—away here*. Something inside her refused the change, something she could not force. She still thought and talked as she had when she first arrived. She could not make the countries change place—back home would always remain *home* to Kristina.

What *was* the matter with her? Kristina put the question to herself, and Karl Oskar too asked her. Nothing was the matter with her, she answered. Did she lie when she said this? Did she speak the truth? She was satisfied with her lot here, she complained of nothing; she had husband and children with her, they were all in good health, they had their sustenance, everything essential, everything they needed to sustain life. They could forget their temporary inconveniences, finding comfort in the good promises the future held out for them in the new land.

Kristina lacked nothing, yet she missed something. It was hard to understand.

What did she miss? What did she long for? Why did she lie awake so long in the evenings thinking about the rosebush and the Astrachan tree at home in Duvemåla? Did she miss the bushes and trees of the home village? There were enough bushes and trees and plants growing around their new home, they grew more profusely than in Sweden, and they bore quantities of fruit and berries, much richer fruit than the trees and bushes in Sweden. She should be well satisfied with all the good things here.

Why did she long so for home? Perhaps it was weakness, a softness in her. Perhaps some childishness remained in her, had remained in her too long: When she had been a married woman, mother of several children, she had secretly put up a swing in the barn and gone there to play. That had been childish. And now it was childish of her to think of rosebushes and trees she had planted in her parental home—to regret that she never again would taste apples from her tree, never see her rosebush bloom outside the gable.

Now she was a grown woman—and she wanted to be a grown woman, she did not wish Karl Oskar to see how childish and weak she was, she did not want to act like a silly girl. That was why she hadn't confided in him. Not a single human being knew what stirred within her as she lay awake these spring nights in her bed.

It was only natural that she longed to see her loved ones, that she missed the life she had been born into and bred up in. Everything focussed in those clear pictures of home—the apple tree and the rosebush in the twilight, all that her longing made vivid in the dark: the family gatherings, familiar customs and ways, the Sundays on the church green, spring and autumn fairs, the year's festivities and holidays, the seasons in the farm-year cycle. Here in the wilderness all was different, here people had other customs, and she lived like a bewildered stranger among people whom she could not reach with her tongue, and who could not reach her with their own speech.

She saw the sunshine, the light of the moon, and the stars in the

302

heavens—it was the same sun, the same moon, and stars she had seen at home. The heavenly lights had accompanied her on her emigration and shone on her here. They were lit at home too and shone over the people she had left behind. Sun, moon, and stars revealed to her that though she was in a foreign land she still shared the firmament with those at home. But she was away, and she would remain away. In this country she would live out the rest of her allotted days, few or many, broken soon or stretching into late old age. Here she would live, here she would die, here she would lie in her grave.

And this was the way it was with Kristina: she could not reconcile herself to the irrevocable. She had emigrated for life, yet it seemed she was still on a journey that would eventually bring her home again.

And night after night she lay awake and measured the road she never again would journey.

—3—

DURING daylight her chores occupied her thoughts, in the daytime she could defend herself. But when she lay wide awake at night, waiting for sleep to engulf her, she was open and unprotected; and then longing and sorrow stole over her. Her evening prayer sometimes brought calm to her mind and helped her go to sleep. Karl Oskar always went to sleep immediately, usually as soon as his head hit the pillow, and often she said her prayer after he had gone to sleep; she wanted only God to hear her.

One evening she made an addition to her usual prayer: She prayed God that He might once more let her see her home and her loved ones. For God nothing was impossible: If He wanted to, He could stretch out His omnipotent arm and move her from North America back to Sweden.

Afterward she lay awake; in her thoughts she was with those at home sitting "twilight." No, her evening prayer did not always help her.

She felt Karl Oskar's hand on the quilt, slowly seeking hers. "Kristina . . ."

"I thought you were asleep, Karl Oskar."

"Something wakened me. Maybe a screechhopper."

"There is no hopper in here tonight." She must have wakened him saying her prayer. "Have you been awake long?"

"No. Just a little while."

She hoped he hadn't heard her prayer.

His hand had found hers: "What is the matter with you, Kristina?"

"Nothing. Nothing is the matter with me. Go back to sleep!"

But her voice was thick and disturbed, so sad that it troubled him. Her voice denied the words she uttered. Her voice said: Yes, there is

303

something wrong. Don't go to sleep, Karl Oskar! Stay awake and help me!

And she was afraid he might hear her voice rather than her words.

"But why do you lie awake this late?" he persisted.

"Oh, I don't know. It's silly and childish. . . ."

She wanted to be strong, as strong and hardy as he.

"Are you—sad? Is something wrong, Kristina?"

"No . . . I don't know how to explain. . . ."

He gripped her hand in his own big, hard hand, he held her hand so tightly that it hurt her. "Aren't we friends, the best of friends, as before?"

"Yes, Karl Oskar, of course."

"But then you must tell me everything. If you fight something, I might help you. Good friends help each other."

She did not answer. A silence fell between them.

Then he said—and his words were firm and determined: "If you want God's arm to move you back, then I'll hold you here with my arm!"

He meant what he said. So, not only God had heard her this evening.

"Yes. Now you know, Karl Oskar." She said this with a slow, hesitating sigh. Then she added: "There isn't much more to say. It was a childish wish that came over me as I said my prayer."

"I began to wonder that time last fall when you cried at the house-warming party. Since then I have wondered how things stood with you. And lately I've felt you don't like it here. You're brooding."

"I like it here. It isn't that. I don't know myself what it is. I'll tell you, and let me hear what you think. . . ."

And suddenly she wanted to confide in her husband, she wanted him to know and understand. It was painful for her to keep such a thing as this a secret, it wore on her mind to suffer a sorrow which she had to hide every moment, had to hide even from her own husband. And hadn't she and Karl Oskar been joined together in order to lighten life's burdens for each other, to comfort each other in trouble? Shouldn't he know why she lay awake nights, what she thought of and played with in her imagination—that she traveled the road back home, bit after bit, mile after mile?

Now he must have the whole explanation: She was not dissatisfied with their new home, or their new country. She felt as he did: They would improve themselves and find security here, if health remained and they managed to struggle through a few hard years. But one country could not be like another country. America could never become Sweden to her. She could never bring here what she missed from childhood and youth in the homeland. She was only twenty-six, and when she thought of all the coming years out here, all the years left of her life, this unexplainable pain stole over her and kept her awake. Only lately had she understood what it meant to move for life. It was something for a soul to ponder.

304

And so at last, this evening, she had prayed for help from the Almighty's arm—wouldn't He stretch it out. . . . Yes, that was all.

"Kristina—"

He had not let go her hand, now he held on to it so tightly that it hurt her: he held on as though someone were trying to snatch her out of their bed, to take her away from his side. But he said nothing now.

She asked: "Karl Oskar—don't you ever feel a longing for your old home?"

"Maybe. At times. Now and then. . . ."

Yes, he must admit, a longing came over him too. It seemed to come over all emigrants at times. But he always drove it away at once. He was afraid it might burden his mind. He needed his strength for other matters. He needed all his strength to improve their lives out here. He was careful, he couldn't spend his strength pondering over what he had left forever. Just the other day, he had seen how dangerous it could be to dig oneself down in thoughts and musings—he had seen a man lying on a bed of wretchedness. . . .

Yes, she knew it well: What she worried over could never change. All her musing and thoughts were of no avail, served no purpose. . . . "But I can't help it, Karl Oskar!"

"No, I guess not." He rose. "I'll fetch something for you."

He stepped onto the floor, and she could hear him as he walked barefoot toward the fireplace corner. She heard him stir in the Swedish chest. What was he fetching for her? Drops? Did he think the Four Kinds of Drops or Hoffman's Heart-Aiding Drops would help her? There was hardly a spoonful left in either bottle, although she had used them sparingly.

Karl Oskar came silently back to the bed, he had something in his hand which he gave his wife. It was not drops, it was a pair of tiny, worn-out, broken shoes, a child's shoes.

She accepted them in bewilderment, she recognized them in bewilderment. "Anna's old shoes."

"Yes. They help me to remember. If I sometimes feel downhearted a little . . ."

"You mean—?"

"Perhaps the shoes can help you too."

"Karl Oskar!" Her voice grew thick again.

"Do you remember the winter the child died? You do, don't you?"

"Yes. It was the winter when I agreed—to the emigration. I have almost regretted it at times. But I still agree. I don't blame you a bit, Karl Oskar. You remember what I said that night on the ship?"

He remembered well, he remembered nothing better: She had said she had nothing to reproach him for, nothing to forgive him for. They were the best of friends. He could remember nothing more clearly than that. For that was the night when he thought she would die.

305

That time it had been she who had taken his hand and kept it firmly in hers. And there between them on the quilt had lain the old shoes, made by the village shoemaker in their home parish, made for their child's feet—made for Anna, who had time to wear out only one pair of shoes while she lived on earth. And now they had the shoes here in America, still aiding them—they reminded the parents of what they had gone through in the homeland: Because of hunger the little girl's life had been so short she had never needed more than one pair of shoes.

Karl Oskar said: Here in Minnesota was their home, here their home would remain. Here they had their children and all they owned, all that belonged to them in this world. In Sweden they owned not even a wooden spoon any longer, in Sweden they were homeless. This was their home.

And if Kristina still felt that she was away, then he would help her all he could to make *away* become *home* to her: "There is something I've long had in mind to tell you," he said. "One day our children will thank us for emigrating to America."

"You think that? You believe so?"

"I feel it. I know it."

"Maybe. But who knows?"

"I know it's true. I'm sure, Kristina. Our children will thank their parents for bringing them to this country when they were little."

"But no one can know."

Karl Oskar persisted: Every time he looked at this countryside and realized how much it could give to them, he felt assured of this: The children would be grateful to their parents. She must think ahead, of their children, and their children's children in time, of all the generations after them. All the ones who came after would feel and think and say that she had done right when she moved from Sweden to North America.

On that thought he himself often lingered, it was a great help to him when his struggles at times seemed heavy and endless. It gave him renewed strength when he slackened. Couldn't the same thought comfort her when she was depressed, longing for home?

"You may be right, Karl Oskar," she said. "But we know nothing of the day we haven't seen."

There was one more matter Karl Oskar had thought over and which he now wanted to discuss with his wife: It was high time they gave a name to their home.

They had lived here an autumn and a winter and soon spring would be over. They ought to name their homestead now that they were settled and would never move away. That day last fall when they had moved in she had said that the place here with the lake reminded her of Duvemåla, that it was almost as beautiful as her home village. He had thought about this many times. They could name their home after her childhood home in Algutsboda Parish. And since he had heard her talk tonight, he was even more confirmed in that thought: They must name their home in the new land Duvemåla. How did she like that? What did she think of moving the name of her parental home over here?

"I—you must know I like it!"

Kristina was overjoyed. Now she took hold of his hand and held it tightly. It was a good idea, this name for their home. She would never have thought of it herself—the name of her own village!

"Duvemåla . . . we don't live at Ki-Chi-Saga any longer, we live in Duvemåla. How lovely it sounds." Her voice was clear, no longer thick and uncertain.

"That settles the name, then," said Karl Oskar, with the intonation of a minister at baptism.

Kristina thought, from now on she would live in Duvemåla. And she would again try to make herself believe she was at home here.

So the first home on Lake Ki-Chi-Saga in Minnesota Territory was named, and the name was given late of an evening in spring as the couple who had built it lay awake in their bed and talked. They talked long to each other; the wife confessed her childish longing and spoke of the light spring nights at home, of the rosebush and the Astrachan tree and the gooseberry bushes and all the things that came to her mind at this time of evening.

It was nearly midnight, and they still lay awake. Karl Oskar said, now they must sleep. If they didn't go to sleep soon, they would wake up tired next morning. And the morrow would bring heavy work—he himself would begin the most important task of the next years: the wooden plow he had made with his own hands, with great difficulty, was at last finished, and the ox team was waiting for him at his neighbor's on Lake Gennesaret. Tomorrow he would begin to plow the meadow, the earth that was to become their good and bearing and nourishing field.

"Do you remember, Kristina? Tomorrow is an important day to remember."

"No. Isn't it a usual workday?"

"It is the fourteenth of April. The day we went on board ship in Karlshamn."

Tomorrow, a year would have passed since they had tramped their homeland soil for the last time. Tomorrow they would put the plow into American soil for the first time.

Karl Oskar immediately fell into deep sleep, but Kristina lay awake yet a while. She listened to the sounds from the bed at the opposite corner of the cabin—short, quick breaths, the light rustle of children's breathing in sleep. It reminded her of Karl Oskar's words tonight: their children would be grateful to the parents for having emigrated with them while they still were little and had their lives ahead of them.

It might be so, perhaps he was right. But one couldn't say for sure, no human could know this for sure—it would be better not to predict anything in advance.

307

What she could predict, what she did know for sure, was that her children would never have to go through the pain of longing which she now went through. They carried no memories from the homeland, her longing would never afflict them, no vivid memories from a past life in another country would plague them. Once they were grown they would never know any other life than the one lived here. And their grandchildren in turn would know even less of another way of life. Her children and her children's children would never, as she did, remember trees and bushes they had planted in a far-off land, they would not ask, Do they still bud and bloom in spring, do they carry their fruit in fall? They would never, as she did, lie awake nights and gaze into the dark for that land where spring evenings are light.

The ones she had borne into the world, and the ones they in turn would bear, would from the beginning of their lives say what her own tongue was unable to say: *At home* here in America—*back there* in Sweden. With this thought, listening to her children's breathing, Kristina went to sleep.

# XXVI

## A Letter to Sweden

*Duvemåla* at Taylors Falls Postoffice in
Minnesota Teritory Northamerica
June 4 1851.

Dearly Beloved Parents
May all be well with you is my daily Wish
Father's letter came some time ago, I thank you for it. I have not written to you because of great oversight, it was a joy to learn you are alive and in good health, the same good holds true for your son and Family in Northamerica.

It has been a struggle right along but all things turn out well for us, I plowed a five acres field on my land last spring, I have seeded the earth with three bushels of rye and two bushels of barley. Besides I have planted four bushels of potatoes, the american bushel is half time larger than the Swedish. All crops in the field grow and thrive it is a joy for the eye to behold.

I wonder if you will ask Kristina's parents to send us seeds from the Astrakan apple in Duvemåla, we wish to plant a new astrakan apple tree here in Minnesota then we can have the same sort of apples, they were so fresh in eating as we well remember, and then we will have moved something from there over here. Sweden has good apple seeds and here is good soil to sprout and grow in, so it might grow to be a large tree in time, with many blooms.

As you see from this letter our abode now carries the name Duvemåla, Kristina holds that name dear I suppose, here it will soon be for her like in her childhood home, we have already full summer and warm

308

weather, I sweat on my hands while I write this the sweat drops upon the paper, I have not much to write about, nothing has happened to us.

Our children are well and healthy, there is long space between my letters but they will not stop, I live far away but no day has come to its end without my thoughts on my dear Home and You my kind parents, your son never forgets his home.

Kindly overlook my poor writing written down hastely by your devoted Son

Karl Oskar Nilsson

## ABOUT THE AUTHOR

*Carl Artur Vilhelm Moberg was born of peasant stock in the parish of Algutsboda and the province of Småland, Sweden. He worked as a forester and farm hand before becoming a journalist and then an author. He has published fourteen novels and fifteen plays, and his books have been translated into seventeen languages.*

## ABOUT THE TRANSLATOR

*Gustaf Lannestock spent his boyhood on a Swedish farm not far from Moberg's home, was graduated from the University of Gothenburg, and has lived in California since 1930.*